THE MEMORY OF STONE

& OTHER STORIES

Novels by Michelle West

The Sacred Hunt
Hunter's Oath
Hunter's Death

The Sun Sword
The Broken Crown
The Uncrowned King
The Shining Court
The Sea of Sorrows
The Riven Shield
The Sun Sword

The House War
The Hidden City
City of Night
House Name
Skirmish*
War*

Forthcoming in 2012 and 2013

THE MEMORY OF STONE
& OTHER STORIES

by Michelle West

Rosdan Press, Toronto, 2011

Rosdan Press
Toronto, Ontario
Canada

This is for my West readers.

Thank you for following my side-paths and small stories, and spending so much time in Essalieyan, a world I love and in which I spend so many hours of my daily life.

ACKNOWLEDGEMENTS

First, and foremost, thanks must go to Hugh Myers. I often thought about attempting to return at least the six Essalieyan short stories to print so my readers could find them again in one place. I *intended*, as self-publishing became more and more accessible (at this point I will never call it easy). But life is always busy, there are always deadlines; I'm sure it would have been another decade before I felt I had the time to actually do it.

Hugh, however, sat down and typed out all of the stories included in this collection from their original sources, and sent them to me; he had offered his help and I had demurred, but apparently this was not entirely discouraging. Waiting ten years after that would have been an enormous waste of his effort.

If the original editors of the various anthologies hadn't asked me for stories, these stories wouldn't exist. Authors often think of stories they'd *like* to write, but they're also working on books they're committed to writing, which have deadlines, and it's hard to justify putting off work on the novels for the short fiction that has no certain home. So thanks also go to Alexander Potter, Larry Segriff, John Helfers and Sheila Gilbert, the editor of my novels at DAW.

Table of Contents

Echoes

Introduction

Kallandras has appeared in every novel I've written in the *Sun Sword* or the *Sacred Hunt*; he is heading his way to Averalaan as I type this, in the final volume of *The House War*. He's one of the earliest of my characters, and his role in any of these books has always of necessity been smaller than I would like. His essential situation is tragic; he is driven by love that will always be scorned, and by a desire to protect those who will not only never thank him, but never forgive him making the attempt.

Music is his forte; he's a Master Bard of Senniel College. In the universe of Essalieyan, this title comes with responsibilities to the Bardmaster, the Bardic College in which he trained, the Kings and the Empire. But if this defines his public face, it is not the driving force behind his life, and this story speaks of that earlier life as an assassin.

Echoes takes place during the novel *Sea of Sorrows*; it's a small interlude during the nights of desert travel.

When Alexander Potter was putting together a collection for DAW Books—*Assassin Fantastic*—he didn't approach me immediately to ask for a story about my sole assassin; Tanya Huff did. She phoned and said, "I've got a story about Bannon and Vree that I want to write, and I figure I can sell it for an anthology about assassins. I want you to write a Kallandras story as well."

I asked her who was going to *edit* the anthology, and she answered, "Alex." So I said the only sensible thing I could: "Sure."

This is that story.

Echoes

WHAT DOES mercy mean?

Kallandras of Senniel College, the most famous bard that the most famous of bardic colleges had yet produced, stirred beneath the growing chill of desert sky. The Sea of Sorrows lay before him, sand dunes rippling out in endless ridges that seemed as solid as stone from a distance. But he knew that the wind would reclaim them, as they did all else in the South.

Senniel College, and the life he had led there, was very far away, ensconced in the heart of the Imperial Capital. The only physical evidence of his time there lay in her case, her strings still. He could not hear music at all, although he listened for it.

Music was the one thing he had found that spoke to him almost as strongly as past voices; that found its way beneath skin, beneath the serene face he presented to the world. But tonight it was absent. They were strong tonight, the old voices.

And he thought he knew why. But he held on to ignorance for as long as he could—and despised himself for it, with an intensity that spoke of the youth in which most of the old voices had their roots. Ignorance served no useful purpose; it changed no fact, it offered no shelter.

"Kallandras?"

He inclined his head in greeting as a figure resolved itself out of the shadows of distant wagons. The dyes applied to his hair for his brief sojourn in the capital of the Dominion of Annagar had been of reasonable quality; their temporary nature only now allowed the natural pale gold to peer through the brown-black so common among the clans.

The Serra Teresa di'Marano stood beside him, the grace of her form encumbered by the heavier clothing that the Voyani chose to wear during their forays into the Sea of Sorrows. Her eyes were dark, her hair the color by nature that his was by artifice.

She did not touch him. She lifted a hand as if she would. It hovered like a moth between them, but in the end, it was not drawn to fire. She said, "I heard you speak."

He lifted a brow in surprise, and turned away in the same instant, to hide the expression, although in truth it was not genuine. In all things, he was as he had been trained to be.

What was a lie after all, when it was not offered to a brother? "I...was not aware...that I had spoken out loud." That was truth. He did not attempt to lie to the Serra Teresa in any way that she could hear—for she had his gift, and his curse. They were marked by their ability to hear all things that a voice could carry—and to manipulate their own in such a way that it might beguile or force obedience.

"It is night," the Serra Teresa said softly. She raised her face to the moon's; the moon was waning slowly. A crescent of darkness grew across the perfect brightness of her face. "At night, we are forgiven our transgressions against strength." She bowed.

"I am not forgiven mine," he replied gravely. He liked her bow because it was so unnatural a movement for a Serra, and yet it became her perfectly.

"Kallandras—"

"Your gift is strong," he told her; he did not look at her again. There were things that he did not wish to share with anyone.

But that had not always been the case.

He heard it because he could not longer prevent himself from hearing it; it was too loud.

Arkady.

His hands trembling a moment in the air, he reached for the only comfort he allowed himself, had ever allowed himself. He pulled, from a battered case, the lute that had been the gift of the Master of Senniel College—an act of faith on her part. And perhaps on his, to accept it. He spoke the lute's name into the still, cold air.

Salla.

But the darkness returned only *Arkady.*

It was over. It was over. He was gone.

His knees threatened to fail him, and with the grace that had seen him through decades, he acknowledged and accepted his own weakness. He sat, knees bent, the bowl of a lute in his lap, his hands, his shaking hands, palm up, as if he were begging for something that he could not even name.

Not beneath the Lady's face.

~

But beneath the Lord's, he had, so many years ago that if memory were weak—it was not, and it was not kind—he might have forgotten it. He sat in the streets of the Tor Leonne's poorest quarter. His father and mother were dead—or he assumed they were dead. He had escaped the slaughter of his family simply because he had been too far from home when it had happened. But he knew why it had happened. Because, across the distance that meant life for him, and death for them, he had heard their screams; they carried words, when words were allowed them.

And words *were* allowed them because the clansmen sought information. He could think of those killers, those deaths, without passion. He accepted what that said about him as he had accepted all things that might once have been considered atrocities.

They had spawned a child with demonic powers: the ability to use his voice to command men to unnatural actions. They wanted that child. He ran, leaving his youth in the Terrean of Mancorvo behind, more than a lifetime away.

Would he have returned to it? No. Not that life. But he had lived more than one. He did not dwell on what happened between death and the Tor; but as he sat, with Salla in his lap, he remembered the shape of the begging bowl in his lap, the pain of blistered skin, the stares his unusually pale hair received whenever someone paused for a moment to notice how much he stood out from the others whose profession it was to beg and plead for the crumbs of the clansmen.

He was careful. He did not use his curse except when the hunger made him weak. He merely sat, letting the advantage of his unusual appearance speak for him.

He had been in the Tor Leonne for three weeks when the old man found him. He had gone from a robust, hefty villager to a slender, gaunt wraith; he had watched his shadow thin with the passage of time. On the second day in which he had gone without food and with little water, he thought that when the shadow disappeared entirely, he would be gone with it, and he was…comforted. He hadn't the courage to take his own life—not then. The courage to destroy life would come later, when he had something to live for.

But his shadow and a taller shadow had converged, and when they remained, locked against the ground, he looked up to see who had cast it. An old man. Or a man he had thought old, from the vantage of youth and hunger.

"Why are you here, boy?"

He had started to speak, and the words had died. He felt their echo in his throat, just as Salla echoed the bowl in his lap.

"This is not the place for you. Can you stand?"

"I…don't know. Yes."

"Good. Stand. Walk if you can." The old man smiled, and the smile was strange; it was…kind. It was not a smile he had thought to see again. It hurt him. He watched his shadow separate from the old man's, and he hesitated a moment as light appeared between them, revealing the colors of dust, of dirt, of summer heat. As simply as that, shadows were transformed. He ran into darkness, his breath catching in his throat after only a dozen steps.

The old man turned. His smile was gone, but the look in his eyes had not changed. "I am old enough to have fathered you. But I am not, and will never be, your father." He held out a hand."In time, if I am worthy of you, and you are worthy of me, I will be your brother.

"And between brothers, nothing is forbidden. No weakness and no strength. If you need help, I will help you. If I need help, you will help me."

Kallandras took his hand.

"What is your name, boy?"

"It's—it's Kallatin." The first lie.

The man smiled as he heard it. "You will learn, in time, to be a much more accomplished liar; your life will depend on it. But you will also learn that there is no need to lie to a brother. Come. You are hungry, and I will have wasted much time if I allow you to perish in the street."

~

Kallatin. Kallandras. Two names, neither of them names he was born to; neither of them large enough to contain all parts of his life. He heard, at a distance, the song his fingers absently forced from the lute, and he grimaced. No small wonder the Serra Teresa had chosen to join him; he played the melody and harmony of a cradle song.

~

The old man led him to a small house. It was nestled between buildings that were larger, but although of modest size, it was clearly well defended, well appointed. There was a small gate around the house, and a door; beyond the door was a hanging in black, red and white. The old man said, "We are a brotherhood that serves the Lady in Shadow; there is little sun in our world, and we have little use for the Lord's ways. If you are afraid of this, leave now, and no more will be said."

"I am not afraid of shadow," he replied. Firmly. Foolishly.

"We have many dwellings, but no home. Come." He did not say, *do not speak of what you see.* The boy passed between the doors as if the doors were sentient and paused in front of the hanging. It was of a flower at night; dark sky, white stars, red blossom. He lifted a hand to touch it; was surprised when his fingers felt linen, cotton, nubbled cloth.

"You are sensitive, Kallatin," the old man said quietly.

"If you know that's not my name, why do you use it?"

"None of us own our names," the man replied. "Kallatin is as useful a name as any." He pushed aside the hanging only when Kallandras' hand had fallen, and he led the way into the dwelling. The house itself was entirely ordinary; there were two serafs who tended rooms in which a man might sleep or eat or watch sunrise or moonrise. They bowed when they saw him, but they did not speak. The old man politely requested food for his visitor, and they disappeared, emerging only a few minutes later with fruit, rice, sweet water, all perfectly arranged.

He *knew* that there was no possible way they could have prepared such a meal in so short a time, but he was beyond caring. If the food were poisoned somehow, if he were to die here, or lose what freedom he had claim to, it was the Lady's will, the Lord's—hunger drove him. He ate beneath the watchful eyes of the old man.

Afterward, he slept.

When he woke, he woke to a darkness that smelled of people, in a room that he was almost certain he had never seen before. The old man was standing in the doorway, as if he knew to a second when the newcomers would wake.

"Welcome," he said, his voice somehow deeper, "to the halls of the *Kovaschaii*. You will train here. But only a handful of your number—three perhaps—will survive the training to become brothers and servants of the Lady."

"What will happen to the rest?" someone asked, in the darkness.

"Does it matter?"

"Yes," someone else said. It took a moment before Kallandras realized that it was his own voice.

"Why?"

"Because if we are to be brothers in all things, what we build here—at our beginning—will define us."

The old man bowed slightly. In the darkness, the subtle gesture was missed by several of the young men who snorted or snickered in derision. He did not know their names, that night. Or ever.

"Sleep well," the old man said, and Kallandras realized that he was, in fact, lying on a hard, flat mat.

~

In the morning—if morning existed in a world that was not ruled, or witnessed, by sky—the old man woke them. He carried a lamp and a torch, but both were unusual; neither flickered, and neither seemed to give off heat. "Please, follow me."

They did. They were nervous, these newcomers; they knew, as Kallandras did, that they had fallen in with the Dark Brothers who served the Lady's darkest face. To cross them was death. To serve them? He had never desired the life of a killer. It galled him. To live in obedience was one thing; to live at the expense of others, different again. But he was not afraid of either the killing or the dying; the shadows had taken the fear from him. He was afraid of failure.

Of loss.

The old man led them into a vast cavern, whose heights and farthest walls were lost beyond lamp and torch's reach. "You will not find this a comfortable room to begin with, but each time you return to it, you will see more clearly. You are now at the heart of the labyrinth. Each step you take from this day forth will bring you closer to freedom from its confines. You may mistep; you may take a wrong turn. These are not fatal.

"But if you do not walk the path, you will never be allowed to leave. You know who we are. You were not chosen because you were fools. Today, you will each be given the first of your many weapons; the most obvious weapon we will give you."

Something touched Kallandras shoulder. He turned. His gaze grazed a strange forehead, and fell until he made eye contact with another boy.

"I'm Arkady," the boy said. His hair was as dark as Kallandras' was pale, and as straight as Kallandras' was curly. But it caught torchlight and lamplight in a way that reminded Kallandras of fine silk.

"I'm—I'm Kallatin."

"You arrived last night?"

He smiled. "If it *was* night. It...wasn't when I fell asleep."

"What do you think of this place?"

"I don't know. I haven't seen enough of it yet."

Light changed its fall across Arkady's hair as he shrugged. "Did you hear what he said last night? Maybe three of us would survive?"

Kallandras smiled. "I don't believe it. It's a test. It must be a test. If we work together—if we stand together—"

"It *was* you who spoke up." Arkady's smile broadened.

"Guilty."

"Well, if he didn't have you killed in your sleep, he couldn't have been offended." Arkady held out a hand; Kallandras took it. For a moment longer than necessary their palms rested together.

$\sim$

The weapons were blades, of a sort, with guards unlike any that Kallandras had seen—they travelled from hilt halfway up the length of the blade on opposite sides, and were sharpened into points at their peak. Heavy and small compared to the graceful length of steel that Southern clansmen carried for all of their adult life, they were straight, where swords curved. They were also deadly.

The first thing the *Kovaschaii* did, in the labyrinth, was to learn their weapons' use. In ones and twos they were taken first to a large, spare room, second to a small room, third to a room with a ceiling that was only barely taller then the tallest of their number. In each of these rooms, they were asked to test the use of their blades. The old man often came to watch them, or perhaps just to watch Kallandras; there were many old men who seemed to come from, and return to, the shadows during the long hours spent practicing nothing more than slicing air. They were allowed, in the end, to spar properly; it was a disaster.

~

"Kallatin," the man who had come to instruct them said. "You will never learn to wield your weapon if you do not practice."

Kallandras nodded. "I am not your equal, Master."

"That is not my name."

Kallandras bowed his head. "I am not your equal. I cannot use this weapon without causing injury, either to myself or another."

"And would you train with false weapons, the way the clansmen do?"

"I was born to a clan, a poor clan. I see no shame in it. Yes."

"Arkady?" The man turned to the boy that he had chosen to partner Kallandras.

For a moment there was long, thin silence; Arkady did not look at Kallandras, did not look at the master. Instead, his gaze fell to the poorly lit shape of his feet, and lingered there in doubt for what seemed a long time. At last, he said, "Yes."

"What did you say?"

"I—I think—I think he's right."

The master's pause was longer than Arkady's. Kallandras did not realize that he was not breathing until breath returned.

The master nodded. "If you do not feel comfortable with real weapons, you may have the practice ones. But we will keep the real until you require them."

~

The old man came in the mornings.

"You do not speak of your gift."

Kallandras did not speak at all. The moment stretched and thinned until the old man broke it by chuckling. It was not the sound he expected to hear.

"Let me speak of mine, then, boy." Kallandras said nothing.

"I can speak in a way that forces men to listen." He paused. "I almost never do. But of all aspects of my gift, it is the one most feared, and with cause.

"Let me speak of the others. Do you sing, boy?"

"No. Singing is for girls," he added bitterly. His father's words. But bitter or no, angry or no, he missed that man; that man had died with the knowledge of his only son's location clenched between closed teeth.

"It is for brothers, not for girls. And no voice is as strong, no voice is a powerful, in either sweetness or sorrow, as the voice of one born with the gift." The old man paused. "I sing more frequently than I command. But I do not sing overmuch.

"But there is one thing that I always do; it is as natural as breathing or sleeping."

Kallandras did not want to hear the old man speak. He was tired. The need for sleep thinned his nerve, robbing him of the composure that he clung to in the face of the Labyrinth and its masters.

"I listen. I cannot help but listen. Every sentence, every word, every syllable, become lines of a map, and between those lines fall cities, if the speaker is careless. I hear a lie almost before it is finished; I hear truth in just the same way. I hear fear, anger, worry; I hear envy, desire, pain."

"Why are you telling me this?"

"I am your mirror, Kallatin. I want you to learn."

He rose, then, and bowed. He did not speak again with the old man that day.

~

Four of the young men had chosen practice weapons; two pairs. The blades were unsharpened, the guards blunted; the weight however was almost the same. They were mocked for it; the other boys, fourteen in total, had chosen to brave the more deadly blades. After all, they were of an age, among their own, where they would have been expected to use blades that were far more deadly than these, and they had trained with swords, or the child's equivalent, when they had had the opportunity.

Unless, of course, they had come from slave stock. The sneer in the words was enough to keep silent any who might have been plucked from that life. It had seemed so important in that small world to appease, or at least slide beneath the notice of, the stronger boys.

During the first week, four of the students—if that's what they were— were taken away from the training grounds. All of them were bleeding profusely from the wounds they had received in training.

None of them returned.

The survivors of each team were paired together. Two of them chose to forsake their weapons, two did not.

During the second week, another four fell. Again, they were taken from the training rooms, and again, they failed to return. There were other injuries during this time, but the boys bore them in wary—or terrified—silence. If they could walk from the session, they walked; they struggled to avoid acknowledging damage done them because they knew that an injury severe enough to bring them to their knees was death.

But no one asked where the injured boys had gone.

～

In the end, of the ten boys who remained, only two chose to cling to their weapons. They were, in Kallandras' opinion, the best; they were confident, and at times savage, but they were dancing on the knife's edge, and they paid attention to every word their masters said. To watch them fight, to watch them *move*, was a bitter joy. The masters watched. They took notes.

What had they said? *Only three.* Eight had already been winnowed by poor luck or poor skill.

～

During that time, the old man would come to Kallandras. He watched as Arkady and Kallandras progressed, but he did not speak or comment on their style, except to point out gross lapses in their technique. If the practice blades were not sharp, they were dangerous nonetheless; they left bruises that were wide across as the span of two hands in a trail from shin to shoulder.

After the training masters had called the sessions to a halt for the day—or night—and the boys filed out to the three rooms in which their meals were prepared, the old man would speak.

"Do you regret your choice?"

"My choice? You mean, coming here?"

The older smile was wry. "The weapon."

"No."

"But you watch Mikal and Torval as if they possessed some magic, some secret, that you yourself would attain if you could."

Kallandras shrugged. "Envy is not the same as regret."

"No indeed, but you are a strange one, to know that so well at your age."

Kallandras looked at the old man for a long, long time. Then he said, "The others are not as careful as you are."

"Careful?"

"You know that I know when you lie."

He turned away; his slender profile was lit from beneath by the soft glow of a lamp that seemed to radiate no heat. "We are granted our gifts and our curses," the old man said at last. "But yes. I know it."

"How?"

"Does it matter? I know that you can hear me; I know that you can hear the things I have found no words for. If you pass the test, Kallatin, you will be without peer in the Lady's service."

"You say that?"

"Yes. Because I know what your curse is. It is seldom that a voice is so strong that it manifests useful power without appropriate training. But power alone is not what the Brotherhood desires. When you watch Mikal and Torval, remember this—lithe, graceful and beautiful as they are, I do not believe they will survive even this first stage of our testing."

~

Arkady. Arkady.

Old man.

The bard's voice was all that remained of his life in the Labyrinth. He did not use it tonight. Instead, he let Salla speak; hers was the only other voice he wanted. The night sky was clear and bright. The stars were cold.

What is Mercy?

~

"What is mercy? Why are we hesitant to shun what remains of it within ourselves?"

Old man.

Kallandras did not think of him as one of the masters until the day he had come to lead them not to one of the three training rooms, but rather, to a large, round room with a domed roof across which, glittering and cold, the night sky seemed to crawl.

Most of the boys didn't understand the question. Kallandras didn't.

The old man looked, momentarily, like any other harried teacher. The man who had been primarily responsible for their weapon training—a man who had never introduced himself, but who did not like to be called master—smiled and turned his face to the wall. Kallandras had the suspicion that he was stifling a laugh—and of all things he had seen in the Labyrinth, it was both most the welcome and the most surprising.

"Let me attempt this again. You," the old man said, pointing at a boy who stood in the back of the group. "Did you spend your childhood dreaming of the day when you would become an assassin? Did you daydream about taking the life of a stranger who has never done you any harm—and worse, by stealth, not by challenge?"

Silence was an effective answer.

The old man did not press. "Let me answer the question for you. For *all* of you. No. Not a single one of you would have been chosen if that had been your desire." There were one or two nods. A whisper. Another. But stillness resumed its grip again when the old man started to speak.

"If the *Kovaschaii* were mountains, you would be standing in the foothills. You will, if you survive, become what we are. We kill. We accept the money of people who desire death, and if it is deemed a suitable death, or a suitable offering, one of our brothers will perform the assassination.

"Do we appear monstrous?"

Silence again, but that was wise.

"You will be killers. You will destroy lives. You know the cost of that firsthand, or you would not be among us. If you cannot find a way to accomplish this task with pride—with honor—you will never leave."

Kallandras listened carefully to each word. The pause between sentences was like a gap between walls that are close enough that a climber might scale them. The old man was worried.

Because he was telling the truth.

~

"What do you hear when you listen to your comrades speak?"

Kallandras tilted his head to one side for a moment and then said, "Exactly what you hear."

The old man's smile was slight. He was always less frazzled when they met one to one. "Diplomatic. I do not ask to gain information, or rather, information about the other students; I do not expect you to spy. I ask because I wish to confirm the level of your abilities."

Kallandras nodded, but he still did not answer the question; let these putative companions give themselves away as they must; he would not do it for them. But he was concerned; they were afraid.

As if he could hear the thought, the fluid lines of the old man's expression changed direction; the smile was transformed into a dour stillness. "They're afraid. Fear will drive them in one of two directions."

"Which two?"

"It is not my test to pass," the old man said. He looked as if he would like to speak more, but as he hesitated, another of the masters came by, and the spell of isolation was broken.

But fifteen minutes after the two masters had left him alone, he heard a familiar voice. **"Watch yourself, Kallatin. Fear seeks a target if it has a weapon."** Kallandras jumped up and ran to the mouth of the great room, but it was empty, and the jagged walls of equally empty, winding hall offered no answers.

~

The eating rooms had never been so quiet. There were usually minor squabbles about seating, food, the quality of food, water, water again, and who would be responsible for cleaning the dishes that were left.

"Hey, Kallatin?"

Kallandras chewed quickly, swallowed quickly, and then spoke. Across the remove of years, he remembered this. On that night, that significant night, he had clung to manners as if they mattered. They had all chosen to cling to their pasts.

"Yes?"

"Which three, do you think?"

"Three?"

"Which three will it be?"

"I think more than three will go on. Or less."

"But they said—"

Kallandras closed his eyes. In the darkness and the silence, it was easy to recall the exact words. "*Only a handful of your number—three perhaps—will survive.*"

Arkady was clearly impressed. "You even sound like him."

"I sound like a tired old man? Thanks, Arkady. Tomorrow, you'll be the one with new bruises, I promise." That had taught him something, although he failed to appreciate the lesson until he was a decade older. Never promise something that cannot be delivered. But at that time, Arkady's snort, Arkady's laugh, was all that he required. They rose from the mats, their knees unfolding almost precisely at the same instant.

"Why are you two laughing?" Mikal rose as well. He carried his weapon with him at all times, and often allowed his hand to stray to its hilt. It did, then. Kallandras shrugged. "Laughter is better than strained silence."

"If you have something to laugh about."

"And if I do?"

Torval rose as well. They were not friends, these two, but they were allies. "Share it with the rest of us."

Kallandras' shrug was less graceful. He had not learned to dissemble; had not learned to flatter or lie; that came later, when death was more important than pride or privacy.

Arkady touched his shoulder.

Kallandras shook his friend's hand away. His own came to rest on the hilt of his practice weapon. Torval snorted in open derision. "Is that supposed to impress us?"

"No. Merely to show you how pretentious the strut looks when you do it yourself."

In the grey of rooms that were never touched by sunlight, color was suspect—but if the flush that stained Torval's cheeks was not glaringly obvious, it was there if one knew how to look.

"What are you planning, you pale-haired—"

Mikal caught Torval's elbow, silencing him. "We know that you talk to the master in private. He speaks to almost no one else. He isn't an arms-master. What does he tell you, Kallatin? What has he offered you?"

"Nothing. Nothing except this life."

"Liar."

Kallandras' turn to flush. "I am not used to being called a liar."

"Get used to it if you are one."

"Kallatin—" Arkady's hand again.

He ignored it. "Or?"

"Or maybe we'll try different partners in the arena tomorrow."

"Fine."

"*Kallatin.*"

Mikal laughed. "Looks like your partner doesn't think so." He sauntered toward the dormitory that housed them all in space that seemed increasingly…small.

~

"Life ends. Whether it ends by your hand, or no, it ends. The only ties that matter are those of loyalty and those of blood."

Kallandras looked at the old man. He was tired. It had been a restless night.

"We will accept any mission that…that we are ordered to accept. But the *Kovaschaii* are not interested in pain or pleasure; we are interested in *death.* You are not a child. You know the difference between a long death and a short one."

Kallandras did not reply. He did know the difference. If he was not careful, he would dwell on it, and the loss of his family would filter into his voice, where it would be easily snatched up by the old man.

"You have made progress with one weapon, Kallandras. I would have you learn another."

"And that?"

"Use what you were born to. Your brothers will not envy you the gift; they will bless you for it because it will be used in our service."

The young man was stony in silence. Stiff. To speak of the philosophy of death was one thing. To speak of its actuality, quite another. He said, after a long pause, "My family is dead because of my curse."

"No. Your family is dead because of the fear of a talentless, ambitious man. In a different land, you would have been valued for what the Lady chose to give you." There was bitterness in his words. Bitterness laced with humour. "And you are in a *very* different land."

Kallandras bowed as he had been taught to in his father's home. "Teach me, then. Teach me what you can teach me, and I will do what I can to live up to your expectations."

"Do I have expectations?"

"Everyone does."

The old man smiled. **Listen then. What I say, only you can hear. Understand the texture of voice that makes this impossible. Understand that it is impossible. Learn.**

~

Do they bless me now, old man? Do you?

~

The master in charge of the first room was waiting for him. Although he was completely expressionless, and his words were smooth as Northern glass, his voice was shaded with disapproval and annoyance. Kallandras bowed as formally as he dared.

"Did Constanso detain you?"

"Who?" For a moment, Kallandras thought he referred to a student; they were the only people in his twilight life who had names he could use. But when the master fell completely silent and his lips compressed into a dagger's edge, Kallandras knew who he meant. He nodded, but he did not speak the name again; it was not wise to remind a man who had the power to grant life or death on a whim that he had made a mistake. "Mikal and Torval have a proposition that intrigues me. They have suggested that you wish to test your skills against opponents that you are not so familiar with. I see merit in this."

Kallandras said nothing.

"Your time here—in these rooms—is almost at an end. The basics, you now have. Anything else you will gain once you complete your passage. It is time." He walked toward the tall table upon which he had set the weapons the boys had originally been given. "Will you take these back?"

He shook his head.

The master nodded as if he was not overly surprised. "Arkady?"

Arkady was paralyzed.

The master took his silence as refusal. "I commend you both," he said softly. "Kallatin, please, join Mikal. Arkady, join Torval, but wait my word." He turned to Kallandras. "I would see the two of you spar."

When Kallandras joined Mikal, he felt as if he had stepped into a different room, onto a different floor. He had spent months training with Arkady. He had received bruises, had left skin on the rough walls and ground of each of the training rooms, had won and lost time and again. He thought he understood the rhythm of the fight.

He was wrong. He understood the peculiar combination of Kallandras and Arkady. Kallandras and Mikal were entirely different.

Where Arkady took a moment to gather and centre himself, to find his knees, Mikal was lunging. He used the points of the guards, and the edges of blade, as if they were lethal. They were. Kallandras leapt out of the way. Arkady was seldom that aggressive, and with reason; Mikal took the back of the hilt in the shoulder as Kallandras spun.

Mikal was tall, his shoulders broad; he had strength and stamina. Kallandras, slender, had stamina; his strength had never been tested in this fashion. He was curious; he had seen Mikal fight with Torval for months, but none of that dance was in his step now; his rage—at what?— was unfettered, and it made him clumsy.

Or perhaps it wasn't rage. Perhaps it was simply lack of caution. He did not consider the practice blade a weapon. If it was not lethal, he could take risks he would otherwise never take.

Foolish.

Kallandras did not draw blood; he didn't need to. Mikal's knee touched the ground when he overbalanced in an attempt to take advantage of an illusory opening in an attempt to draw blood. The master called the match and sent them both to the wall, calling Arkady and Torval to take their place. Before they began, he lifted a hand.

"The deadliest weapon does not make an opponent deadly. It may, however, make him foolish. A lesson should be taken from this; take the right one." He lowered his hand.

Torval and Arkady began to circle each other. Arkady was pale; his breath was too shallow. Kallandras wanted to shout at him; to correct him. *You know better than this!* But the master's grim expression was a command. Torval was not Kallandras. Arkady was not Kallandras.

"Your friend won't last the round," Mikal said, conversationally.

Kallandras said, equally tonelessly, "That arrogance has already failed you once. Learn from the failure."

Mikal's jaw snapped audibly shut. It was the last sound Kallandras allowed to distract him from the fight.

Arkady could not see past sharp blade, ground point. Torval struck once; grazed Arkady's slender thigh. Cloth parted; blood welled. It had not been a particularly graceful strike, but grace was not as useful as success.

Arkady, he thought. *Damn you, Torval is not playing a game. You're better than this—*

Another misstep. Torval drove Arkady back, and Arkady, mesmerized by blood and the glint of light across polished steel, let his guard slip again. But he did not fall to his knees. He faltered, righted himself, continued.

Kallandras reached for his practice blade, and a hand clenched his wrist when his fingers brushed the hilt.

The master's hand.

"Our purpose here is not to kill each other!" he snarled. He could not suppress the rage that broke between words to crawl to the surface.

"It is not for you to judge your purpose," the master answered. His tone was cold and dark, but something beneath it reached pale-haired boy that Kallandras had once been. Pain. He bowed, then, in order to retrieve his wrist. And heard the clash of weapons.

Arkady, you fool! Bend at the knees. He's not half the fighter I am,

and you can beat me! The edge is illusion; the guard points are illusion; the only thing that counts is the block and the counter. See me if you must see his face at all; see my weapon if you must see anything.

The words died into stillness as they left him. He *felt* them go. But he had not felt his lips move. And the master's eyes were upon the fight. He offered no censure.

He didn't hear me.

No. For just a moment, fear came; fear of fire, of swords, of death. But behind that, satisfaction. Arkady had come to life. The stiffness of fear left his limbs; the fear of bleeding—of being carried away by masters, never to return—went with it.

Who's the old man now, Arkady?

"Damn you, Kallatin!" Arkady shouted back. It was not, strictly speaking, forbidden, but the master frowned. His glare travelled the distance between the two boys. Only Kallandras saw it.

But he didn't care. Arkady had heard him. Arkady was safe.

After the fight, the master nodded. He broke up the pairings of the others, but as Torval and Mikal were the only two who fought with true edges, the contests were even. Arkady ungraciously allowed Kallandras to tend the two wounds he'd received.

"Scars are attractive to the right people," he told Arkady, as he pulled the bandage taut around the thigh.

"And we see the right people down here?" Arkady laughed. "You saved me out there. You know? I—I heard you, I heard you speak."

"You're lucky that's all you heard," Kallandras said darkly. "If I were closer I would have slapped you."

Arkady laughed. The laughter walked the edge of hysteria without falling off. "I owe you."

"There is no debt between brothers."

"You're too ugly to be my brother."

Kallandras laughed. "If we ever face each other again, you'll pay for that."

~

"Did you interfere in the fight today?"

They sat on either side of a low table in the mid-meal eating room, but it was just after the meal had been cleared away. Kallandras looked away.

"The master was most specific."

"If you already know the question, old man, why do you ask me? I have no desire to walk into your traps."

The old man laughed. "But you walk into them nonetheless. I—am surprised. You should not have been able to do that, not so quickly."

"I had to."

"Did you?"

"Torval would have killed him." He was silent for a moment, and then he added, "Or he would have wounded him badly, and that isn't much different, is it?"

The old man bowed his head a moment. When he lifted it, his expression made steel look soft. "No."

Although Kallandras knew—they all did— what must have happened to the injured and the fallen, the bluntness of the single, cold word cut him; he took a moment to gather breath. He did not bother to hide what he felt. The old man would hear it in the words that needed to be said. "Why? If we are to be brothers—"

"If you cannot leave the scene of a battle of your own accord, you will die, and better so. The *Kovaschaii* are almost immune to torture, but they are not immune to magic. We guarantee our clients privacy, because in the end, we force them to reveal much about themselves. We cannot afford to risk exposure and destruction."

"But the scene of a battle is *not* the training ground."

"Kallandras, it is a test. You insisted on the practice blade. You endured mockery and scorn because you did not desire to injure your partner. He accepted this. The others did not."

"But they—"

"It doesn't matter why. Some mistakes are fatal. You of all people should understand this."

"This is a…harsh lesson."

For just a moment, the old man's face softened. "It is not the harshest you will learn." He reached across the table, and then let his hand fall to the flat, unadorned surface. "I have spoken too much."

"You have said almost nothing."

"I have used few words," the old man countered. "Where you are concerned, they are not the same. When I first passed all tests—" He bowed his head a moment, and Kallandras heard small fissures in the surface of his voice; cracks that memory would widen, judging by the look on his face. He rose. "I envy you the chance to rediscover the brotherhood."

But not the cost. Not the cost.

~

Over the next few weeks, they moved from the three training rooms to others. Long, narrow rooms in which it was impossible to swing a weapon. Rooms where the floors were sloped from edge to centre, like a giant, stone funnel. Rooms in which stairs started nowhere and ended in the height of the wall.

They also fought in the largest of the rooms, and honed their response to flight—both their own and their target's.

To Kallandras' eye, they had improved—but the masters grew dour and silent.

"Soon," they said, in their own ways, "it will all be over. Soon."

But no matter how soon that was to be, the training continued; Kallandras forgot what daylight looked like because the reality of shadow was much more visceral.

"But they said only a few of us would—"

Kallandras lifted a hand. He was not an authority, but when he spoke he could make people listen. "They said probably. It's not as if they'll set a limit of two or three and kill the rest of us. It's a test."

"A test to see who is the fittest?" Mikal snapped.

"Perhaps. But I think—"

"No one cares what you think."

Arkady rose. "I do," he said.

"You are barely a separate person. He tells you what to eat, when to breathe, when to piss."

"He tells me everything I need to hear; he lets me decide the rest for myself," Arkady snapped back. "Unlike the way you treat Torval, your seraf."

Torval rose as well. Hands touched the hilts of weapons and an ugly silence robbed the room of everything but harsh breath. The old man entered, and movement returned. But it was strained.

Kallandras bowed.

The old man said, almost against his will, "The weapons are not for use outside of the training rooms."

They nodded the way children nod when they're not listening.

Later, in the quiet of long, half-smooth halls, Arkady turned to Kallandras. "Aren't you afraid?" he demanded, his voice both low and urgent. It was clear to Kallandras that Arkady was; also clear that he felt no need to hide it.

"I am more afraid of being ordered to take my first life—to make my first kill." It was true.

"Kallandras—they're all so tense now. They don't even look at us as if we're going to be their so-called brothers. I wake up in the morning—every morning—and I thank the Lady that I'm not dead."

Kallandras did not point out that a dead person had no thanks to offer. Instead, he said, "What do you expect them to do?"

"Take us away," was the blunt reply. "Just like they did with the others."

"No." Kallandras said quietly.

"No?"

"If they do, they won't take us without a fight. There are three masters here. There are ten of us."

"They're *Kovaschaii*, Kallandras."

"True. And maybe we stand no chance against them. But if we're to die anyway, without a word or a struggle, why not stand together instead of dying alone?"

Arkady's words were always full of the nuance of emotion. But he did not speak. He met Kallandras' eyes in the poor light, and his own glimmered unnaturally bright.

The old man did not come the next morning. He did not come the morning after, or the morning after that. The masters spoke very little. In the absence of a familiar voice Kallandras felt the tension that had infected Arkady and the others as if it were a disease. Something was going to happen.

~

"After dinner tonight, you will confine yourself to the sleeping chambers.

On the morrow, we will come for you, and we will choose among you."

"C-choose?" Arkady said.

The master frowned. "That *is* what I said. Those who are chosen will leave the Labyrinth. Those who are not, will not. We have need of the Labyrinth for the newcomers."

Ah, memory. The voices of his brothers, bound to him by ceremony, oath, blood and his own desire—*to never be alone; to never have to face the world without someone trusted at one's side*—did change, subtly, with the passage of time. So did memories. As a young man, so much of what he had learned after being accepted by ritual and ceremony had loomed so large. Now, he remembered his beginnings. What he chose to remember ten years from now, if he lived, would be different again; he could not predict it.

But ten years from now, Arkady would not be dying.

∼

Darkness. Always darkness. Everything began when the shadows were too dense. Sound. Scuffling, the huff of breath that speaks of shock; silence. But something woke him as he lay across the mats in the dormitory. There was little light, but as the old man had promised that light had become enough to see clearly by with the passage of time.

There was blood on the floor. The mats were slick with it. It dripped from two blades, and as Kallandras rose, those two blades came round. He knew that he could not take his eyes off these two, but his gaze slid past them anyway, risking death for a glimpse of death; his own death. The deaths of his…brothers.

Mikal's hands were wet. Torval's chest, also wet.

Kallandras shook his head in denial—just as he had shaken his head when wind had carried the sounds of his family's death. He had thought that he would never have family again, and he had found the promise of something more. But that promise would never be fulfilled—not by the boys here. He reached for his blade, practice blade.

"You don't stand a chance against the two of us," Mikal said conversationally. But he did not look at his hands, or at the sleepers who would never wake. Their bodies were still—of the injured, they at least would not be carried off and put down.

Torval's eyes were glinting as well. His hands were shaking.

They were not, Kallandras realized, madmen. They were frightened, and they had chosen this way to appease their fear.

As if they could hear his judgement, they said, "But we don't have to fight. Help us, Kallatin, and there is room for you when the masters come tomorrow. They said three."

He said nothing. But with their words, the room's focus changed. If they wanted help, they had not yet finished their work. He saw them at a remove of years: inefficient. Emotional. But in the Labyrinth, he had also been both of those things.

When he spoke his voice filled the room; there was no space that escaped the command he put into the words.

"WAKE!"

They did. Not a shred of sleep remained; they were on their feet in an instant. Some rolled, hands hunting for the blunted weight of practice blades. Some leaped.

They were quicker than he had been to take in the events that had occurred while they slept. There were cries of dismay, of anger, of outrage—but there was no room for fear.

Not theirs.

"You would have done the same!" Mikal shouted, as he backed toward a wall. "They're going to choose in the morning—they're going to pick who lives and who dies!"

"And you thought you'd help them?"

"I didn't come here to die!"

"None of us did," Kallandras said softly. He lifted his weapon. Blunt. Heavy. "You betrayed us."

"There *is* no us!"

Kallandras stepped forward. At his back, there were a handful of boys; he was not sure how many. More than two; probably four, judging from the way Mikal and Torval had chosen to stand.

"You have no right to judge us."

"You had no right to kill them."

Mikal's laugh was strained, terrible. "I had every right—all we're going to do for the rest of our lives is kill people."

Kallandras hesitated. Every word that Mikal spoke was true; every word struck home in a way that a simple weapon had failed to do in their earlier combat.

"If we can't kill here, when our lives depend on it, where can we kill?"

"Anywhere else," another voice said. A familiar voice. The old man. For the first time, Kallandras noted that the old man did not wear the robes of the heartlands; he wore black; night's color. He pushed the door of the sleeping rooms open and stepped into the room. The other masters followed them in. Kallandras spoke.

"*To me,*" he said. And the four—there were four—obeyed instantly, although he had put no command in the word. They held their practice blades, and if they were blunt and unblooded, they were not without danger.

Mikal and Torval turned to the door.

"You have failed us," the old man said quietly.

Mikal's voice contorted into a thing halfway between roar and scream. Torval had always been the more cautious of the two.

The old man gestured with both hands. Mikal charged, and the old man stepped out of his way; he ran into the hall and stumbled as he attempted to run. There was a thud and a crash, a clatter of steel against hard stone. In the torchlight, Kallandras could barely make out the toe of his boot. Torval did not run. He slumped. Fell.

The old man bowed to Kallandras. To the other four. "Welcome," he said softly, "to the brotherhood. There is much to be done before you are presented to the Lady, but you have earned the right to be presented."

But Kallandras shook his head.

The old man's brows rose until they were obscured by hair.

"I'm not ready to leave yet."

"The Lady is waiting."

Kallandras met the gaze of the old man and held it for several heartbeats before he turned away. He looked closely at the four who waited—and it was clear that they did wait—for his word. None of them were Arkady. He walked past them then, quickly.

His heartbeat was loud enough for two. Loud enough for two. "Arkady?" Silence.

One of the masters lifted a brow; the old man lifted a hand in response, although he had not looked back to see the slight shift in expression. "Kallatin," he said quietly. "The time has come to leave."

Arkady, answer me.

The silence was broken by something like a cough. "K—Kall—"

"Enough. Shut up now." Kallandras knelt on the floor beside the pallet. It seemed impossible to him that Mikal could miss. But Mikal was not, then, a killer. Only another desperate person struggling to stay alive.

"W-what happened?"

"We have to go, Arkady."

"Kallatin," the old man said. His voice should have been harsh; it was surprisingly gentle. "What I said was true. If he cannot leave on his own, he cannot leave."

It was not the only time he would ignore Constanso, although it was the first. He looped an arm beneath Arkady's arm and brought him to his feet.

"Kallatin," the old man spoke again. "You make this hard on yourself."

"That was not my intent. How far must he walk?"

"Pardon?"

"Are we never to seek medical aid? Are we never to recover from a wound if we evade capture?"

The four were brothers; whether or not the Lady accepted them, they had already accepted Kallandras. They looked to him, and he shook his head; they stepped between his exposed back and the masters of the Labyrinth, although they had all seen Mikal and Torval die.

The old man's smile was slight. "You remind me of my youth. Very well. He must walk from here to the centre of the complex, where we first gathered. The Lady will decide—if he survives that long—whether or not she will accept him."

"Arkady, can you hear me? Don't speak. If you can walk down the long hall and through the doors, there will be help for you. I can—I can help you, but only with my words. Decide."

Arkady coughed. Blood spilled from his lips, like a black fountain in the poor light, but he managed to hold himself steady. "I'll...walk."

Walk, Arkady. Step with your right leg. Yes. Now with your left.

The old man looked at him. But he said nothing as Arkady began his awkward, painfully slow stagger through stone corridors. Kallandras hated everything about the brotherhood at that moment. It was the last time such hatred or anger toward his own would even be conceivable.

Arkady fell twice. Both times, Kallandras forced him to his feet with use of a command that he was far, far too weak to fight. When Arkady stumbled a third time, Kallandras snarled and grabbed him by the shoulders.

"Arkady," he said. "I won't do this without you. We are brothers before we are anything else. That's what *I* was promised. I will start here as I mean to continue. If you lie down here, the masters will be forced to kill you, and I will be forced to kill them, or try."

Arkady coughed and then smiled weakly. "You are such a stubborn bastard."

But Kallandras could not smile in return. His heart was strong enough for two. It had to be. *Just a few more steps.* They were so close he could see the cascading wall of candles that glowed beyond the open doors. They had never been there before.

The room was full.

It was full of men in dark robes, of men in white robes, of light and the harsh shadow bright light cast. Across the floor, inlaid in gold, five points of a star. Without thinking—and even decades later, he could not understand why he did so—he caught Arkady under the shoulders and knees, and lifted him off his feet as if he weighed nothing. He heard the old man's voice as if it came from a great distance, heard other unfamiliar voices raised in whisper, raised in surprise. He passed them all, left them gaping, ran to star's center, and carefully laid Arkady to rest upon it, arranging his head in the uppermost point, his arms and legs to the sides. Arkady said, "Can I sleep now?"

Kallandras nodded.

And then he drew his dull, blunt weapon, and he held it high.

The old man came to stand beside him, and Kallandras saw that in the flicker of a thousand lights, his eyes were filmed with unshed tears. "That will do you little good," he said softly. "But take this. You have earned it." And he caught Kallandras' wrist in a grip that could not be broken. He pried his nerveless fingers from the hilt of the practice weapon and laid the hilt of real one into his palm instead.

The brothers were beginning to chant.

The floor, rather than growing darker or brighter, grew hazier as he watched.

"You must use the weapon," he said softly.

"Why?"

"You must offer her blood. Arkady is bleeding; you are not."

"But—"

"Do it now, Kallatin."

Kallandras dragged the knife across his left arm, biting into flesh, but not vein. He had no desire to bleed to death.

"Call her."

"Who?"

"The Lady."

"But I—"

"Call her before your friend dies, and you may be able to save him. The only mercy we know is The Lady's."

He heard no lie in the old man's voice, although he heard many other things. He lifted his chin, and trembling, he began to do the only thing he knew he could do better than any man present save perhaps the old man. He *sang*.

There, in the broken darkness, his eyes blurring, he accepted his curse as the gift it had always been. He sang to praise the Lady, to praise the Moon, to praise the shadows that had given him life when the sun was harsh and blinding. He sang to call her forth, although he told her that he was weak and insignificant by comparison to all of the others that had come before him to serve her. And he dared to sing, when he paused to draw breath, of his love for the brotherhood that served her, and of his desire to save one who belonged in that service, if she deemed him worthy.

He put all that he had learned into the singing of that song, and when the song was finished he was on his knees, straddling Arkady's too-still form.

And she came. The mists had crept up from the ground to his shoulders on all sides—saving only where Arkady rested within the confines of gold.

Her hair trailed like liquid night down her back and joined the mist that rolled in on all sides, like a phantasm of the sea; her raven sat upon her shoulder, watching them all as if it was possessed of the spirit of a hawk. "You called me, young one. You called me very boldly."

He had never heard death in a voice so clearly. For a moment all breath was suspended as he absorbed what he'd heard, and then he drew breath again as he looked at Arkady's still face. He had summoned death—he understood now, why the brotherhood who served this Lady performed the acts they did—to save life. But it didn't matter. He was done running from what she offered.

"Your pardon, Lady."

"Perhaps. Let me see the one you guard, young one."

He bowed his head and gained his feet. Arkady was not cold, and he had not stopped breathing; there was nothing else that Kallandras could do for him.

She leaned down, and Kallandras stiffened, but her hands merely grazed Arkady's cheek. "Your song is sweet," she said, "even though you are not yet mine. Join me, and I will grant you what you desire."

He bowed. "What must I do to join you, Lady?"

"You will know," she said. "Come. The bowl is waiting for your blood. The others are already there."

He swallowed. "And Arkady?"

"Is that what he calls himself?"

"Yes, Lady."

She reached down and caught his limp hand. "Arkady," she said softly. "I have need of you here. I withhold the journey of death from you until such a time as you have earned it. Serve me well." She pulled him to his feet and he came, blinking as he met her gaze. His jaw fell, not in fear, but in wonder. He could not even speak.

Together, Arkady and Kallandras joined the old man before a basin carved in stone. It seemed a miracle that they could have failed to notice it the first time they were here; it was not large, but everything about it seemed to glow with a star-white crispness. Kallandras saw that a thin layer of blood covered the basin; he added his own to it without hesitation—but he reached out to catch Arkady's hand after the blood had fallen. Arkady smiled.

"Give me your name," the Lady said, and he jumped back. "Give me your name, boy, and I will guard it against all use. Your truest identity will be within me, and only I will know of it. Not even death will find you when it is your time to die.

"I will find you," she continued, when none of the six spoke. "And I will return your name to you when I lead you in safety to the Halls of Mandaros. We may speak, then. We may rejoice, or cry, or laugh. But I cannot take your name if you have no desire to give it." She lifted a hand;

dropped it through the air as if it were an executioner's blade.

The six boys cried out in terror as they felt something jump *through* them. And then they cried out in shock and surprise as they felt what followed: The thoughts, the hopes, the fears, of the men who gathered in this room, watching.

What is this, what is this, Kallandras?

I—I do not know, Arkady.

Tell him, an unknown voice said. *Tell him Constanso.*

He was afraid, and the fear was strong and cloying. But to the fear came comfort, a wordless offer of wisdom and knowledge that was not his own.

You are brothers, the old man said. *You are our brothers. The Lady accepts you. He was crying, quietly. It has been four years since we have had new brothers emerge from the Labyrinth. Four years since we have found those whose understanding was stronger than their fear.*

My name? From out of the darkness, her hands came to caress his cheeks; to draw his gaze up to meet hers. He saw all of the night sky, and he had never seen a night sky with such grandeur and such depth. He had forgotten just how much he missed the sky. He spoke his name into the night she brought with her, and she caught it, gently, as a movement of lips against her brief kiss.

You are the Lady's servant. We are the Lady's servants. And Kallatin, there is a joy that waits us at the end of our lives that makes us fearless. You will never be alone again.

And when I die?

No matter where you are, no matter how dark or how isolated, you will not die alone; we will be with you, always, as we are tonight. We will hear your name, no matter how far away we are. In the green Deepings; in the heart of the Sea of Sorrows; in the ice of the Northern Wastes—there is no distance that can separate us or keep us from your side.

When you take your first life, we will be the hands that guide you; when you suffer your first doubts—or your hundredth—we will listen and offer comfort. You are one of us now, and nothing can remove that save the Lady herself should she so choose.

He felt a sharp and terrible pang, like a premonition. *Has that ever happened?*

The old man's laugh was rich and warm; it seemed to echo and linger long after it had passed. *It has never happened. Who could be one with us and betray us?*

~

He rose. *I could, old man. In all of the history of the Kovaschaii, I could. I loved my brothers much, much more than I loved their Lady.* He bowed.

And then, although he knew it would not be welcome, he spoke a single word.

Arkady.

He lifted Salla as he rose. There were deaths in the desert that lay before them, and he had been given all the time he could expect for this singular act of mourning a loss that was three decades old.

He set his lute in her case; closed his eyes, and then lifted his shoulders, straightening them into a perfect line so that no one would see the burden he carried.

And he heard it, on the wind, free from fury, contempt or loathing.

Kallatin.

Huntbrother

Introduction

This is another story written for Alexander Potter, for an anthology about dogs—albeit dogs in a fantasy or science fiction setting, since it was a DAW anthology. When he asked if I had a Hunter story I could write for him, I leapt at the chance—because there was a story that I wanted to write.

When I finished *Hunter's Death*, I didn't exactly end it where the novel now ends. I was completely caught up in the characters and the world—enough so that my first thought, upon seeing the cover for the novel, was "Where's Stephen??". I wrote pages after the final scene that ends the novel, seeking some sort of peaceful resolution for poor Cynthia of Maubreche—and in the end, it was my editor, Sheila Gilbert, and my husband, Thomas, who gently pointed out that the book *had* to end where it ended. They were completely right, and I saw that—but I still found it very hard to let go. It's a danger that one always confronts when one becomes so emotionally involved in the reality of one's character's lives. It doesn't happen with every book; sometimes I know the end, and it is the end. But it's happened at least twice that I can think of.

(The inverse is also true. There are times when I think: This is where the novel ends, and the ending as conceived is too abrupt. I would have ended Sun Sword in a different place had it been any other book but the last one, for instance. I'm trying to be careful to elide possible spoilers for anyone who hasn't read that book yet, because the spoilers will also pretty much spoil the whole thing.)

I went on to write the six *Sun Sword* novels, because the *Sacred Hunt* was the prologue in a longer series of novel arcs. I've always known that Cynthia's son plays a very important role in the world of the Empire of Essalieyan. He hasn't appeared on the pages beyond this story and a single (unnamed) instant at the end of *Sea of Sorrows*. But he's important to the final arc of the world as a whole.

I couldn't write Cynthia's story, or any part of it, in the context of the later novels. I had considered trying to write it as a prologue, but structurally, it didn't work (and, at twenty thousand words, it's a very,

very long prologue). I wrote it, instead, in this novella.

Readers of the previous books will find the beginning of Stephen of Maubreche's story in this one—but I hope that they'll also find some closure for Cynthia of Maubreche as well.

Huntbrother

A N OLD STORY: girl who must marry for duty falls in love with boy who cannot fulfill that duty. The boy goes away to war, and war takes him; he never returns.

But this history was slightly different. The boy was given leave to return, in the casement of his god's flesh, and the girl, leave to spend one night with him. The night was glorious.

The morning was terrible.

And after?

$\sim$

The mirrors were covered in cloth; dust nestled in the folds made of tarpaulin's fall. The chandelier, likewise covered, hung above the great table and the fine, old chairs, casting shadows; it had offered no light in the outer chambers of these rooms for months.

Nor should it. Cynthia had refused all guests, and all visitors; had adorned herself in the colors of mourning, the deep black, with edges of green, brown, and gray. She wore a veil when it suited her, and it suited her this day. Too old to be sent to her room, she had nonetheless chosen to retreat there, for Lady Maubreche, her mother, was in a mood that was just shy of fury. Her proper, brittle voice had fallen into ice, and the space between each of her evenly pronounced words was an attempt to maintain the facade of a civility she certainly felt her daughter did not deserve.

As Cynthia had made her way up the grand staircase, its finery almost too ostentatious for the nobility of Breodanir, she had met her father, Lord Maubreche. His hair had grayed only over the last half year; his beard had turned white. The hunting injuries he had sustained during the Sacred Hunt would never leave him; he had neither the youth nor the vigor to fight their slow decay.

He had had very little to say. His daughter's condition, the doom that had been placed upon her slender shoulders, had robbed him of wrath. Of hope.

But not of affection.

It was the affection that was hardest to accept, for it was couched—and offered—in a hesitance born of pain. He expected her to reject him. She wanted to.

But she knew that death waited, and soon, for this man who had once been the pride of the Master of the Game, the King as Hunter. He had been offered the rank of Huntsman of the Chamber, and he had taken his dogs into the Sacred Woods by the King's own side.

He would never do so again.

And the certainty of that made her want to rage against the resignation she saw in a face that had once defined strength. This man had taught her to handle his dogs, although she would never love them so dearly as he; this man had brought her the books that she craved, and given her the horses that even his stableboys had difficulty taming. He had given her every freedom that a daughter could be granted, and some unwisely, as her mother had often told him.

But he could not give her more. What was left her was duty, and he could not ask her to fulfill it. Except in this way, eyes rounded and narrowed, hand upon the banister.

"Lady Eralee will come at the end of the twoweek with her son."

She nodded; she did not trust herself to speak.

"Your mother bids me remind you."

And you are to run Mother's errands now? But she did not say it. Instead, stiff, she nodded and mounted the stairs that led to her only privacy.

~

She rocked a while on the bed, her arms crossed against her chest, her head bowed. The tears that she had shed at the death of Lord Stephen of Elseth were gone; gone because she willed them gone. As he was. She had seen his corpse, and even the ceremonial dressing that bound him together, that made him whole, could not disguise how terribly his body had been mauled.

By the Hunter. By the Hunter God.

Aie, but it was not the savagery of the death she hated, for it was a death that every Hunter Lord, every huntbrother feared—and faced—within the Kingdom. Only by death was the Hunter God assuaged; only by such a death were the lands made fertile, and its people fed.

It was simply the death itself. Stephen had left her on the evening of her debut; Stephen had promised to return. And in some sense he had; the God himself had brought what remained; spirit, soul, ghost.

She had taken what he offered, desperate, pathetically grateful for the moments, the hours, that were hers. But in the end, Stephen of Elseth had no way to return to the mortal land; he would travel to the Halls of Mandaros, there to be judged for his life, and his life's deeds.

And she, Cynthia of Maubreche, returned home.

Returned home.

Lady Eralee was not a predatory woman, and it was for this reason that Cynthia found her presence a comfort.

She greeted Cynthia in the chambers reserved for the most important of dignitaries; the servants nicknamed it the King's room, although it had another, older one.

The older woman was dressed simply. She wore high collars and a gown that fell from shoulder to floor. This was not the current fashion, but Lady Eralee was old enough that elegance counted for much. "Lady Cynthia."

She noticed the dark colors of mourning Cynthia chose to wear; she was no fool. But she did not respond to them, did not offer anything but the silence of sympathy.

"Lady Eralee." Cynthia's curtsy was perfect.

"I trust you remember my younger son. Corwin, please, Lord Maubreche has promised you inspection of the kennels and the runs. Attend us now before he arrives."

Lord Corwin of Eralee was, by Hunter standards, a handsome man. His hair was dark and thick, and his eyes bright and wide; his lips were full, and were often turned up at the corner in a smile. His nose had been broken at least once, but it didn't mar the line of his face.

He turned from the windows and bowed.

Cynthia was impressed in spite of herself; the bow was perfect. She wondered what dire threats Lady Eralee had made to ensure such perfection and decided she didn't want to know.

"And my son's huntbrother, Lord Arlin."

She curtsied again, but when she rose, she met Lord Arlin's eyes. They were nothing at all like Stephen's. Lord Arlin was not as dark as Lord Corwin; his hair was a brown that would pale in sun and darken in winter, and his eyes were an odd shade of green. His skin was dark with sun, and the creases around his eyes would deepen with time. He wore a beard, where Stephen had worn none.

Nothing about him reminded her of the dead.

And yet, there was something about him that spoke to her in a way that no one but the dead had.

She had met no less than six Ladies who had made the offer to Maubreche on behalf of their Hunter sons. And of the six, Lord Corwin had the two strongest advantages: His mother, with her obvious affection for him, and his huntbrother.

"I must apologize, Lady Eralee, for my conduct during the Sacred Hunt."

"No, Lady Cynthia, you must not." Her eyes were kind. "It is I who must apologize. I understand that mourning must take its course. Believe that time heals all but the fatal wounds. Believe that, in time, the memories will be gentle.

"And forgive me, for I do understand this truth at my age, but in spite of this understanding, I am here, with my son. Corwin," she said, her voice taking on some of the steel that *must* be hidden beneath the kindness of her words. "Attend us."

He came.

Arlin had never left.

"My son is a Hunter."

Cynthia offered a conspirator's smile. "I've lived with a Hunter Lord all my life."

"With a Hunter of the Chamber, Lady Cynthia."

"Honor or no, he would rather be with the alaunts and the lymers than within the confines of the manse." She smiled.

Corwin smiled as well. His smile was a Hunter's smile, but it was not shorn of kindness.

"I would not hold him," Lady Cynthia said. "And I hear my father's heavy tread upon the stair. He will join us soon, and he is *most* excited to have a visitor who will appreciate the value of the Maubreche kennels. We have had many, many Ladies visit over the last six weeks and only two have troubled themselves to bring the sons they hope to marry."

"My thanks, Lady Cynthia, for your understanding," Lord Corwin said. Almost before the door to the hall was open, he was through it. He paused, one foot on either side of the doorframe. "Arlin, are you coming?"

"I would prefer to sit; I have not yet recovered from last week's hunt."

Corwin's brows drew down in a single thick line. But the retort he might have made was killed in its entirety by the fixed smile on his mother's face. He left.

"I have never envied the life of a huntbrother," Cynthia said softly.

"And I," Arlin replied, "have never envied the life of a woman who will sit in judgment upon the seat of her lands."

It was not what she expected to hear, and she rewarded the words with a hesitant smile. "It makes us hard," she said. A warning.

"It makes you human, I think; I am aware that there is a difference between a mask that is worn and the face beneath it."

"And mine, Lord Arlin?"

"Yours?"

"Do I wear a mask now, or do I expose the face beneath it?"

He laughed. "It is true, what is said of you."

"Arlin," Lady Eralee said.

"No, Lady Eralee, I am not so easily offended. Gossip—where it is checked and informed by affection—is a simple fact of the life of *any* house. I am aware of what is said of me in this house—but I admit that I am less aware of what is said beyond these walls.

"What part of what is said is true, Lord Arlin?"

"That you are as bold and direct as a Hunter, Lady Cynthia."

"But hopefully not as…distracted."

He laughed.

She was surprised that she could like the sound of his laugh, although she could not quite bring herself to join it.

"Lady Cynthia," he said, rising, "I have taken the liberty of bringing something of value to me. It is not a gift, for you have not accepted our suit, and I would never burden you with an obligation. It is a…loan."

She was curious.

He reached into the folds of his jacket, and drew from the pocket a small book. Bound in leather, she saw that it was much read; the leather itself had cracked and chipped in places.

A book. She took it in hands that shook. Opened it gently. There was an inscription so faded that she could not read it, but above it, the title of the book. It was called, simply, *A Life*.

"I haven't read this," she told him.

"Very few have. It was written by a young man who once apprenticed to Omaran the Maker. It says much about Makers, but more about art, and although it has little in common with my life in Breodanir, I have found that it speaks to me."

A book. "I thank you, Lord Arlin, for lending me something you so obviously value." Thinking, as she said it, of all of the days she had met Stephen while she hid from the young ladies of the court in the quiet stacks of the royal library. Another life.

"Lady Eralee, I am honored to have seen you again. You are always such a joy. I find your youngest son the epitome of a Hunter Lord, and I believe that—should my parents approve—he would make a fine Lord Maubreche."

Cynthia rose then, the ghost of Stephen of Elseth painful in his sudden presence. "I am called away, but Lady Maubreche will join you shortly." She turned her head to one side.

Arlin rose as she rose, and he stepped toward her; she shied away when he raised his hand. "I apologize, Lady, if my gesture has caused offense—"

"No," she said, meeting his eyes although her own were heavy with water, "no offense at all, Lord Arlin."

~

Six months passed in peace. After Lady Eralee's visit, Lady Maubreche enter-tained the noblewomen who had come, aware that no formal engagement had yet been announced; she had not, however, required her daughter to be in attendance for such meetings. In her severe fashion, Margaret, Lady Maubreche, could be kind.

But after six months had passed, that kindness had changed to something harsher: fear. With fear came anger, for the Lady Maubreche had no easy way of containing the things that were beyond her control, and she could see—anyone who thought to look could now see—that Lady Cynthia was with child.

~

If her mother was surprised—and outraged—her father was not. And perhaps that was why he dwindled.

But when Lady Maubreche chose to confront her wayward daughter, he intervened. He often intervened in the affairs of his Ladies, especially when those affairs were tainted by raw fury. He had always been a brave man.

"Cerle," his wife had said, offering him a rare warning.

But he had simply shaken his head, forcing his shoulders to stretch to an almost forgotten height. "Margaret. Come. I have something to show you."

"What can you have to show me that cannot wait? Your daughter is in disgrace. All that we have done—all that we have arranged—will be undone, and publicly; Lady Eralee will see this as a betrayal of her trust. And it is."

"Our daughter is not the only woman whose heart has overruled her head; she is young, Margaret. You were young once, and I have always been aware that I…would not have been the husband of your choice."

That silenced his wife a moment, and it surprised Cynthia, for Margaret, Lady Maubreche, was the epitome of Breodanir nobility. "Come," he said again quietly. "If Andrew were here, he might have shown you what you must see. He is not, and I must accept that duty."

Andrew, huntbrother to Lord Maubreche, and been taken, these many years past, by the Hunter God in the Sacred Hunt. But his name still had power.

For that reason, it was seldom invoked.

Lady Maubreche hesitated a moment before she took the arm her husband had offered her.

"Cynthia," her father said. "If you would accompany us?"

What her mother accepted, she could not refuse. She nodded, although no like arm was offered to sustain or guide her, and she trailed after her parents as she had not done since she was considered a child in Maubreche.

They wandered, of course, into the the gardens. There was not a room in the manse that did not have the ears of the servants, and some dramas were best played out on a private stage. But the gardens were not their destination; what lay beyond them, in the heart of the Maubreche responsibility, was. The maze, the hedges of the Master Gardener.

On a day like this one, the sun half-veiled by passing clouds, the maze cast scant shadow; what drew the eye was the life of the hedge. Not the greenery, although there was no finer hedge in the whole of Breodanir, but rather the details contained in the clipped command of shears. There was, about the hedge, a mystery and a grandeur that had silenced even the most voluble of Maubreche's many guests.

Perhaps it was because the maze grew. It changed. It seemed a thing of life in a way that even the living were not. Among its hedges, one could see the hesitant face of a doe, her child, leaves carved and cut in a way that suggested wide eyes and delicate face, beneath her forelegs. One could see the flight of birds, suggested by the rustle of branches that did not, in fact, rustle; could see the little signs of captive life.

But beyond them, beyond these living miracles, these growing statues that changes as the days changed, lay something that was hidden from the eye of the casual visitor: the hedge-wall.

It was to the wall that Lord Maubreche now went.

Lady Maubreche was still silent, but the quality of that silence had changed. Cynthia knew it well; it was kin to her own, and contained an unspoken dread that was not—quite—fear.

The history of Maubreche could be seen here, and unlike the outer hedges, there was no sense of life's urgency in the living carvings. Year after year Cynthia had seen the men and women who had earned a place upon this hedge, and they did not move, did not seek to break free of the confines of the branches and roots that told their story.

She could see the eyes of Hardann the Black as he stood upon the cliff's edge, gazing out upon the vast hills and forests of his domain; could see the savagery of the expression of one of the earliest of the Maubreche Hunters. She could see dogs—Aswine, the finest that Maubreche had ever produced—holding a crazed bear at bay; could see the sundered horn at his feet, the wounds—green, but gaping—in his side.

More. More, and she knew it all.

But her father did not seek to offer her a lesson from the history of the oldest of the Breodani families; the time for that had passed, with child-hood. It was the first time he had truly acknowledged that her childhood was over. The distant past gave way to the near past.

It was almost over.

As if he could hear what she did not say, her father turned; the line of his shoulders had fallen again, and he walked with a pronounced limp, gifted him for his valor at the King's side in the Sacred Hunt.

"No, Cynthia," he told her gently, "it has only just begun." He lifted an arm, and Cynthia could see her mother's hands rise, although she could not see her mother's expression; Lady Maubreche's back was turned toward her daughter in the stiffness of what had, a moment ago, been fury.

Cynthia walked around her father and came to stand by his side.

To see, upon what had once been the unshorn, unsculpted branches of the last stretch of the wall itself, the image that had caused her mother to raise hands to mouth.

She saw herself.

Saw herself, in formless robes that she had never worn, and by decree, would never wear: they were Priest's robes. Their color was green, as the hedge was, but their form and shape was unmistakable.

Is that what I look like? She approached this woman, this other Cynthia, and found that they were of a height; the maze was tall. But this woman's expression was one that Cynthia had never seen upon her own face. Not peaceful, not exactly, but free of the misery and the pain of loss that had guided the last half year.

Yet it was not this that stopped her mother, nor the fact that beneath even the trailing robes of a Priest, her pregnancy was so advanced it could not be hidden, could not be denied.

It was the hands upon her shoulders, the head above her head.

Her eyes rose slowly.

Above her image, carved as the statue in the maze's heart was carved, was Breodan, Hunter God.

She had seen him. She had heard his voice. She knew that the statue no more captured his essence or his truth than this clipped and tucked artistry.

But she knew, also that that statue was now. That the face it wore was the face that the Hunter God presented to his people in effigy. She turned away then.

She had not seen this. She had not come here since she had left, six months ago.

She swore that she would never come again, but she swore it in silence, for words spoken aloud had power and exacted a price, and she was not willing to expose herself to the wrath of Breodan.

"Cynthia!"

Her mother's voice. She ignored it for another ten steps, but when it came again, she turned like a beast brought to harbor.

The fury was gone from her mother's face, and with it, the color.

"Why did you not tell us?"

She had nothing to say. For just a moment, nothing. And then cheeks burning, she met her mother's eyes defiantly. "He came to me," she said, voice soft because there was no other way to force the words out. "He came to me as Stephen. Stephen of Elseth.

"For one evening. Just one."

Her mother looked stricken.

"And in return, he asked of me one thing. He did not command it. He did not compel it. But he *asked* it, and who of us have ever refused what the *Hunter God* has asked?"

"We—we—must call the Priests."

"*No.*" Her voice was louder now.

"Cynthia, the Priests *must* know. If you bear the son of the Hunter—"

"I bear Stephen's *son*," she said, the words raw, the lie rawer.

But that was not what the god had promised. He had offered her no lie. He had offered her no comfort. *The child will be mine; I contain the spirit of Stephen, but the flesh is gone.* It hadn't mattered.

Her mother released her father's arms and crossed the perfect grass. "Cynthia," she said, her voice a voice that had not been heard in Maubreche since Cynthia was a girl.

"Don't pity me. I don't want your pity." Cupped hands caught the sides of her face. Warm hands. Her mother said nothing at all.

~

Not that day. But later, when the awe and the compassion had once again taken its place in the depths of Lady Maubreche's shuttered heart, words came.

"Cynthia."

Cold words. "Lady Maubreche."

"What do you think you're doing?"

"I am dressing," Cynthia said coldly, "to meet Lady Eralee and her sons."

"You are not a child," her mother replied. "That dress will not be acceptable. Look at you."

"I chose this dress for a reason."

"You look as if you might bear a child at any minute, and you've months before your time."

"I will bear a child," Cynthia said, with a calm that fooled neither. "Am I to dress as if this child is the product of grief and histrionics? Am I to hide him?"

"Lady Eralee is not, as you well know, apprised of your…situation." It had been a bitter point of contention between the elder and the younger Ladies. "I should have overruled you. Your recklessness—"

"I am *not* reckless!"

"You are." Her mother's hand rose, palm exposed, as if it were weapon, or worse, as if it were all of her rage. Rage, Cynthia accepted with a bitter grace, but what lay beneath that rage, and that urgency, she could not force herself to closely examine.

But her mother did not strike. The hand fell, and with it, the line of her mother's shoulder. Lady Maubreche looked *old*.

"The healers are not certain that your father will survive to see the birth of your child." Just that.

Her mother's face was a wall now.

Cynthia stood, but the blood left her face, and her knees bent toward carpet and hard floor. She did not accuse her mother of lying. Could not. "But—but he—"

"The infection that came of the wound weakened his heart. I confess I am not a healer; I do not understand the whole of the details, and I have heard them time and again. Your father," she added bitterly, "will listen to no one."

"Why did you not tell me?"

"Because I am old and foolish," Lady Maubreche replied. "And because I raised no fool; I had hoped you might notice it yourself."

Cynthia's words slipped away from her, water through cupped hand.

She stared at the lines around her mother's thinned lips.

"Yes," her mother said, sparing her nothing. "We have no time to wait, and none to waste. When Lord Maubreche at last succumbs to his stubborn—" she turned her head a moment, lifting a hand in warning. "When that happens, there must be a Lord Maubreche to take his place.

"Think, daughter. Think of what you choose to do. I cannot turn Lady Eralee away; two weeks of travel separate our territories, and the winter is already approaching. If she does not come now, we will have to wait until the spring."

"Margaret, are you shouting at the poor girl?"

Lady Maubreche turned as the door creaked open upon the face of her Hunter Lord.

"I am discussing the duties of the afternoon with the woman who will one day continue the work that I now do," she told him, the chill in her voice more of a threat than the winter.

~

The argument might have continued; in truth, it might have had no end.

But that day, the dogs had come in from the runs, leaving their kennels like a stream of muscled flesh and glistening coat. They were silent, the alaunts; silent and determined. But they came.

Through the runs, over the fences that served to mark their territory, out of the huts and houses that were tended with such care. Black bodies, brown bodies, white and gray; sable, with patches of lighter colors. They had run up the path to the main house, and they had thrown themselves against the doors with deafening thuds until Sartay had chosen to open them.

The dogs had run *into* the hall, nudging the door wide to allow themselves free passage. They had run unerringly up the stairs, Hasufel at their head, and Onma, the best of the lymers, a leap behind. They had come to Cynthia—herself no great champion of theirs—and laid themselves, almost on top of one another, at her feet.

"Hasufel! Onma!" Lord Maubreche said, the command in the words undeniable.

Hasufel, the pack leader, raised his muzzle. He uttered the first sound the dogs had made since they had gained entrance into Cynthia's chamber. He whined.

And then he rose. Rose and placed his great forepaws gently against the swell of pale blue cloth, beneath which lay flesh and child. His paws were not perfectly clean; they left a mark against the fall of fabric; a dog's footprint. A signature.

Lord Maubreche met Hasufel's eyes; the whining grew in pitch. Cynthia saw the peculiar expression that spoke of Hunter's trance cross her father's face. More than that was lost; she could not take her eyes off his alaunts. There were reasons that they were not kept in the house, and not all of them had to do with the strict demeanor of the keeper of the keys.

Perhaps because the dogs drew her attention, she missed the subtle shift of her father's expression; what was left, when she turned to face him, was something akin to surprise. He walked across the room, closing the distance between them, and then, as Hasufel before him, he lifted a hand and placed it gently against the crest of her belly.

To his wife, he said, his intonation low, his words a growl, "Let her be."

Just that. And Lady Maubreche bowed her head, wordless.

In the face of Hunter business, the greatest of Ladies could not be judged weak for leaving the arena.

~

Thus dressed, thus marked, Lady Cynthia of Maubreche met the mother of her future husband for the seventh time.

That Lady had taken the trouble to arrange her skirts upon the settee in the King's room. She looked up as Sartay opened the doors to announce the presence of Lord and Lady Maubreche; her smile was pleasant, the expression that Cynthia remembered.

She wished, for just a moment, that she had taken her mother's bitter advice. For the smile froze on Lady Eralee's face so completely Cynthia wondered if it would ever return.

"Lady Eralee." Cynthia executed a curtsy that would have made her mother proud in any other circumstance.

"Lady Cynthia." The elder woman's smile was pinched and forced.

"You look well."

"Lady Eralee," Lady Maubreche said quietly. "Lord Corwin. Lord Arlin." She offered them a full curtsy. "You honor us with your presence. I assume that Lord Corwin would like to inspect the kennels?"

But for once Lord Corwin's attention did not seem to be upon the kennels, the alaunts, the Hunt. Where his mother's face was pale and hard, his was unschooled; his mouth was open in what seemed a wordless parody of shock.

"Forgive us," Lady Eralee said coolly, "if we came at an awkward time." Beneath the surface of her chilly words, her meaning was plain. She desired an explanation. Now.

Cynthia could have let her mother speak. It was Lady Maubreche's right, and responsibility, in such an uncomfortable situation. But instead, she lifted a gentle hand.

"Lady Eralee," she said, with a calm she did not feel, "Please accept my apologies."

"What I accept, Lady Cynthia, has yet to be decided." Her frown was now pronounced. Cynthia could not recall a time when she had seen Lady Eralee so furious that her anger could not be contained behind a civil facade.

"I bear a child," Cynthia continued. "And I *will* bear the child to term."

"That much, Lady Cynthia, I can see. We were not informed of this… development. And I can be certain that the child is *not* my son's."

"No." Cynthia replied gravely.

"Had you no desire to accept my son's suit, you might have chosen to be more forthcoming and less insulting. May I ask whose child you carry?" It was not a polite question.

Cynthia was silent. She looked to Lady Eralee, straightening the line of her shoulders. And then, she looked to Lady Eralee's son. To Lord Corwin. To Lord Arlin beside him. She studied their faces, and if what she saw there did not bring hope, it did not destroy it. Hope was a bitter thing.

Lord Corwin met Cynthia's eyes. Held them. "Lady Cynthia," he said, drawing toward her. "How long have you known that you carry a child?"

"I knew," she told him, "the night of his conception."

"Why did you see fit to hide it from me?"

Not from you, she wanted to say. But she was of Maubreche; she chose her words with care. "I deemed it too great a risk."

"A risk?"

Was tired of choosing them with care. "Yes, Lord Corwin." She knew she should speak with Lady Eralee, for in the end, the decision would be hers. But Lord Corwin now stood close enough that she could see no one else.

"And that?"

"Of the six men who have made the offer to my mother, you are the only one I wished to accept. I am aware that my situation is tenuous; I am aware that I must marry. I am aware that for the sons of lesser families than Eralee, or of greater ambition, my condition—no matter what its apparent cause—would be no obstacle. If you choose to withdraw, we will begin again with one of the others. But—"

He reached out slowly, as if she were an injured alaunt, and placed his palm against the curve of her belly. His hand was warm; beneath the multiple layers of cloth, she could feel the heat.

"My apologies," he said, his unblinking eyes the peculiar windows of a Hunter Lord's face. He bowed head. "I did not mean to interrupt."

"I had hoped—I had hoped that you might forgive me."

"But you did not speak."

"No." She closed her eyes a moment.

"Why?"

"We—" She could not speak of her father's death. Could not.

"So...if I accept your hand in marriage, I am to be the keeper of another man's child." His face was shuttered now.

She looked for condemnation in it; found nothing at all to hold on to. Was surprised at the pain this caused.

"I know what you must think of me—"

"No, Lady Cynthia, you do not. Arlin?"

Arlin rose from his place beside Lady Eralee on the settee. He bowed to Lady Cynthia, his face concealing more than Lord Corwin's. She closed her eyes. Heard his words in the darkness.

"I told you," he said softly, "that she was wounded."

"And this?"

"What do you think, Corwin?" Impatience, in the words. Sharp impatience. "When the alaunts are wounded by boar or bear, they do not lightly suffer anyone's touch. Look," he added, "at your left hand, if you require proof. You bear the scars. But the alaunts serve you, and you alone."

She could end it. She could tell them the truth. But...but there was something she *had* to know. And because of it, she bore the humiliation of their assumptions.

"And you would accept her, after this?"

"You know my answer. But it is not, in the end, my decision. She is not like many of the other Ladies we have met."

"No, indeed. Not one of the others would risk her future and her fortune in such a fashion."

"Yes. Because they are careful; because they are calculating. Were she different there would be *no child*. She will also be a good deal more powerful than the others you have met."

"Speak plainly, Arlin. You seem to love words."

"She has too much heart, and she has too much will; what she feels, she feels strongly. Yet I believe that if we accept this, she will give you what few of the others *could* give."

"And that?"

"In time? Love." He looked at Cynthia then, and she met his dark eyes; saw a compassion in them that she wanted, desperately, for her own. "And a son."

"True. Maubreche is not know for fecundity; perhaps this can be seen as proof that *my* line will be established here."

"Lord Corwin—"

But Lord Corwin turned to Cynthia's father, "Lord Maubreche," he said quietly.

"Lord Corwin."

"It would honor me greatly if you would allow me inspection of the kennels that will one day be mine." His smile was sharp.

Her father's brow's rose; for just a minute, Cynthia thought he would growl. Instead, he laughed. "The alaunts are in the runs, but they have been forbidden the forest stretch for the day, for it seems they thought it acceptable to charge *into* the manse."

"Into the manse? Why? Was there some danger to you?"

"To me? No." The old Lord Maubreche turned the most gentle of gazes upon his only child. But he did not speak of what had happened. Instead, he said, "If you care to view a pack of hostile, unhappy running hounds, the honor would be mine."

"As I said, old man," Corwin said, with a wolf's sharp grin, "I desire to see what will be mine."

Her throat was tight. She felt tears at the edge of her eyes, her open eyes; felt breath desert her. She closed them, and again, in darkness, heard words. This time they were her own.

"Lord Corwin?"

"Lady Cynthia."

"The child I bear is Breodan's."

~

Later, when the engagement had been announced and the agreement written, signed, sealed by wax and the crests of the two families, Lord Corwin looked up from the table. His Hunter eyes were bright and keen; he was on the hunt, even surrounded by furniture, carpets, long curtains, and thick windows.

"Why did you not just tell us the truth? It would have spared you much."

Lady Eralee placed a thin hand over her son's; the contrast in color was the difference between their responsibilities. "If you do not understand, ask Arlin."

"Arlin doesn't understand it either."

"Ah, well. Arlin *is* a man, even if he is the finest of huntbrothers."

Corwin looked annoyed. It was an expression that only the Lady Eralee could easily provoke.

"Forgive them, Cynthia," she added, using the family name. "I am proud of them both; for a Hunter, Corwin is a fine person."

"Truly there is nothing to forgive, Lady Eralee."

"Call me Amanda."

"Amanda, then. There is nothing to forgive. Lord Corwin's question is a reasonable one."

"Very well. Since you are so keen to be charitable to the man who will be your husband, I must assume that your kindness is an act of loyalty, and such loyalty is always a balm to a mother's heart, even if it is in this case misplaced."

"You tell us, then," Corwin snapped.

"Is that the neatest signature you can make?" His mother said with a sniff, greatly enjoying herself. "Very well, I will take it upon myself to answer your question. There are very few among us who do not desire to be loved. Or to be trusted.

"If she could appear thus before you, with no word and no explanation, and you could offer acceptance, could believe that some extenuating circumstance drove her to this situation, you would prove—to her—that some trust exists. You accepted her for *herself*."

"Well, who else would I accept her for? She's no one else." He was annoyed.

"Lady Eralee—"

"Amanda, dear,"

"Amanda—really, I think Lord Corwin is correct. I was foolish."

"Besides, it proves no such thing," Corwin continued. "I could have accepted it if I wanted a house of my own, lands I could claim and rule. My acceptance might have been a matter of practicality. And greed."

His mother sighed. "Did she not say, of the six, she chose you for a reason?"

He rolled his eyes. "Do not," he said to his wife-to-be, "spend too much time with my mother. I would not have her infest you with her wordplay."

~

One month later, they were married. The ceremony was not small, but Cynthia allowed her mother to choose the dress, the veil, and the accoutrements in which she would be seen. She no longer cared if her pregnancy—which was well advanced—was hidden to the best of the dressmaker's capabilities. All that she wanted, she had achieved.

She was nervous.

Corwin was not. But Arlin made up for his composure.

Breodani weddings, were not a simple matter of two people; they were a binding of three. The bride and the groom might stand together, but in the procession, it was the huntbrother who led the way, and when they arrived before the Priest, it was the huntbrother who gave over the symbols of the joining of their houses: the chalice, the rings, and the key.

Lady Eralee had obliquely threatened poor Arlin with six different torments if he dropped anything, stepped on Cynthia's train, or worse—

much worse—allowed the dogs to disturb the ceremony.

For the dogs had their role. They were as much part of a Hunter's flesh as wife would be. Perhaps more.

But Corwin's dogs were silent throughout. They stood in the room at the top of the nave, waiting; they watched, heads raised, ears peaked, as the Priest began his incantations. Cynthia was certain they were thinking of food, but one glance at her husband's face said otherwise; he was deep in trance. She hoped the Priest would not be too offended.

Iverssen had performed many Hunter marriages; if he noticed this breach, he spoke above it.

But when the joining was done, when the chalice had been filled, first with wine and then with the blood of the three supplicants—Hunter, huntbrother, and wife—the dogs rose as one, as if called. They walked quietly, and with a processional air about their movements, until they stood before Lady Cynthia. Then, as one, they lifted heads, elongating throats; they bayed. Even she, born to Hunter but not to Hunt, understood what they offered, and she was moved by it.

Corwin, however, was not, and they were kennelled for the twoweek after the ceremony was concluded.

~

When Cynthia's child was born, he was born in silence, and his wide, golden eyes, crouched in the red wrinkles of a newborn's face, looked out on the world with curiosity. Corwin and Arlin haunted the room that the midwives had grudgingly allowed them to enter, and it was Corwin—not Arlin—who had taken the babe from the arms of the midwife; Corwin and not Arlin, who had lifted the child with an awe and an open expression of wonder that Cynthia would never forget.

He had taken the long, soft squares of swaddling cloth, and with shaking hands—huge hands, in comparison with the babe's—he had swaddled him tight. Then, before the midwives could stop him, he bent and placed lips upon that wizened brow.

"This child," he said softly to Cynthia, although he could not take his eyes from the babe, "is your son. But allow it, Cynthia, and he will be mine; I will raise him, and I will teach him the ways of the Hunt."

She wept, then, because he was Hunter Lord, and almost incapable of lying. She said, for the first time, the pain and exhaustion of hours of labor loosening her tongue, "I love you, Corwin of Maubreche."

And his eyes had widened further, his sun-darkened skin still capable of reddening.

Arlin had come to sit by her; had taken her shaking hands in his. His smile was gentle.

She had been happy, then. In truth, she would have remained happy.

But from the moment her son could walk, he had been drawn to the maze.

~

Although she was tired after the baby's birth, as the midwives had warned she would be, she was calm; she felt graced by the absence of pain and the absence of burden. The babe slept—the midwives also assured her that this would not continue—and she herself passed from waking to sleeping with ease. But on the third day, her father woke her at twilight. He entered the room with a swinging lamp in hand, and held it aloft, pressing one finger firmly against lip. It was both a request and a command, and Cynthia, for the first time since the baby was born, rose from the birthing bed. In the darkness, she dressed, and then she joined him.

He walked slowly, and he paused several times. She heard the rise and fall of his chest as he labored for breath, but she did not injure his dignity by offering him aid.

They walked, together, toward the heart of the Maubreche maze, and there, in the darkness, they paused before the statue of the Hunter God. The moon did not cast his shadow, but it lit him softly; he looked less forbidding in the evening than he did during the height of sun's light.

"There is something you must know," he told her quietly. "About Maubreche. About the Hunter."

She nodded, understanding fully what he meant by this; his time was almost past.

"The first of our line was, like your first son, born of the God. I do not know how; I have not had the ability to ask him. You, I fear, have spoken with the Hunter far more often than even his Priests; there is little that I can teach you that you do not already know.

"But this place is the heart of his worship. This is what I was told by my father before his death, and what my father was told by his; it has passed in an unbroken line to all of the Maubreche blood.

"The hedge-wall," he added quietly, "is almost complete."

She nodded.

"You have seen yourself in its leaves and the cuttings of the Master Gardener. What you do not know is this: when the last of the hedge is complete, the task of the Gardener is at an end."

Her brows rose.

"The Gardener is older than the Kingdom," he told her quietly. "And he swore his oath to the Hunter when Maubreche was a man and not a great family. He has labored for centuries upon this work."

"What is his work?"

"The history," he said quietly, "of Maubreche; the history of the first— and the last—of the Hunter's chosen family." He bowed his head. "I did not understand it, Cynthia, when I was told. It was not clear to me. My father was taken by the Hunt, but he knew, before that Sacred Hunt, that he would not return to these estates. I asked him how he knew, and he told me he couldn't say. I realize now that this wasn't a matter of choice.

"Because I know, and I don't know how, or why. It doesn't matter. When I...found you here, on the hedge I understood. The Hunter has waited centuries for another child; birth was the beginning of our line, and birth, in some fashion, is closure to that tale.

"Your son will fight an enemy so terrible that he is not named. But it is in preparation for that fight that Maubreche has stood, these centuries; it is for that fight that the Hunters have waited, that their oaths have been given and taken."

"My son is—"

"Yes," her father said, his face grave with pity and horror. "He is a babe. I've held him, even though my arms are so weak they can barely keep a lamp aloft. I know how slight he is, how vulnerable.

"But he is Breodan's Hope," he closed his eyes. "In this garden, in the Heart of this maze, he is safe. But if he stays within its confines, he will have failed not only Breodan, but all of Maubreche and its ancient history.

"We've waited for your son, Cynthia." He bowed his head.

She stared at him, sorrow and anger blending until they were inseparable, a weave she would wear for the rest of her life.

"But waiting or no, we have had no way of discerning his worthiness. He must take a huntbrother," he added.

"Of course! He's Breodani, Hunter-born."

"Yes. And he must learn what Hunters often fail to learn: the value of the people he must protect. Without that knowledge, without that guidance, he will fail us all."

She swallowed. "Let me do it," she whispered.

He frowned, but it was gentle. "So has every parent said since child was born, and not only within Maubreche. But we cannot protect our young in any way save this: We can teach them the value of love, of trust and trustworthiness. Not more, and not less."

He bowed. "Your son's road will be strange and difficult. He is of the Hunter God; we cannot forget this. But he is *also* mortal; he is still a child. What a child needs, he needs." He walked to where she stood, and leaning down, kissed her upturned brow.

"I am proud of you, daughter," he said quietly.

~

Two weeks after the birth of his first grandchild, Lord Maubreche passed away.

Lord Corwin became in name, Corwin, Lord Maubreche, and Lady Cynthia, Cynthia, Lady Maubreche, heir to its vast responsibilities. Her mother had promised her that she would grow to meet the needs and demands of Maubreche, and as often was the case her mother had been correct.

When Stephen was well into his seventh year, the arguments began.

"He needs a huntbrother, Cynthia. He is our oldest son. He will be eight in six months; he will be expected to take the green and the gray of the page; he will be expected to make his vows. Iverssen is waiting."

"I know."

"Then give me leave to find a suitable boy. The streets of the King's City are full of them. Let me hunt there."

"Not yet," she answered softly. The answer would become less soft with time.

"You cannot coddle him!"

"He is not like other Hunters. He has the eyes of the God."

"He has the eyes of the God, yes. But he *also* has the duties of the Breodani! Would you deny him the heritage of his people?"

"No! Nor would I force him to take vows that he is not yet capable of making."

"The Hunter's Law—"

"The Hunter's Law guides Hunters," she said, and it pained her. "But our son—"

"You mean *your* son, is that it?"

His anger was sharp; the words were harsh. What he had promised, from birth, he had lived up to. He loved Stephen. Had always loved him. Because of it, she knew that he could not let it rest; he was Hunter, after all. But She said, "It is not yet time, Corwin. Be content."

"Content?"

"Breodan has bid us wait."

Her husband fell into a grim silence. He would break it, again and again, as the years passed, for he felt her refusal as a wall between himself and the child of his heart. And it was.

~

If Stephen had not been so adept with the dogs, perhaps the argument would have—like so many of their arguments—been left to wither, growing the cold edges and hidden barbs of all such unresolved pain.

But the dogs adored Stephen. At least it seemed so to Cynthia; to Corwin it was much, much deeper. When an alaunt appeared, sidling out of the runs, to sit by Stephen's feet, it seemed natural to her; to Corwin, it was not. Because the dogs, in all things, had their hierarchy, and the dog that was also first to abase himself in the joyful abandon of an anxious pup was no pup. It was Hasufel.

With the death of Cynthia's father, he had—with initial reluctance—become Corwin's dog.

But he was Stephen's liege.

He would take his portion from the hands of the master of the game, but he would often take it *to* Stephen, and Stephen would quarter it for him, feeding him from hand as if Hasufel were an imperial falcon and not the finest of the running hounds Maubreche boasted.

The truth of this allegiance could not be denied. The awe it caused, among the Hunters, even less so.

Corwin's anger simmered, boiled, simmered, and boiled. In the end, they could barely speak of Stephen. Only Arlin stood between them, and it caused him some bitter pain.

Aie, they waited. Stephen passed his eighth birthday, and his ninth. On his tenth, Corwin's anger knew no bounds, and he left—without Arlin—to hunt the dogs made wild by the temper he could not contain.

When he returned, he was subdued but the anger and the helplessness of the situation did not leave him. His son, his oldest son, was not yet allowed entrée into the world of Hunter Lords.

It would have been natural for him to turn his attention to Robart, his youngest. And he did, for Robart was now seven, and fast approaching the first of the many ages of majority within Breodanir. But his success with Robart, and the introduction of Mark—a scarred young boy with an unruly tongue and a rough sense of loyalty—as the first huntbrother of the Maubreche kin, had not calmed his anger.

Because the anger was based in fear. Fear for Stephen of the golden eyes.

She hated his fear, but she loved him for it. She accepted his rage as if it were weather, a storm that she could predict but could not deflect. Was it not her own?

~

But the day finally came. It was a day much like any other, but it was punctuated by the presence of guests—guests who were as much kin as people could be who did not bear Maubreche blood. Gilliam, Lord Elseth, and his unearthly, wild wife Espere. They had come on a social visit, or so Gilliam said—but there was about him a tenseness, an anger, that she had not seen since they had first met, and Stephen of Elseth had stood between them, loved by both.

Her Stephen, her own son, was called to the house from the runs. But he failed to arrive. And after an hour had passed, Lord Corwin had looked up, bleakly, at his wife.

She closed her eyes. "Yes," she told her husband, her voice subdued and quiet but without any hint of gentleness, "I will go and fetch him."

~

Lady Cynthia lifted her skirts and began to walk, with purpose, toward the maze. Purpose was required. She knew that today the maze would give way to the land that the Hunter God opened on occasion for those of his blood. Knew that grass and hedge and flower bed would become gray and insubstantial; they were mortal, things not meant for the odd landscape of the world between the realm of the gods and realms of man. She turned the corner, following the line of the wall by the shadow it cast upon tended grass. When that shadow changed, lengthening into something slender, she looked up.

Met the silver-gray eyes of the Master Gardener.

She bowed at once. In no other garden was a gardener afforded such a genuine gesture of respect.

He returned that bow gravely. "Lady Cynthia."

"Master Gardener."

She did not speak his name because she did not know it. Had never known it. When she had been younger, she had asked it of him, as she might ask it of the other children she met. His answer was a stiff, cold silence—an indication that she had breached social protocol. She had not asked again.

"I—I come looking for my son."

"He is at the Heart of the maze," the gardener answered. He raised his hands; they were empty. He carried no shears, none of the tools of his life's work.

She did not ask him why. But he stood before her, immobile, as if he were a gate, locked and barred against her passage. "Am I to be forbidden the maze now?" Her voice was cool.

"No, Lady. But it would be prudent if you chose to return to your guests."

"My guests wait upon my son," she told him quietly.

"He will come," the gardener replied. "But he speaks, now, with his father."

She felt the cold, then; the sun could not pierce it. Gathering her shawl about her shoulders, she stepped forward.

"I was never terribly prudent," she said quickly. But her voice shook. At a decade, memory slept. But it had never died.

"Then I will not stop you," he replied. But his eyes were cold.

~

The mists rose at last above her face, obscuring the maze, with its intricate, secret hedges, its indictment and its promise.

She bowed her head; felt the sweet air of the Between in her lungs. This was the Heart of Maubreche. She had come to understand it in a way that none of her predecessors had.

She could not see Stephen.

But in the shadows that no sunlight cast, she saw the Hunter God.

As always, she turned away from the sight of him, steadying herself. The God was not a man, although he bore form similar to one; he was not a beast, although the great tines of antlers rose from the perfect smoothness of his forehead. He was not a giant, although he was tall; he was not simply beautiful in the way men can be.

But he suggested all of these things, as if mortality were a dim and tarnished echo of his glory, and when he turned his eyes upon her, they were of gold and fire.

"Lady Cynthia."

"Lord." She bowed. She bowed deeply.

"You have waited," he said gently. "And by the reckoning of my people, you have waited long."

For what? But she did not ask.

"For the time when your son is able to hear my voice without the crutch of Maubreche and its hallowed ground; for the time when your son is able to make himself heard across the wilds of the mortal plane. He has my gift," the God continued. "The oldest and the greatest of my gifts: His is the power of the oathbinder."

Oathbinder.

"Honor," the God continued, his voice the multitude, the crowded murmur of young and old, of man and woman, of sorrow and joy, anger and peace, birth and death: a song; a God's song. "What is given, as oath, to my son, will be binding. Only death will end it."

What does that have to do with the Hunt?

"He will take his place among his people," the God said, speaking as gently as a gale could. "I have watched our son. I have spoken with him. I have judged him where judgment is possible. What he is, he is. What he will be…

"It is time."

"And his huntbrother?"

For just a moment an expression solidified upon the God's face. Compassion. Or pity. "You have defied convention before."

She closed her eyes. "When?" she asked, without opening them.

"Today. Today, Cynthia, and believe that had we any other choice, we would make it."

"We?"

"The enemies," he answered, after so long a pause she though he might not offer words, "of the Lord of the Hells."

She was Lady Maubreche now. In her youth, she had been another girl—but the Between was a funny place; it existed outside of time.

And outside of time, in her heart, she was Cynthia. The Hunter's gaze moved her to a bitter fury.

"Have I not given enough?" she whispered, through clenched teeth. "This boy, *this* Stephen, is mine; he is all the remains to me of—of—" Her hands were fists; they shook.

"You have given," the Hunter God said quietly, the multitude fading, "what only Maubreche can give."

"Then do not ask more of me!"

"It is not of you, in the end, that all will be asked." Pity.

She hated pity.

"You will find your son," he said quietly. "And he will be with you some little while yet."

~

Stephen was golden-haired. Golden-eyed. His skin was the pale white of a Northern clime, unusual among those born to the heat and the sun of the Hunt. His face was slender, his chin pronounced; his cheeks were high, and if color was to be found in his face, it was there. He was tall, or seemed tall, for his age, but that was simple illusion; he wore his height well because of his slender build. Only his eyes spoke of his parentage, and no craft on her part could dispel their truth.

Those eyes were round now, and unblinking; they had been touched by the God, and they burned brightly. Even when they narrowed in confusion, as they did now.

"Mother?"

"Lady Maubreche," she said, correcting him automatically.

He grimaced. "We have guests?"

"Yes. We still have guests."

"How long was I gone?"

"Not...not long," she told him quietly.

"I'm sorry." They were probably his first spoken words; they were certainly his most common ones.

His wince brought her no pleasure; no sense of the superiority of experience or knowledge that separated them. His eyes lost a hint of their brilliance, and none of their color, as his vision turned inward.

"Why did you leave, Stephen?"

"I heard the Hunter," he answered quietly.

Answer enough. "Are you finished, then?"

He nodded quietly. Offered her his arm, as if he were already past childhood. She accepted it with gravity.

"Mako is angry," he told her.

"Mako is always angry." Although Stephen had not taken the first of the Hunter's Oaths, and was therefore not legally allowed his pack, his pack had nonetheless formed. It was one of the few facts of Stephen's life that made Corwin happy, and Cynthia accepted it gratefully.

Of Stephen's alaunts, Mako was the wildest. She had no fondness for him, nor he for her; everything was his rival for Stephen's affection. She smiled briefly. "I can't imagine what he's going to be like when you finally take a huntbrother."

His arm tightened. "Mother?"

This time, she offered no correction. "Yes?"

"Are you ready?"

It was an odd question. An honest one. "I don't know." She didn't. This son, this Stephen, was far more like a huntbrother than a Hunter in temperament, and if something would slowly transform him into a Hunter, she wasn't sure she wanted to see it. Although the dogs were indisputably his, they had never robbed her of his company or his attention; they were not his obsession, not the signal truth by which he might claim, in the end, his title and the fullness of his power. She was afraid to lose him.

Afraid to see Corwin or Gilliam when she gazed upon her son's face; afraid to lose the very little she could see of the man she had once loved, and at such cost.

Afraid, because in the end, if he was Hunter Lord, she would surrender him to the Sacred Hunt that might claim his life.

"No," she told him, pensive now. "I'm not. But I'm not certain I will ever be ready."

~

When they reached the lawns, Cynthia stopped. She reached for Stephen's shoulder, gripping it tightly enough that his breath came out in a hiss.

Lord Gilliam stood, and by his side, bristling, stood Espere, his truly wild wife. Her lips had come up over teeth, and those teeth, long and white, were bared. He had taken her as wife over his mother's muted objections, and she had never been given the full duties of a Lady of Breodanir. Instead, his mother, Elsabet, continued to fulfill the Elseth duties.

At Gilliam's side, Corwel, the third of his dogs to be so named, crouched, belly low to ground, throat vibrating with growl. He was not cowed; he was tensed to leap.

And only his Hunter Lord's command restrained him; Cynthia knew it, although she had not been witness to the command. She might have picked up her pace then, for it was one of a Lady's many duties to ease tension and hostility; the Hunters could often be like their dogs when matters of implied territory broke the thin veneer of civility.

But there were no other Hunters present.

There was a Priest, or perhaps a mage, someone of medium height who hid behind the folds of a voluminous robe. The robe itself was strangely dyed; its cloth was of a deep blue that suggested midnight rather than darkness. The cowl of that robe obscured the stranger's face.

But Gilliam's expression made Cynthia wary.

"Oh, no," Stephen muttered. "Mother, let's hurry."

"Do you—do you know this man?"

"She's not a man. And I know of her, but I've never met her before. I'm sure she's met me."

"Stephen—" He placed a hand upon the hand that restrained him, and gently pried himself free. But instead of hastening to the distant tableau, he turned to his mother, offering her the expression that reminded her of his namesake. "You don't have to like her," he said softly, "but for my sake, don't judge her. You've paid all the price the Hunter demands, but nothing that you—or I—will ever pay will be as harsh as the burden she carries."

"Who is she, Stephen?"

"She is the Wyrd of Mystery," he answered, his eyes glowing softly, as if he were looking at something that she would never be able to see. "And she carries a God's burden. But she's not a God, Mother, no matter how powerful, or how distant, she seems. Remember that, if you can." He hesitated a moment, and then said, "And remind me, when I forget."

Not if, but when. Cynthia nodded.

"Come," she said hearing the Hunter's voice. "Let us greet this unexpected guest."

~

The woman—and she was a woman—turned before they reached her. Her face was as pale as Stephen's, but where his hair was golden, hers was the color of pitch, with a hint of snow's frost about its edge; where his eyes were golden, hers were the color of winter violets, housed and grown in glass.

"Lady Maubreche," she said, inclining her head.

"Don't speak to her, Cynthia," Gilliam snapped. Anger there. Tension in the line of his jaw.

Lady Maubreche replied. "She is a guest, Lord Elseth; I can hardly fail to tender her the hospitality due a traveler."

He snarled. Like an alaunt, as tense as Corwel beneath his feet.

"It was because of *her* that Stephen died."

Cynthia froze. Stephen of Elseth. Stephen.

Gilliam was Hunter; Gilliam did not lie. Had he learned that trait, she would still have heard truth in his words; they were raw with pain and the loss of more than a decade. That loss, more than any other thing, bound them.

Before she could ask, the stranger said, "It is true. It is because of me that Stephen of Elseth traveled to Essalieyan. Because of me that he met the Hunter God on the day of the Sacred Hunt."

Cynthia struggled to remember the words her son had just spoken, but they passed through her mind like water through cupped hands. She had no words to offer.

"It was because of his oath," Stephen of Maubreche said into the terrible silence. "If you helped him, if you guided him, the truth of his oath was offered by Stephen of Elseth alone, and he chose, in the end, to abide by it. You accept much, Evayne a'Nolan. But I am Breodan's kin, and I will not allow you to dishonor Stephen of Elseth's memory. He chose."

Violet eyes widened. Beneath the slender point of stiff chin, the glinting silver of metal caught light; she wore a pendant, shaped like a small flower. It seemed odd to see it there; Cynthia had expected a medallion, some emblem of office or rank.

"Fair words," she said at last, and her voice was all of midnight. "But tell the whole of the truth, if you use truth, Stephen of Maubreche."

"I have."

"No, You have not. Stephen of Elseth was *oathbound*, yes. But he swore his oath when he was barely eight; he offered a child's promise. He did not understand the price he was expected to pay—either to carry out the oath, and have peace, or to reject it. Can a man truly be said to have made a choice when he is doomed by words that he does not have the experience to understand?"

"Yes."

"You are your father's son," she said bitterly.

"Both of my fathers. And he understood his oath before the end."

"Would you have killed him, had he failed?"

"No. I am not the God."

She closed her eyes. Closed them, and it came to Cynthia that this stranger, this Evayne, had known Stephen of Elseth. And had loved him, in her fashion.

She felt a pang, something akin to pain or jealousy. But she was Lady

Maubreche. "Evayne a'Nolan," she said quietly, "you have come today for a reason."

"Yes, and it was not to be corrected by a boy." But she smiled as she said it.

The smile was heavy. "You look like Stephen of Elseth," she told the young Maubreche Lord. "And you have some of him within you. I…had not expected that."

Stephen approached her, passing Gilliam and Espere, passing Corwel. He stopped a foot from her, well within the sphere of personal space that was never breached in polite society.

"I'm sorry if it makes things harder for you." He meant it.

The stranger's eyes widened again, and then they narrowed. "I am not so young a girl as I was then. I will never again be that girl."

"I haven't had your experience. If the gods are kind, I will never have it. But…my mother is your age, and she still remembers what she was, and what wounded her. Some wounds never become scars," he added, "because they never heal."

"You are, indeed, of the god-born," the stranger said. "Or I know little of boys."

"He has always been quick to speak and subtle," Cynthia said at last, with quiet, uneasy pride.

"My apologies, Lady Maubreche. Time is of the essence, and I am needed elsewhere."

"But you came upon some urgent business?"

"Indeed." And she lifted the folds of her cloak, opening them wide. Cynthia caught a brief glimpse of what lay within, and she blanched, although later she could not say why. "Come," the stranger said quietly. "Come Nenyane."

From out of the swirl of midnight, a young girl emerged.

She made Stephen look ruddy; her skin was the color of snow. Her hair was so pale it was silver, and a silver that was unkind; it was not the pale of blonde, but rather the color of platinum, of age, cold and harsh. Her eyes were wide in the white of her face, gray as storm.

Cynthia went forward immediately, hand outstretched as if the girl was in danger of breaking. She could not know what experience had scarred the girl, but the color of her hair could not be natural. Had she thought Stephen was slender? Not compared to this child. She was knife thin, all bones and angles.

"Nenyane," Evayne said, "this is Lady Maubreche. And this is her son, Stephen of Breodan, Stephen of Maubreche, what have you heard of Nenyane?"

Stephen barely heard the question. His eyes were golden, round, clarity to storm. He lifted a hand, palm out. The girl stepped out of the lee of the storm of robes, and the folds of cloth fell at once. She had eyes only for Stephen, and when she lifted a hand, it was the mirror image of Stephen's shaky gesture. Their fingers touched.

In the bright clarity of daylight, shorn of the mystery of night and the shadows of twilight, Cynthia thought she saw a light flare where their fingers made contact. It was brief; she could not be certain that she had seen it.

Or would not be.

"Nothing," he said at last. "Except that I'm her Hunter. And she—she's the huntbrother I've been waiting for."

"Yes," the stranger said quietly. She turned, took a step toward the gardens, and disappeared, but the girl she had brought forth remained.

~

What she expected from her husband, not even Cynthia could say, and she knew because she tried to give it voice. Throughout the speech of the stranger in her fell robes, throughout the speech of the son that was not his son, he had waited in silence.

Nor had he spoken when the girl had come forth from robes that should not have hidden her, no matter how thin and gangly she was. But when Stephen spoke the single word *huntbrother*, Lord Maubreche had risen, the silence a shield and a cloud. He meant to storm off, but before he reached the edge of the green, he turned.

Cynthia met his gaze; saw in it an equal measure of shock, and a terrible bleak anger, before he continued on his way to the kennels. She would have followed him; she started across the green to do just that.

But two hands touched her. Arlin's.

And Stephen's.

She let him go.

~

Gilliam of Elseth was silent. Brooding. It was a state with which Cynthia of Maubreche was acutely familiar. She had seen him thus for the better part of a year after his return from the far East; had seen him thus at every Sacred Hunt thereafter. Only when he was soothing the temper of his wild and inexplicable wife did that darkness leave him, and for that reason, if no other, Cynthia placed some value upon Espere of Elseth.

For Lady Maubreche and Lord Elseth had come, over time, to an unspoken understanding. Of the bereaved, they were the two who felt the loss most keenly. Stephen of Elseth was gone, and only in memory was anything of him retained. That was their responsibility, Cynthia and Gilliam: the memories.

Cynthia had given Stephen a son. Had insisted upon naming the boy after the dead. The name was a compulsion, for Gilliam of Elseth, and he had undertaken some responsibility for his huntbrother's namesake, even when he knew that in form, in truth, the boy was son to the creature that had killed him.

But this, this was difficult.

"Lord Elseth," Cynthia said quietly.

He turned his glance briefly upon her face. "It can't be done," he told her. "You know that."

"Is there law against it?"

"Hunter law," Gilliam answered. "I know that his eyes mark him, Cynthia." No formal title offered in return for the use of his; he desired no distance. Probably didn't understand why she would. "I know it. But Breodan's law is Breodan's law."

"He is as close to Breodan as any Priest who has ever undertaken to follow the Hunter God," she replied, with a calm she did not feel.

"She's a girl."

"I had noticed that."

"There is a reason they aren't called huntsisters."

"She is not a Hunter Lord," Cynthia replied. "She will never lay claim to that title. Not for her are the dogs, or the trance; not for her the claim of lands, and the responsibility that goes with it. She will be what Stephen was—a child that is forgotten. A child in need of a home. Would you have me deny her that?"

"A home? No. Give her a home, by all means. But what you desire, you cannot give her. She is not Breodani. She is not—"

"No huntbrother has ever been blessed with the gift of the God," she continued, offering reason, logic, the persuasion of a woman who sat upon the seat of judgment. "A huntbrother has always been the human face of the pairing; a huntbrother, trained to the peak of his abilities, has at his disposal only ingenuity, loyalty, and affection. Does it matter, in the end, whether she is a boy or a girl? She does not have to *be* a Hunter. She only has to offer the Hunter her support and oath."

"And will she swear the oath?" he snapped. Espere turned, although she stood some fifty yards distant. He cursed, but quietly, and forced himself to be quiet.

"She is to be huntbrother. She will swear the oath."

He closed his eyes. "Lady Maubreche," he said, finding the formality and the distance that had, moments before, eluded him. "He *is* Stephen's son, to me. I don't care about the color of his eyes. I don't care about the Priests. I don't care about the Hunter. I heard what he said and I know what I heard.

"If not the girl, then no one. He will never be a Hunter."

She had him, then, but it brought her no sense of triumph, for what he heard, she had heard.

~

"He knows, Cynthia," Arlin said. The lamplight shone at her back, reflected in twin circles on the curve of the high ceiling above her. Before her, curtains drawn and sheers hooked aside, the widest and longest of the windows reflected some of that light; she moved closer, losing reflection. The night was clear.

"I know," she said bitterly. She pressed her head against the cool glass. It would get colder still before winter's end. "I know it." She bit her lip. "Arlin—"

"He has to deal with it in his own way."

And what of me? She wanted to cry. She said nothing. He came to stand behind her, his hands upon her shoulders, light as a feather, as a bird's wing. "You've waited," he said at last, acknowledging the bitterness she could not put into words.

But such acknowledgment was often the key to what lay locked in silence. She closed her eyes. "Yes," she said at last. "I've waited. I've waited through all the arguments, all the anger, all the pain. I've waited for the moment when Stephen would finally find a huntbrother and make his vows. I want—"

"I know." Arlin was more generous with words than she. Not really like Stephen at all. "Peace," he said. "An end to the fighting."

"I wish Corwin could speak to the Hunter."

"There is only one way that he will ever have that chance. Do not wish for it, Cynthia."

She bit her lip again. A girl's gesture. She hated it. "I do love him," she said at last. "I still love him."

"And he loves you."

"As he can."

"And he loves his son. Both of them."

"Yes. But it shouldn't be like this, Arlin. It shouldn't. All that love, turned inward like a weapon, turned outward in anger—all that love, a growing divide. It shouldn't be."

She lifted her hands. Caught his gently and disengaged them, turning to face him. "And you, between us, trying to heal the rift."

"I love you," he said quietly. "Both of you."

"And Stephen?"

It was Arlin's turn to stare beyond the panes of glass. "Yes," he said at last. "But, Cynthia, Nenyane is not..."

"Not?"

He shook his head quietly. "I don't know," he said at last, with a marked hesitation. "But I think it best for Maubreche that Robart not be neglected."

She felt the cold then; winter coming early.

~

Mark, Robart's huntbrother, was not kind to the newcomer. He himself, newly arrived, was not yet comfortable in his position—as if the rank of huntbrother could somehow be snatched from him, and his life be returned to the streets of the city from which he had come. He knew that, among any pack of children, there must be a victim, and he did his best—in subtle and not so subtle ways—to make sure that it wasn't him.

She found it hard to forgive him this, although she understood it; it had not been long enough since he had been the hunted, in his own way.

Robart did not go out of his way to welcome the girl either, and this too, Cynthia understood, although she accepted it less readily. Robart was his father's son, and his father's most vocal supporter and he knew that Corwin was not pleased with her presence.

She also knew, although it pained her more, that Robart stood both in awe and in envy of Stephen's strange position within Maubreche: Stephen was the Hunter's son. His golden eyes marked him, as did the loyalty, slavish and inexplicable, of the alaunts and the lymers. Stephen was not allowed near Robart's hounds; Stephen was not allowed near Corwin's pack. They were brothers, and although it happened in some families that brothers held little affection for one another, she hated to see it happen in hers.

If Stephen felt pained by this enforced separation, he was careful not to show it—but although he was marked in all ways by his birth and his blood, Cynthia knew that he was a boy, with a boy's sensitivities. In that, he was like his namesake.

The girl herself was more of a difficulty.

She spoke rarely, as if words and their use were foreign and achieved only with struggle and a deliberate attempt to remember their use. When she was willing to speak with Cynthia—and that was seldom—she became instantly mute when any questions were asked about her past. Cynthia had encountered some of the same resistance from Mark, but she found Mark's silence less threatening; he had not arrived in the dark clouds beneath the folds of an enchanted robe.

Nenyane ate little, slept little, and often disappeared for hours at a time; Cynthia could find her only when she asked Stephen for his aid.

And Stephen himself?

He was entranced by the girl. He deferred to her in too many things. He called her out to see the dogs, and he tried to teach her what he himself had not, in theory, been taught. He protected her.

And that was not, in the end, the role of the Hunter.

~

Three weeks after Nenyane's arrival, the first of the snows fell.

The letter that Lady Maubreche sent to the Queen herself had made it to the roads before the snows; the reply would not be tendered—without the use of the mages the Order of Knowledge granted—before spring.

She could not honestly say what the reply would be, for it asked permission to break the most ancient of the laws of the Breodani. Winter was therefore cold and unpleasant in the Maubreche house.

But Nenyane had found a use for the time.

~

"Cynthia."

Cynthia looked up from the desk at which much of her work, for the winter, would be done. She looked up a little too quickly, and perhaps a little too eagerly, for Corwin seldom entered her study. Or her bedroom, these days.

But the hope died when she met his gaze, and she composed herself as only a Hunter Lady could. She rose stiffly, setting quill aside. "Lord Maubreche."

"I want you to see something."

"Is something wrong with the alaunts?"

"No." He held out a hand—or started to. But the gesture was aborted; the hand fell to his side. "Come."

The tone of his voice brooked no refusal.

She walked with him, leaving the large room in which she worked, leaving the halls that led to their separate chambers, leaving the towering heights of the second story.

The descent led her to the great hall, and the great hall passed by, mirrors and tapestries unheeded; her husband's stride was wide, and she had to step quickly to match the pace he set.

She wondered where Arlin was.

Stopped wondering as she heard, in the distance, the sound of metal against metal.

Her eyes rounded, her brows rose and fell. This much she could not keep from her face, and Corwin noted it in silence. Too much silence, these days.

The sound grew louder; much louder.

She knew where it came from: the training rooms that were, at the moment, empty. Robart was eight; not until he was nine would work with swords begin in earnest. And Stephen was not a Hunter—not a page, nor a varlet; the room was closed to him.

He *knew* this.

But it was Stephen's voice she heard, Stephen's sudden curse, from beyond the closed doors.

Without another glance at her husband's face, she placed hands firmly on the doors and pulled them wide in a single motion. They did not move silently, but the noise they did make was lost to the louder crash of blow and parry: Stephen was upon the floor, and at his side, gray eyes flashing, Nenyane.

She looked, to Cynthia's eyes, like a dancing blade—all angles, all lean, cold steel. Her white hair was bound tight, pulled from her face and her eyes. Stephen's, shorter, fell across his forehead in a sweaty, damp patch.

The blades, to her measured but inexperienced eye, were not sharpened; they had the weight of true swords, but not the edge.

Still, weight of that kind, carelessly handled, could cause death or injury less cleanly than edge, and she drew a single sharp breath. "What is going on here?"

Not even the din of this practice battle could dampen the force of her words. Nenyane froze at once, and Stephen jumped back, lithe and quick, from the reach of her still blade.

"Mother!"

"And Father," she said coldly. "Stephen, what are you doing?"

"Sweating," he replied. "And bruising a lot."

Her lips thinned. "There is no weaponmaster in this room."

He snorted. It was not the reply she expected.

"Stephen?"

"You haven't seen her fight," he said darkly. "She's—she's—"

"Nenyane." The girl turned her narrowed eyes upon the Lady of Maubreche. She bowed.

"Are you teaching my son swordplay?"

The girl nodded. There was no hesitance in the motion; none of the reticence that Cynthia had come, with experience, to expect.

"And you are qualified to be his teacher?"

Stephen knew better than to answer his mother's question. He knew her mood well.

But he answered anyway. "She is," he said. His voice was subdued. "She's better with the sword than—than she looks like she should be." The words had the force of wet paper. But he spoke steadily, and without cringing.

"You know that this room is forbidden you," Cynthia said. She felt her husband's shadow presence at her side. Did not turn to him for support.

"Yes."

"Then what are you doing here?"

"It's the only room that's big enough, and empty enough. We could have used the ballroom, but—"

Her brows rose. "Stephen!"

He bowed his golden head, closing eyes that were nearly the same color as his hair.

Corwin stepped past Cynthia. It was not what she expected, and it was *not* what she desired.

"Girl," he said, for he called her nothing else.

Nenyane looked up. Her pale face was smooth and dry; her eyes were startling. She put up her blade, but she did not drop it or lay it at her feet, as Stephen had done.

"My son is not a boy who has seen much swordplay. His opinion is therefore suspect. Mine is not." He walked to Stephen's side, but he did not so much as meet his son's eyes. Instead, he bent and retrieved the blade the boy had set aside. "I would spar with you."

It was not a request.

"Corwin—"

"Now."

"I am not here to teach you, Lord Maubreche," Nenyane replied, but she began to move carefully in what was an obvious circle around the Hunter Lord.

"You are not here to teach *anyone*," he snapped back. "But if you will do so, you will first convince me that what you have to teach will not be harmful—or incompetent."

At that, the girl's eyes widened.

In the pale, gaunt lines of her face, the expression was sharp and bright.

"Nenyane—" Stephen began.

But his father waved him to silence, the motion so abrupt, it too, was a command.

Stephen was well enough trained that he obeyed. But he came to stand by his mother's side, and his right hand tugged a moment at her elbow. A child's gesture. Her child's.

She looked down. But in truth, it was not far down; gone were the days when she bent just to place her ears close enough to his mouth that she missed none of his words.

What she saw in his face gave her pause.

"I'm not good enough with a sword," he said, the words hushed enough they were clearly meant to carry only to his mother. "And I'm old, she says, to start training."

"Old?"

"If it were up to her," he said with a grimace, "I'd have started when I could walk."

"It is not up to her."

He winced. "Mother—"

She looked across the floor at her husband's face. "Only Arlin," she said quietly, "could stop him now."

"If I call *Hasufel*—"

"Do not call *Hasufel*."

Stephen swallowed. And then, in a bitter voice that was years beyond his age, he said, "He's never going to accept her, is he?"

And she heard what lay behind those words. *He's never going to accept me.*

She placed one hand upon his shoulder; the gesture was not gentle, but the ferocity behind it was born of her desire to protect.

"He has always done what he feels is best for you," she said, punctuating the words with a shake. "But he is a Hunter Lord, and the only thing he understands is what he *is*. He loves not the title, but the life. And he cannot conceive of a crime worse than this: depriving you of your place in that life." She paused, and then added, "and depriving you of Arlin, of a huntbrother, is the greatest measure of that life."

"Then the Queen—"

"It is not in the Queen's hands." Cynthia replied coolly, "as you well know. If she chooses to grace us with her support, she may make her pleas on our behalf. That is all."

Stephen swallowed. Then, just before the first of the clashes of steel robbed them of words, he said, "I'm sorry."

But steel had the whole of her attention.

~

Corwin was not an indifferent swordsman. He had had years with which to hone this skill, and if it was not Hunter's trance, if it was not the use of spear, it was still an important part of his early training.

But Cynthia could see, from his stance, from the first strike that came out of that peculiar stillness, that he intended to take Stephen at his word; his eyes were light, his movements quick, his breath quicker. He had called Hunter's trance, and he resided within its preternatural speed.

Nenyane did not seem to notice. She bent into her knees, and when Corwin charged, she snapped to the side, dodging the strike by the simple expedient of being above the crescent it traced in air. Her limbs, like the limbs of a bird, remained hovering for just long enough. When they touched down, she was in motion. Her blade was in motion.

Corwin parried, but the parry was clumsy; the strike had come at his back, and he had only enough time to deflect it, no more. He was forced back three steps. His eyes widened. His lips thinned.

He growled.

Stephen, by Cynthia's side, flinched and covered his face.

Corwin struck again. Nenyane was gone before the motion started. She did not press him; she was simply not there when he chose to strike. But by allowing him the attack, she chose not to end the evaluation. There was no fear in her.

Corwin gathered speed. The shape of his shoulders changed; he bent into his knees, approaching with caution, but still approaching. He had passed beyond testing; the Hunter's trance informed the whole of his vision. She was his game.

Cynthia was grateful for the absence of the alaunts. She watched, because she could not—as her son had—look away.

And she saw Nenyane in flight. Saw the girl's sword respond to her arms as if it were an extension more natural than limbs or hands. She parried every blow, but the blows were heavier. If Corwin had remembered that she was a child at the start of their bout, he forgot it.

"Stephen—"

Her son peeled fingers from eyes and met his mother's gaze.

And while she looked at the golden flash of her son's eyes, she heard the crash of steel against steel in the background; it was followed by silence.

She looked up.

Corwin held the jagged remnant of the practice blade in his right hand. His left was empty.

Nenyane waited.

"Corwin!" Cynthia shouted, as her Hunter began to circle the girl again. "Enough!"

He shook himself then. Struggled with the hunt, with the Hunter's imperative. Slowly, too slowly, he looked at what he held.

He stepped back.

Nenyane remained where she was.

The Hunter Lord bent slowly and placed the ruin of blade against floor. He rose, stiffly, and bowed.

"Your son," Nenyane said quietly. "May I teach him?"

His only answer was silence, and he did not stay long to offer it. He swept past wife, past son, past training room.

Cynthia watching his retreating back. "Yes," she said softly. "Yes, Nenyane, you many continue to teach him."

~

That day marked a turning point, although it was subtle, and only in retrospect did Cynthia note it.

Corwin was no friendlier than he had been—but he was suddenly present, a shadowy grim figure, taller than either his son or his son's chosen huntbrother. He often watched while the two practiced in the training room, and after a week—only a week—he began to offer Stephen his own observations. Nenyane herself did not seem to notice this intrusion; she spoke only when she thought Corwin in error, and thankfully, that was seldom.

"She's too damn skinny," Corwin said at dinner two weeks later, winter piled against the windows in faces of snow. He still did not choose to speak the girl's name, but Nenyane looked up anyway.

"Am I?"

"You've no weight behind you," he replied. "You can lift a sword—Hunter alone knows how—but you can't lift a simple chair without straining."

"I have no need to lift chairs."

His brow rose. Cynthia's surprise was more easily masked; Nenyane had spoken more at this meal than she had at any other.

"You don't know what you'll need to lift," he snapped back. "Can you lift a boar, when it falls? Can you help Stephen to lift it? Can you help him to drag a deer to its resting place? In your duties—in the duties you think you will earn—you will need strength."

She raised a white brow.

Stephen, hearing the question she didn't ask, nodded.

"How am I to gain this strength?"

"Eat," he said. "Eat more."

She looked at the food on her plate with a vague air of suspicion.

Again, Stephen nodded.

"But Lady Maubreche eats and surely she is no stronger than I?"

Arlin was taken by a sudden coughing fit. Robart snickered. Mark was sullen. But Cynthia herself smiled. "I am not allowed upon the Hunt," she said quietly. "And I can, indeed, move chairs when the necessity arises." Nenyane shrugged.

But she began to eat, and throughout the winter, the gaunt contours of cheek, the sight of skin over bone with little flesh to cushion it, began to recede into memory. With weight came color; a blush to the cheek, a pink to the tone of skin. Her hair was white, and would remain a winter color, but her eyes lost some of their silver light, their edge of hungry intensity.

~

The only chore that winter required of those who had not yet taken their title was the cutting of wood. The wood itself, dead, had dried over the course of the summer and the autumn, and required only the gentle urging of an ax blow to split.

When Corwin was not called away by the duties of the winter hunt, his voice was often raised in the woodshed.

"How is it," he snapped, "that you can handle a sword with such ease? You've almost chopped your feet off *twice* in the last half hour!"

"An ax," Nenyane snapped back, "is not a weapon. And these," she added, nudging the logs with what looked suspiciously like an ill-humored kick, "are hardly *foes.*"

"The cold is a foe," Corwin countered, taking the ax in hand. "It is always a foe. Fire prevents it from claiming lives, and without wood, we have no fire. Come, Nenyane."

Cynthia forgot to wrap her shawl more tightly around her shoulders; for a moment, the only sound that entered the shed was the howl of wind outside the crack in the door that had granted her entry.

She could see Nenyane's unusual hesitance.

"And foe or not, your enemies won't care where you took your wounds. If you have no feet, you can't run. If you cannot run, you will never be given leave to take the ceremony and swear the oath."

Nenyane glared at Corwin. It was…a young girl's glare. Corwin came to stand behind her. "Your feet," he said sharply. He would always speak sharply, but the fact that he spoke at all was precious. "Do what I do. Plant them apart like this. And here," he added, his arms above hers. "You must hold the ax with your hand here, and here. Do you have it?"

She nodded.

"Good. Stephen? The log."

Stephen shuffled a log on the stump upon which it would be split. It teetered a moment, and he righted it.

"Try again."

~

In the winter, the hay in the lofts of the alaunts had to be changed with care, for the dogs were often restless. They wore winter coats, of course, and their kennels boasted the warmth of fireplaces. The pages were to tend to those fires, and although Mark and Robart had attained that rank and Stephen and Nenyane had not, Corwin suddenly decided to order them see to the comfort of the alaunts that served Stephen.

Here, too, her husband was often an unwelcome presence—to Nenyane. To Cynthia he was something entirely different, although it was not her duty, and would never be, to tend the hounds.

She had a mother's visceral fear, a mother's joy and it was balanced between these two that she made her way to the kennels. Villagers often crept into the kennels in the late winter to sleep with the hounds, and the hounds, accustomed to this intrusion from the time they were puppies, bore it with arrogant grace.

But the winter had not yet grown so cold and the wood supplies not yet squandered, that these villagers were witnesses to Corwin's harsh lessons. "Nenyane attend!"

Like an insolent hound, she drifted to stand by his side, her gaze touching Stephen's first, as if for reassurance. He nodded. Words seldom passed between them, although the Hunter's bond had not yet been established. Their language was a language of gesture and expression that would serve them as well as the bond the God blessed.

Nenyane was taught to turn the hay, and was taught to tend the fire. The last always fascinated her, and Corwin came close to blows in his frustration, for she failed to hear him when she was given to the spark and sputter of cracked black wood.

But he had grown cunning; he refused to allow Stephen to stay by her side. She had to learn to listen to The Hunter Lord, and if the lesson was slow to take, it came with time.

~

"Corwin, what are you doing?" Arlin's voice. Cynthia, shivering, turned.

Her husband held the chains and leather bindings used to couple the lymers. "What," he said, through clenched teeth, "does it *look* like I'm doing?"

"It *looks* like you're trying to teach Nenyane how to couple the lymers."

Nenyane glanced up. "He is."

"Thank you, Nenyane."

"Is he doing something wrong?"

"You will find, with experience, that Hunters are almost always doing something wrong. It will be your duty, as huntbrother, to ensure that they do not suffer for that wrongdoing. Or that they aren't caught."

Her frown was a child's frown. It came easily to her face, and often stayed for hours.

Stephen laughed, and his laughter caused her eyes to narrow. "She's afraid of the dogs," he told Arlin casually.

"I am *not* afraid of the dogs!" she snapped, heated now. So many words from a girl who had initially offered none. Cynthia might have hoped she could learn less of Corwin's intonation, but she was simply grateful to hear them at all.

Corwin snorted. "You are," he said. "And they know it. They're not as skittish as horses but they're a good deal more devious. You have to learn to hide your fear."

"I've nothing to hide!"

He smiled. For just a moment, the chains idling in his hands, his expression was warm. "Then come, and try again. Leave Mako; take Cebran and Rain, and bind them."

Stephen started forward, and his father said, without looking up, "If you do that again, I'll throw you out. This will be her duty. She *must* be able to handle the dogs."

"Mark didn't have to go *near* the dogs until after the ceremony."

"Mark is a boy," his father replied, the smile quenched. "He has nothing to prove."

~

When Corwin came that night to her chambers, Cynthia was surprised. But his expression was grim and shuttered as she set quill and paper aside.

"You work late," he said.

"There is work."

"You waste light."

She smiled. "You sound like my mother."

His brows rose for a fraction of a second, and then his face thawed. "Or mine," he said, almost rueful. He stared at her for a long moment, and then he stood and crossed the distance—all of the distances—that lay between them and took her in his arms; his clothing and skin were cold with winter.

He did not apologize in any other way. She didn't expect it. But she found the hollow beneath his shoulders that best fit the curve of her cheek and stood there until the bit of winter had vanished.

"She is difficult," he said, speaking into her hair. "I thought she was slow or addled. But she is no fool. She is *not* a hunter."

She said nothing.

"But there is already a bond between them that I do not think can be broken. I know," he added, with grim amusement. "I've tried."

"Corwin—"

His arms tightened. "He's my son," he said quietly. "What man wants less for his son than he himself enjoys? Cynthia—this girl can stay by his side. She has to. I understand that now."

For just a moment, Cynthia thought she could see a glimmer of the peace that had eluded them both for so many years.

"But let me find him a *legal* huntbrother. A true huntbrother will understand what they have and accept it—"

She pulled herself free from his arms and turned away.

~

"He's not what I expected."

Cynthia nearly dropped the books she was carrying when she heard the words; they were Nenyane's. She looked around quickly; there was no one else in the study. No Corwin, no Arlin, and most significant of all, no Stephen.

With care, she righted the books by their spines. With Nenyane, it was best to appear to give no more than half one's attention.

"I'm not sure that you're what he expected either."

At that, Nenyane offered a smile. It was slight, but it was there. "You love him," she said, after a pause.

"He *is* my son," Cynthia replied.

Nenyane nodded. Her gaze was distant, but it was not sharp, and the harshness of the early days had left it entirely. "Corwin loves him, too."

"He is Corwin's son," Cynthia said. She set the books upon her desk and turned, leaning against the wood lip.

"But he's not."

"He is in any way that matters."

"Do you believe that?"

"Yes."

Nenyane frowned. "He is Breodan's son."

"Is that why you came?"

For just a moment, Nenyane lapsed into a familiar silence. Cynthia expected her to leave, but after a while, the girl nodded.

"We can't afford to make any mistakes," she said quietly. "We have so little time."

"We?"

Nenyane shook her head, and Cynthia let the question drop.

"But he's young, younger than I thought he would be."

"You're not that old, Nenyane."

"Aren't I?"

On impulse, Cynthia took the girl by the hand and led her to her dressing room. There, she paused in front of the mirror, hands on either of Nenyane's shoulders. "Look," she said quietly.

Nenyane did. Her eyes widened as she stared at herself. She shook her head a moment, and white hair spilled out of her loose braid.

But she did not say anything else. After a while, Cynthia left her there, staring as if everything about her image was foreign to her.

~

It came to Cynthia, as the snows melted, that Nenyane was afraid.

They were *all* afraid. The roads would be open within days if they were not already open from the capital. And the road would carry the Queen's message. Although the Queen did not make Hunter law, her advice would carry its weight; in such a way, warning could be given to noble families without the legal censure the King's words would, by nature, carry.

But such a fear was not Nenyane's.

She came to visit Cynthia while Cynthia busied herself with seedlings that would eventually find their way to the garden. It was not real work; the Master Gardener would, no doubt, dispose of most of the results of such labor. Still, it kept her hands busy, and she required that busyness. The silence was difficult.

She became aware of the girl after some time had passed, and rose, hands wet with dirt.

Nenyane's eyes were wide and almost haunted. "Lady Maubreche," she said.

"Nenyane?"

"You must come. You must gather your—your family. *Now.*"

"My Family?"

"Everyone. Everyone in the House."

Cynthia rose, wiped her hands on her skirts, and *ran.*

~

She found Stephen in the kitchen arguing with the cook and his assistants. Her presence stilled the harsh flow of incredulous words.

"Ellias," she said bowing. "You are *ordered* to leave the kitchen. Take what you need for warmth."

Her son shook his head.

"But come *now.*"

"Come? But where? What has happened? Is there a fire?"

"Worse," she said softly, seeing the color—or lack of it—in Stephen's face. "Go at once to the maze. Wait for me there; I will lead you to its heart."

He paled, then, and he bowed instantly, obedient for the master where he had been truculent with the son.

~

She met Corwin and Arlin as she raced up the stairs.

Corwin's face was grim, his lips set. His eyes were already the peculiar color they took when he had summoned a light trance. "The dogs," he began.

She shook her head. "It's not just the dogs. Empty the household, Lord Maubreche. Send everyone to the maze, and do it *now.*"

He did not question her, but he glanced at the face of their son.

"Where are Robart and Mark?"

"In the kennels," he said.

"Good. Tell the alaunts to get them to the maze."

"The alaunts will—"

"Corwin," she said, her voice rising.

He nodded again. She loved him then.

~

She had no time to take a head count; no time to take a tally. But she thought—and prayed—that she had not missed anyone. They gathered, some shivering in the cool of early spring, and they waited upon her word.

Nenyane and Stephen stood beside her.

Robart and Mark stood with Corwin, and she could see from Robart's excited bounce that he knew something *big* was happening.

"Forgive me," she said, raising her voice so that it carried. "But we are in some danger, and we must harken now to the Hunter in the maze. Follow me, and if you get lost, follow Stephen; we know the way, and if we lead you, you *will* arrive in safety. Do *not* touch the hedges. Do *not* disturb the gardens."

They nodded. She was proud of this obedience, and grateful for it. She turned, skirts still dark with new dirt, and began to walk as quickly as she could without breaking into a panicked run.

Corwin's voice rose and fell at her back; she did not turn to see why; she trusted him.

The maze opened before her, and she followed its twists and turns, its broken walls, as if they were the halls of her childhood. They were. She felt safety in their presence, although she was exposed to sky and the brisk bite of wind.

But she stopped, once, at the hedge-wall. People bumped into her, driving her forward a step; her hands brushed branches that were only beginning to bud.

She did not come here in winter. She expected to see only bare branches, the skeleton of bush. But even in this exposed state, she could see what the Master Gardener had carved. Could see where her place upon the hedge was. Could see, clearly, that something else had begun to take shape and form in the wall.

It wasn't human. It wasn't even close.

No, she thought. *This is old. This is part of my other life.*

But she *knew*.

She picked up her skirts and she began to run. At her back, her servants now followed in utter silence, for they had eyes, and brains besides; they had seen exactly what she had seen.

They did not name it. They did not pray. Instead, they sought the shelter that only Maubreche could provide.

She broke into the Heart of the maze, her eyes raised to meet the eyes of the stone Hunter God.

Something spoke.

"Well, well," he said, turning, his long leather wings unfurling in an expanse that seemed to go on and on, "you took your time. We were beginning to think that we would have to hunt you."

In the heart of the maze, three creatures stood. She had seen their like only once in her life, at the side of the long dead Stephen of Elseth. And she knew how kind her memory had been, because this reality was so much worse.

~

She found voice before she found weapon, although she reached for both at the same time. "*Sanctuary!*" she cried.

The creature laughed. "It only works if we're on the *outside*," he said.

But she felt some distant answer to the single word.

"Your God has ascended," the creature continued. "He has left you here, to the mercy of *our* God. And our God has chosen to make this realm his home. There are always a few…difficulties…in such an arrangement, and we have been sent to smooth them out."

He lifted a taloned hand, a slender arm; they were the color of night. At a distance, he might have been beautiful, in the way predators are. But there was no distance here.

Fire flew from the tips of his fingers.

At her back, the household staff began to scream.

~

But the fire did not reach them. It lapped against the old, wet grass that had been blanketed by snow for months. the grass burned anyway, tracing the edge of a circle that began at Cynthia's feet.

The creature frowned.

With a confidence she did not feel, she said, "You are in the Hunter's domain. Go, now, and you will be spared."

His eyes widened. He turned to his companions. "Kill them," he said.

"Kill them all. If the boy does not fight, spare only him. Do you understand what you are being offered, boy?"

She knew who that boy was, but she did not turn to look at him; instead she drew knives, one in either hand.

But the boy—her son—replied. "Yes," he said quietly, his words drawing her glance where the demon's could not, "I do. My first test."

He was ten. Almost eleven. He was a child.

But he stepped out from behind the broad girth of the cook, shaking himself free of that man's large hands. In his own, he carried a sword.

She had not seen it when she had summoned him. Had not seen it in the kitchen, nor at the edge of the maze. But it was there, and it was not the only sword drawn.

By his side, her eyes a pale silver to Stephen's gold, stood Nenyane. She too, held a sword.

The creature laughed but the laughter was short and sharp, and it died quickly. Where he was oddly compelling, his laughter was simply ugly.

"Kill them all," the creature said, and pushed off the ground, seeking the vantage of height in which to do battle.

Cynthia turned to face Ellias, the man who had tried to protect her son. "No matter what it says," she told him, "no matter what it does, do not try to leave the Heart of the maze. If it is not safe here, it is far, far less safe anywhere else in Maubreche."

Ellias nodded grimly, and said, "All right. But we're going to have a discussion about my salary after this is over."

The faintest of smiles tugged at her lips and was gone.

~

Nenyane leaped to the the right as the creature dove; Stephen stayed his ground, the tip of his sword tracing flat, brown grass.

The creature did not, however, attack them; instead he focused the whole of his attention upon Cynthia.

She threw her knives. It was a skill, and one that she had been taught in lieu of sword. One dagger skirted the underside of the leathery wings; the other sank into flesh.

The creature snarled.

But he was one; there were three.

Stephen's sword came up as the second creature took to the air; there was a clang, as of steel against steel, and talons came away without leaving a mark. Stephen was driven back by the impact; the cook caught him, righted him.

He almost paid for the interference with his life, but the winds in the maze's Heart rose sudden and terrible, and the creatures, airborne, were driven back.

"This is the work of a lifetime," a familiar voice said. "I will not have you carelessly damage it."

She turned at the sound of the voice, and then looked up. *Standing* upon the thin branches of bushes that should never have supported his weight was the Master Gardener of Maubreche.

In his hand was a blade that seemed to be made of blue fire. Gone were clippers, shears, trowels; gone was the nondescript clothing in which he worked, day by day and year by year. He wore something that must have been armor, but it conformed so perfectly to his slender frame, Cynthia thought she must be mistaken.

"Lady Maubreche," the Master Gardener said, "you once asked my name, against all convention, and I did not choose to answer you. I am sorry to answer you now, and perhaps you will better understand why I chose silence when you have my answer.

"I am Caralonne." He lifted his left arm, and a shield suddenly graced it; it was of the same metal as the sword, burning brightly in the daylight.

The creature upon the winds shrieked in fury. "*Caralonne?*" it spat. "But you are dead!"

"I see that you are as observant as you always were," the Master Gardener replied coldly. "But you are *not* in your element here. Choose the air, and it will devour you."

Wind swept across the clearing of the maze's Heart. It forced the creatures back, and they dove to earth, finding purchase against the unnatural howl.

But the gale did not touch Cynthia or her people.

Instead, a different howl did.

The alaunts were coming.

~

Stephen and Nenyane *moved*. Before Cynthia could stop them—and she would have, and knew it was wrong—they crossed the flat ground, blades flashing in the sunlight. No blue burned those edges, but the glint there told her that these were not practice blades. Her son was wielding a man's weapon, and at his side, his huntbrother wielded one, too.

First blood: Stephen's. It fell when talons raked his arm, splitting the thick winter fabric as if it offered no resistance. His blade replied, and the creature snarled; it had extended its arm too far in an attempt to deal a fatal blow.

Nenyane's blade bit to bone; second blood was a good deal more dear than first had been.

The creature sprang up; the wind battered it and it came down at once.

Cynthia turned to look at the Master Gardener. He was watching, his gaze intent, his sword readied. But he did not leap down from the hedge-wall; he did not choose to join her son.

As if he could hear her, he said, "Stephen is correct. This is his test." But it was not a child's test; to fail was simply to die.

"You have your responsibility, Lady Maubreche. Do not desert it."

He's a child, she wanted to scream. *I'm his mother!* But she was silent. Her weapons were gone; her responsibility remained. But she could not turn away.

The dogs came through the maze, snapping at the servants who stood in their way.

At their head, horn in hand, was Corwin; at his side, spear readied, Arlin. They were like, and unlike, Stephen and Nenyane, but they moved with a single purpose.

Cynthia could not interfere with Stephen. She could not—had no desire—to call Corwin back But she *did* reach out to grab Robart and Mark by their collars; enough was enough.

Robart snarled, but Mark went limp instantly. He was terrified; he had come this far because his duty and his loyalty lay with his Hunter. She loved him for both his loyalty and his fear, and she drew them both close.

"If you do not still *this instant*, I will hand you to Ellis," she said, into Robart's ear.

"But Stephen's there, and he's not even a page!"

"Stephen is Breodan's son. This *is* his place." Driving the wedge between her sons more deeply into place and regretting it, she spoke.

"Mother—"

"I would have stopped him," she said, mouth by her youngest's ears. "But I can't. You're *eight*. He's *eleven*."

"He's *ten!*"

"Enough. I need you here. If they fail, there will be no one to protect us. Do you understand?" She shook him to punctuate the words.

But they had their desired effect.

~

The battle raged. Everyone moved so damned quickly it was hard to take it all in, but Cynthia bore witness. She bit back a cry when Arlin fell, and did cry out when he rose, bloodied, his hand upon the haft of his spear. The dogs leaped past him, snapping at the demons, and she knew that they would lose at least one of the hounds.

But she was unprepared for that hound to be Hasufel. He was the link between father and husband, between husband and son, and he was older now, too old to be pack leader. But not too old to be Hunter's hound; not too old to give his life in the defense of his many masters.

He did not even cry out when talons sliced through his windpipe, felling him in a single blow; his jaws still gripped tight about the leg of the demon, and Arlin and Corwin used this momentary pause to time their attacks. The Maubreche spear pierced the creature's chest, lifting him an inch off the ground.

Nenyane and Stephen were besieged by the two remaining demons; if there had been any question who their target was—and there hadn't, but there had been hope—it was dispelled.

Stephen was cut again, and this wound was deeper, but he did not lose his footing; instead he leaped clear of the strike that would have ended his life, and returned it, taking the wing at pinion. The wings of these creatures were as much a threat as their talons; he had crippled it for the moment.

Nenyane removed its head and turned, shouting Stephen's name.

He flattened; something passed over his head. Something red and bright. A sword. One of the demons had drawn sword in the maze.

Nenyane screamed at the demon in a language that Cynthia did not understand. The demon froze an instant and then turned to stare at her, incredulous. It was a costly mistake, for she did not pause, and in her wake, her Hunter was also moving.

But Nenyane took the first of her wounds in that meeting; Stephen escaped unscathed. The creature did not.

The dogs gathered around Stephen were his own. Rain and Cebran snarled, but they did not leap, and it took Cynthia only a moment to realize why: He had given them orders. Hunter orders, in the silence of a trance that she knew he had not yet learned.

They traced a circle around the creature, snapping and growling, but they bounded out of his way when he brought his sword to bear.

And then the creature was attacked from behind; Arlin had managed to remove his spear from the chest of the demon, and he had found an opening in the space between the great wings.

It was not over in that instant, but Cynthia drew breath, for it was over.

~

The Master Gardener stepped lightly down from the hedge. He landed just beyond Stephen, gaining his feet with a nimble grace that did not suit a gardener.

"Breodan-kin," he said, and he bowed. "You pass."

Stephen, bleeding and breathing heavily, looked up at the face of the Master Gardner as if he did not understand his words.

"It was a simple test," the Master Gardener continued.

Stephen glanced at the bleeding body of Hasufel and said nothing.

"You will lose much, much more than Hasufel before this is over," the Master Gardener said, but his words were oddly gentle. "Do you understand what the test was?"

Stephen frowned. "We killed them," he said at last.

Nenyane, by his side, and bleeding just as profusely, rolled her eyes. "He's not really stupid," she said to the Master Gardener. "But this is his first real fight."

Stephen turned on her. "If you're so smart, you tell me."

"He offered you your life," she said, "if you left."

Stephen's frown spoke clearly.

Nenyane laughed. "You don't remember?"

"Of course I remember. But—"

"But?"

"Not much of a test," he said. He set his sword down then, and walked over to Hasufel. He lifted the alaunt with as much care as a slender boy could; Hasufel's blood darkened his shirt, mingling with his own until they were one and the same.

"No," Nenyane said. "But I never said demons were *smart*."

But Stephen didn't hear her. He was crying.

～

In the somber silence of the Maubreche spring grounds, they buried Hasufel. The standing stones that existed upon any Hunter Lord's domain still bore the trace of ice from winter's passage, and the ground was barely thawed; Stephen and Nenyane had to *work* to dig the grave in the lee of the ceremonial stones.

The healers, accustomed to Hunters, kept their outraged complaints to a bare minimum; Stephen's wounds were not healed, and he was in no way whole enough to undertake such an arduous task.

But he did the work. Nenyane's months of eating and training had indeed given her the muscle necessary to move chairs—and earth. She did not complain about wielding a shovel to fight with dirt.

Instead she glanced at Stephen as she worked; he did not meet her gaze.

Cynthia watched in silence. Her hands were balled fists at her sides; she had attempted to offer Stephen comfort, but she knew that he would take none. Time would give him what he required, or nothing would; he had never lost a hound before.

Corwin and Arlin bore witness as well. They offered their help, but only obliquely, and neither man seemed surprised when Stephen curtly— even rudely—refused them. They *had* suffered the loss that Stephen now suffered, and they accorded Hasufel the respect of their open sorrow.

It was the only thing they could offer Stephen.

～

Three days later, the Queen's letter arrived, carried by a man who wore the livery of the Master of the Game. Hunter Green, the darkest of colors. Cynthia recognized him immediately.

She took the Queen's letter and retired at once to her chambers, followed by Corwin and Arlin.

They waited in a hushed silence as she broke its wax seal. The silence grew as she read; she did not speak the words aloud. But these two, they knew her. They knew the subtle nuances of her expressions well. What had been written was there in the stiff lines of her face.

She looked up; met first Corwin's and then Arlin's eyes before handing them the news.

Corwin did not read the letter. Instead, he cursed roundly. "I'd better go," he said quietly. "Arlin?"

Arlin looked up from the Queen's response, his expression bleak. "Where?"

"To the King," Corwin snapped. "Where else?"

"The King has spoken," Arlin replied, lifting the letter. "Through his Queen, he has made his decision. Will you challenge the Master of the Game?"

"And his Priests?"

"Even if the only forum we're given is the Sacred Hunt, then *yes*, damn you. They didn't see what we saw," he added. "They weren't there for the fight in the maze. If they know about it, they'll change their minds."

His huntbrother offered him the loyalty of silence.

"You saw her," Corwin continued, speaking to his brother. "Without oath, without ceremony, without any bloody *training*, they are what they are. And I'll be damned if my son is denied his life because of a set of stupid laws."

Cynthia's eyes widened. "They're the Hunter's law," she said, muted.

"No," he said quietly. "I thought that. But I know what I saw, Cynthia. I know what I felt. Will Lord Elseth stand as witness to a ceremony that does not have the King's blessing?"

She was almost shocked. But she gathered herself quickly, "I believe," she said, choosing her words with care, "that Lord Elseth would die before he would fail Stephen of Maubreche."

"Good. Write to Lord Elseth. I will write to my mother and my brother. Stephen doesn't know the horn calls; he didn't sound the hunt. But he *hunted*. He's earned his title.

"And we'll give it to him. If we have to break the Priest's laws, we'll break them. He's *Breodan's* son. What the Hunter God accepts I'll shove down the throats of everyone else."

She reached up and placed her hand against his mouth, stemming the flow of his words with regret. It was seldom that he spoke this freely. "He is *our* son," she said, with a quiet pride.

"Cynthia—"

She shook her head. Walked into the circle of his arms, although he had not—yet—lifted them. She was careful to touch him gently, and after a moment, he bent his head and kissed the top of her hair.

"Yes," he said at last. "He is. Our son. And if I come to an understanding of things less quickly than you, Lady Maubreche, I *am* a Hunter Lord. I will fight for what is mine."

The Black Ospreys

Introduction

Women of War is the only anthology Tanya Huff had any hand in editing, at least that I'm aware of. If it isn't, it's the only one for which I was asked to write a story. In fact, I was asked twice, because Alexander Potter also asked if I had one to contribute (technically, I suppose I was only asked once, as Tanya pretty much said, "you're writing a story for this." She can, because we worked together in the bookstore full time for many years before she moved out of the city).

What makes it particularly fitting, though, is the character of The Kalakar.

I first met Tanya Huff when I was hired to work at Bakka Books, by then-owner John Rose. She was the manager. She had sold some short fiction to *Amazing*, and had a finished novel making the rounds; I had sold nothing, and in fact, started work on my first novel that year. Tanya has worked the writer's panoply of jobs—and one of those was as a cook in the Navy, because she figured when women were allowed to actually join ships, it would be the support staff first. She's practical that way.

One of the things we'd do, in those early years, was talk about writing. Tanya in particular would talk about the book she'd be working on next (whereas I was still trying to finish the one I'd started, which ended up being four books). And one of the novels she meant to write—which she, of course, no longer remembers—was about a leader of a unit of mercenaries. The thing that stuck with me was the leader was a woman who never left anyone under her command behind. People were loyal to her because she was worth that loyalty, and she returned it. I can still hear her voice as she described this military captain of men.

Fast forward *quite* a few years, and I am working on *Broken Crown*. When I created Ellora, The Kalakar, I could only see Tanya Huff. This very seldom happens to me, but I described her as I saw Tanya (although, to be fair, my writer brain does not possess one tenth of Tanya's verbal wit). Ellora is, of course, important throughout the whole of *The Sun Sword*.

Tanya's read all of these books. She didn't notice anything unusual about The Kalakar, the woman who created the Black Ospreys. But when her unofficial son finally read these books many years later, the first thing he asked me was, "Is The Kalakar based on Tanya?". Stewart clearly paid attention. Then again, we both have the advantage of seeing her on the outside.

When I was asked for a story, the origins of the Black Ospreys came to mind, and in particular, Ellora's part in both their creation and their survival. And I wrote it for Tanya. And, of course, she didn't notice.

(Tanya said, after reading this introduction: "I'm kind of stupid that way. But, in my own defense, Ellora is *significantly* cooler than I will ever be."

This is actually completely untrue.)

The Black Ospreys

THE AVERDAN VALLEY AT NIGHT: moon low and red, stars bright. Light enough to see by, no torches required, although they were lit and carried. The earth was broken, the scent of newly turned dirt almost overwhelming.

Commander Kalakar stood at the side of one of her oldest friends, Commander Allen, called the Eagle, and with reason. His eyes were bright in the darkness; bright and keen—but they were dark as well. He touched her shoulder, just that; no words necessary, and therefore none offered. Standing side by side in companionable silence, they could count the dead.

Not accurately, of course; that would come in the morning, and the days that followed. And she would be there, for all of it. Looking for her own House colors among the fallen, looking beyond the crest of sword and rod that signified loyalty to the Kings, and the Kings' army.

"Ellora."

She nodded quietly.

"The master bard has offered his services, if you require them."

She wanted to say no; the dead couldn't hear his song, after all. But she bit back the word, held it, transformed it into motion. A nod. Some things best left unsaid could be, for now. The living would remember that a master bard of Senniel College had been present upon the field. And the living—most of them—would care.

She didn't give a damn.

Verrus Korama AKalakar joined her as Commander Allen took his leave. He was injured, but not incapacitated, and he carried pen, ink, the slate across which paper would be laid. For the names. For the names, most of which she wouldn't remember, to her shame.

"We won," he said softly. To remind her.

"We always do," she replied. Heavy words. She let pride seep through them and fall away. "Where is Duarte?"

Korama closed his eyes.

~

In the South, over a dozen years past, they had come for war. The Empire in whose army Ellora AKalakar served hadn't started it, but they responded to its call. She had crossed the stretch of water that knew no natural divide, in the large, long boats of the Empire of Essalieyan. At the head of the armies were three Commanders: Devran ABerrilya, Ellora AKalakar, and Bruce Allen. They were known as the Flight, three great birds of prey, Northern birds: Eagle, Hawk, and Kestrel. She flexed those wings now, as if she could stretch pinions and return to the safety of perch and hood after a long hunt.

But she had unleashed the fourth: Ospreys, the Black Ospreys. It was to the captain of that disbanded unit that she now strode, stepping carefully over the remains of fallen horses, men, broken weapons—the detritus of success. The stench didn't bother her; her nose had gone numb with exposure. The living had already been culled from these fields, this broken, terrible place that was the aftermath of magic. Some would return, but in dignity.

Some, never.

So many Annagarians here. Once they had been her enemies, or the sons of her enemies. It made no difference now; they looked at her, numb, and the fact that she was a woman upon their fields, in the depths of their valleys, failed—at last—to register. Some men drank, and some sang; Northern words blended with Southern until she couldn't separate them. Nor did she try.

She was an officer, after all. She had accepted that duty almost the day she had accepted the service of men; gods only knew what those men held sacred. She knew what she did. She had learned to cultivate tunnel vision with care.

Tonight, the tunnel was long and dark.

Primus Duarte AKalakar was alone. And not alone. Hovering there, at the edge of his grief, and enmeshed in their own, stood the men and women who had once served the Kings—served *her*—as Black Ospreys. They paid their respects, in as much as they knew how, to their fallen. Duarte, holding the body of Sentrus Alexis AKalakar, knelt in their center.

Ellora had crossed this valley before to reach him. It had almost been easier then. The twelve years that separated that passage from this one were at once insurmountable and flimsy.

~

Duarte AKalakar looked up. Looked past Cook, past Fiara, past the listing banner of the Tyr upon the field. His grip tightened briefly. He did not want to let go. Could not, he realized, hold on. He had been called Primus for more years than he cared to count, and it all came to this, this moment. Loss. His fingers brushed hair from the face of a dead woman. His lips touched her forehead. Hard to believe she could be at peace now; she had never been at peace before.

"Duarte."

He rose, carrying Alexis. Listing, like the banner, under her weight. He would miss her anger. It was the first thing she had offered him, when they had met in the South. He had been AKalakar. She had been Alexis.

Cook, seeing the Kalakar, offered his arms, and Duarte hesitated. He wanted to carry Alexis home.

But home, he realized bitterly, had *always* been in Averda. In the Dominion of Annagar, the land of their enemies, when the creation of the unit had first been sanctioned. He handed Alexis, with care, to Cook; Cook had always been the largest of the Ospreys, and against his broad and bloody chest, she looked small. Diminutive. She had always seemed that way to him when she slept—and only then. He paused. Put her long blade in slack hands. Cook shifted her body so that it lay against her chest.

Primus Duarte AKalakar stepped through the small barrier of the living, and went to meet the woman whose House Name he bore.

~

Duarte had not been born AKalakar. Nobody was. He had been offered the name when he had arrived in the office of Ellora AKalakar. She was not, then, the ruler of House Kalakar, but it was acknowledged that she was damn close. Her hair was a pale, thin gold, shorn so it rested in a wave above blue eyes; her face was round, her bones wide, her lips slightly pursed in annoyance.

She was surrounded by paper. If there were any order to the piles that littered the huge surface of her desk, it was an entirely intuitive order; he didn't doubt that she could find what she wanted, but he *did* wonder if there was anything of value to be found there.

It was clear that she wondered the same thing.

"Duarte Sorrelson?" He nodded. He was dressed in the robes of a different order, and from the tightening of her expression, it was not an order she favored. Then again, the magi did little to make themselves popular with anyone outside of the Order of Knowledge. He had made certain to wear the symbol of the mage-born across his chest; it hung there, quartered moon, each quarter graced by the iconic symbol of one of the four elements.

"AKalakar," he replied. As she did not tell him to sit, he ignored the fine, empty chairs that girded the visitor side of that desk, biding time, as if it were a test.

She pulled one piece of paper from the wreckage, glanced at it, and let it fall. "You've come seeking employment."

He nodded.

"You are a member in good standing of the Order of Knowledge."

He hesitated for just a moment, and then said, with the barest hint of a frustrated smile, "The words good standing would probably be contested."

To his surprise, she looked at him, really looked, as if he had said the first thing that made him worth looking at. "You don't look like a mage," she said at last.

He shrugged. "Lack of gravitas?"

"Lack of slouching. Lack of beard. Lack of hubris." She stood then. "Understand that I am not looking for a House mage. We have enough of those."

As it was not yet clear what she was looking for, Duarte chose to be respectful; he said nothing.

"You are aware that House Kalakar maintains a large House Guard?"

He nodded. It wasn't exactly a secret.

"Do you have problems with the concept of military authority and military discipline?"

"Not the concept, no."

She raised a pale brow. "Sit."

He sat.

"You were trained with the warrior magi?"

He raised a brow. "The Order of Knowledge does not commonly discuss its constituent parts with those who are not members."

She shrugged. Waited for a different answer.

After a moment, he shrugged as well. "Yes."

"You are not, I see, considered powerful for one mageborn."

It was almost an insult. "No, I'm not."

"And you were considered somewhat unorthodox in your approach to your studies within the Order."

He nodded again. Assessing her, being assessed.

"The Kalakar House Guard is in need of a mage."

"I believe it has two."

"It had two."

"And now?"

"Now it is in need of at least one." There was no humor at all in her smile. There was, however, a challenge. "How good is your Torra? '

"Almost flawless."

"Good. That would be useful; mine is lacking." She paused, and then added, "A number of my soldiers speak the language well enough for the type of diplomacy they'll be involved in."

"How long?"

Her smile stilled. "How long?"

"How long until the war is joined?"

She said, "You're bright for a mage."

He waited.

"Two months."

He nodded. "You have other applicants, no doubt. I'm interested in the post."

"I have five applicants," she replied. "I can second several if necessary. You understand that you will be part of the Kalakar House Guard, should you accept this post?"

He nodded.

"Familiarize yourself with our rules," she told him. "There will be paperwork to sign. I will have it delivered to your domicile." She paused, and then added, "Members of the Kalakar House Guard are offered— and expected to take—the House name."

So, he thought, that was true. He tried not to look eager. It fooled neither of them.

Commander Kalakar met him in silence on the field. She did not ask about Alexis; she could see the answer in every shift of exposed muscle. His face. His hands.

But she offered him this much. "She was mine."

He nodded bleakly, saying nothing. The sky was bright, and the possibilities of the future were, as they always were for the living, endless. The dead walked a different road, and short of following Alexis, it was a road closed to them both.

He was not yet tired of living.

But he understood the honor she obliquely offered Alexis AKalakar, and he hesitated. Once, there would have been none.

~

The border skirmishes that characterized diplomacy between the Southern Dominion and the Northern Empire had done little to prepare the armies of the Twin Kings for the savagery of the battle itself.

Months, months spent at sea and on dry land, hoarding food and guarding supply lines, had brought them to Averda, for it was in Averda, at last, that there was any purchase upon the heart of the Dominion's gathered forces.

Whole units of enemy Annagarians had been destroyed to the last man, for they failed to understand an offered surrender. Whole armies had been offered up as carrion, and among the fallen, many of the Imperial officers and soldiers who had worn the Kings' colors with such early pride.

This was expected; war was war.

But the actions of the enemy within this war were almost beyond comprehension. Whole Imperial villages had been razed, their occupants destroyed, their bodies left in smoking ruins: men, women, and children all. The South employed slaves in almost all levels of life: they had not seen fit to take slaves from these villages. They had left death, and death was ugly.

Not beyond imagining, for a mage.

But for the soldiers? The laws that prevented like deaths chaffed and strangled, and in the end, many of the Kings' own were offered to the gallows for the actions of reprisal.

It was to the gallows that Duarte looked, as they were erected. But it was to the woman he owed his allegiance that he at last went.

~

"Give them to me," he asked Commander AKalakar quietly. He forced deference into the words, and it was not entirely feigned. Having seen Ellora AKalakar at the head of the House Guards that were her pride, he had discovered that she could lead men anywhere, and they would follow. Because she was almost one of them.

She was writing. On the field, there were few things that were so necessary that they needed to be signed by a commander. Among these were writs of execution. Each commander was responsible for signing the warrants of those men whom, in the opinion of the military police, deserved death. It was considered a formality.

Duarte meant to test this supposition.

Exposure to Southern sun had darkened Ellora AKalakar's skin and her complexion; exposure to Southern warfare had darkened other things. She looked up from this task, Verrus Korama a shadow by her side, as he always was.

"What do you mean?" She asked him, half bitter. "Will you serve as official executioner here?"

"Yes," he said, stark word offered in the darkness of shadowed tent. There were stockades being built, but it would be days before they were finished, and the hewing of wood, the lifting, the fitting, would occupy the army for some time.

"Why?" She set the papers aside, staring at him.

"I've listened to the Annagarian prisoners," he told her quietly. "You all have."

She nodded.

"They are convinced that the Northern armies are too weak to wage war," he continued softly. "The presence of women upon the field only strengthens this belief. We will slaughter the whole of the Dominion without shaking that certainty if we continue to fight on the terms that we have."

"We are the Kings' army," she told him firmly. But she lifted a hand, and after a moment, Verrus Korama chose to retreat.

"And how many of our own—how many of our civilians—will we sacrifice in the name of those Kings? The Kings are *not here*. But we are."

"Tread carefully."

"I am. But you are signing writs of execution for two women and one man, and I think, AKalakar," he added, using the House name, and not the military title, "that I can make better use of them."

She said softly, "What use? If I grant you this request, there will be some difficulty for me; Commander Devran ABerrilya is not noted for his tolerance of poor discipline."

"A better use than gallows fodder, although it'll end—for them—in the same way." He was silent for some time. "We need a different way to wage war."

"What different way?"

"Their way. We need to speak their language." He did not flinch; he did not move. He did not fail to meet her eyes. "You cannot ask this of your regular units."

"Ask what?"

A game. But he was adept with words. "That they become your personal monsters."

Her pale brow rose. "I accept no monsters in my service, Duarte AKalakar. I accept men and women who accept *my* command."

"They will," he replied. Games, all games, these words. He knew what he had to do. Had come far enough in this war, and with this woman, that he was willing to do it. To be her sacrifice. "But they have already proven that they have the strength—or lack of moral fiber—to do what I think must be done."

"And that?"

"Change the face of the conversation." As if war were just that, no more.

Verrus Korama returned when Duarte AKalakar left the tent. He stood in the same spot that he always occupied; to the left of her back, his hand upon his sword. His expression was smooth and neutral; he was her calm. She had none. The hand that was raised above the inkwell shook. She understood the anger that had driven these soldiers to their acts of desperation and rage; to rape, to disembowelment, to desecration of the not quite dead. To execute them, however, was the order of the Kings. Distant kings.

"Well?" She asked, without turning. Without signing the documents.

"You know what Commander ABerrilya will say," he said quietly.

"I don't give a rat's ass about Devran."

She could feel the Verrus' smile; it would be brief.

"Castration of prisoners of war is considered a capital offense."

She said nothing, waiting.

"But I believe that Commander Allen might listen if you choose to make your request. These executions will not be popular with the men."

"Will we win this war?" She asked him. Because she could. Doubt, in the silence of her own space, was her own business.

"Not without loss. Perhaps not without the loss that Duarte AKalakar envisions."

"You must know what he intends." Because she did. And she had never been a woman who ascribed to the theory that the ends justified the means. Pragmatism warred with something else, and she knew that it might win. That it would be costly. How costly? Ah, that was the question. "If we lose," she said, to herself, exposing all, "then all we will be are—"

"Monsters."

She knew a moment of anger, then. But she had always been a pragmatic woman. An intuitive one. She understood everything that Duarte AKalakar offered her, and she had never expected that offer to come—if it came at all—from a mage.

"Call Duarte AKalakar back to my tent," she told him quietly.

Primus Duarte AKalakar faced the Kalakar, arms shorn of the weight of the dead in a way that he would never be. "This was her home," he said at last. His words were bitter, but his voice was soft.

After a moment, she nodded "Yes. This was. She was never at home in the peace of Averalaan. Not after the war."

Because this was honest, because they were two officers alone, Duarte relented slightly. "Not before the war, either. She came looking for death. She didn't much care whether it was her own."

"Only the first time," the older woman whispered.

Because this, too, was true, he said nothing.

"I made you a promise."

He nodded, remembering it.

~

Alexis Barton. The first name on the list of three. Fiara Glenn, Auralis, no family name given. It was to Alexis that he had gone first, and perhaps, had he chosen a different person, things would have unfolded in a different way.

But he hadn't.

He had crossed the grounds trampled to mud by the boots of Imperial soldiers. Had listened to their whispers, their curses, their Weston phrases of anger. Even their songs, delivered in anger like a prayer to the god of war. Which god, which war, no longer seemed to matter. This he expected. But Alexis? He could never have expected *her.*

She was knife thin; the ocean passage had been unkind. Her skin was dark and red; it appeared that the sun had been unkind as well. But her face, like the face of a bird of prey, was bright-eyed, unhooded, and she met his gaze with contempt and defiance. She knew that the gallows were being built, alongside the stockade; could see the wooden beams, some too new in her opinion, as they were raised by ropes and battered into standing shape. She could even see the graves that they'd be granted: traitors' graves, in foreign soil.

Her hair was dark and lanky. What food she had been afforded remained, rotting in the sun; she had taken the water, no more. She had been stripped of rank—sentrus, he thought—and the colors of the unit that she had come with. He knew the unit, or rather, could look it up; it was written beside her name.

As was her crime.

"Alexis Barton," he said, as if he were calling roll. Her eyes narrowed. She'd been stripped of regulation weapons as well: short sword, daggers. He doubted she had the strength to pull a bow. But even without these, she was dangerous.

"That's my name," she said when it became clear he was waiting for an answer.

"You stand accused of breaking the edicts of the Kings."

She shrugged. "The Annies don't read enough Weston to know the edicts."

"No. You understand that the civil treatment of prisoners is one of the things that differentiates us from the enemy?"

She spit. "Not the only thing." Her back was to the pen; she faced him, her knees beginning to bend.

He lifted a hand, and fire flared in a bright ring around her feet. It was a warning. It was the only warning she would get. But her brows rose, and she chuckled. "They sent a mage?" She whistled. Low whistle.

"You are not a member of the Kalakar House Guards," he told her grimly. "But you *are* a member of the army under her command. Your behavior here reflects upon her. Do you understand this?"

Her reply made clear that she did, and that it didn't matter. He almost smiled. But the humor would be lost on this Alexis.

"You served the Kings," he replied calmly.

"Look where it got me."

"Could you do it again?"

She stilled. She always stilled when she heard something worth listening to. "Any time."

"Your sentence will be held in abeyance, should you choose to serve." he told her quietly.

She looked at him as if he'd either sprouted another head or had started talking in Torra, the Annie tongue. "Abeyance? Big word."

"But not one with which you are unfamiliar."

She shrugged. "I'm familiar with a lot of words."

"I am Primus Duarte AKalakar," he told her quietly. "And if you choose to accept my offer, you will be a sentrus in my company. You will wear my colors, and the only law you will serve is my law."

"And what law is that?"

"War's law," he replied grimly. "And the Kalakar's."

"What about the Kings?"

"They're not here."

"Then who do you serve?"

"Commander AKalakar," he replied. "Choose."

She shrugged. It was her way of saying yes. He knew it, and would come to know it better, in time. "If you do not prove useful, the gallows will still be your home."

She reached out and grabbed his hand. He almost burned her, but something held him back. "This isn't our war," she said, voice low. "It's *theirs*. They called it. They made the rules."

"Yes," he replied, tightening his hand; replying to her unexpected grip.

~

Fiara Glenn had been more difficult. Her rage was harder to contain, and he had endured fifteen minutes of it before he cut her short. The offer made was curt; he was under no illusion. Those that made their way to the gallows could not *all* be of use. Some, the gallows would claim. He could not be certain that she wouldn't be one of them, and he chose—carefully—not to care.

But when she found out that Alexis was his first sentrus, she folded suddenly, swallowing fire as she tried to remember basic discipline. He knew then, that they were either friends or co-conspirators. Wasn't certain if this was a good sign or not.

And that left only Auralis. The man who would one day be known as the Bronze Osprey, with his bitter anger, his dark past, his desire for death. Duarte had seen men like him before; men who weren't truly aware that the death they wanted was their own.

Auralis had almost found it, and if he wasn't at peace with it—and he wasn't—he was almost unprepared to have it snatched away. He hadn't spoken a word. Confronted by, confounded by, Duarte AKalakar, he had simply nodded, as if he had expected no less.

~

"Where is Auralis?" the Kalakar asked, as Duarte sifted his way though memory walking slowly.

"I don't know. With Kiriel."

The Kalakar said nothing. The memory through which he walked, she now walked, and it was just as tortuous a passage.

~

By the end of the week, he had ten men and women in his service. They came from different units, and they were wary, ugly, angry. Only Cook was peaceful, although he had not yet earned that name; he was Jules from the Free Town of Morgan, and if he had a family name, he wasn't sharing.

Of the men, Cook had taken most easily to army life. His place upon the gallows had been secured by a berserk and terrible rage, one that took him in fits, and left him shaking, almost unaware of his surroundings. Shorn of this rage—as he so often was—he became an odd peace-broker. His size guaranteed his safety, but only barely. His fists did most of his talking otherwise, but without the rage to drive him, he never hit first. He almost always hit last. Cook was unique. He was humble in his acceptance of the offer of service over death.

The rest?

Given that they walked on the edge of certain death, and at that, at the hands of their own, it was hard to instill in them the respect due the Kings' army. Duarte didn't bother to try; that respect would render them useless for his purposes.

Commander Ellora AKalakar had come to visit.

Duarte had not expected her, and was genuinely surprised when she interrupted his training run by the simple act of observing it. He was barely aware of her presence, but Auralis and Alexis stopped almost instantly, as if disturbed by the shadow she didn't cast; the sun was high.

He could still see her clearly as she was that day.

"I know why you're here," she told them, taking up a sitting position on a large, round rock and crossing her arms. It would have been easy to mistake that comment, and many of his ten did. But Duarte looked at her carefully.

"And I've come to tell you this: You serve me. I am Ellora AKalakar, commander of the third army. You are the walking dead." She had their attention. Held it. "You have committed crimes for which the Kings' military police would see you executed. Fair enough.

"I believe you're worth more than that. You are not a part of the Kings' army, upon this field. You are part of the Kalakar House Guard."

Duarte's attention was riveted on her. When he had approached her, he had chosen caution; he had couched each phrase with care, so that she might have the opportunity, in the end, to disavow his small company.

But it was not just his attention. The words *Kalakar House Guard* had a power, both within and outside of its ranks, that had not yet become myth. It was a near thing, though. Because it was known that Commander AKalakar's House Guard was her family. The whole of it; she had no children, and had disavowed all ties of kin when she had chosen to take the House name. And she had done it gladly.

"What you will be asked to do in the name of this war, only the gods know," she continued. "But you will be asked it, and more, in my name. You will *be* AKalakar, and you will be counted as AKalakar."

Duarte closed his eyes.

She rose. "There are three birds of prey upon this field. The eagle, the Hawk and the Kestrel. I offer you the unenviable position of becoming the fourth, fleet and small." She gestured, and Verrus Korama came to stand beside her. He held a standard, which he unfurled before their eyes.

It was not well made; there were few enough who could be spared for such endeavor. But it didn't matter. Upon the field of Kings' Gray, wings stretched, claws extended, flew a black bird. Black Osprey.

A whisper went up among his men, his women, these handful of criminals that had yet to become a working unit, if it ever would.

"Your crimes are you own," she told them. "And I will not ask you to detail them; they are your past. It is your present—and your future—that will define you. If you came to the Ospreys by the paths of the gallows, you have come, unknowing, to House Kalakar. If this war is to be won, we must alter its face; we must build our own legends, our own nightmares. Build as you must, and *only* as you must.

"I demand service," she added. "And loyalty. They are the only things I will ask of you; they are *not* the only things that will be asked of you. But serve me loyally from this point on, and that is all that will grace your service record at the end of this war.

"You are *mine*," she told them. "And if you have success in this war, you will *be* mine. I will not disavow you, and I will not desert you; all roads that lead to the gallows start—and end—with me."

She left the standard pole planted in the ground, and shored up by rock. She left without another word. But words followed in her wake.

~

"House Guard? You take a risk," Korama told her, when they were well away.

"I have to," she replied. She stared at her mailed hands; the sun was bright and unrelenting. "And if we take the risk, we take it openly. Duarte is no fool; what he needs from me, I can't yet say. But I can give him what I can." She paused, and then smiled grimly. "We need to let them hunt," she said, seeing clear sky. "We need to learn to speak a different language."

War's language. Death's language.

"You never did care about keeping your hands clean."

"Not much, no, but then again, I don't have to. Some other poor bastard will be cleaning off the blood."

Not all of the men seconded to the unit were part of the third army, and this caused strife almost instantly. Devran ABerrilya surrendered none of his dead, but Commander Allen chose to trust the instincts of Commander AKalakar, and in the weeks that followed, more men and women, execution papers unsigned, were taken from the shadows of the gallows.

Some of the men, Duarte almost rejected out of hand. He read their records, and he understood that he could make no easy use of them. But one use did suggest itself, and in the end, with reservations, he accepted them.

The raids upon the supply lines had been ferocious, and worse, the Annies were burning their own stockades as they anticipated lost ground. Food, always an issue with an army of any size, was in scant supply and the heat of the Southern summer, drier than the season that graced Averalaan, made men mad. The colors of the Black Ospreys were stitched upon surcoats that had been grudgingly surrendered by quartermasters across the encampment in ones and twos. Armor was returned to the Ospreys, and with it, weapons. Their attitude hovered between surprise and arrogance. He expected no less.

It was his duty to train them; his training was difficult. He had learned enough magery in the Order of Knowledge to test their reflexes; to test their ability to move silently and without detection. He was not a kind taskmaster, but he didn't have to be; popularity was not his concern.

Fear was. Fear could either make a man very smart or very stupid.

Alexis AKalakar was not a man. And she was not afraid. Not of Duarte, and not of the commander. She offered him the respect due his rank—but it was an ungainly, imperfect respect. The Ospreys had not been chosen for their ability to dress well.

When they numbered fifty-five, he began to teach them the shorthand that would be become their silent language; it was almost the language of thieves. It was certainly the language of assassins. They took to it as well as the uneducated could be expected to: very.

"This is a lot of training for not a lot of work."

He looked up from the paper he was examining. They were, as always, writs of execution. Without replying, he handed them to Alexis. He couldn't have said why, had she asked. But she was Alexis. She didn't. Instead, she took them. Leafed through them, her dark eyes focused, flicking over the spares lines that described crimes, names, units.

"AKalakar?" she asked him, when she had finished. It hadn't taken her all that long. He wondered, for the first time, what she had been in her life before the army. When she had joined. Although the army had always been open to women, few indeed were those who picked up sword and stood in recruiting lines.

"AKalakar," he replied. "And Commander Allen's. Commander ABerrilya will send us nothing."

She shrugged. "Given his reputation, it's probably just as well."

It surprised him. "Why are you here, sentrus?"

"To pass along a bit of friendly advice." Her expression was at odds with the word friendly. Her voice was thin edge.

He nodded slowly.

"Keep an eye on Kreegar."

He nodded again.

She set aside five of the writs. "These," she told him quietly.

"You know them?"

"One of them. But I'd take a risk on the rest."

"The others?"

"Fiara will kill at least two of them."

"If she does, she's dead."

Alexis smiled grimly. It was the only way she smiled, but it changed the landscape of her face. "I know." She turned from the tent, stopped bent slightly, in its flaps. "But Fiara, you can trust."

He almost laughed. "Not a single one of you could follow the orders you were given, not even when it meant your death otherwise."

"Maybe we didn't like the orders." She shrugged. "Take 'em if you want. Fiara can look out for herself."

He stared at the papers for a long time, musing. In the end, he kept five.

~

Where food was scant, alcohol was less so. It was a mystery to Duarte, who seldom drank; a mystery and a great annoyance. The first time, he chose to overlook it. Two men were sent to the infirmary with wounds that would render them useless for at least two weeks. The second time?

He shed his forced nonchalance. Drinking after battle was a time-honored tradition. Drinking right before it, time-honored as well. But this? He found the men—and woman—who were drinking and he set the alcohol alight. There were cries of surprise and pain as bottles dropped and cracked, some shattering where they hit the sparse rock along the plateau. Alcohol made men brave.

And stupid. Terribly stupid.

One, scarred, ugly in ways that had nothing at all to do with appearance, took exception to his loss. He recognized the man: Kreegar. Alexis' gift. His dagger glinted in the dying blue fire as he rose swiftly, his Weston a smattering of words that would make street thieves proud.

Duarte, dressed in the finery of a Primus of the Kalakar House guards, lifted a brow. "Put it down," he said quietly. It was not a request.

Kreegar swore. He wasn't drunk enough to stumble; he certainly wasn't drunk enough to slur his words. Just enough to be foolish.

He lunged at Duarte, who didn't bother to move.

In all, the Kalakar Primus was underimpressed. They had trained with him. They should be aware of what he could do, by now. Of course, they hadn't seen it all. He was their Captain, Primus Duarte of the Kalakar House Guards. He was also their last jailer.

He used fire that would have been almost pathetic among the Warrior mages of the Order of Knowledge, seconded to the Kings. And while the fire burned, and Kreegar screamed, he stepped in with his sword. It was not his favored weapon. Favored or no, it did its work. It passed through

Kreegar's chest with unerring accuracy.

And Kreegar? Passed on to the Halls of Mandaros, where judgment awaited him.

All sound died; the wind seemed to hold its breath as he watch the twenty Ospreys who now lingered around him in a circle. If they chose to attack him, it was over.

He could see indecision at play across many faces, some more familiar than others. If the gallows hadn't held them back, death wouldn't. The silence strengthened, thinned, grew oppressive.

It was broken by Alexis, who turned to her companion. "Pay up," she said, holding out a flat palm.

Her companion was Auralis. "Pay up?"

"You said six days. I said three."

"It was four. The way I see it, there are no winners."

"Then open your damn eyes. I was closer. You owe me."

Fiara laughed. "Don't mess with him, 'Lexis."

"The hells. Pay up," she added, sliding her dagger out of the sheath.

"Sentrus," Duarte said coldly.

Everyone started at him He stared at Alexis. Her expression shifted instantly into a clean anger, but she jammed her dagger back into its sheath. She was fond of it; she didn't want to lose it.

Or have it embedded in her chest.

"The rest of you, back to your tents."

Fiara whistled; she made a fist and pumped it once. "Sentrus," she said, managing both syllables without a sneer.

Alexis still faced Duarte. After a moment, she said, "Do I get a raise?"

"My tent," he said, still cold, "Now."

~

All studied casualness was gone the minute the witnesses were. Alexis faced him across his pathetic excuse for a desk. Field desks were terrible, unless you were a commander. It was a rank he would never attain. And he thanked the gods daily for that fact.

"You've been here three weeks," he told her quietly. He did not refer to her promotion. "I've had Dunbar confined three times; I've broken up eight fights. I've killed three men, including Kreegar."

She lifted a hand. "Permission to speak freely?" she said, with a trace of humor.

His raised brow told her how much he appreciated the attempt. "Granted."

"Nine fights." He thought, for a moment, that had he actually been a commander, the army would be a *lot* smaller. "Nine, then. Your point?"

"Give us something else to fight. Soon."

"Sentrus—"

"Alexis will do."

"I decide that."

She shrugged. "Whatever. You can add a stripe or a quarter circle to the arm. Or the armpit. It won't make a damn bit of difference. No one trusts you. No one trusts each other. You have no idea if we ever will."

He nodded quietly.

"But with people like us, there's only one way to test it. We're not theoreticians. We're not even army. We're just…your cadets." She said the word with a grimace. Lifted her hands, signaling, of all things, retreat. "We only learn one way, Primus. We don't know what you want. We can guess. Some of us are pissed off about it; some don't give a damn."

"What do you 'guess' we want?"

"You want us to fight like the Annies fight. We're ready to do that." She paused, and then added, "But we're not ready to sit, to wait, to be picked off because we're stupid. Give us a fight."

He nodded quietly. "Sixty-seven men and women. You're one decarus. Who will the others be?"

Her brows rose and then lowered, as if they were wings.

"Not Fiara," she said at last. "And if you repeat that, I'll kill you."

"You'll try."

"Even odds. I've seen you fight. But unlike Kreegar and half of the rest, I paid attention."

He nodded grimly. "Continue."

"Auralis, maybe. You'll have to bust him down, but he'll do."

"That's two. I need at least five."

"Margie. She's grim, but she's got enough discipline to keep things in line unless all hell breaks loose. Stepson."

"Stepson? He's a—"

"Psychotic, yes. But fear works. He knows you'll kill him if he blinks the wrong way; you've been itching to do it. That's what four of us? Put Cook up as well."

"Cook is—"

"Bloody big."

Duarte hesitated for just a moment, and then he nodded again. "Don't let the tent hit you on the way out."

She muttered something rude under her breath. It was a start.

~

Ellora AKalakar liked maps.

Which was good; she had to look at a lot of them, and some were of question-able accuracy. She made marks on them, pinned flags to them, removed flags from them, watched as whole river boundaries were redrawn. Birds were the scouts of choice for the Northern army, but a bird's-eye view was not always accurate, and very, very few people could get information from conversation with birds. She found some amusement in watching them try.

Then again, she found mages more or less amusing in general. They were obdurate, arrogant, overweening in their vanity; they fretted about things that she hadn't worried about since the vagaries of youth had been shaken off with a vengeance. With the exception of the warrior magi, they were all considered elderly, although she privately thought much of that age was like carefully applied make-up; age and wisdom, or age and power, were often conflated among mages.

That, and she liked their beards.

Had she hated the magi, she would have found them amusing anyway, because Devran ABerrilya could not abide their presence for more than an hour at a time. He was not a man given to outburst; instead, he used silence like a blunt instrument. He was positively glacial on this particular day.

It was the first time she had pinned a black flag to the map. She thought he might reach out to sweep it away, and apparently, so did Bruce Allen; the Eagle hovered between them, his shadow like outstretched pinions, while the mages talked among themselves.

At length, however, they finished, and they turned their attention to the maps that held them all. The Terrean of Averda and the Terrean of Mancorvo were the most detailed portions of the map; there were only two passages into the Dominion, one through each. But Mancorvo's pass went through the mountains; Averda's did not.

It was therefore in Averda that most of the battle was likely to be fought.

"What will your Ospreys do?" Commander Allen asked quietly.

"What they have to."

"And that?"

She shrugged. "Change the face of the Northern army."

Devran's face grew slightly pinched. "The face of the Kings' army does not require changing."

"We've had this argument," Commander Allen said. He Looked at Ellora, his gaze keen. "You're sending them into the heart of the Annagarian front."

She nodded. "They're few enough."

"They won't make it," Devran replied.

Her turn to shrug. She did; it was artless. "They were carrion anyway. What do you care?"

"They broke the Kings' laws."

"The Annies don't care about the Kings' laws, and we're not in the Empire."

"I *said* we've had this argument."

Devran rose. "Will you let her play these games?"

"They're not games," she replied evenly.

He ignored her. He often did. "Her men are barely part of the army; they serve *her*. I do not want our command structure to devolve into a personality contest."

"You command your army," she told him. "I'll command mine."

"You will answer to the Kings."

No, she thought, but she didn't bother to say it. She looked at the markers and pins. I'll answer to their wives, their children, their parents. If they have any who give a damn.

～

Sixty-six men and women were not a small force, unless held against the balance of the Imperial army. Primus Duarte AKalakar watched them warily. Truth? He didn't like them. They didn't like him. He was counting on the fact that they hated the Annies more. He had tested this hatred a handful of times, culling their numbers; choosing, with deliberate care, the men who could best serve as examples by dying. He was not a torturer; he generally killed quickly. He did not kill officially.

That would require paperwork and time, neither of which he had in abundance.

No, he thought, as Alexis lifted two fingers in the silence of the occasional snapped branch. It would require *distance*. It would make him just another servant, albeit one with rank. This way, he was master, or no one was.

It was close.

With the Black Ospreys, it would always *be* close.

By killing swiftly, and without any compunction, without any sign of hesitation or remorse, he made the game deadly. More, he made it clear that they were his.

He waited a moment. Alexis lifted her left hand, and flattened her palm. He lifted his own, then, as if he was a conductor, and brought them together. She nodded, left her men, her fingers dancing wordless in the air.

She had learned quickly. And she moved.

He was almost captivated by the speed and silence of that graceful motion. His eyes were still on her when she reached his side, and she noticed; she noticed everything. Her brows rose in amusement, but her eyes were steady and unblinking when they came to rest upon the village. The valley contained it. Here, between the perch of too many trees, they could see the planted fields, and beyond them, the huts that were home to the Dominion's slaves. Beyond those huts, a stone manor, the only such dwelling, and behind it, the tall structures that were, in theory their target. Granaries. They were guarded; he could see horses moving in the distance. They were more easily counted then men. In fact, in Averda, they were counted and prized more highly then men.

He did not look at his hands.

Alexis did. And she smiled. They had traversed the forests with care, avoiding the mounted patrols and guardposts that the Annies relied on.

The Imperial army was a theory, now; the Ospreys were surrounded, in all directions, by the forces of the Tyr'agnate of Averda. Callesta.

Learn to speak a different language, he thought.

He glanced back once. Just once.

The night would be filled with sounds of terror: laughter, screaming, the cries of the dying. Some of them would be his; most would not. Twisted fate, then, that the ones that would linger longest, in memory and nightmare, would be those that were not.

But they were parchment, paper; they were the things upon which the first of the Northern messages would be left. Over the corpses of the dead—the many, and the helpless—the banner of the Ospreys would be the only moving thing by night's end, and it would move by the grace of the Southern wind.

Wind was the only thing the Southerners seemed to fear, and the wind carried the Black Ospreys.

~

Ellora AKalakar looked up as Verrus Korama entered her quarters. He was quiet, which was not unusual; like Devran, his silences were often more telling than his speeches. He handed her a tube; she touched it. Beneath her hands, it warmed, waiting. She spoke a phrase, placed her thumb against the edge of the tube that would either open or explode, and waited.

This was Duarte's work.

Korama waited while the tubing fell away; waited while she uncurled the missive it contained. He even waited while she read it, his posture pitch-perfect, as if it were the only grace-note in a particularly grim second act.

"Kallos has fallen," she whispered. The paper fluttered to her desk. She did not touch it again.

"There was resistance," he said, when it became clear she wouldn't.

She understood what he offered, and refused to accept it. "There would be," she replied, black humor edging all of the syllables. "Any bets?"

He frowned. "Don't," he told her quietly.

"Don't?"

"Don't think like an Osprey. They have that luxury, AKalakar. You don't."
Luxury. "Did anyone survive?"
"In the village? Possibly. At night, it would be hard to be certain."
She didn't ask about prisoners.
She didn't ask about anything. She had come to war, and with her, had brought the certain callousness that any officer must. She balanced on its edge.

~

"Kalakar."
She had not looked away from Duarte.
"The Ospreys were born here," she said quietly.
"And they were laid to rest in the North," he replied, equally quiet. "We surrendered the colors there. We thought it wouldn't matter." His shrug was dismissive. "We were never a peacetime unit."
She looked at him, gave him that much. The darkness hid many scars.
"This was a different war."
"A cleaner war."
"Duarte—"
"Alexis will stay in the South."
And you?

~

By the time they were sent to the third village, word had spread. The Northern armies were known, in the South, by the visage of the Osprey, and its wings were black.
The prisoners that the rest of the army gathered—and admittedly, they were few—spoke of the Ospreys in bitter, implacable Torra. They spoke of little else, and the words were both curse and promise.
You could have painted targets on their backs, Duarte thought, gazing at his unit. But they would have been small targets, and at that, in constant motion.
The Annies thought they numbered in the hundreds. In the thousands. They thought the wind carried them. They thought the Lord of Night blessed

them. Duarte was willing to admit that if there *was* a Lord of Night, they worked in his shadow.

He thought about clipping their wings.

But it was only thought. And if he didn't join them in savagery, if he didn't join them in murder, he gave them the opportunity to vent their rage, to plant the seeds of a different rage in their enemies. Anger made fools of all men.

Even Duarte AKalakar.

~

The villages around the granaries became focal points for the Tyr's cavalry units. The valleys were not kind to horses; the Ospreys, who used them seldom, less so.

They added *horsekiller* to the long list of epithets they wore as badges. They took their greatest losses in that enterprise. And they suffered the bitterest of their divisions there. Men, women, and children? They were seen as mirrors. Their deaths were markers, the oldest variant of an eye for an eye.

But the horses were harder. Not for Duarte, and not for many of the Ospreys. Fiara, however, was livid. As if the horses were helpless, and the children were not.

Alexis reined her in; it was close.

Duarte felt the first hint of unease, then; he was prepared to kill Fiara—but he didn't want to kill her. Wanted, in fact the opposite. It was unexpected. Unaffordable.

The Ospreys had lost and gained men; the gallows were empty, their shadows paler and more peaceful than the shadows the Ospreys cast. But each new Osprey that survived Duarte, that survived the insane and suicidal missions that Duarte himself chose, became AKalakar. The name meant something to them.

But not, in the end, as much as the Black Osprey did.

He hadn't expected that.

He didn't expect, truth be told, that *any* of them would survive this enterprise, this terrible act of madness that their war had become. There were even moments—all of them silent—when he welcomed the thought.

War made killers of men and women.

His embraced them. They were his.

～

Commander AKalakar waited.

She watched the Primus as he crossed the plateau; watched the silence that enfolded him. He did not seem to be aware of it; he was aware of his armor, his steps, the path that led to her and from her.

By his side, in the ragged surcoats that now meant almost everything to the Annies, the Ospreys walked across the camp as if they owned it. She could almost understand why Devran hated them; they were feared. They knew it.

Primus Duarte gave a curt order to the woman who stood closest, and she, in turn, transmitted that order. Hard to imagine that men who could swagger in such a ragged line could also come to so abrupt a halt. But they did, and they watched Duarte recede as she watched him approach.

She said, "You don't look so much the mage."

His smile was slightly lopsided. His eyes were ringed dark, his hair flat against forehead and skull. Like the rest of the mages upon the field, he decried helms, and he never wore them.

She couldn't argue with success. "Primus."

He snapped a brisk salute. He was probably the only Black Osprey who *could*. "Commander."

"Report."

He did. She forced herself to listen. It wasn't as hard as it might have been; there was fascination in his words, and because of it, they were fascinating. She could trace the spiral path of his flight, and it made her uneasy.

He waited, and when the silence stretched, she realized he had finished speaking. And would never finish. The man who had come to House Kalakar seeking employment was almost entire absent.

"Duarte," she said, without thought.

He waited.

"The Ospreys have been noted by the Tyr'agnati of both Mancorvo and Averda. The Tyr'agar himself has, for the first time in the course of this war, put a bounty on your heads."

He allowed himself to nod.

"The Tyr'agar is in control of the field." She paused, and then added, "He is not the equal of his generals." She wanted to tell him that he could stop. Wanted to, and knew that it was a lie. He had what they wanted: the attention of the Tyr'agar. Now? They had to focus it, hone it, keep it.

"Your men are the face of the army," she whispered.

And saw his reaction, clearly. Turned away.

~

"You're drinking."

Duarte looked up from the lip of the canteen, Alexis stood in the lee of what could charitably be called a tent. The months that had worn away at his reserve, draining what could equally charitably be called youth, had not touched or tarnished her. She moved like a cat, a hunting cat.

When she moved. It was clear that tonight she didn't mean to.

He shrugged. Stared at the canteen. Something as civilized as a glass had long since been rendered useless. "It's a habit I've picked up," he told her. She shrugged, stepped into the tent. He could not remember the day; could barely remember the month. But he would remember her, always.

"I've got nothing against drinking," she told him, taking the canteen from hands that had gone nerveless, "but they say you shouldn't drink alone."

"They don't say anything to me," he replied, smile hollow but present, as if his face were a mask.

"They do," she said. All humor had left her slender face. It took him a moment to realize that she was replacing the canteen's stopper. "I think you've had enough."

"For what?"

"For now." She set it aside, Or rather, tossed it aside. Her eyes were dark, keen. She took a seat beside him. He really had had enough; he didn't speak.

She surprised him—she always would. Caught his hand between hers. Her arm was dressed, her shoulder dressed; she had almost been killed by the crescent blade of a Southern horseman. Almost didn't count for much.

Cook was a bit of a medic. He certainly wasn't much of a cook.

"What have you done this time?"

She laughed, and the sound was startling; it was clear and high. Most of her laughter was guttural, visceral.

"I won a bet or two. I busted Auralis down a rank," she added.

"You can't."

"I can't. You can. And did."

"Funny. I wasn't there."

"It was. Funny," she added. "He missed."

With Alexis, it was hard to tell how much of her humor was based in fact. He didn't ask.

"What did *he* do?"

"He pinched Margie's backside."

Duarte laughed. It, too, startled him. Enough that he fell silent, staring at her hands. They moved across his skin, fingers drumming, silent language. A question. The wrong question.

"Yes," he said, shaking her off. "I'm fine."

"Did you hear that we're wanted men?"

"From Commander AKalakar. Where did you hear it?"

"From just about everyone. The Tyr'agar was enraged when we left the horses—"

"Enough, Decarus."

She stopped instantly. Because there was death in the tone. Even for her.

When she spoke, she was cautious. The way people who stepped on the mage-fields were. Each word was deliberate and slow. "It's not easy, is it?"

His expression didn't change.

"You were a city boy. You were always a city boy. Look at you now. You had money," she added bitterly. "You must have. Maybe even a family." She shook herself free of the bitterness; it was a touch too close to dangerous.

"Now you're surrounded by murderers, thieves, rapists. Every day, and every night. You almost have to be one, just to get by." She paused. "But you're still there, on the thin side of the edge, behind an officer's rank."

"I don't keep my hands clean."

"No. You don't. But outside of the fighting—where there is much—the only people you've killed have been Ospreys."

"And what would you have me do, Decarus?"

"If you were any other man, I'd tell you to join us," she whispered. She looked at the canteen; he caught the bent profile of a nose that had been broken at least once and was lovely because of it.

It wasn't what he'd expected. Alexis never was.

"And as I'm not, as you so quaintly put it, any other man?"

"Don't." She stood. "I didn't understand you the first day we met. And after the first village, I thought I might. But by the third?" She shrugged. "I wouldn't bet money on anything you might do. So I've been watching you."

"I've been watching you."

Her smile was a brief, sly flash of teeth. It was a miracle that she still had them. "Not in the same way. Or maybe not only in the same way."

Dangerous ground, here. But he rose as well. "What have you seen?"

"You've come as far as you *can*. The rest of us? We can go farther, Primus. Some of us—Cook, Amberton—can pretend it's in the name of duty. Most of us don't bother. But most of us aren't thinking either. Most of us haven't figured out that we're here because of you. Oh, we know we'd be feeding the vultures." She paused, watching him. He let her worry.

But worry had its own rhythm, "Most of us think you need us because we're killers. Most of us think you don't need anything else from us."

"They're right."

"But most of us don't understand that we need you because you're *not*." Her hand touched the canvas beside the tent flap, and she winced. "You've let us fly," she told him, looking away. "But that's only half the hunt. Some of us are finally ready to land, Primus."

She looked, for a moment, weary. But only a moment. "Hood and jesses," she said softly, as if the words could actually mean something to her. "Rein us in."

"There's only one way to rein in the Ospreys."

She shrugged. "I know." She started to leave.

"Decarus." Pause. "Alexis."

And turned back. "We know what we *are*," she said quietly. "Make us something *more*."

"If it weren't for what you are—"

"Duarte, we can go on like this until the army slaughters us all—doesn't much matter which army. But *you* can't. I'm not asking you to do this for our sake—hells, I don't even know what 'our' means. I'm not even asking you to do this for my sake, because I can keep going with the rest. I made my choice, the first time. You gave me a different choice, and I made that one, too. I thought it would help."

He had never asked her why she had done what she had done. Didn't want to ask now. "And did it?" This was as close as he would come.

She shrugged, looking bored. Bored Alexis was at her most restless, her most dangerous. "We fear you."

"With reason."

"But it's more than just fear."

"Maybe for you."

She shook her head. "Not just for me, Duarte. Take the risk, now. Now is the right time."

And he did. He reached out for her wrist, caught it, held it. She almost pulled away. But she didn't. He drew her back, into the tent. And she stayed.

~

She was the first of the Ospreys that he loved. The first that he trusted. Of the latter, he would find a handful more, over the swift passage of days. The former? He could take another lover if he wanted to part with his balls. Alexis never made a verbal threat, but it was clear, by the end of the following three days, that she was his.

Or more accurately, that he was hers.

This did not come as a surprise to the Ospreys, much to his chagrin. Fiara was smug enough to let slip that she'd won a betting pool, and Alexis' icy stare was enough to let him know what the betting pool had been about. It should have angered him. It amused him instead, and short of contemplating the rage of the man who had forced them all to war, there was little that did.

He took what he could get.

And found that in the taking, his position had changed. It was a subtle change, for Duarte himself remained much at a distance, ready to kill when judicious pruning was required, but he was trained by the Order of Knowledge; he noticed it.

Alexis had not precisely made him one of them; no more had he made her stand apart. But the line that had separated them blurred, and he realized that she had become the dark face of a den mother, daggers in hand, death waiting her displeasure. And by association? He could not think of himself as father. But she spoke for him, and he allowed it.

He was busy thinking of other things that she'd said. How to rein in the Ospreys without clipping their wings and diminishing their shadow?

Now, he thought, was the time to take risks. But they were Alexis' words.

~

"We're Kalakar House Guards."

He was prepared for the stares he received, but not prepared to listen to argument; since his expression made this clear, no one offered any.

"We're Black Ospreys, first and foremost, but Commander AKalakar has always made it clear that we're part of her personal force." He paused. Let the words sink in as far as they could; given the Ospreys, he was lucky if they scratched the surface.

"The House Guards won't argue with her. But they won't accept us as soldiers. Or hers."

"We don't need 'em."

Flame shot out in a thin stream; it was met by a curse that did not quite elevate into a scream. Warning shot. He didn't usually give them.

"We're baby killers," he said. "Looters. Rapists. They don't think we know how to wield swords. They don't think we know how to fight a war."

"We're fighting an Annie war."

He held his hand.

"We've been fighting an Annie war on Annie terms," he told them. "And on their terms, we've done some damage. But we've done damage to slaves, buildings, a couple of horses."

"And their riders."

He shrugged. "Three men. Four. Against sixty."

They were the Ospreys' favored odds.

"We've proven that we can go where the House Guard can't." He paused. Gazed out at the Ospreys who lounged against trees, flat rocks, open ground. For just a moment, he regretted the absence of Commander ABerrilya, because this was the Osprey idea of discipline, and it was a pity to waste it.

"We wanted fear. We have it. The fear of every slave girl and child in the Dominion."

This, this was not what they wanted to hear. Too bad.

"But because we've proven that we *can* survive, it's time to up the ante."

"To what?"

"We want," he replied, "the fear of the men who count."

"The Tyr'agar has a price on our heads."

"Yes. For property damage." One or two grim chuckles. Better than he'd hoped for.

"But now we start in earnest. Are you ready for that? You, Sorren? Fiara?" The latter nodded. The former looked suspicious. He wondered which of the two was the smarter. "Are you ready to actually fight? Can you watch each other's backs when the people are running toward you, rather than away? Can you kill men who have a good chance of stopping you?"

Auralis AKalakar laughed. "I can kill pretty much anything that moves. Do they scream?"

"I don't know."

"Why don't we find out?"

~

Verrus Korama came, as he often did, when the sun was fading and the sky was changing hue. But there was something in his posture this eve that made Ellora take notice. She frowned. It was an open invitation to discussion.

Instead he handed her a report. It wasn't sealed; it wasn't magically keyed. Not Primus Duarte's, then. She took it, and held it before the glow of burning oil. "What is this?" She said, when her eyes stopped halfway down the page.

"I believe," he replied quietly, "that your Ospreys are stretching their wings."

"Has the primus lost his mind?"

"There are those who would argue that happened months ago."

Her frown was deeper than his; light made it more severe. "He took on their cavalry scouts in broad daylight."

"Apparently."

"With pit traps."

"Apparently."

"How the hells did he dig them without being seen?"

Korama shrugged. "He's mage-born."

She snorted. She'd had enough of mages long before she'd set foot on dry land. Her eyes caught the thread of Weston that she'd abandoned, and she read, her pale brows rising and falling as her eyes crested the words. In the end, she laughed.

"The main body of the three armies were nowhere near the scouting party; the scouts were returning from the front. It's unlikely that they expected this level of aggression within their own territory. The Ospreys took casualties," Korama added.

"I can see that. How accurate are these numbers?"

"Ask the birds."

She'd sooner ask the birds than the mages who flew them. She flipped the paper over. Turned it down and read on. The last page was written in a bold hand, thick, dark strokes of ink above the plain signature of Commander ABerrilya.

"Yes," Korama said, before she could speak. "The Commander wishes to know why you chose to deviate from your plan."

"Tell him to get stuffed."

At that, Korama's brow rose. Predictably and comfortably. "I will tell him," he said stiffly, "that he was busy on the front, and you did not have time to confer with him about your change of plans." He turned to leave, and spoke without looking back. "Primus Duarte has changed the direction of the war; I believe it is his intent to change the face of the Black Ospreys."

Ellora said nothing. A lot of it. But some tightness of chest relaxed, and she could allow herself to admit how worried she had become. Not for the war; that was its own burden. For Duarte. For the House Guard.

"Verrus?"

"Commander."

"Tell the quartermaster the Ospreys have lost their standard again. Tell him we need a dozen." It was their calling card, after all.

⁓

Auralis was swearing. In and of itself, that was not unusual. He was, however, swearing at the Ospreys under his nominal command. His swift action in the attack upon the scouting party had regained him the rank of decarus, and he seemed determined to make the most of it while he had it. Gods, knew, with Alexis' temper and Auralis' open lack of respect, it probably wouldn't be long.

But the tenor of the swearing was unusual. And because it was, Duarte listened. That he used magic to do so annoyed Alexis.

"Would you prefer I go in person?"

"Yes."

She was in a mood. He could squelch it with a curt, cold word, but chose instead not to make his night miserable. He gestured, cutting the magical ties that girded the small encampment, and rose. Alexis followed, like fate. Or fury.

"…your armor is practically moving on its own!"

Duarte's brow rose. He glanced at Alexis. She smiled, but it was brief.

"We've done *three times* what the rest of the damn Kalakar House Guard couldn't do once. Shale, you lazy bastard, where the hell is your kit?"

There were no latrines to be dug; the Ospreys, as always, were on the move. But three of Auralis' men were on kitchen duty by the end of the tirade. Only one attempted to argue with the decarus; he was in Cook's tent. A reminder, as Auralis made clear, that there was a step lower than sentrus.

"This is your work?" Duarte asked Alexis, as they watched the men begin their practice.

"Not mine."

"Why did he mention the House Guard?"

"Because we're part of the House Guard," she said, with a thin smile, "and he's a competitive sonofabitch."

"There's something you're not telling me."

"Love, there's *always* something I'm not telling you." But she caught his hand and squeezed it before letting it drop. Alexis' idea of a public display of affection usually involved bruises.

"Cook's men?"

"Medic tent."

"We don't have a medic tent."

"We do now."

"Alexis—"

She said, voice low, "Cook is willing. He's knocked six heads together, he's broken two ribs, blackened three eyes. The men," she added. "He doesn't usually try to hit the rest of us."

"Alexis—"

"You told them what they had to do. You killed two men. They listened." She looked at his face without touching it. "I want the rest of your cache," she added.

"My what?"

"You're not drinking so much."

"Alexis—"

"It's worth money."

He shrugged. She laughed. One or two of the Ospreys looked up at the sound.

"You're enjoying this."

"Yes," she told him, smile creasing her lips. "You aren't?"

"I'm the primus," he replied, with what dignity he could salvage.

"You are. But you take your chances with the rest of us. It's enough, Duarte."

~

The Ospreys lost no battles. They were chosen with care, with the subtle magery that had been, in the end, unsuitable for the warrior magi with whom he had chosen to study. They struck quickly, moved quickly, burned forests when they needed an easy way to retreat. They carried food enough for lightning strikes, and lost days to foraging, but the days they lost were also days in which those who would walk again could take the time to find their feet.

But they always traveled back to the army; Duarte always made his report. Commander Ellora AKalakar spent more time with him in the presence of the House Guard, and he in turn, more time in the company of the House Guard. It was not always easy.

But the last time they returned, their numbers winnowed, new members waiting, the Kalakar took him aside in full view of the House

Guard, and asked him the most significant question she had yet asked where others could hear her speak.

"Where are the fallen?"

The question made as much sense as any officer's questions did; Primus Duarte stared at her for a moment, as if trying to translate the words into a language he better understood.

"You've spent little time in the ranks of my House Guard," she said, pitching her voice so that it carried. The wind helped. "So I'll make myself clear. Bring the fallen home."

"It will cost us time," he said at last, as the full import of her words made themselves clear.

"Bring them home," she said again, "or tell us where you left them."

"Beneath the banner of the Black Ospreys," he told her.

She nodded. Turned to Korama.

~

Aside from the growing outrage of the quartermaster, Ellora heard few complaints. And she listened for them when she walked among her own. The House Guard spoke quietly of the Black Ospreys, but every now and then, they let the unit's colors blend with their own.

The black bird of prey was scattered across the front. The Ospreys chose to leave it when they left the scene of battle. It was their signature. And it was hers.

~

Devran ABerrilya was in a sour mood. Although she knew it was petty, she was satisfied. Commander Allen was diffident and calm. The map spoke for them.

"He's shaken the confidence of the Tyr'agar," the Commander said. "The Tyr has moved two of his armies onto the plateau, and one into the valley."

"Valley's no good for cavalry," she said with a frown. "Better for magic."

"There isn't a surfeit of magery from within the enemy's rank." He circled a large area of the map. "We can approach the army on two sides."

"When?"

"Three days. Maybe four."

She nodded.

"Commander AKalakar?"

"Commander Allen."

"Good work."

~

"The dead don't give a shit," Auralis said, with a grunt. Fiara's complaint was more succinct.

"The commander does."

"Tell her to carry them."

Duarte's expression was about as soft as stone. "She does," he said. And surprised himself by believing it. No one else offered any argument, and this surprised him as well. The Ospreys had taken the time to bury their dead when they had it. They no longer left the wounded to fend for themselves. Once or twice, Duarte himself had stepped in to cloak the retreat of those who dragged the fallen behind them; he could not hide the blood trail left for long, but it was always long enough.

It took them an extra two days—two day's worth of food—to reach the army base.

The Kalakar was waiting for them.

The House Guard, in full dress, was behind her.

She ordered the House Guards forward, and they obeyed in silence, joining the Ospreys; the difference between the field and the camp evident in the state of their surcoats, the length of their stubble, the overall *smell* of a road that was carved by feet alone.

The House Guards took the dead. They handled them with care, with a solemnity that even the Ospreys couldn't have managed. Or so Duarte would have bet—which was probably why he didn't.

The dead served as a reminder to the living. They were accorded the full honors of the fallen, and if the medals that decorated them briefly meant nothing at all to their corpses, if they should have meant nothing to their comrades, they did.

~

"We need the Ospreys," Ellora said quietly.

"Where?"

"With the House Guards."

"With the army?"

She nodded. He waited.

"We need the colors," she said, surrendering. "But you built them, Duarte. I would never have said that they would become what they've become. I would have been willing to bet," that word again, "that they'd give up the flag to the House Guard."

"They might."

She raised a pale brow. Her eyes were a shade of gray-blue, clear, far-seeing. "Ask them," she said. "But ask carefully. Don't be surprised at their answer." She paused. "And don't kill them for it, either."

~

"She wants *what?*"

Duarte faced Alexis across about five feet of space. No desk to hide behind, no chair to sit in, no bed to lie on. The sun was high above them, and around them, in the loose, languid circle Commander ABerrilya so despised, the Ospreys waited.

"The Tyr'agar has moved his armies into position," Duarte said, speaking, as Ellora AKalakar had commanded, with caution. "This could be it."

"What could be what?"

"The Annies aren't well-organized. The Tyr's armies are, but they're not the only men on the field. We'll have armies across the plateau and in the valleys, and the commanders think the Tyr'agnate, at least, will be present in the valley."

"And the Tyr'agar?"

He shrugged. "Less clear. We're not a large unit. We aren't accustomed to working within the main body of *any* army. We're not used to battlefield orders. The Commander recognizes this.

"But she wants our colors to fly on the field. I think," he added, taking a risk, "that if it were up to her, they would be only our colors."

"And she'd take the colors without the *unit?*"

"Yes."

"Sounds good to me," Auralis said, stretching. Duarte considered busting him to sentrus before Alexis could. It had become a bit of a contest—one of many. "But then again, I wouldn't mind mooning Commander ABerrilya."

The mention of his name always had an effect on the Ospreys. Usually it wasn't useful. Today, it might be.

"Realistically," Duarte continued, "it's the Osprey that bears weight. There probably isn't a man in the Annie armies that won't recognize it. And there probably isn't a man in the armies that won't make straight for it, either. Not a good bet."

"You'd let her do this?"

He met Alexis' cold, cold glare. "She isn't standing the unit down," he said at last.

"But the House Guard *aren't* Ospreys. We are."

"We're sixty, give or take a few. They number in the hundreds, and within the third army, even that's insignificant. But the Black Osprey isn't."

"No."

"One Decarus."

He turned to face the others.

Auralis shrugged. "I'm in, if you are."

Two, Cook nodded. Fiara spit. Margie smiled.

"They're ours," Alexis said, meaning it. "Whatever that bird means, we made it. Where are you going, Primus?"

"The commander is waiting," he said, with gravity. "I'll tender her our response."

～

Twelve years later, Duarte stood beside the woman who had taken her House, becoming the Kalakar in the process. Across the long, dark stretch of broken valley, trees riven and fallen over bodies that it would take days to recover, he could see the standard of the Tyr'agnate of Callesta. Ramiro kai di'Callesta stood beneath it.

"Do you hate him?" Ellora asked. It wasn't really a question.

Enemies become allies, and allies, enemies, with the turn of time and circumstance. "No. What we did, we felt we had to do. And what he did showed his mettle, even then."

"He was younger. He lost his father in early fighting."

"He was no fool. Not then. Not now."

"No," she said softly. Remembering. "He knew what the colors would mean to the Tyr'agar, and the armies of the South." She was careful not to use the derogatory term Annie. But for the moment, it was difficult.

~

Sixty men. Three standards. It was overkill. It was, in retrospect, an early target. It was also the only target worth striking in the South. Black Osprey. Northern Osprey.

Northern army. They were to be positioned in the valley in two days' time. Two days was a *long* time, for the Ospreys. Too long to listen to the military patrols. Too long to pretend that they had a hope of maintaining Imperial discipline. Duarte had them on training runs through the valleys' height—the valleys that the Imperial army had claimed as their own. Beneath the heights, the fields lay, and behind them. The blackened ruins of villages that had been destroyed by either side. No food there; nothing of value.

He reined them in; they let him. They really were birds of prey. His, he thought. But he thought, as well, of the Commander.

She wanted the standard; he'd given her the unit. He wondered if she would surrender the latter to battle. The Black Ospreys had done what no unit had honorably done in the history of the Empire. What better way to lose it? To the Annies. To the real war.

She could say a eulogy as she laid the colors to rest.

Alexis touched his shoulder, and he turned, catching her hand. Thinking of death, of her death. It hurt him in ways that he had never thought to express. Wordless, she kissed the side of his face. "Do you trust her?" she asked, her lips beside his ear. The reason, he realized, for her open display of affection.

"She left the choice to us," he replied. It wasn't much of an answer.

"She'd be rid of us," Alexis continued.

He put a finger over her moving lips. "Don't go there," he told her.

"I'm not allowed to go where you go?"

He realized that she might hit him, but took the risk anyway; he caught her and held her tightly, her chain shirt making marks across his chest.

~

But they didn't have time to reach the field before that battle started. Hubris, on their part really. If they could go where the enemy was, the enemy could approach them in a like fashion.

They had warning, but not much; they were in the place where the valley narrowed, and the trees along its twisting paths made poor haven for cavalry. The sound of horses were few, the snapping of branches, the sounds of any unit's movement.

But the banner that appeared from between trees that had grown apart, as if they were an open palm, was no Imperial banner. It was red, and across it, the sun in gold shone, eight distinct rays catching and scattering light. The standard of a Tyr'agnate.

And the Tyr'agnate, much like the Ospreys, did not suffer his standard to be raised when he was not upon the field.

Poor field, narrow field. And through it now, the war horses of Averda came, great, armed destriers. Crescent blades had been drawn in silence; Duarte had just enough time to wonder how long they had waited.

He lifted his voice in a cry that had nothing to do with training; it was primal, but unmistakable: his own. He had magic; he used it, sent a flare straight up, where it burst in a gout of traveling flame, like a blossoming flower.

The army was close; he knew it was close.

But not so close as the Tyran of Averda's ruling lord. Against men such as these, the Ospreys had only triumphed by planning, by stealth, by ambush.

And the canny man who ruled these lands—who had lost so much to the Ospreys—had at last learned to speak their tongue. There was a precious irony in that. And death.

~

Auralis drew both swords, roaring as he did. The dignity of rank deserted him, as did the months of training, discipline, the months of odd leadership that he had been forced to surrender and return to, like a child's bouncing ball. Around him, the men and women who had started to panic froze; they knew what this meant, and the familiarity of it provided what Auralis himself no longer could: command. Authority.

He had no fear.

Instead, he laughed, wild and reckless, and he used the cover of trees to advantage against the horsed men who came with their swords. Had they polearms, it might have gone differently.

But even without, Duarte could count, could add, and could certainly subtract. He turned to Alexis, an instinctive movement that had nothing—and everything—to do with the ambush. She was already gone. He wanted to grab her, to hold her, to hide them both. But it was wrong, and had she remained, she would have failed the Ospreys.

She knew it, damn her.

He used fire where fire could be used; he used the ability to hide where it could be used. Both strategic. This was not unlike an exercise, except in one regard: death was certain rather than a danger.

He welcomed it, as Auralis had done, but for different reason. There were no slaves here, no women, no children, no old men. There were killers. Northern killers, Southern killers, with almost nothing to separate them.

The Ospreys began their plummet.

~

Ellora AKalakar saw the flare as it erupted in the sky. So did the rest of the army. As a body, the army moved slowly. Not so the Commander. Verrus Korama was by her side in an instant.

She pushed past him, but he caught her arm.

Held her gaze.

So many things, in it. Too many. She knew what he offered, and she hated herself for just a moment, because she saw, clearly, that after the war the Ospreys would be a liability. Had always known it.

"I told them," she said, tearing herself free. "They're mine. Call up the House Guards—get them moving. Now." His smile was its own reward; he was gone almost before she'd finished speaking but not before she'd drawn her sword.

Hold on, Duarte. Hold on.

~

He didn't count the fallen.

He could barely count the living. Mages were seldom required to stand in the middle of the battle; they had other uses. Fiara was wounded, but the man who had wounded her was dead; she could not bring herself to kill the horse that she had injured.

He could, and did.

He sent fire skyward again; it was the last time he could afford to spend power on such a display. He had never bothered with horns; none of the Ospreys had. Theirs had been a language that was best used in silence. Now? Screaming. Death. Slaughter.

"Alexis!"

She was there. Gone. He drew his sword, and followed her, forcing himself to think. To use the talents that had been too meager for the warrior magi, in a different life. He called the Ospreys to him, pitching his voice in Weston, aware that in so doing, he was also calling the enemy.

But the Ospreys arrived first, and he saw that Cook carried both the standard and Margie. Only the standard would remain; he could see death clearly where Cook wouldn't.

There were trees on all sides; they were a narrow formation that would make the horses impossible to utilize. Men would have to dismount, to fight here.

And they did.

Minutes might have passed; he couldn't say. He cursed the commander in silence, but only in silence; he saw that the Ospreys had planted their standard—*his* standard—in the damp, thick ground of the forest shade. They surrounded it as if it were the only thing that mattered.

To the Annies, it was.

They began to carve their way toward it. They didn't have time to be vicious; where they could spare movement or motion, they were, but they were focused. On the standard. On the Ospreys who, twenty now, protected it with their lives.

It had always been something worth killing for. When had it become something worth dying for?

~

She hadn't used the sword in years. Not this way. But she used it now, and by her side, her House Guard, silent and grim, used theirs. She had not waited to gather them all; she had taken only those who were already prepared to fight.

They were prepared. The moment they glimpsed the standard of the Tyr'agnate, the moment realization dawned, they were hers, an extension of her rage and her anger. An extension of her pride. She lost them as she fought; the living stepped over the injured and the dead, moving inexorably down the flank of the eastern valley toward its center.

Bowmen would come; they would come late.

She paused for just a moment, and lifted her horn to her lips.

~

Duarte heard it.

He thought that loss of blood and loss of power must have addled his wits; that hope must have crazed them. The Annies didn't like to fight women, but they had long since stopped thinking of Ospreys as women. Fiara stood bleeding and Alexis stood beside her; they were back to back, holding short swords. They might have fallen had Auralis not intervened; Duarte couldn't.

He had been left to guide them, his words reaching them over the din of clashing sword, the rush of sound. It was almost too much; his hand gripped the standard pole for balance, and the Black Osprey fluttered against his forehead.

Three men fell; he could clearly count the Tyran that approached. They, too, were injured; their armor was rent, their swords notched and bloody. They hardly seemed like men at all.

But neither had the Ospreys, in their early evening flights. Fire flared at their eye level, glinting off helms as they fell back. One more, he thought grimly. Just one, and he would be finished.

But it didn't come.

Instead, seeping through the encroaching ranks of the Callestan Tyran, came surcoats and colors he recognized. Men, he thought. And a woman.

Although she was yards away, a hundred yards, maybe, he could see her face. She was not a mage; she wore a helm. But her skin was pale, and her movements certain; her eyes were blue and clear. She was a commander; it was almost impossible that she could be here, at the forefront of her House Guards, face bleeding where Annies, had tried to slow her down.

But she kept coming, and as she did, he heard the Ospreys raise voice, saw them find a strength that had almost abandoned them. They called out her name, as if it were a battle cry and not a prayer.

She had come for them; they were hers.

And Duarte AKalakar surrendered them with a tired grace.

~

Two thirds of the Ospreys were dead when the Callestans called their retreat. Scattered among them, dying, were Kalakar House Guards. Cook, bent among them, treated them all as if they were his. He looked once to see the standard, and he offered it the grim salute of a nod, no more.

The commander of the third army made her way to Duarte AKalakar, and only when she reached him did she doff helm. Her face was a mess. It would heal, and given her medics and her resources, it would heal well—but he memorized the new wounds that cut across familiar silver scars; these had been taken, and given, for the Ospreys.

She said, "You didn't think I'd come."

It was a gentle accusation. As gentle an accusation as she was capable of making.

He bowed head. She raised it, bending to lift his chin. "AKalakar," she said. It was the title of all men—and women—present. "Take your standard. Take the men who can walk beside it. The third army is waiting for us." She grimaced. "And probably not with a lot of patience."

He stared at her for a long moment. "I would have spared you this," he said at last.

She said, "I know. But I'm Ellora AKalakar." She lifted her head, and added, "If I'm not mistaken, that's Decarus Alexis AKalakar, and she's waiting for you."

He turned, in pain, and pain was good.

Alexis caused more.

~

He stared at the Kalakar now. Helmless, in the dark, she might have been the same woman. The same woman under whom the remains of the Black Ospreys had served; the same woman who had taken them, broken, into the House Guards when war had at last come to its close. She had not left them to die within the valleys; she had not abandoned them before the military tribunal.

But in the darkness at the close of this second war, she surrendered at last to the inevitable. "You served me," she told him.

Past tense. He heard it clearly; it was deliberate.

"Yes."

"Who will you serve, now?"

"I don't know." He bowed to her. "But Alexis belonged in the South, Kalakar. This was her home, and I brought her back to it."

"She changed."

It hurt him. "So did the war."

"Duarte—"

"I don't want to leave here here," he added. "Not alone. She was the heart of the Ospreys."

"So were you."

He shrugged. He had to take his leave of the Kalakar, and it was a parting that he had foreseen twelve years past. When it had failed to happen, he had sworn he would serve her forever.

So much for oaths.

"Alexis is waiting," she told him gently.

He nodded.

"And the House Guard is waiting as well."

And nodded again. "Let me carry her," he said.

She hesitated for just a moment, and then she gestured. Verrus Korama came to stand by her side, as he often did. He carried something in his hands, and she took it from him, dismissing him as wordlessly as she had summoned him.

Turning to Duarte AKalakar, she gave him what she carried: The flag of the Black Ospreys.

The Weapon

Introduction

I wrote this story for John Helfers, for his anthology, *In The Shadow of Evil*. Interestingly enough, the cover painting for the anthology was the original concept sketch for the anthology *Summoned to Destiny*—a concept sketch based on my story in that anthology, *The Colors of Augustine*. The artwork was deemed too dark for *Summoned to Destiny*, which was supposed to be a YA anthology, and the artist actually asked me if he could use the painting for John Helfer's anthology. Which was very considerate of him, but entirely unnecessary.

Most of the novels that take place in Essalieyan also take place in Averalaan. Since the premise of the anthology was to write about a milieu in which evil had the prominent position, I thought I would write about Veralaan, the woman after whom the city was named. The first day or advent rites that occur on the first of Veral are a celebration of the choices she made in the very confined circumstances she was in. Those choices lead to the style of rule and governance that the Empire now enjoys.

The Weapon referred to in the title is Veralaan, herself. She is the Baron's only daughter, and because his rule is much contested, he leaves her in the Mother's cathedral on the Isle. His is a reign of terror and fear, and while the Mother's many priestesses and servants adhere to worship of the Mother, they've all felt his shadow, and they all bear the scars.

What would you do if you were given the daughter of the man who had murdered your family? How would you feel about her? Given the oaths sworn to The Mother, what would happen to that child within the cathedral?

The Weapon takes place during the period of the Blood Barons, as they were affectionately called. In *The Hidden City*, and actually in at least one of the *Sun Sword* novels, mention is made of the first day rites, and of the festival of The Ten. *The Weapon* is the story behind the first day rites.

The Weapon

I.

I N THE QUIET of isolation and a long-nursed pain, a woman knelt, praying to her god to give her a child. Because she was golden-eyed, she could be certain that her pleas were heard, for she was Daughter to the Mother—and because she was certain she was heard, she was also certain that Mother rejected her supplication. As a child, growing up in the certainty of knowing that the Mother *could* hear her, she had often pitied those who would live their lives in uncertainty. Time had eroded pity, or worse, begun to turn it inward.

The gift of god-born children was rare indeed in the small and fractious Baronies, for the Barons rooted them out without mercy, often destroying whole family lines in an attempt to destroy those who could willingly, inexplicably, consort with gods whose offspring might challenge their rule.

Only in the temple of the Mother, where healing was offered—and controlled—were such slaughters avoided. But even in these temples, the god-born were rare.

A miracle, denied those who lived in the shadow of the Baron's rule. After all, what parent willingly offered a babe to death?

Mother, she thought, rising. *Grant us your child. I am no longer young, and I must raise my successor. Grant us a child.*

But the Mother was silent.

～

The Mother's Daughter seldom summoned her Priests and Priestesses to this room, this hall. But when she did, she did so for a reason: blood did not cling easily to marble.

"Amalyn," the Mother's Daughter said, to the youngest of her attendants, "I want you to go to the Novitiates."

"But—"

"Now. The Novitiates will know, when the Baronial carriage empties into the Courtyard, which member of the family our visitor is. I *do not* want them to panic."

"But—"

"Amalyn. You are barely out of their ranks; they know you, and will trust your reassurances."

"And if I have none to give?"

"Find them."

Amalyn's eyes closed. It was a type of surrender. She backed her way out of the nave, toward the door that led to the rooms that housed the novices who served the Mother. They were crowded now. Every person that the temple could save, they had—and proof of it could be found in the cramped quarters the Priests and the Novitiates shared.

"You wouldn't be the only Daughter of the Mother that the Blood Baron has killed—"

"You *will not use that title*," she said, her voice as cold and severe as any autocratic noble's. "If it is my time, it is my time."

"We can't afford to lose you—" Her words died as Amalyn struggled not to say what they all knew: There was no other god-born child in the temple.

"Yes," the Mother's Daughter replied quietly. "We can. But we cannot afford to lose the cathedral; we cannot afford to have the name of the Mother silenced across the lands." She hesitated and then added, in a more gentle voice, "We serve those who have no other hope. And because we have obeyed the rule of our Baron, Lord Halloran Breton, we are the only church that has not been destroyed or driven underground. Our responsibilities are to those who have no value to the Baron. And because we can heal, child, we have value."

"Our oaths," Amalyn whispered.

"Oh, yes. If the Baron kills any of those who serve the Mother at my command, I will close the healerie to his entire clan. But if that happens," she added, with just a hint of fear, "you must be ready to flee; if we serve no purpose, we will become as the others."

"But you could flee *now*—"

"Hush, child. The Baron sent word that he wished an audience; it is not his way to be so tactful when he desires a death. I am content to wait upon his command." Amalyn left. Only when the door swung shut behind her did the oldest of the Priests bow.

"Iain," the Mother's Daughter said, granting permission to speak.

"Why has your agreement with the Baron never extended to your own life?" He said this with quiet respect—and managed to imply several decades' worth of reproach in the almost uninflected statement. He was good at that.

She shrugged. "It's enough to protect those who serve." And then she exhaled. "Not even the Baron can be offered affront without exacting a public price, and what better victim as balm to his pride than the Mother's Daughter herself?

"Let the temple stand," she added softly.

No one was certain whether or not it was a prayer.

~

Baron Halloran Breton was, in these times, a man to be respected. Of the Barons, he alone had managed to subdue his neighbors, binding them in ways that she did not care to imagine to his cause. And his cause?

He had not yet named himself King. But even casual analysis of the geography of his campaigns made clear that he desired a kingdom; he was first among equals, if he held any man to be his equal.

He was not a handsome man. This much was a known fact. But he might have been, had the cast of his expression been less forbidding. He was tall, and he wore his height as if it were a mantle. Age had not lessened him; it had broadened his shoulders and crafted lines across his face that made clear he was a man of little humor.

He traveled with four guards.

It was one third of even the most minimal number that she had seen him use before, and this gave the Mother's Daughter pause. But not so much pause that she did not bow. The Priests and Priestesses who served her chose the more expedient gesture of obeisance; it was certainly the one with which he was most familiar. They adorned the floor, the robes across their supine backs a spill of thick cloth. A cloth not so fine as his, and not so stained by travel.

"Is this hall secure?" he asked as she rose.

"We have not the soldiery you have at your disposal," she replied quietly. "Nor the wizards. But inasmuch as it can be, Lord Breton, it is."

His eyes were already roving the vaulted ceilings; torchlight flickered a moment across the dark of his eyes, reflected there. *Caught there*, she thought, *as if he had swallowed it in his youth.* She knew the Mother's pity then, but was wise enough to hide it; his father, the previous—and very dead—Lord Breton, had been a famously cruel man.

And Lord Breton had decided, in the end, to abide by the life his father had chosen for him. He had learned fear first, and when he had passed beyond it, he had never forgotten the price fear exacted. Fear was the tribute he desired; fear gave him a measure of power.

But no peace, no security.

He turned to the guards at his back; they were perfect in every way. Silent, grim, obedient, they responded to this slight gesture, and turned from the hall. He met her gaze, and his own flickered across the exposed backs of the most trusted of her servants.

She understood the command in his glance.

"Leave us," she said quietly.

They rose, not as perfect in their discipline as the soldiers of the Baron. But they offered no argument. When they were gone, he turned to her. "Mother's Daughter," he said coldly. "I have granted you willingly what few Barons have chosen to grant even greater temples than yours. I have seen the worship of your goddess spread across my cities and my towns, and I have done little indeed to stop it, although I, as the rest of the Barons, have little use for the gods."

She said nothing.

His smile was thin. "You are in the prime of your power. I have seen it before. I have also seen the decline of such power. Age, in the end, will leave you bereft; will you pass willingly from the halls that you rule?" Before she could answer, he lifted a hand. "They are words," he said, "no more." He stepped toward her, and she saw the mud leave the soles of his boots. "I do not understand you. I believe that you feel you understand me. And perhaps you do. I have let you spend your life upon my people in return for services that the mages cannot render me, and I am satisfied with our bargain. I have given you those who have chosen to break my edict; I have killed them, in your stead, so that your hands might remain bloodless. I have seen your servants," he added, "and they do not all bear the blood of your Mother; there are those who would raise hand against killers; those who would rise up to the status of executioner.

"But you keep them contained, and they are protected while they serve in your name."

"In the name of the Mother," she said at last.

"Oh, indeed." He paused; his hands slid behind his back and he stood there, staring at her, the harsh lines of his face tightening. "I am not certain that you will be a suitable guardian," he said a last.

It was not what she expected to hear. It was, in fact, probably the last thing she expected to hear.

~

When he had first taken power over the corpse of his father—a phrase that was not exactly literal, as there wasn't *enough* left of his father to technically be called a corpse—he had come to the temple, bleeding, burned. Twenty years ago, and she remembered it still. She had been a simple novice, albeit golden-eyed.

The Mother's Daughter of that time had offered him the respect of obeisance in front of the congregation that had gathered—that still gathered, huddling now in their pews—before the Mother's altar.

Skin dark with ash and sweat that he had not bothered to remove, he had gazed at them all, hawk to their rabbit; she had watched, from the doors that led to the nave, thinking that he might destroy the service to demand the healing that was his by right of power. Thinking, if he were not granted it, that he might destroy more. He certainly looked, to her practiced eye, as if he were in need of healing.

But he had confounded that expectation. Into the spreading, uncertain silence, he had walked as if he owned the temple. "I am the Baron Breton," he said, and the exultation in his smile did not quite penetrate the quiet dignity of those words.

The Mother's Daughter bowed. She rose, but not quickly, and moved to stand by the altar, placing her palms against its surface.

"You have not flourished in the reign of my father, but you held your own. I respect that, Mother's Daughter. I desire your company; I will tour my city before the waning of the day." He paused for a moment, and then his gaze crested the bowed heads of the men, women, and children who were wise enough not to meet it. But Emily Dontal, golden-eyed novice, was not so wise, and she met those dark eyes beneath those singed, bleeding brows, and almost forgot to move.

"Who is the novice who attends you, Mother's Daughter?"

The Mother's Daughter said nothing; he had expected that, but his lips thinned.

No, she thought. Seeing him, understanding now that he desired a death to mark the beginning of his reign, to mark his prominence. She had stepped forward, ignoring the gaze of the Mother's Daughter to who she owed both service and obedience. The latter she forsook for the former.

"I am Novice Emily Dontal," she said, bowing. Bowing low. She might have knelt, but she thought if she did she would never rise.

"You are golden-eyed," he replied.

"I am the Mother's."

"Good. You are the first of your kind—with the exception of the Mother's Daughter—that I have seen in the temple, and I have had occasion to visit during my youth. You will accompany us as well."

"Novice."

"Mother's Daughter."

"You will stay by my side, and you *will not* speak."

"Mother's Daughter."

~

She had learned much, in traversing those streets.

The new Baron Breton had come to the temple with a small army. He led the men, the Mother's Daughter by his side, through the streets, proclaiming his rule. He led them to the heart of the high city, and there, he set them free, for in the high city were the men who had gained great fortune in the service of his father.

There, she knew, his sole living brother resided. And he, too, was not without his men. She had read of war. It was something that was fought over distant plains, and distant patches of land. This sudden terrible knowledge: this was the Baron's gift. To her.

It was a scar she bore still. The soldiers clashed, and this, at least, she could bear in silence. When the first volley of quarrels flew from the distance of buildings, when they pierced armor and men fell with grunts or screams, she flinched, and the Mother's Daughter gripped her shoulder like a vise. But she could witness this, mute and still.

It was after. It was after the one army had been defeated, and the Baron's brother beheaded, that the slaughter had started in earnest.

~

"Emily Dontal," the Baron said quietly, calling her attention back from the bitter recess of memory although her eyes had not left his face. He was older, and he did not come injured and in triumph to these halls.

"Yes," she replied, "that is what I was called."

"But it is not, now, what you are. Mother's Daughter, do you understand the gift I gave you when first we met?"

She did not, could not, answer. She could still hear the screaming.

"I have spoken with the Witherall Seer."

She kept her face schooled. It was difficult.

"And she has told me that my blood-line will rule these lands; they will fashion not a Kingdom, but an Empire, and it will stretch farther than even the lands the Barons now hold." His smile was slight.

"Why have you come?" she asked, weary now.

"Ah, that. I am not the man I was when I took the Baronial throne. I have buried three wives," he added quietly.

As it was widely rumored that his first wife had attempted to assassinate him, she expected no open show of sorrow.

"I am in negotiations with Baron Ederett, to the far South. If these are concluded successfully, you may receive an invitation to a wedding."

Again, silence was the only response. It seemed, however, to be the incorrect response.

"My oldest son is much like my brother in his youth. My younger sons are canny." He shrugged. "It is...surprisingly bitter, to see them arrayed against each other in such a fashion. They are attempting to become adult in the Baronial Court, and if they survive it—they have sacrificed pawns and slaves in their games—they will emerge stronger for their testing.

"But the Court at this time is no place for a child." And he gestured.

The cloak that he wore fell away, its weave a weave invisible to the eye. When it was gone, a small child stood at his side. She was, to Emily's eye, perhaps three years of age, pale and slender, her hair still blonde, eyes still blue, in the way of children. She did not speak. She did not touch her father.

"This—this is—"

"This," he said turning to look down upon the child's head "is Veralaan. She is, as your spies may have told you—"

"I play no games in your Court—"

"Not all spies are paid, Mother's Daughter. Some come to you because they *feel* they are doing the *right* thing. They have hope of you, of your Order. They do not understand that you are content to sit, as dogs, if you are given the appropriate bone." It was an insult.

She smiled anyway, and the smile was genuine. It annoyed the Baron.

"She is," he continued, "my only daughter. The child of Alanna, my third wife."

The child said nothing at all.

"Your wife—it is rumored that she died in childbirth."

"Ah—that is the word I was looking for. Rumor. Yes, that was rumored." A shadow crossed his face. It was a terrible thing, that shadow; it spoke of death, in every possible way. And had it been on another man's face, she might have been moved to pity. As it was she struggled with self-loathing, because there was a part of her that enjoyed his pain.

"It was not, as rumors are often not, entirely true. But it is true now." He put a hand on the top of the child's head. His fist was mailed.

But gentle, she thought, and again she was surprised. "Go," he told the girl. "This woman, she is your new mother. Her name is Emily, but everyone here will call her 'Mother's Daughter.' You must learn to call her that as well."

The child did not speak. But she was, as were any of his subjects, obedient. She crossed the marble floor, her stride small enough that the hall seemed truly grand. Truly empty.

"You are weak," the Baron said to the Mother's Daughter. "It is because of your weakness that I am uncertain of my choice. But it is also entirely because of your weakness that I feel that my child will be safe here. You do not understand politics, Mother's Daughter, and you have been wise enough not to play.

"Therefore no one will tempt you, and I believe that even were the child my only heir, were the child a son and of use, you would still protect him with your life and the resources that I have chosen to leave at your disposal.

"Do not fail," he added softly. He turned from the hall.

The child started forward. "Daddy!"

He hesitated. She thought he might turn back, but the hesitation was his only show of weakness—and at the risk of exposing even that, he had sent all of his men away.

She caught the child in her arms, and the child kicked and screamed, as children will who understand that they are being abandoned.

∼

Iain was appalled. Amalyn was bitterly, bitterly angry. Norah was silent, and the silence was chilly. "Melanna?" Emily asked quietly. She held the child in her arms, for the child's terrible frenzy had, at last, given way to an unshakable sleep.

Melanna, wide, round, her cheek scarred from a different life, looked at the child's sleeping back. Her face was entirely composed; no hint of humor, of desire, of hatred, marred her expression. It made her, of the Priests, the most dangerous. Hard to deal well with things that one could not see.

"His men killed my son," she said at last. "When he was but two years older than this girl." What did not adorn her face informed her words.

"We have been ordered to protect her," the Mother's Daughter said carefully.

"We serve the Mother," was the perfectly reasonable reply.

The child stirred. Emily began to shift her weight from side to side, her arms around the child. The warm child. She, Mother's Daughter, would bear none. Had never thought—until this moment—that she might find solace in the act.

"We have no experience in raising children," Iain told them all. But his eyes were now upon Melanna. "The Mother has not seen fit to grace us—"

"No," Melanna said. "I will *not* do this." She turned from them and strode out of the small common room, her hands in tight fists.

Iain watched her go. "Mother's Daughter, is this wise?"

"Wise? No." Her arms tightened briefly. "It is not wise. But less wise is refusing the Baron's request. Inasmuch as he can be, he is fond of this child. I believe…he was fond of her mother."

Amalyn snorted, and Emily frowned. "She is but three years old. If she is her father's daughter, she is also her mother's. We cannot judge her. And she is no son; she is merely a daughter, and without value."

"He has shown himself to be without mercy when the children of others are involved."

She knew. She remembered. "And will we show ourselves to be, at last, a church made in his image? The Mother will turn her face from us, and without her blessing, without her power, what then can we offer the people?"

"Justice."

"We are not the followers of Justice," the Mother's Daughter said firmly. "Nor of Judgment."

"Melanna will not accept her."

"Melanna is the only woman here who has borne and raised children. She has served the Mother for ten years. Perhaps this is her test."

~

But she had not been truthful with her priests, and this was its own crime. She took the girl to her room and laid her in the small bed, staring at her perfect child's features, at a face which would change, again and again, with the passage of time. Would she be beautiful? It was impossible to tell.

She had prayed for a child. But not this one.

What will we do with you, Veralaan? What will you become to us? She understood Melanna's desire. She felt no like desire; death was not her dominion.

But she had in her hands a child born to power, a child born with the blood of Barons in her veins. It was true that the Mother's Daughter had never become involved in the politics of court—why would she? Between one contender and the other, there was only the difference of competence; there was no difference of desire or ambition, no intent to change, merely to own. What matter, then, whose hand raised sword, lowered whip, signed law?

But here: here was temptation.

It was not only Melanna who was to be tested, but also Emily Dontal, the child who had become woman in the streets of the city, on the day that Lord Halloran had become Lord Breton, Baron of the Eastern Sea.

A child was unformed, uneducated. A clean slate.

And upon such a slate as this, *so much* could be written. She had not told her most trusted servants the words of the Witherall Seer.

Mother, she thought. *Guide me.* And she lowered her face into shaking hands, because it wasn't a prayer for advice; it was a prayer for absolution.

~

The child would not eat for three days. She would drink milk and water, and Iain informed the Mother's Daughter, with increasing anxiety, that he was certain she shed them both with the volume of her tears. Those tears had ceased to accompany loud wails, desperate flights toward the door; they became, instead, the silent companions of despair. She did not like the robed men and women who ruled the temple; she did not acknowledge the men and women who labored in the Novitiate. She was not allowed to sit when the congregation gathered, but Iain was certain she would take no comfort from the hundreds of strangers who made a brief home of the pews either.

In the end, it was Melanna who took the girl in hand; she was not gentle. Not with the child, and not with the slightly anxious men and women who gathered around her, almost afraid to touch her unless she had finally exhausted herself and lay sleeping.

"You'd think the lot of you had never laid eyes on a child before!" It was custom to lower voices when exposed in the cloisters. Melanna often flouted custom when in the grip of disgust, and as she had come late to the Novitiate, she was often forgiven this flaw. "I can understand her, at least—she's just been abandoned by her only living parent. The rest of you?"

"It's not our custom—"

"And when the Mother grants us *her* child, what then? Will you leave all the cleanup to me?"

"Melanna—" Iain began again. He retreated just as quickly, his hands before his chest and palm out in the universal gesture of placation.

"You're a man," she snorted.

He had the grace to roll his eyes when she wasn't looking, and she the grace to pretend she wasn't actually looking. "Damn you all. I'll take her."

~

Daughter of the Mother, and not daughter of the god of Wisdom, Emily Dontal observed. It had taken two weeks, a mere two weeks, before Melanna intervened. Emily had intended to allow it, for she wanted Veralaan to feel isolated, and she could think of no better guardian than Melanna in that respect.

And for a while, it worked. But it was a short while.

~

She came upon Melanna in the smallest of the chambers used by the Novitiates for quiet contemplation and prayer. As Melanna was no longer a Novice, she was surprised to come upon her there, but not nearly as surprised as she was when Melanna looked up, and the dim lights of the brazier shone across her wide cheeks.

Even in the darkened shadows of the room it was clear that her eyes were reddened. She lifted shaking hands and made to rise, and the Mother's Daughter gentled her by lifting her hands in denial.

"Why are you here, Melanna?"

Melanna said nothing.

The Mother's Daughter waited, and after a moment, she drew closer. Melanna was upon her knees; she had surrendered the advantage of height. Of more.

She said, "I wanted the Mother's guidance."

Emily nodded.

"The child—Veralaan—"

"I know it is difficult—"

"No, Mother's Daughter, you *don't*." Her voice broke. "My son was older," she added. "Older than Veralaan. I thought—" She lifted her hands to her face again, callused hands.

"If it is too difficult a task, Melanna—"

But the woman shook her head and rose. "I can manage her. She's just a child." Her tears had dried.

The Mother's Daughter watched her go.

∼

But she came to understand, as the days passed, what the difficulty was. It was not in caring for the child of the man she most hated; it was the child herself. Although Veralaan was still quiet, sullen and easily frightened, she understood that Melanna had been appointed her care-taker, and she clung to Melanna whenever they were together. Melanna would extricate herself as she could, bending to free the folds of her robes from the three-year old's fingers.

But she would stop, spine curved, as the child spoke; no one else could hear what Veralaan said. Melanna would speak harshly in reply; harshly and loudly. The child would cringe. But she would not let go; once dislodged, she reached, again and again, for the comfort of this angry attachment.

∼

When Melanna almost missed dinner for the first time—and it would have been a disaster, because the Priestess supervised the chaos that was the kitchen—Emily Dontal *knew*.

Melanna came late to the kitchen, Veralaan in the crook of her right arm. It was the first time that she would carry the child with her in her many headlong rushes from one place to another, but it was not the last. She tossed young Ebrick off his stool without ceremony, paused to criticize him for removing half the potato along with the peel, and then set Veralaan down in his place.

The child started to cry, but the tears were quiet.

"Veralaan," Melanna said, shoving her hands through her hair, "I *don't have a choice.* If I leave this lot to cook, we'll be eating dirt and burned milk for the next three days!"

Veralaan nodded, folding her hands together; they were small and white. But she still cried.

"Hazel, what do you think you're doing with that? The milk will just cake the bottom of the pot! Pay attention! Veralaan, we can go back upstairs when I've finished. I won't forget the rest of the story. But I—EBRICK!"

Emily had never seen her quite like this, and watched in silence from the safety of the door.

Veralaan said something, and Melanna bent to catch the words. Her face froze a moment, and then she smiled, but it was a tight, tight smile.

"Yes," she told the child, lowering her voice. "His mother finds him, and brings him home."

Small hands were entwined in the fabric of the older woman's robes before she'd even finished her sentence. "Veralaan, I've told you a thousand times not to do that. Not where people can see you. These are the Robes of the Mother; they're to be treated with respect." She was busy prying those robes from small fingers as she spoke; it was a losing battle.

In the end, she sighed and hefted the child again in her right arm, lodging the bulk of her weight against her hip. She turned and resumed the marshaling of her beleaguered forces, carrying Veralaan as if she were some sort of precious mascot.

~

"I don't understand it, Iain," the Mother's Daughter said, over the same dinner.

"What don't you understand?"

Had they not been quite so isolated, she would have guarded her tongue; she was the Mother's Daughter, and inasmuch as she could be wise, she was expected to personify wisdom. Given that there was *already* a god that did just that, she thought it a tad unfair.

"Melanna."

He was quiet for a moment, which was often a dubious sign. At last he put his knife down and pushed his plate an inch forward. "Emily," he said quietly. Her name; a name he almost never used.

She met his gaze and held it. But he did not look away. Had she desired it, he would have. Or maybe not, she thought, as his expression continued to shift.

"Was that not your purpose in giving the child to Melanna to foster?"

"What purpose?"

"She will never have another child," he said quietly. "The injuries she sustained made it certain."

"I know. I was there."

Grave, now, he said, "You have given her the only child—save perhaps one, if we are blessed—that she will ever be allowed to raise in peace."

"I gave her," Emily replied coolly, "the daughter of the man responsible for the slaughter of her family."

"Yes, and so, too, did she see the child."

"And she cared so little for her son that she could—"

"That is unworthy of you, Mother's Daughter. Worse, it is a thought unworthy of the Mother." Not since she had been in the Novitiate had he dared use that tone of voice on her. It brooked no argument, allowed for none; he was rigidly certain.

"I do not know what you intended. I do not wish to know. Leave me with the illusion of your mercy. Melanna will grow, from this. She will remember things that will hurt her, but once she is past the pain, she will remember things that will define her."

"She will love this child."

"In time, Emily, accept that we will *all* love her."

"She is the daughter of—"

"She is a child. Whose child has yet to be determined; it is not in blood and birth that such decisions are made, but in the life itself."

"Iain—" She held out a hand. It shook. "I have looked long and hard at this city, harder still at the Baron who rules it; I have evaluated, as I can, the foreign Barons who bark at the gates. They are of a kind, Baron Breton and the others; if he loses his war, there will be death and slaughter, before and after. I cannot see a way out of this darkness if not through her. If blood and birth matter little to the Mother, they matter to those whose power destroy our people, generation after generation.

"I saw her as a gift. As an opportunity—perhaps our only one. I thought to be a weapon-smith."

He placed his hand across hers. "Have you spoken with the Mother?"

She shook her head. "I know my mother. I *know* what she'll say."

His frown was edged with humor. "There are other ways to fight," he said at last.

"In stories," she replied bitterly. "In song. But in song, the god-born walked freely among the villains, carrying the blood of their parents, and using the power it granted them. Where are their like now? We do not even have a god-born child of our own—" She choked back the words, the bitter fear. "I have seen those who would be heroes. They were not gentle men, and they were not kind, but had they succeeded, they might have been better rulers. If she is soft, if she is weak, what favor have we granted her? What good have we done ourselves? She will be killed by her own naivete. Had she stayed with her father, she would be capable. If we love her, will that not in the end make her a victim?"

"Let the definition of weakness be made by men like Baron Breton, and you have already lost; make of her a woman who can stand against him upon his own ground, and you will simply make another like him. Perhaps she will be beholden to you; perhaps she will kill you, as Baron Breton killed his father. I cannot say."

"If we—"

"But if we have no hope, Emily…"

"Hope did not save Melanna's child."

"No," he said quietly. He did not speak again during that meal.

～

Prayer afforded hope to those who gathered at the Mother's altar; it afforded little to the Mother's Daughter. But in the end, she *was* the Mother's Daughter. She watched as Veralaan grew, claiming, as Iain had predicted, the love and affection of the Priests, the Priestesses, and the Novices. Melanna was her protector and her guardian, and each time the child was introduced to a newcomer, it was by the side of the ferocious Priestess, whose grim and loving demeanor made clear what would happen to those who judged her for her father's crimes.

In a different world, this might have produced a different child. But in this one, not even Melanna—as she had learned so bitterly once—was capable of protecting a child completely.

~

When she was six years old, Iain began to teach her how to read, how to write, and how to comport herself as a young lady of wealth and power. The former, he had done in the Novitiate for years, but the latter? Not for a lifetime. Melanna hated it, of course. But Emily insisted on it.

"Why?" Melanna demanded.

"Because she *is* the Baron's daughter."

"Why Iain?"

"Because he is the *only* son of a noble family to grace these halls."

"It's no damn kindness to remind him of it. It just reminds him—"

"Of what he's lost?"

Melanna fell silent. It was a mutinous silence.

"Melanna, if he is unable to teach her, he will tell me. Trust him." She paused, and then added, "trust yourself. Trust Veralaan. To understand the odd customs and the graces of the patriciate is not to become what they are; if that were true, Iain would never have come to the Mother.

"He cares for Veralaan. Let him do this one thing for her; you have done almost everything else she requires."

"I don't see why she *requires* this!"

No, Emily thought, but did not argue further. *You don't want to see it.*

~

Emily Dontal used the excuse of the temple's care to keep her distance from Veralaan, but it was a distance that time eroded so slowly she couldn't say when it broke at last, and she, too, was swept up in the joy— and fear—that came of caring too much for a child.

But she knew the exact moment she became aware of it, and she did not forget.

Iain had, uncharacteristically, bemoaned the lack of a "proper" staircase. The cathedral boasted stairs, but they were subtle, and meant to be traversed with silent dignity; he wanted something that would lead from the heights to the altar in full view of an audience.

And he was embarrassed by the desire.

"She's graceful," he said lamely, "for a child her age. But she has to practice the stairs," he added, his voice wilting even more, if that were possible. "It's the one time when all eyes will be upon her."

"She's seven, Iain. And at that, a quiet seven. I'm not sure she'd be happy if all eyes, as you say, were upon her. We found the funding for the harp that you requested. We found funding for the dress. But, Iain, the funding to add such a staircase is well beyond our means."

He winced and lifted a hand. "I'm sorry, Emily. She reminds me of my youth, that's all. I see so much potential in her—" He shook his head. She stared at him.

"There was a time," he said softly, "a time in my life when I could see beauty and it wasn't tainted. She *is* that time. I have learned to appreciate beauty in more subtle forms. I see it daily in the struggles of the Mother's children. But this is different.

"And she's the Baron's daughter. She has to know how to make an entrance."

"Iain—"

One of the Novices burst into the room, throwing the doors wide. "Mother's Daughter!" she cried, all ceremony cast aside by panic. "Come quickly!"

"What has happened, Carin?"

"The Baron's men are in the healerie!"

"What? Why?"

"Three of the injured. They want to take them."

The Mother's Daughter stiffened. "Iain."

But he was perfectly composed now, and he followed where she led. The halls were long and narrow in her vision; the lights were dim. She had seen this many, many times. "Carin," she said sharply, "who is in the healerie?"

"Edwin. Harald." She hesitated and then added, "Rowan."

Rowan was healerborn. Emily Dontal lifted her robes and ran toward the bend in the hall that would take her at last to the bitter scene she had supervised so often. But as she rounded the corner, Iain her shadow, she saw that the doors to the healerie had been left open, and in the frame of that door, she saw a broad, bent back that she could not help but recognize. Melanna.

She slowed; a collision and its subsequent lack of dignity would hold her in poor stead. Melanna did not seem to hear her; she had to touch the older woman to get her attention and when she did, she forgot why she wanted it; Melanna was so tense were it not for warmth she might have been a statue.

"Priestess," the Mother's Daughter said cloaking her voice with the weight and authority granted the god-born.

Melanna shifted slightly, providing barely enough space that one adult might slide past her. But her hands came up in fists, and as Emily stepped into the healerie, she saw that Melanna's face was white, bleached white.

And she saw why in an instant.

Veralaan was standing in the healerie. She wore the deep, dark velvet that had been so costly, and her hair had been gathered above the nape of her neck; were she not so short, she might have been years older.

Rowan was crouched beside one of her patients. The child. Why was so much that was bitter twisted around the lives of children? But the child was unconscious, and Emily thought it unlikely that he would wake before this was over. And it would be over. The Baron's men were not to be denied. It was the harshest of lessons that the novices learned, and it was repeated over and over again, the birth and death of hope.

Gathered just beyond the door at the other end of the healerie were the Baron's men. They wore the surcoat of Breton, and carried the swords forbidden to any other citizen of the city. They had lifted their visors, but they did not remove them; they numbered eight. Eight men, to take two who would not wake and one who could barely walk.

But she saw the subtle signs of hesitation in their stance, and she moved forward. Because she did, she could clearly hear Veralaan's voice. The ceilings in the healerie did it no justice.

"Why are you here?" Veralaan demanded, her arms by her side, her shoulders straight, her chin lifted.

"We've come for those three," the soldier replied. "They are wanted by the Baron."

"They are in the temple of the Mother," she answered evenly, the words so smooth they bore none of the stilted effort that spoke of practice. "They came seeking sanctuary and healing, and we granted it."

We.

"It is not yours to grant," the man said. He shifted his blade.

"It is the Mother's right," Veralaan replied. She lifted a slender arm, a child's arm. "And you are not welcome here if you come to disturb the Mother's peace. You can lay down your arms, or you can leave."

His eyes widened. So, too, did the Mother's Daughter's, but none of the men seemed to notice. Their attention was captive to the girl.

Iain, she thought, *you need no staircase here.* But she walked forward until she stood to one side of Veralaan.

"Mother's Daughter," the man said, a hint of relief in the words, "we have come to take three criminals to the courts of the Baron."

"But you have not taken them?"

"They can't," Veralaan replied coldly. She did not look up to meet Emily's gaze; her eyes were fixed upon the man who seemed to be in charge. "They are not noble."

"They serve the Baron—"

"And I," she continued, brooking no interruption, "am. I am Lady Veralaan ABreton, and I have ordered them to leave."

"Mother's Daughter—"

Iain had come up behind her, as he so often did. "Lady Veralaan is entirely correct," he said, speaking to her, but pitching his voice so that the intruders might hear him. "The laws of the Barony are quite clear. Lady Veralaan ABreton is a noble, and she has given these soldiers her command."

"Only the Baron may command us."

"Then take the men," he replied evenly, "and offer public disobedience and insult to your master's only daughter."

The moment stretched out. The Mother's Daughter waited. She had meant to put a hand on Veralaan's shoulder, as both warning and protection; she would not have dared now. She saw the indecision upon the man's face, and saw it, inexplicably, shift in a direction that she had *never* seen in all her years of service.

He bowed, stiffly and angrily, to a seven-year-old girl. "We will take word to our Lord," he said, just as stiffly, when he rose. "And you will see us again."

"Send my love and respect to Baron Breton," Veralaan replied calmly, "and tell him that I look forward to his visit."

She stood in the same perfect posture until the men backed out of the healerie. The silence that surrounded her seemed like it might never be broken again. Not even the one man who was awake could speak.

When the last of the soldiers had left the healerie, Veralaan turned to Rowan. "Please close the door," she said quietly.

Rowan rose instantly, and tendered the Lady Veralaan a perfect obeisance. She also obeyed.

"Lady Veralaan," Iain said, offering a perfect, shallow bow.

She looked at him, then, lifting her chin to better meet his gaze. "Did I do it right?" she asked softly.

"You were perfect," was his grave reply. "But I think that—"

"They are not allowed to enter uninvited into *my* home. They are *never* allowed to enter my home uninvited." And then she walked over to the unconscious boy who slept on the mat upon the floor. "He's younger than me," she added quietly.

At any moment, Emily expected the child to crumple, to show the strain of the confrontation.

"What could he have done to my father, at his age? There must be a misunderstanding."

No one spoke. They should have. And if they did not, the Mother's Daughter had that responsibility. But the girl's desire for her father, her love for his memory, was something that, bright and shining, not even Emily desired to tarnish. It came as a surprise to her. Bitter surprise.

Melanna ran into the room. But even Melanna hesitated awkwardly on the outer periphery of Veralaan's sheer presence. "Veralaan?"

"Lady Veralaan," Iain said, his tone as severe as Emily had ever heard it.

Melanna glared at the side of his face, but it was a helpless anger. She had watched her charge from the frame of the door, powerless before her power.

"No, Iain," Veralaan said quietly. "She is Melanna. She can call me whatever she wants." And she turned to Melanna, "I'm sorry."

Melanna looked confused.

But Veralaan, clear and confident as children could sometimes be, had no intention of allowing her the grace of confusion. "I'm sorry that I wasn't with you when your son died. I could have saved him. You would be happy, then."

Everyone froze again.

"You loved him," she continued quietly, "more than you love me."

Melanna bit her lower lip. She sank to her knees in the healerie, and she held out her arms—looking, in her roundness and her sudden pain, like one of the few perfect paintings of the Mother. "Not more than you Veralaan," she whispered.

Veralaan walked slowly into Melanna's arms, and disappeared as they closed round her back. "Never more than you."

The Baron did not come.

II.

"LADY VERALAAN."

The young woman so addressed arched both eyebrows and rolled her eyes in mock frustration. The Priestess who attended her almost snickered. But she didn't speak, and after a moment, the Lady Veralaan ABreton turned almost regally. "Yes, Iain?"

"We have kept the Courtier waiting for as long as we can safely do so. He is, if I recall—"

"Lord Wendham," she replied curtly.

"Lord Wendham, then, and if you know that much, you know he is seldom given to patience."

"He has come to visit *me*," she replied coolly. But she rose, wiping bloodstains from her hands upon the apron that hid her clothing. "And I have duties in the healerie that I consider to be more important." But for all that, she spoke quietly. "Mother's Daughter?" she said at last, and Emily Dontal, silent until that moment, nodded. The years had aged her. But not unkindly.

"He will wait, Lady Veralaan. Your reputation precedes you, and if you do not tarry for *much* longer, he will pretend not to be insulted." She paused and added, "Rowan is capable of watching the healerie."

"Rowan," the healer said curtly, "is also capable of speaking for herself, Mother's Daughter." She turned to Veralaan, and offered the young woman a brisk nod. "I can watch the healerie. But I'd appreciate it if you didn't tarry." Her grim eye fell upon the pallets, the floor, the crowded confines of the room that was her life's work.

Veralaan offered her a perfect bow. An unnecessary one. Rowan accepted it; long years had come and gone in which the arguments about form and necessity had at last been eroded by Veralaan's tenacity. But as Veralaan left the healerie—by the interior doors—Rowan turned to the Mother's Daughter, her gaze shadowed.

"Do you know why Lord Wendham has come?"

Emily Dontal frowned. "No."

"I believe I do, Mother's Daughter. There will be a funeral that Veralaan will be required to attend."

"Whose?"

"I'm not certain," she replied quietly. "But there has been death in the streets in the past two weeks, and if I had to guess, I would say the funeral of one, if not two, of her brothers."

The Mother's Daughter closed her eyes. But words didn't require vision.

"She's learned more here than we could have taught her had we planned it all," Rowan continued, speaking words that should never have been spoken. "She's seen, every day, what is done in his name, by his men. Or by those who serve him. She knows. No one speaks a word against her father. None of us speak of the wars—not in the temple. But the injured who come to us speak when they dream. The dying? She tends their injuries; she knows how they were caused, and even why. She hears.

"I was against her working in the healerie," Rowan added softly. "From the beginning, even after she saved those three lives, I was against it. I do not know when that changed, Mother's Daughter. But it has. Her presence here—it does something that my power can't."

"What?"

"It gives people hope."

"Rowan—"

"Hope for the nobility. Hope for Breton. It is a bitter hope—to me— but not to all, and it has spilled from the temple into the city streets, traveling—like hope does—by whispers couched in awe. People know that if they can reach her side, they are safe." She paused, and then added, "if she is taken from us, that will no longer be the case."

~

At fifteen years of age, Lady Veralaan ABreton presided at her father's side over the burial of two of her brothers. She wore the black and the white, and it was edged in the color and power of gold; she wore gloves, and a dress so fine it would have fed the temple's beggars for two years. She was tall and straight, slender with youth, and her eyes remained utterly dry.

The Mother's Daughter was allowed to attend her, and accepted the insult conveyed with this permission. No other Priests or Priestesses were likewise allowed to be present. It was just as well. This close to the highest echelons of power, it was almost difficult to breathe. There was no grief offered the dead; their mothers had gone before them to the Halls of Mandaros, and their father? Grim and dispassionate. She offered no blessing; was asked to offer none.

But she saw how the Lords of the Breton court circled Veralaan, and she did not like it. The girl herself, however, seemed above them; if she noticed that they eyed her like jackals, she paid them no heed.

In fact, she paid only one man respect: the Baron Breton. And he was graceful and perfect in his reply. But distant as well.

"It is a pity," he told her softly, but not so softly that Emily Dontal did not hear the words, "that they attempted to prove their power when they had not yet mastered it."

"Lanaris is still heir," Veralaan replied. It was the first time—the only time—that Emily was to hear her speak her brother's name.

"For a while," was his bitter answer.

And two weeks later, when healers had come at the Baron's command, and failed to emerge from the bowels of his dungeons, Lanaris ABreton passed away. Rowan was white with anger, and with a bitter admiration. "I would have healed him," she told Veralaan, as she cut bandages into the long strips that were most useful in the healerie. "I would have healed him and been damned."

"They didn't."

"No. And they will never heal anyone else as a consequence of their choice."

"What does it mean?" Veralaan asked, in the pause that was wedged by anger between the gentle healer's words.

"It means that Baron Halloran Breton is now without heir. He has a wife," she added, "who has had no issue. This was less of a concern, before."

Veralaan said, with a shrug, "He will find another wife."

∼

He needed one. He had come through war to rule the Baronies to the North, the South and the West; he owned the seas. His armies were like legend and nightmare, and where they traveled, they were not forgotten. While he lived, he held them all.

But not even Halloran Breton would live forever.

As Veralaan had so coldly said, he found another wife. But when she was pregnant, she died of poison. Many, many men perished in her wake.

He came to the temple one evening, with four men. He came on horse; the carriage was slow and noisy, and it afforded lookouts the ability to grant warning. But he did not enter the temple; he waited at the door as if he were simply another supplicant. If he did not wait with grace, he did not wait with ire, and Lady Veralaan ABreton agreed in due time that she might speak with her father, Lord Breton.

He left his men at the doors, and they fanned out, brightly burnished fence beyond which, for the duration of the interview, no one living would pass. Emily Dontal led him from the door to his daughter. She did not ask him why he afforded Veralaan this courtesy; he did not offer. But he looked aged, in a way that she had never seen him aged. Not with the death of his sons, certainly, nor the death of many wives.

She led him into the small chamber, and when she made to leave, he lifted a hand. It was an imperious gesture, but he did not follow it with words; instead, he met his daughter's level gaze. She nodded.

"Please," he said, with just a trace of irony, "stay, Mother's Daughter. What I say may be of concern to you in the future." He did not add, *do not interrupt.* Nor had he need. She bowed to him, and moved to stand beside the wall farthest away.

Veralaan did not run to him; she did not smile or lift arms. She regarded him from a distance. If he noticed, he said nothing—and Emily thought it unlikely that he *did* notice. It would pain Veralaan, but she had grown strong enough over the years to hide pain from all but Melanna and Iain.

"I will be brief," Lord Breton told his only living child, "because your safety is served best by brevity. Your existence here has long been known, but it has never been of grave consequence. I fear that this is about to change, Veralaan. There will be, among the Lords who serve me, men who will offer you much if you will consent to marry them. There are those who would not bother to ask your consent, were you not now in the hands of the Mother. They will not risk her wrath at the moment—if they choose to fight among themselves, they may well need the blessings of the Mother.

"I know them all. I know their weaknesses and their strengths. I have chosen two who I believe are likely to be able to hold what I have built. They could simply take it, but I think they are canny enough not to spend men where it is unnecessary. You are the bloodline," he added quietly. "And therefore, your presence by the side of the right man will signal legitimacy."

She looked at him. "I am to marry?"

"Not yet," he said quietly. "But soon. You will know. Choose wisely." He hesitated for just a moment, as if he might say something more. But he was Halloran Breton; in the end, he retreated in silence, taking nothing of her with him.

And when the door was closed, Veralaan turned to Emily Dontal. The presence —and the absence—of her father cast long shadow; some hint of the wild fear she had shown as a young child now darkened and widened her eyes. She raised her hands, and they shook, but she did not bring them to her face; she held them out before her, turning them so that she might inspect their palms.

~

The room was cold and quiet; the thin door was shut. There were chairs around the table, because they had chosen the dining hall for their meeting; it was one of the few rooms that could easily seat them all.

They sat in a tense silence, one punctuated by sudden motion, by words that almost demanded voice. Emily Dontal waited until she was certain that no one would speak.

"This is what we expected, isn't it?" she asked them all. Melanna's glare was tinged with red, although she did not cry. "This is why we trained her. This is why we taught her. She is *the Baron's daughter*. Did any of you truly think that she would spend her life here?"

It was an unfair question, for it had only one answer.

"Iain?"

"I have studied the Lords of the Baronial Court," he said quietly. "My sources —and they are few—have given me what information they can."

"And you trust them?"

"Not at all. They understand why I have requested the information, and they seek their own advantage from the giving." There was no bitterness in the words. "Of the men that consider themselves powerful, I think I know the two of whom he spoke."

"And they?"

"What would you have me say, Emily? That they are *good men*?" Ah, bitterness there. "That they will be *kind* husbands?" And all of Melanna's rage, but cultured, quiet.

"Yes, if it were true."

He rolled his eyes. "In a different story, Mother's Daughter. In a different world." He drew the circle across his chest, a jittery fidgeting motion. "But if she must choose—"

The door that led to the kitchen swung open.

In it, hands by her side, stood Veralaan. "I won't," she said softly.

She had heard everything.

"Veralaan—" Melanna rose almost blindly.

"I won't. Do you think I'm stupid? Do you think I don't know? One of them will be responsible for my father's death."

Ah. "Veralaan—"

"And even if they're not, what difference will it make? I know their names. I hear them every day, in the healerie. I know what they do, in my father's name. I know what they will do. Am I expected to leave the Mother's heart so that one of them may rule?"

"If you do not," Iain said, without fire, "they will war among themselves. And in that war, there will be more death than even you can imagine. You have some power, Veralaan. If you choose—"

"I won't. I will never marry." She lifted her hands; they were fists. "Why didn't you train me to wield sword, Iain? You know how. Why didn't you teach me about armies, about strategy? Why did you—all of you—let me labor here, let me think I was making a difference?"

"You *are* making a difference, Veralaan."

"And when I leave?"

They did not lie to her. And, because they couldn't, they said nothing.

~

Six months later, Baron Breton passed away, leaving behind one living child. She was a girl, and although in theory she was heir, it was tenuous theory; no one would follow a woman. But as Baron Breton had surmised, the Court did not immediately fall upon itself, although there were deaths. They decided, instead, that they could wait for Veralaan to make a choice. They signed treaties in blood to that effect: they acknowledged *her* as Breton's only heir.

Word began to arrive in the hands of trusted emissaries from all stratum. Letters were followed by gifts, and gifts by requests for audience.

Iain saw that Veralaan's wardrobe suited her station, but he also demurred when presented with these requests; the Lady Veralaan, he said, was in mourning for her father, for her much loved father, and she could not entertain others until the period of mourning had passed.

It was not—entirely—a lie, although Veralaan did not cry or weep. She refused, however, to meet with these men. And for a year, they accepted this refusal with outward grace. But it was a thin veneer.

~

The first girl who came to the healerie with a message from one of the Lords had two broken arms. The girl could not be more than eight years of age, and she was weeping and frightened—but she was alive. Veralaan was not in the healerie, and Rowan and Melanna managed to keep this from her for a day and a half.

A day and a half was all it took for the next injured victim to arrive. After that, there were a dozen, and each man, woman or child carried a message for Lady Veralaan of the Mother's Temple, writ in broken bone, in gaping wound: a simple greeting.

Veralaan tended them all herself; she insisted on it. She wept with them, and openly begged their forgiveness. It was the only time she would do so.

Iain said, quietly, "what one lord does, they must all try. But Veralaan, if you accede to these...requests...they will never stop."

"And if I don't?" she asked. She was bone-white.

"I can't say," he replied at last. "If they kill, the message will never reach you."

"What would you have me do?" She turned to Rowan, hair now gray, skin as white as Veralaan's, and for the same reason.

"I—I can't advise you, Veralaan." She turned away.

"Rowan!"

"I think Iain's right. Start, and it will *never* end. All they will have to do is fill the healerie with the dead and the dying, and whoever can do the most damage will, in the end, be the one who holds the most power over you." But her hands were bunched fists as she said it, and the cloth around her legs shook as she shoved those fists into her lap.

Melanna tried to drag Veralaan away, as if, for a moment, she were once again a three-year-old child. Veralaan shook her off without speaking. But her face did not regain its natural color.

"Don't do it," Ian told her, "If you do, they will know that you're weak."

"And is this how strength is defined?" she asked, staring at the closed doors of the healerie, her voice very soft.

"In the Baronies, yes."

~

One day passed.

Melanna wept quietly, her voice shorn of bark, and therefore of strength. Emily put an arm around Melanna's shoulder. "Why are you standing in the hall?"

"Veralaan won't see me," was the choked reply. "She sent Iain away as well, I'm afraid of what she'll do—"

Emily held Melanna tight. "We are all afraid," she whispered. "I prayed. The night she came, Melanna. I prayed to my mother for a child. For the child she has long denied me. I always wondered—I wonder still—if it is because of my weakness, my anger, my inability to simply forgive.

"I don't know. Perhaps the gods do listen to those who aren't born with their blood; Veralaan came after the prayer."

"There is no god of Mercy," Melanna said bitterly.

"No. Only the Mother."

"Where are the *other damn gods*?" Melanna snapped harshly. "Where are the heroes? Where are the men who could stand against those—those—" She lifted a hand to her face.

"You know the answer," was the bitter reply; they were of a mind this evening. "But I—"

"She won't see you."

"She will," the Mother's Daughter said, without stiffness or determination. "Because she sent for me."

"Don't—" Melanna gripped Emily's arms. Her wide fingers would leave bruises there, but it was unintentional. "Don't let her do it."

"She cannot stand to see them suffer because of her. To see them suffer? Yes. Because she has practically lived in the healerie when she has not been learning how to be a Baroness, she has grown calluses, as we *all* have. But this is new. Until now, they lived *because* of her. She is young, and her heart is not scarred enough. I do not think she will survive this."

"We should have done things differently. We should have—"

The door opened, and Melanna choked in her rush to contain the rest of the words. But she stared at Veralaan's pale face. She lifted her hands to touch it, and Veralaan, instead of withdrawing, lifted her own, catching Melanna's beneath her youthful palms.

"You are my mother," she said quietly.

Melanna, already given over to tears, cried more of them.

"And Emily, you, too. Amalyn, Rowan. Even Iain."

"Not father?"

"No. I would never disgrace Iain by calling him that." The words were bitter, but the bitterness was a ripple. "Mother's Daughter?"

"Lady Veralaan."

"I require your presence in the inner chamber."

"The inner—" Emily's eyes widened. "The Mother's chamber?"

Veralaan nodded quietly.

"Veralaan, the Mother is *not* of this world. She cannot offer you guidance, and she cannot protect you. She—"

"She cannot even hear me, if you will not intercede," Veralaan said. "I know. I know all of this, Mother's Daughter. And I know that Rowan is also right. But I can't—I can't go into the healerie again. I can't—" She stiffened. "It won't end with strangers, even the strangers to whom you've dedicated your life. If injuring—and disfiguring—outsiders won't work, they'll try insiders. We'll lose Novices. I might lose—" For a moment, the younger Veralaan was there, in the wide eyes, the frightened eyes, of a child who had been abandoned by her father. "I've made my choice."

"What choice, child?"

"I am not a child, Mother's Daughter. I am Baron Breton, by the acknow-ledgment of the Lords of the Baronial court. And in the end, it was not a request. You will accompany me to the inner chamber."

"There is no magic in the inner chamber, Veralaan."

"No, Mother's Daughter."

"Then why?"

"The Mother will hear you. And when you call her—if you call her—she will come." She turned to Melanna and hugged her tightly. "Tell Iain—"

"I won't. I won't tell him anything. You want to tell him something, you *have to be here to do it.*"

~

The inner chamber. The room in which the prayers of the Mother's Daughter were made. It was a small room, with a modest ceiling, stone walls, and a small altar. Upon the altar was an empty bowl, an empty basket, a small candle; things that were entirely modest and ephemeral.

"It is not a very fine room." The Mother's Daughter came to stand by the altar; she did not kneel.

"What need have gods of finery?"

"Ask men who envy the gods the power they think gods possess," was the bitter reply. "What do you wish me to ask of my mother?"

"I don't," Veralaan said evenly. "I wish to ask it myself."

The Mother's Daughter was silent for a long moment. "Veralaan—I can summon my mother. And in reply, she will summon us. We will walk in the world that is neither man's nor god's. It is...not an easy place to endure."

Veralaan, however, was young; she would not be moved. "Call her."

And Emily Dontal did.

The mists ate away at the floor; they severed the walls from their moorings, until only the mists themselves remained. They were not gray, not black, not white, but all of these things, and interspersed with them, colors, muted and moving as if at the behest of strong breeze. But none of these things moved Veralaan; she endured them as if they were simply a matter of fact.

Emily was impressed.

But when the Mother came, Veralaan lifted chin and looked up, and up again, for the form the Mother chose was not comforting, and not small; she was tall as the skies of mist, her arms long, her shoulders wide. She came carrying no baskets; she came attended by no beasts of burden, no emblems of unearthly authority. She wore the workaday robes of a field laborer, and her face was lined by sun and wind.

"Daughter," she said to Emily. "Why have you summoned me?"

"At the behest of one of your Novices," was the quiet reply. "And no, Mother, I do not know why."

"Ah, daughter," the Mother said quietly. She spoke not to Emily, but Veralaan. "I have long watched you, through the eyes of my only child. What do you wish of me?"

"This world, this place," Veralaan replied. "It is said that time moves strangely here."

"It is true. Time is of passing consequence to my children, but it does not touch me."

"And if I spent time here, would I age?"

"You are mortal."

"If I were willing to age, would time pass beyond this place?"

"In mortal lands?" The Mother frowned. Emily could feel it as if it were weather, a storm. "Why do you ask this, child?"

If Emily's use of the word had caused offense, the god's use did not. "Because I have no time. Beyond this place, your followers are dying because men with power seek my attention."

"They seek more than that."

"Then you already know why I ask."

"I wanted to be certain that you did. What would you have of me? I am no warrior, and I am bound to my lands, as you, in the end, must be bound to yours."

"I want a son," Veralaan said.

Emily almost stopped breathing.

"I want a golden-eyed son, a god-born child. I was not trained to war," she added bitterly, "because I am a daughter. I cannot fight. I cannot lead armies, even if there were any willing to follow. Everything I am, I have become in your service.

"But I am not without strength. I am willing to bear such a child, and to raise him as I can—but only in the lands between; if I bear him here, he will die."

"If you bear him in the lands between, you might, child."

"I am willing to take that risk."

"I cannot give you the child you seek."

"I know. But you are sister to many gods, and I—" She struggled now, with the words. "And I wish you to intercede on my behalf with one of your brothers."

"Which one, child? The fate of the god-born is death in your lands, and there is not a god who easily surrenders his children to death."

"I know," she whispered. "Not even a man as monstrous as my father could do that."

The Mother was silent a long moment. "If you are willing to live in the half-world, there may be among us those who are willing to offer what you ask. But child—those born to the blood are driven by it. Which god would you choose?"

Cartanis, Emily thought. Surely Cartanis, god of just war. But Veralaan was silent. After a moment, she said, "Which god would you choose for me?"

And the mother laughed. It was a low, rich sound, a sound carried by a host of voices, a multitude of emotions. "It is not a question that I could answer," she said, when she had stopped. "But think long on what is missing in your world, and perhaps you will find the answer you seek." She held out her arms, her huge arms, and gathered Veralaan in them, as if she were a babe.

"Emily," she said, when she had pulled Veralaan from the ground that the mist obscured. "You have done well. You have struggled, and you have chosen to love this child as if she were your own."

"No, Mother," Emily said, bowing her head. "I had no choice. But the others? Melanna, Iain, Rowan—they are worthy of the praise you offer me. They love her. And they will be grieved indeed to lose her."

The Mother's smile creased; it blended with sorrow.

"Loss defines us," she told her only blood daughter. "But more than that, what we choose to lose defines us. I will go. But wait here, Emily."

~

Emily Dontal knelt by the altar. The mists had parted and dispersed, and in the absence of her mother, she felt the world as the grim, dark place it was. No dint of labor could lift that darkness. It was said that the gods had once walked the world, and she bitterly regretted the fact that she had not lived in those times.

But one could not choose.

Mother, she thought, as she pressed her forehead to stone. Her vision was skewed by a thin sheen of water; there were tears there that she could not shed. She had been bidden wait, and she was dutiful. She waited, feeling, now, the cold of stone in her bones, the ache of age.

She did not see the mists as they returned until they had all but covered her. But she stood as they did, so that she might see her mother again.

It was not her mother who stood before her.

It was a young man. And beside him, another. Two. They gazed down upon her, for they were tall, and their eyes were bright, golden. That light seemed to burn the mist away, and she was captive to it, although—had she been vain—she would have known that those eyes were kin to her own.

"Mother's Daughter," the man to the left said quietly. He offered her a hand, and she stared at it for a moment. Then she took it.

"I am Cormalyn," he said quietly. "And this, my half-brother, Reymalyn. We have heard much about you, and we are honored to meet you at last."

She shook her head, almost in wonder. "You are the son of Cormaris, Lord of Wisdom."

"I am."

"And your half-brother, the son of Reymaris, god of Justice."

"I am," the second man said, speaking for the first time. "And I am capable of speaking for myself, although my brother is the better with words." He too, offered her a hand.

She felt her throat constrict.

"We are the sons of Veralaan," they said in unison, "and as she is, by acclaim, Baron of Breton and therefore the Eastern seas, we are her heirs, and between us, the legitimate claimants to the Baronial lands."

But she could not speak. *Veralaan*, she thought, staring at the two.

Cormalyn's smile was gentle. "It is hard, for my mother," he told her. "But hard, as well, for you. Or it will be. She is coming, Mother's Daughter.

But she is not what she was, and you must warn the others."

"I—"

But they stepped to the side, and between them, as the last of the mists left, she saw Veralaan. No: she saw through time, down a stretch of more than a decade and a half, to see the woman that her Veralaan might become: Stronger, wiser, but almost silent in her isolation. Her hair was still blonde, and it was longer, and the features of her face were unmistakably her own; she did not look old, but she was no longer a fifteen-year-old girl.

She was a woman.

She had borne these two, and she had raised them.

"Mother's Daughter," she said quietly, as if speech were foreign to her. She held, in her arms, a blanket, but she wore the same dress that she had worn on the day—this day, some half an hour past—she had left.

"Veralaan!" Emily said, pushing past the two men who had at first seemed miracle and were now merely adornment. She held out her arms wide, but Veralaan stepped back. She smiled, to show that it was not an act of rejection.

"My sons," she whispered.

"You were always an ambitious child," Emily said with a wry grin. "Two?"

"Wisdom. And Justice. Because we need both." She added, with a rueful grin, "I was never really good at making choices unless they were obvious."

"What will you do?"

"I will summon the Baronial Court, Mother's Daughter. They will come, and they will meet my sons and their fathers."

"You would—you would summon your fathers? In the court?"

The two men said nothing, but they looked at their mother.

"I speak too freely," she said with a pained smile. "I am accustomed to the company of those for whom silence is no barrier. I…have to learn again, Emily. Will you…will you let me stay here, when I abdicate my throne in favor of my sons?"

"Veralaan—they are two men."

"Yes. But they were raised by their fathers, and they know things that not even you, Mother's Daughter, can know. They will build an Empire.

The Witherall Seer foretold it; my father went to the Seer before he brought me to your temple, and I listened to what she said, although I didn't understand it at the time. But it has to be the *right* Empire, or else, what's the point?" She took a step forward, and then stopped. "I almost forgot." And she held out the blanket to Emily.

"What is this?"

"It is a gift from the Mother, although she wept to part with her."

And Emily Dontal closed her eyes. "I do not think my arms are strong enough," she whispered, afraid to open them.

"I do. There is work to do, Emily. I cannot promise that it will be without bloodshed and death. But you've always done what needed to be done, and if my sons are driven by Justice and Wisdom, they will *always* need the mercy of the Mother, the compassion of her Daughters. Take your child. I want—I want to see Iain and Melanna. Because they haven't changed."

And Emily's arms closed round the infant whose eyes, golden, were a reflection of her own. Mother's Daughter.

Warlord

Introduction

This is the first of the short pieces I've written that were set in the universe of the *Sun Sword* novels, and it features the domicis, Avandar. When I was asked to write a story for the anthology *Battle Magic*, I was hesitant, because although my books often contain battle scenes that take up hundreds of pages, I'm not actually fond of battle; they're always a struggle to write. I like the events and the interactions that lead up to a conflict; I like the ramifications and aftershocks that occur as a result of one. But it's like the moment of a gunshot; the shot itself isn't the point; it's what lead up to it and what happens after it that makes it compelling. Unless you happen to be the person being shot at, which of course is different.

But Avandar and his past, alluded to in the books, but never fully explored, have always interested me, and I agreed to write the story with the understanding that the mage was trained for war, but that the war itself would be more internal.

This is not all of his story; given the fact that he's lived for longer than any of my mortal characters combined, that would be impossible in this space of words. But it does give insight into his character that might not be as clear in the novels.

I think, in the interim between the conception of this story (and it was written before *Uncrowned King*) things have shifted a bit, because they do between conception and execution for me; they grow and they develop dimensions I didn't see when I first conceived of them.

Warlord

E CAME down from the mountain on the day the sun rose between its peaks in a curtain of orange and crimson, a gesture of near-forgotten glory. He had some wealth with him, and in some quantity, although he had taken care to make certain it was easily carried and easily hidden. He dressed for the weather, although the cold never bothered him, and carried a pack—emptied—that observers might believe had once been filled with supplies. He wore no obvious weapons, although he might have chosen to arm himself with a sword had he taken the southward pass; to the Dominion, a weapon defined the status of a man and he was not above vanity, although the sword was no true weapon. He had his birthright, and with it, he had destroyed whole armies. Those fires were not banked.

It was time, again; time, but still too early.

He had woken the previous day, and the day before it, from the nightmare that had haunted his life for so many years now it had become, in some fashion, his closest companion—the only companion he was allowed. At dusk, having thrown off sleep by a monumental act of either will or cowardice, he would be wreathed in old ghosts, and the blood on his hands would glisten darkly as he listened to old cries.

The ghosts had driven him for years, and as always, he had retired to the finery of his mountain confines to wait out their long decline. Half-mad when he arrived—always that—clothing rent and torn, blood across his chest, his hands and the length of his face not covered by untended beard, he would plunge through the mystical wards that separated his mountain vastness from the cold, the wind, the snow, and the presence of any other man.

There, surrounded by the finery of lifetimes, awash in the reflection of magelight against crystal, gold and silk, he would recover from his wounds.

But the deepest of the wounds seldom left completely.

As a younger man, his rage had fueled the healing; as a younger man, it had been easier to foist the import—and impact—of his actions upon his enemies and allies. If, he would reason, they had not attacked or if they had done as they were ordered... But he had been younger, then. The pain was easier to twist into rage, and rage was by far the more comfortable. Unfortunately, with age came a certain understanding, a certain self-knowledge, and a distinct self-loathing. A man so enraged was an easy pawn, and he intensely disliked being the servant of any other man.

Intensely.

But he was tired.

And the dreaming was different, this morn. Different because it had followed the course of three nights, unchanging; different in that the ghosts of the dead were escorted, were called back, by the visage of a woman in robes of blue.

He disliked gods on principle; they were, of a type, rulers, and made of men—men and their own flesh and blood—groveling servants. And they, in their time, had destroyed more than his life by their curse and their geas, by the edicts they had *no right* to pronounce upon him. It was no surprise that he recognized the hand of a god in the figure of the woman.

"It is time," she said, her voice low and deep, yet still loud enough to be heard clearly over the terrified accusations of his dead, all his dead. "The battle that you've trained for all your life is about to start. They will find you; they have always found you in the past."

He could not make out her face in the folds of cloth that framed it. Shadows, there, darkness of her own.

"And am I a pawn," he said stiffly, "to be ordered into a life I've chosen to leave?"

"You have never," she replied, "chosen to leave it. Never." And so saying, she pulled a glowing orb from the confines of her sleeves. "Or perhaps you do not remember your beginnings."

He lifted his hands. Pulled back. He knew what the orb was, although it had been a long, long time since he had seen one.

"You are weary," she said, as the light faded, as the implied attack ceased. "And I understand weariness. Will you not, at last face the truth?"

"I have tried," he said bitterly.

"Have you?"

"I have lost everything that I have ever cared for. I have surrendered all, again and again. And I am still as you see me. I am still as I *was*."

"Perhaps," she replied softly, "it is time to seek the truth of that fact. Go North, and East. Seek service."

"Have I not served in my time?"

Her eyes were violet ice; he saw them, saw the hint of pale, icy cheek, the hint of moving lips in shadowed face. "You have never served any master but yourself. After all these years, do you not understand that truth?"

The first night, he might ignore the words, although he heard the truth in them clearly. And the second night. But the third night, he accepted the sign of Fate. He stirred himself, and left his mountain fortress far earlier than he would have chosen to otherwise depart it: The loss was still fresh, and the pain still too close, and the voice and face of the woman he had loved was still locked in accusation and madness whenever his memory was unkind enough to return to her.

~

"The life of those who serve is not an easy life, and if lived correctly—and it will be, by those of you who finish your apprenticeship—it is not a life of glory." The man who spoke paused a moment. Frowned. "I realize," he added stiffly, "that you are in your first year here. Manners, however, are not the preserve of the well-taught; they are a *requirement* within the guild halls."

It was a threat, of course, and it worked; the unruly, unacceptable, thoroughly disgraceful lot of boys that the guildmaster had seen fit to send him fell silent as they contemplated life outside of the future employment the guild offered.

And that was the problem.

They saw it was a *job,* and while it was that, it was also more, this gifting of service, this dedication of life. It was a vocation.

Most of these boys wouldn't make it past their first year. If they somehow managed that, it was unlikely they'd persevere beyond the first year of their apprenticeship. They were like young weeds, and it was his task to strengthen the garden; he'd grown used to the job over the years.

The door swung open, exposing his students to the faint noise of the hall. Just what they needed. Another distraction.

"Sir?"

Ellerson frowned at the familiar young man. When the boy didn't cringe, the old man assumed it was important. He put on his this-had-better-be-good expression—although when he taught it was never that far away from his real one—and nodded at the interruption.

"I expect," he said, as he walked across the room, "that you will be ready for the history test when we resume."

~

Although the classrooms in the guild hall were modest, the building itself hosted rooms that only the finest of the Ten's mansions could boast; it was to these that clients came with their requests, seeking the service of a domicis. Most had temporary needs, and often of an exceedingly dull and transitory nature; they wished to impress a certain group of the right people for a certain season.

Ellerson was a practical man; he understood that the guild prestige derived partly from the money that men and women such as that were prepared to spend for the sake of appearances, and he treated them with courtesy and deference. But it was not in his nature to accept their offers.

Truthfully, it was not in his nature to accept any; he was of an age where he felt his service was suspect, and he had taken a well-deserved retirement after the lingering death of his last master.

All of which should have been beside the point, and none of which usually was. When he was summoned at all, he was offered a task by the guildmaster, and one refused the guildmaster only rarely. Always at some risk.

He found the door ajar. Waited a moment to see just how formal Akalia was being. But no attendant peered out; no one waited to greet him in the stuffy uniforms that younger journeymen were forced to endure when Akalia was entertaining clients of money and power.

Ellerson grabbed the door's authoritative handle and pulled it open.

"Ah, Ellerson. We were waiting for you. Please, come in." Akalia frowned slightly, pursing her well-weathered lips. Ellerson noted the expression, but he was frowning as well.

There was a man sitting in the armchair in front of Akalia's ancient desk. The desk itself was spotless—hardly its usual state—and there was a decanter and three cut crystal glasses which were reserved only for the finest of the patriciate.

Or at least those who considered themselves among the finest. Ellerson had met many, many such men and women in his life. He had also offended quite a few.

"Before you start," Akalia said quietly, raising a palm in a gesture that was part command, part surrender, "let me say that I realize that you are a) retired and b) far too curmudgeonly to be asked to serve a member of the minor or major nobility even if you weren't."

The man in the chair raised a dark brow in an otherwise perfect face. It was too perfect by half for Ellerson's liking; too haughty and too well-formed, unblemished by the heat of the sun or a day's honest labor. It was also completed by the finest clothing he had seen in perhaps five years— give or take a year for the Princess Royale—and a modest collection of rings which, thrown together, were the only quirky thing about the man. They were not fine, the rings, or rather, not all of them were; they were a mishmash of styles and materials that clashed rather than complemented.

"Ellerson," Akalia said, looking dowdy and unkempt by the unavoidable visual comparison to her visitor.

Ellerson stiffened; he couldn't help it. Instinct shored up his shoulders, his chin, the line of his nose. "How may I be of assistance?"

"You might start," she said, just slightly less stiffly, "by being less formal. This is not an interview, Ellerson. This man is not a prospective master." *And if he were, I'd never invite you to meet him without several days of coaxing and preparation first.* The unspoken sentence was several degrees louder than the spoken one, and followed by a brief, perfect frown. She was good at that; she, too, taught unruly boys.

"Ah." Ellerson relaxed. Slightly. "Your pardon. Akalia knows I'm retired, but occasionally seems to forget. I am Ellerson of the guild. Whom do I have the privilege of addressing?"

The man rose. "Avandar," he replied. "Avandar Gallais." He did not bow; nor did he extend a hand. But there was a warming of expression that might not be missed if one were paying careful attention.

Ellerson waited; the time passed. At last, Akalia cleared her throat. "Avandar Gallais," she said quietly, speaking to Ellerson, although the older man hadn't taken his eyes off the visitor, "has come to...join the guild."

200 — MICHELLE WEST

"Impossible," Ellerson said flatly.

"Impossible?" the visitor said, raising a dark brow. "I have failed at very little that I have attempted in my life, in spite of opposition."

"You see what I mean, Akalia?"

"Ellerson—"

"And I have offered, of course, to pay for the privilege of being taught the...guild's vocation. Service, I believe."

"Akalia."

"Your guildmaster seemed to think that my money was good, and my intent not obviously damaging."

"*Akalia*, may I speak with you in private?"

"No," Avandar Gallais replied, "I do not believe it would be suitable. I am...unused to having my future discussed when I am not present to mount my own defense."

Ellerson said, coldly, "I-was-not-speaking-to-you. Should you, for reasons that completely escape me—and should any sane teaching member of this guild—find your petition acceptable, you will have to endure far worse than merely being discussed when you are not, as you put it, able to mount your own defense. Do I make myself clear?"

The air literally crackled.

Akalia's face dropped into her hands.

Ellerson's face froze into rigid, unpleasant lines. "If that is supposed to impress me," he said, "it fails. You are certainly not the only mage domicis—or would-be one—to cross this threshold. Certainly the most arrogant, and the least suitable, but not the only, and not the first. Now if you are at all serious, I have two words of advice for you: Get out."

To his surprise—and judging from her apprehensive expression, Akalia's—Avandar Gallais did just that. Slowly, to be sure, and with the icy stillness that spoke of barely-checked anger. But he went.

~

"Why?"

As the guest absented himself, Akalia relaxed. "Why what?"

"Why do you want to accept him? There is no possible way that service is any part of that man's calling. Forcing others to service—and quite probably unpleasantly—yes. But serving? Taking a master and making that life the only life? Akalia, not even you can believe this."

"No," she said softly. "I don't." She rose, then, and went to the windows nested between ancient, very fine shelves.

"He reeks of power. It clings to him in every possible way. Had he come to request the services of a guild member, there are three I would immediately suggest. I would also inform the three, should they choose to apply, that I would consider their chances of surviving their service to be vanishingly small."

Akalia nodded absently.

"Akalia, I find your lack of response distressing."

"I concur," she said, again quietly.

"We have enough trouble finding acceptable students among the desperate rabble that come seeking some skill for employment. Would you put a man of this nature in this classroom?"

"No."

"Then?"

She turned to face him, eyes hard. "I would pull you from your classroom Ellerson, and I would put him entirely in your care."

"If he's going to learn *in* the guild, he'll follow the guild procedures. Is that clear? The students have to be house broken; I don't care how old they think they are. Akalia—" Ellerson stopped. "It's not just the money."

"No."

"And it's not his status. You don't recognize his name either."

"No."

"Then what? If you're going to saddle me with this task—a task, mind, that I think will be impossible to successfully complete—I will at least be offered the courtesy of truth."

"I had a dream, Ellerson," she whispered. "I had a dream, three times."

He lifted a hand to his face. "Gods," he muttered. "You're going to make the next four years of my life miserable for the sake of superstition."

"Yes."

He didn't bother to ask her what she would do if he refused. "Very well. Avandar, you may return," he said, quietly and dryly, to the empty air.

Avandar Gallais stepped into the room.

"And if I catch you doing that again, I'll throw you out of the guild myself. I am your teacher, and if you are here to learn, you *will* learn. If it kills us both."

Avandar raised a brow. "It won't," he said at last.

Unfortunately, Ellerson could hear the unspoken part of Avandar's sentence as easily as he could Akalia's.

~

Avandar attended classes. That was the first calamity.

At about the time the tabletop beneath his hands began to sizzle and blacken—causing an offending young adolescent to think better of his comments about age and stupidity—Ellerson had already decided two things. First, that the classroom was not the suitable place for a man of Avandar's abilities, and second, that Avandar was perhaps not as familiar with the laws of Averalaan as one grew used to assuming everyone was.

He excused Avandar, continued to teach the class, and when that was finished, dismissed the boys under his tutelage as if, indeed, he dealt with mages every day.

After that, he sought Avandar out.

The new students were given quarters within the guild halls, rooms with a bed, a window which varied in size depending upon whether or not the boy in question was expected to live on his own or in a grouping of such young creatures, and the usual shelves and desk that had endured for so long they were proof that carpenters really were forces unto themselves.

Avandar had been granted a privilege reserved for few first year students: A room of his own. And given the depth of the black singe marks on wood that seemed to have melted beneath his spread palms, Ellerson considered it wise. Certainly wiser than when Akalia had first suggested it.

He knocked.

Avandar opened the door.

"I suppose you know why I'm here."

He stepped out of the way, letting Ellerson into the admittedly tiny space before closing the door upon them both. "Yes."

"*You* are a man. *He* is a boy."

"He is a lucky boy," Avandar replied coldly. "In my youth I lost many... friends who learned the lesson he survived."

"Mockery is not considered a capital offense."

Silence.

Ellerson walked over to the pristine bed. "I'm old," he said, by way of preamble, "And I refuse to have this conversation standing up." He sat. Avandar did not; instead he walked moodily over to the window and turned half toward it. His profile was a shadow with elements of color; he looked neither in nor out. Significant, that.

"Why are you here?"

"To learn how to serve."

It was not quite what Ellerson had expected to hear. "What do you think that means?"

Avandar turned toward him; his face was haloed by a sunlight harsh enough to shadow his features completely. Ellerson kept the smile off his face, wondering if Avandar had chosen his place by the window for just that purpose. *My eyes aren't what they used to be*, he thought; *but I don't need to see your face. I can hear enough of you in the words.*

"To suborn my will," the shadow said. "To suborn my will to another's. To take orders with grace. To live in the shadow and glory of another man while taking credit for nothing." Northern winters were warmer than his words. "To stand in shadow."

"Avandar Gallais," Ellerson said, his voice oddly gentle, "this is not the quest of a man of your nature, of your stature. I understand what you think you will learn from the guild. What I don't understand is why you want to learn it."

"Why is not your concern."

"Why is the only concern I will have for the next four years. Most boys come searching for money. The balance come because they're young and insecure and they'd rather attach themselves to greatness than take the risk of becoming great themselves. Some come because taking orders is easier than thinking of orders to give; some because they think the domicis are well paid house servants. Pedigreed. Expensive.

"In our first interviews, we attempt to discern the why; to place the boys where they are likely to have the most success in questioning their own motives. Not," he added dryly, "that at this age there is much success in that.

"But you—you are a man who has attained his power."

Ellerson straightened his shoulders. "You realize that we have no writ to protect you from accusations of rogue magery."

"There are…mages among the domicis?"

Ellerson shrugged. "Being domicis does not convey immunity from the illegal use of magic."

"This is not public property."

"No. I see you have some inkling of the laws that you are breaking. Let me make it clear: There will be *no* unauthorized use of magic in these halls. Another such incident—even one—and you will find no teacher."

Silk rustled as Avandar Gallais—if that was indeed his name—brought his arms up across his chest.

"Why are you here?"

"I will not answer that."

"Very well. Tomorrow we will avoid the classroom. I have errands to run on behalf of the guild; you will accompany me."

"As…errand boy?"

"As that, yes. I do not find your method of dress appropriate for the station you are to assume. If you have difficulty choosing the correct clothing, you may come to my quarters after dinner."

The man nodded.

Ellerson knew he'd burn in the Hells for eternity before asking for help.

~

Averalaan was not a small city. It was not, in the estimation of most Imperial travelers, a city at all; it was a vast island of humanity, folding in and farther in upon itself, that harbored *everything* anyone might desire to see in a lifetime. Magery; money; the famed bardic College of Senniel; the Holy Isle upon which *Avantari* rose, circled by the three most important cathedrals in the land; Southern silk and Northern furs, exotic spices, gems, and the work of Makers.

The trees here were taller than all trees but those found in the deepings, where men seldom traveled, and if they were surrounded by cobbled stone and man-made stalls, by house and horse and cart and dog and donkey, they were no less grand for exposure.

Avandar Gallais did not condescend to notice them. Which meant either that he had visited the Common before—which Ellerson doubted—or that he refused to display the weakness of awe to anyone. It was interesting.

As they walked—more slowly than Avandar would have liked, judging from his slightly sour expression—Ellerson observed. Not Avandar, but rather the people who moved out of his way. Women stopped, or stared at him from under the shadow of umbrella or awning; some very few gawked, but not even the young were moved to act foolish. Men also moved; the elderly and the wise. Young boys pretended not to notice him.

There were men who smelled of power, and Avandar was one of them. A domicis.

Ellerson put a hand up to his forehead to massage the wrinkles from it. They were unbecoming.

In four years we hope to accomplish what with a young man? Civility, for one. A better understanding of the life of a domicis. A clear acceptance of the value of service, and of what service itself must mean.

This man did not need to learn civility; he understood it, and would practice it or not as flawlessly as he probably practiced his magic. Ellerson thought that a month would be long enough, and four years too short a time, to teach him what service *meant*.

He was lost in thought. As teacher, and not domicis, he took the luxury of such reflection. He would remind himself of this later.

But something caught his attention: the tone of Avandar Gallais' voice.

"And I tell you, ADarias, that you have approached the *wrong* man. Do I make myself clear?"

"You are not the mage who calls himself AGallais?"

"Have I not just said so?"

"Three times." A man wearing House Darias colors drew himself up to his full height. "Three times. I seldom give a man a chance to lie to my face three times. But I am in…a tolerant mood." He lifted an arm, this House crested man.

Something was wrong with the gesture. It was innately foreign. But the Houses were not constrained in who they chose as members; the Ten did not birth their family; they adopted it, choosing merit instead of bloodline to carry the name. At least that was the theory.

Four men stepped out of the crowd. They, too, wore Darias crests, but

again, the crests were odd. More significant—much more significant—
were the swords they unsheathed.

Ellerson cursed.

The Common was crowded. Too crowded for a fight of this nature.
He himself had barely mastered the use of a sword—if master was a
word that applied to his ability to lift a blade without losing fingers or
toes to it—and he carried no weapon.

But he thought they might brazen or at least speak their way out of the
difficulty until he saw the expression on Avandar's face.

A cool, an icy, smile. A gesture of welcome, almost of relief.

"I will tell you again, ADarias, that you are making a mistake. You are
seeking a man. I am not that man. Let us say that in theory you are
incapable of making such an irresponsible mistake. Let us say, as your
ego decides, that I am, for whatever reasons of my own, lying to you.

"If I were the man you were seeking, and I refused your request—a
request which you have not made and which I have not heard—what do
you think the wisest course of action would be?"

Ellerson couldn't see the ADarias' face, but he could hear, in the reply,
the same chilly pleasure, the same recognition, that marred Avandar's features.

"This, of course." He lifted his arms again, and this time there was no
mistaking the utter wrongness of the gesture. Ellerson was a man who
had learned over time to trust his instincts. He moved. "While I admit a
certain surprise at your foolish reluctance, there really is only one course
of action, Warlord. We couldn't leave you alive to join our enemies."

Magic.

Fire.

Death.

~

The battlefield was alive with magic. The winds carried it. The fires
burned with it. The swords—drawn under a sun not quite bloodied by its
fall—reflected its light, glowing and burning where they struck. All
around him, in the fresh air of a bloody spring dusk, the dying screamed,
their words an accusation, a cacophony of voices that he could not
recognize, they'd been twisted so badly by pain and fear.

The trees cast long shadows where they still stood; many of their thick, ancient trunks had been splintered by the movement of earth, sudden and sharp, beneath their great roots. He felt it coming, a distinct, a distant, surge of power beneath his feet. Bodies flew to either side, a press of momentary flesh, stilled where it fell—or swallowed by turning earth.

He smiled. Sometimes he chose to play games with his enemies. Sometimes he pretended to give them the advantage; sometimes he let them see fear where none existed. They were fools; they believed in their own power although they had heard—they had all heard—of *his*.

But today, he felt no such desire. Enough of toying. He had come to the city to cleanse himself of war, and the war had come—as it always came— to him. This time, it wore the guise of an old, old foe, and an older ally: Demon. *Kialli* and its kin; one greater, four lesser. Had he so chosen, he could have seen them from miles away, and, in truth, had he suspected their presence so strongly, he would have called the power forth instead of letting it slumber so uneasily.

But it woke; it always woke. That was his curse and his gift.

"Impressive," the *kialli* said.

"Indeed," Avandar replied, cool now. He lifted his hands, palms up. No one would have mistaken the gesture for a surrender. His fingers snapped down, making fists of his hands. The four lesser demons snapped just as easily, spraying blood—then nothing at all—into the crackling air.

The *kialli* lord drew his blood-red sword; its flames were dull in the harsh light Avandar's magic cast.

"I tell you now," the would-be servant said coolly, "that I have no battle with you. I am here for my own purposes, and until you cross them you are of no interest whatever to me.

"It is the last chance I will give you; you are insignificant otherwise. But choose, and choose quickly."

The *kialli* were creatures of power and arrogance; there really was very little choice to be made. They closed, warrior-mage and demon, and where they touched they could not be seen for the crackle and glow of brilliant light. The earth thundered beneath them, the winds howled, the air snapped with lightning.

And when it was over, when the maelstrom had cleared, Avandar Gallais stepped out of the floating dust and the shattered ruin of the

Common ground. He was not unblooded; he granted the *kialli* some respect for that. But he was, as always, undefeated. As always.

He had come down from the mountains too early.

He had known it when he left them, driven North by the ghosts of the dead and three dark dreams. But the dead had become tricky over the passage of centuries; they waited until the battlefield loomed around him then snuck out of the shadows and debris, finding bodies, lingering in the whimpering screams of the dying.

He found the boy that way.

Found him bleeding to death, his chest a puckered, blackening wound that would not hold until a healer could be found. Young boy, not more than four years old, and beside him, arms broken on impact, his mother or grandmother. Hard to tell; the magic had scarred her face completely. The boy was not wild with pain, nor yet with fear, but he was wild with the desolation of abandonment, and no magic that Avandar Gallais possessed—or had ever possessed—would bring back the dead.

He should not have touched the child; that was his first mistake. But his body had given in to the glory of the fight and the satisfaction of the kill; it was satiated now, and other things had room to play.

He knelt by the boy. Reached out for him, his long sleeves sticky with blood that had not been shed in decades. *This* blood, his own, he was not used to seeing. But the boy's blood—the blood of others, had become his life. *Was* his life.

In the foreign, Weston tongue, the boy cried out for his mother. Avandar Gallais spoke a few words, a few comforting words of enchantment, and then, after a second's pause, snapped the child's neck cleanly.

He had done it countless times before, but he had always had time to recover; had given himself that much. The ghosts were so strong in these streets. Almost without thought, he held the child's corpse to his chest, tucking the lolling head beneath his chin.

There, in the dimming day, Avandar Gallais began to weep.

And it was weeping that Ellerson of the guild of the domicis found him.

~

They did not speak.

Ellerson, because he could think of nothing at all to say at the sight of a child in the broken city streets, and Avandar for his own reasons.

The magi were summoned. The magi arrived.

The witnesses—the few that had somehow stayed near the scene and survived it—were unclear about what had happened. They had seen men wearing the awkward crest of Darias, they had seen another man, taller and prouder of bearing, and they had seen the earth break, the sky rain fire, the trees snap like kindling on a hot, dry day. Not that the port city had many of those.

Ellerson's duty was to the guild, and not to the magi; to the guild, and not the magisterial guards. He did not speak, except once, and that was to say that in his considered opinion as a longtime member of the domicis guild, the House Colors that the five men wore were so sloppily put together they were obviously forgeries. That much was true.

Avandar said nothing. He rose as a witness, spoke as a witness, lied as a witness. The magi who had come to question him took his name and his occupation—apprentice guildsman—with some surprise, but the surprise was clearly not one of recognition.

"Come along, Avandar," Ellerson said, when the magisterial guards were finished questioning him. "It is time, I think, to go home."

Avandar looked up, beyond the fringe of Ellerson's remaining hair; looked South. He staggered to his feet, looking once over his shoulder at the unknown child the magisterial guards were bearing away on a simple cot.

"No," Ellerson said softly, "not South. To the guild, apprentice." He was gentle. He had not thought to be gentle with this man. "We go to the guild. Come. Follow me." Even in gentleness, he could not bring himself to touch his student.

Avandar pulled himself up to his full height, as if stung by the softness of Ellerson's tone. He followed.

~

Every life you take will become yours, Warlord. Its power, although not its knowledge, will be your strength.

And what price? What price will I pay for this gift? I am a man, and I will not give up my life to night or darkness in order to prolong it. I will not feed like an animal upon my own kind; I will not play kialli games or dance Arianni dances.

Do you think you do not prey upon your kind even now? No, do not answer. You are wiser than I thought you would be—an interesting sign. I cannot confer eternal night; I cannot change your essential nature. If you fear either from me, be easy. That is not my intent.

What is your intent?

To give you immortality, Warlord. War is an interest of mine, and you will keep it alive.

~

He woke to a darkened room. His arms ached. His chest hurt. The stench of the dead was in his nostrils, and to breathe he must rise, must seek the open air. The bed he left behind; his step to the window was almost, but not quite, flight. He threw the latches off, pushed the window up, sought the open air. The dream was thick and heavy and he had seen it often enough that he knew what would follow.

He would stand, at the foot of a god, waiting.

The mists of the halfworld where god and man might meet, if not as equals, then not quite as slave and master, would be thick with a life of their own, sensuous and disturbing. They had never seemed so immediate before; it was almost as if his answer would make him part of them, part of their dominion. His first intimation of immortality.

That part of the dream he could face. But what followed was harder.

He was almost grateful for the knock at the door.

"Come," he said, knowing that Ellerson would bring light with him; knowing that he would stop at the threshold a moment before stepping across and closing the door behind him. Knowing that he would come alone.

"Avandar."

"I...often have trouble sleeping."

"I rarely do."

"That does not surprise me." He lifted a hand to touch the peak of the window frame. "It was perhaps...to attain such easy sleep that I came to you." He turned; the light that Ellerson carried was a muted, simple lamp.

"My turn to stand behind the light, and you in it, is that it?" the domicis asked quietly.

"Even so."

"Tell me."

"There is not much to tell."

"You killed that child."

He turned away again. "I have seen enough of the dying, old man. That child was already dead. I spared him a few minutes of isolation, fear, pain. You would have done the same had he been a dog."

"Yes. Had he been a dog." The night was harsh. "You killed the five men."

"They would have killed me."

"True enough. But your battle killed some thirty people, at best count."

"So few?" The windows were airless. "I have killed thousands, in my time."

"In *your* time," Ellerson replied. "Not on *mine*." He set the lamp down. "Tell me why you've come, Avandar Gallais, and I will do what I can to help you. Refuse, and I will likewise refuse. This was a game, to me, and I repent of it; it is now clear that I have accepted a task whose failure will be too costly. I can step back, or I can go forward.

"I am prepared to wash my hands and step back."

Avandar Gallais stepped into the darkness and stared a long time at the older—at the younger—man's face. "You are not what I expected, Ellerson of the domicis. I will tell you what I may tell you. If it is enough, it is enough."

Ellerson stood quietly, seeking to take no comfort by seating himself. He was, in his way, like the mountains that Avandar Gallais called home.

~

He spoke first of his dream. He had thought to be interrupted, but Ellerson did not offer him that comfort, except to say, almost dryly, "you accepted, of course."

"I was a younger man," Avandar replied, as if that were answer enough. In a way, it was. "Younger," he said, "and less sure of my power." His hands, shadowed, were still visible in the night of small room and single window. "I am sure, now, of nothing but power."

"You aren't a god."

"No. But if I killed no other men in my life, I would live as long as one. As far as I've been able to determine, the length of life is year for year: One potential year of their life for one actual year of my own.

"I said I did not wish to feed upon my own, but I have, and if I do not hunger for their lives, I hunger for the thing that takes it most: war. Dominion." His hands dropped. "I had an Empire, of a sort, when I chose to accept the god's offer.

"And an Empress, a woman of beauty and power in her own right, a partner of consequence." This, then, was the second part of the dream, the part that defined his existence, that made him understand the mercy of gods. "She was fair, Ellerson, as your Northern snows; the sun could not bite her. Her hair was dark, the blue-black of night, and her eyes were dark as well; nothing cold at all about them. She was as tall as I, harder and more determined, and she had turned her talent and her energy to the study of magery so that she might be my equal." He laughed bitterly. "My equal. I indulged her shamelessly. She was the jewel in the crown; the crown itself." He looked into the dim light, the old man's stiff face. "I tell you this because I am a fool, and I am too new from loss. I will kill you if I hear it spoken of, because it will have to have come from you."

"If I choose to accept you, Avandar, what you say will be as close to sacred as words can be."

Truth, there. "And if not?"

"If not, I will take your words as a confidence between a lord and the man who has chosen, for this single night, to serve him as only one of the domicis can."

That surprised him. He was silent a long while, unsure of whether or not the silence was due to his wife or this strange man. "She was the first kill," he said at last.

Ellerson said nothing.

"She knew what I had done. I do not know how, but I assume the god's servants told her. Did I tell you that she was like the fires themselves? Hot, scorching, blistering—sudden in her anger and her fury, sudden in her love. She felt betrayed; she felt abandoned to mortality by me, by the only man she had chosen to love.

"She came to me in fury, and she—who had honed her talent at my side and knew better than any what my weaknesses were, attempted to destroy me. I tried to speak to her. To speak with her—she was beyond reason. A day, two days, and we might have spoken and had peace of one sort or another, but there was no peace offered.

"I did not intend to kill her."

"But you did."

"Worse, Ellerson. When she died, I felt it. The life that left her, the magery that had been her pride—and mine—came to me as if they were swords and I was the only sheath they had ever known. I had doubled my life span, and my power, in a single blow.

"But she was not just any woman. She was of an old, old line, and had in her the blood of the firstborn. It was not above her to place a curse upon the gift that had been given me. *You have chosen victory over love,* she said, *and this is what it will buy you; eternity. You will come to curse it, for you will hold nothing that you value until the day you choose another man's cause over your own. As you have conquered, so must you serve.*"

He did not kneel; did not sit. But the stiffness left him. The nightmare of death, her slack blistered face, the shock and the anger melting into hurt and denial. Nights that he could not leave the dream quickly enough he still woke screaming at the feel of her life bleeding into his. He had tried so hard to stop it.

But his pride was part of his power; he could not scream in front of this old man. He spoke instead, quickly to cover the pain, to pass over it, "She was the first of six wives who attempted to take my life. It…makes a man cynical about love and the fair sex."

"Did you kill them all?"

"No. Not after her. But I didn't love them either; not that way. In the case of my wives—or my children—I let executioners deal with their deaths. I could not quite bring myself to claim them."

"Your children?"

"Sons, mostly. They tired of a father's Imperial grip, and as my life would extend infinitely beyond theirs, they saw no better way to free themselves. I will admit that I had some sympathy for them; they were young men much like I had once been.

"I built Empires, and after a while, I left them. To my sons, to their sons. Once in a while to my daughters. But it pales, as time passes. We live—we who are mortal—in a world of 'ifs.' Imagine, Ellerson, that you have finally lived the perfect life.

"I chose to absent myself from war for a time—albeit a short time—and to find a woman who might be wife not to the Warlord, but to a soldier, a common man who had cunning and strength to recommend him. It was not a guise that suited me well, but I wore it. And I found such a woman, and I lived with her. I joined the army of the man who ruled the city in which we lived; it was long ago.

"War came." He fell silent for a long moment. "She was lost to the war; my son was lost to it. I remained. I conquered. I made my enemies pay, and with every life I took, the time of my return to her—to any of the people I loved—grew more distant.

"Was I a good man? What does the word mean? I have never understood it, and I understand it less and less with time. In my youth I did things that I could not speak to you of; I am not proud of them now, but I do not judge them, and those injured are so long dead it is hard to believe that any other judge exists. But I am not what I was.

"It is tiring, to watch every person you love wither and die. Whether they die attempting to take your life, or die because you have chosen to join battle—and I have chosen many battles, and I have held many of my children as they lay insensate with pain, unaware of me, of my presence—they die and I remain. I am *tired*, Ellerson. I have come this way to fulfill her curse and have peace.

"I tried. I tried it on my own. I lived what I thought was a life of service. Three lives. It was not, apparently, enough. And it came to me that I did not understand service; that I could not understand the conditions of her curse enough to be free of it. I had heard of this…unusual guild long before you were born, and I had thought to recover from my last life and come to you here for instruction."

"You've come here to learn enough to die?"

Avandar smiled softly. "Not the way I would have worded it, had you offered me the choice, but yes, I believe that is what I said."

"You realize," Ellerson said quietly, "that the magi would kill for the opportunity to speak with you. That the historians would stand in line, beg and plead for years on end, for a chance to listen to what you might say."

"I would speak to them in tongues that have long since died," Avandar replied, "if I spoke at all. There is some history that is better left buried; I would bury my own if I could. Will you aid me?"

Ellerson was quiet. "I cannot answer you tonight, except to say this: I may not be able to give you the peace you desire, but if it is in my power, I will point you in the right direction."

⁓

Pride.

Pride was the root of all great falls, in both story and religious text. In that ground where old religions faltered and fell into the realms only children now knew, it was a sin so often warned against that the children themselves had lost the sense of its grandeur and its greatness; in their language it was a crime much like theft.

But Ellerson was no longer contained by childhood. He stood in the darkened classroom, framed by door, the lamp's oil burning dangerously low. After a moment, he walked through the door to the room that was his preserve, his territory, his hallowed ground. He paused in front of a desk that still held the scorched and blackened marks of two palms.

Closing his eyes a moment, he listened to the tenor of Avandar Gallais' voice. How could a man such as he learn the value of service when in truth he had never done anything but rule? Even in this, his desire was his own, a thing apart from a master or mistress.

And what had Akalia seen in the Three Dreams, that had driven her to accept what was plainly otherwise unacceptable?

I am too old for this, he thought, and set the lamp in the cradle of burned wood.

He knew what he would do, of course, because he could still hear the man's voice breaking and breaking again, like water against the seawall, the new corpse of a child held against chin and chest.

⁓

"Service in the guild is not the service offered by a servant, or a guard, or even a Southern oathguard. The Chosen of Terafin, who lay down their lives, and make of their lives their duty, are not—could not be—domicis. Do you understand this?"

"No."

The one good thing about Avandar: He was honest to a fault. Ellerson could understand how a man of his nature had somehow stood still for long enough to learn the art of magery. His focus was astonishing.

"To be willing to die for a cause is *not* what the heart of service is about. Young men scattered across the globe throw their lives away—uselessly and usefully—on a daily basis. They neither know, nor understand, the heart of service; they offer themselves, and they are accepted." Here, the sun cast a shadow. It had taken Ellerson the better part of two weeks before he was willing to appear in public with Avandar Gallais again.

But the days were long and lovely and he found this student so oppressive he almost had to get up and walk around to escape the sensation of being caged with a hungry beast. Avandar himself did not seem to mind the interruption, although he did not appear to understand it.

"First," Ellerson said, as they walked by the seawall, a place where few people ventured, "there is the matter of inclination. *I* am not a man interested in serving power."

"And yet you are with me."

"I will teach you, but teaching has different constraints. I would never serve a man of your nature."

"Why?"

"You are a man of power, Avandar, and service to power is its own responsibility. I am not willing to become what I would have to become to be useful to you."

"And what have you served, then?"

"This is not about me, and the question is therefore impertinent—but I will answer it. I have served merchants in my time, in particular three who sought to achieve some status within the patriciate. They were not well-bred, but they were cunning and they were decent enough."

"And you taught them manners, one presumes?"

"That and more, although they did not hire me to teach them." He shrugged. "I cannot speak of them further; it is part of the code. But I have been hired on contract, I have fulfilled my contract and I have returned to the guild."

"I do not understand."

"No, I suppose you don't. There are two ways to offer service. The first is for a term: a year is usually the shortest, and five the longest. The second is for the life of the master—or mistress—who requests a domicis. These are always people of power." He looked down at the sea, which was oddly still beneath their feet.

"Why do you make the distinction?"

"A domicis must protect his master and mistress, and that protection takes many forms. He must be aware of their needs, sensitive to them, and able to respond by either presence or absence, without the need for formal spoken word. He must understand what they desire when they themselves *do not understand it*, and this is one of the most difficult things a domicis learns to do.

"It is part of our art, to understand people." He turned to look at Avandar Gallais. "You were called Warlord; you understand people in a fashion, but I would say given your long years of experience, that you actually understand less than the students who remain with the guild after the first three years of their lessons."

It did not surprise him when Avandar Gallais bristled. He wondered, almost idly, if the man would melt the stone beneath his hands.

The stone did not melt. After an uneasy moment, Avandar Gallais spoke again. "Pretend for the moment that I am such a student. That I have been judged ready and worthy. To whom would you…display me?"

He will never be ready for this. "A person of power, Avandar. A man or a woman who has need of the talent you display—a man or woman who can take the flow of your power and bend it to their life without being so bent by it they lose *that* life."

"In other words," the mage said, showing a humor that always surprised Ellerson, "no one."

～

The days grew longer; grew shorter; grew longer again. There were no more mages, no more attacks; the streets had become so safe that Ellerson— had he been a different man—might have forgotten what he had witnessed in the Common.

But two things happened to change that.

The first was a visit from an old student. An old student who had, as many did, sought service to a woman of power, and who had been found acceptable by the Terafin herself—the most powerful woman in the realm, after the Kings. He was curious; he was always curious when his students returned to him seeking advice or favor. Morretz was not a man who did either.

"Morretz," he said, as he took a seat. "Akalia says you have an unusual request?" He was suspicious of any unusual request Akalia placed before him, but he was not suspicious of Morretz.

"Very."

"You know I've retired from all of this nonsense."

"Of course."

"Which is why you had Akalia call me in, no time for more than a quick change of clothing and a hasty gathering of personal items?"

"Not precisely."

"Then tell me. Precisely."

"The Terafin wishes to hire you, for a contracted period, not for life. You will have a wing of the House proper, and it will be your domain; you may choose your own servants, if those provided do not meet your approval, and you will, of course, be given a generous budget out of which to operate. You will be offered the sum of not less than two thousand crowns for a period which may be as short as two days and as long as two years."

"Two *thousand* crowns? That is rather a lot. Am I to serve some nefarious criminal?"

"Ellerson, The Terafin might not be aware of your particular choices in masters, but I am—I assure you that we would not house a nefarious criminal under your care."

"The patriciate is composed of them."

"However," Morretz continued, knowing him well, "we would certainly not shy away from asking you to serve a petty criminal."

"I beg your pardon?"

"A girl. Possibly of age, but most likely fourteen or fifteen by her size and look." Pause. "She came off the street of the older holdings. With her den."

~

"Akalia, *tell me.*"

Akalia looked *old*. She lifted her head and met his eyes with a fraction of her usual vigor. "That girl," she said softly, "needs you."

"More of your dreaming nonsense."

"No, Ellerson; part of the original. I am tired of this, in a way even you would find difficult to understand." She rose. "But Avandar Gallais was sent to us for a reason." She frowned. "Morretz saw him. He was not particularly pleased to renew the acquaintance."

"He didn't mention—"

"Don't ask him. And don't ask me."

"I cannot possibly accept the care of this girl—although I admit my curiosity and my inclination are both piqued—while having the care of Avandar Gallais."

"No."

"And you would let me take service to the girl?"

"Yes."

"Why, Akalia?"

"You must answer that for yourself. Will you do as I have asked?"

"He will not be pleased."

"No, but he will accept it. I have already seen to that."

~

Teaching was a type of service; Ellerson acknowledged this in one corner of his mind. One corner was all he had left for it. The Terafin manse—the manse upon the Holy Isle itself—was not to his liking, and setting it straight, with the required frosty tact, had taken concentration, energy, and speed.

But he was up to a task of that nature, and when his new master arrived, he was ready for her. Ready, and not ready, prepared and unprepared. She was as Morretz had said, a girl not quite fifteen by the look of her, but beneath the wild fringe of humidity-curled hair, and above the bruised circles that ringed them, her eyes were bright and sharp; free from the hard edge that the street often put there.

He bowed formally, and she stared at him as if he were a different form of life. He was. "I am Ellerson," he said. He waited a moment, and then added, "I am the domicis." Pride was such folly; it was clear that she had no idea of what the word meant. And he was heartily tired, at that moment, of attempting to explain it. When one of the unruly young men at her back called for food with manners that would have embarrassed soldiers on the field, he led the way. Time to teach them all that they needed to know later. For now, food, shelter, the hint of home.

What had this to do with Avandar?

Nothing. Ellerson was here as domicis, and it was almost a pleasure to let the responsibility of Avandar recede. He had this one, this Jewel Markess, and she was a child in which he could see possibility.

~

A day later, a day, and he had the answer to a question he wished he had not asked.

A day, the girl with her den, her den in the silence of shock that magic often leaves in its wake, the word *demon* whispered but never spoken aloud. He sat with them in the darkness of an evening around, of all things, a kitchen table. And he knew, when they spoke, that what he had to offer them would not be enough.

But he watched this girl, this Jewel, speak. He watched her speak to the white-haired boy, Angel, the dark-haired boy, Carver—children who were not quite children. Watched her struggle with her own fear in order to calm theirs.

You are a leader, he thought, as a face framed by the lamplight he would come to understand she best loved sank toward the tabletop, *and you will be a person of power.*

~

The Henden that year was dark; the darkest month that Ellerson had ever known, and he had known many. He had not had word from Avandar Gallais in the three months leading up to it, and wondered, as he advised and guided the young Jewel Markess, if Avandar Gallais and the Guild of the Domicis were still together.

He was fond of the girl, but more than that, he could see that the power that she would take was fast coming, faster than he would have liked. *I have never served a man or woman of power*, he thought, *but you Jewel Markess, are the first one that I will regret walking away from.* Almost, he did not. He was fond of her, as he had never been fond of a master; her sharp temper and salty language aside, she was a mistress worthy of service, one not aiming for power, but destined for it nonetheless. And when she had it, would she even understand what it meant? Would she know how to protect it, how to nurture it, how to remain true to herself while wearing it?

Those things, he could teach her. But he had come to understand that he could not keep her alive in the deadly world of House Politics for long enough that she might learn.

This is why you sent me, Akalia, he thought. And returned in secret to the Domicis Guild. Akalia was waiting for him.

"Well?" she asked softly.

"Yes," he replied.

"She is, I hear, a young girl."

"Yes. Young for her station, old for her age."

"Would you give her to Avandar?"

The old man laughed. "Not easily, no. But I would say that they will be evenly matched in their fashion. She is not a girl, Akalia, she is—"

The door swung open. Avandar Gallais strode into the room. It was expected, at least by Ellerson. "You have found me a master," he said, with a terrible confidence.

"I told you," Ellerson said, "Never to do that again."

"And I might play at apologies, Ellerson, but I have waited many lifetimes. I do not wish to wait another. Come. You have found me a master, and she is a master of power; I will take what I am offered. Now."

Ellerson and Akalia exchanged a single glance, and the glance spoke volumes. But the old man remembered how that imperious voice could break, and he saw the young woman who he thought might not survive the House itself without the aid of a powerful and completely trusted domicis; he rose.

Jewel was going to hate him. To hate them both.

"Very well, Avandar Gallais," he said softly. "But I must warn you now to be careful; she is not what you expect, and she will judge you for the next decade by what you do when you first meet."

~

When Avandar left the Domicis guild hall for what he hoped was the final time, he carried very little with him. But he carried history, and history was heavy.

The old man walked beside him almost stiffly.

"You are worried." he said, because he understood Ellerson that well.

"Yes."

"Why?"

"This girl—she's not what you expect."

"I have seen many women, and many girls, in my time. You have already said that she is a master who requires *my* service. What else should I know?"

"You are not ready to serve, Avandar. I do this with misgivings, but I feel that—for reasons I cannot explain, either to myself or to you—you will be of aid to each other in the years to follow.

"She is…young. She is not—" Ellerson fell silent. "Avandar, remember: first impressions." He paused. "It is not our way to discuss our masters. I feel, however, that I should warn you—"

But the words were like gnats; he brushed them aside. The sea wind carried the tang, the taste of freedom. He walked quickly, and Ellerson walked slowly, and together, by dint of ruffled compromise, they reached the Terafin Manse at more or less the same time.

~

Avandar Gallais was shocked.

To see the girl—for she was a girl, no more—seated uncomfortably before Ellerson, her eyes half-filled with defiant tears, was perhaps the most disappoint-ing event in his life. To hear Ellerson speak to her, as if she were somehow a weak child, was worse. But to know, to *know* that this was to be his fate—to serve *this*—was almost more than he could bear.

He would have left the room, but The Terafin's domicis, Morretz, was present. They had met before; clashed before. The younger man had, of course, lost. He was an enemy, if one beneath notice, and Avandar did not show defeat or weakness in the face of an enemy. He stood his ground.

But he could not believe that this…urchin…was to be his *master*. He rebelled against it, until the power within him made more noise than the speech of the people around him.

No. Wait. Think. He took a breath. The power sometimes drove him, and *he* was its master, not the other way around. Ellerson had tried to tell him something about this girl; he had not listened. He listened now, trying to sort out the buzz of half-remembered words. Minutes passed before the right ones returned to him.

She has the sight. It had been centuries, longer, since he had encountered that power, but it had always intrigued him. Perhaps something could be salvaged from the ruin of his plan.

Turning to The Terafin, he said coldly, "This is the one?"

"Yes."

"Good."

He let the power go; it jumped from the skin of his gently pointed fingertips in a fan of light and fire toward the girl.

Who was not there to greet it. He heard drawn sword; heard the crackle of Morretz' magic, saw the stiffening of The Terafin's fine features. And he smiled.

"That," The Terafin said icily, "was unnecessary."

"For you, yes," Avandar replied, turning to the only person in the room who would normally be worthy of his attention. "But it is not you who will devote your life to the services of this one."

She was close to refusing him that opportunity; he saw it clearly in the frost of her unchanged face. He was not used to explaining any of his actions. But he swallowed his pride. Turned to the girl who was even now lifting herself from the carpets beneath the large, expensive table that graced this library. "My apologies." He turned back to The Terafin, gauging her reaction.

Morretz spoke; he replied. It was an insignificant exchange; The Terafin's reaction was the only one that counted.

He was therefore extremely surprised when something struck his shoulder. Something sharp, hard, with enough of an edge to bruise, although not enough to draw blood. Eyes widening, he turned in the direction of the missile, his gaze sweeping groundward for just long enough to note that what had hit him was, in fact, a simple book.

She stood there, defiant, bristling, her cheeks flushed with anger and just a hint of triumph. He saw her age, and he saw beyond her age, and he thought: *No, I have been here before, and I will not do this.* For her eyes were dark and of fire, and he had thought her unworthy of notice until that moment. Now, he thought her beautiful.

It hurt him.

"It seems," The Terafin said, her voice as smooth and neutral as his would have been under similar circumstance, "that you are not the only one to test, Avandar."

"No," he said softly, seeing now some of what Ellerson must have seen in this young woman, this Jewel Markess ATerafin. "Just the only one to fail. Your pardon, little one." He was only slightly surprised when she bristled at the term of almost affection. "Terafin, I accept your contract. I will serve this one."

The Terafin raised a brow slightly, and then nodded. "Jewel, this is Avandar Gallais. He is of the Domicis and has come to fulfill the obligation that Ellerson felt he could not."

"W-what?"

"I am," Avandar said gravely, "your domicis."

"I won't have him!"

The Terafin's voice chilled several degrees. "You will. This interview is at an end." She turned, sweeping out of the room, followed by Morretz and the Chosen who attended her always.

Jewel was left in her wake, flat-footed, deflated. He had seen that before. Knew that in her, it wouldn't last long.

What am I doing? He almost turned and followed The Terafin out. Because he recognized in Jewel something that, in time, he might come to love. And he loathed the loving because it was the source of all grief, all loss, all damage.

She turned to him. Mutinous. Certain—as he was certain—that she had no choice but to follow her Lord's dictate. "*You* serve *me*, is that clear?"

"Oh, absolutely," he replied, speaking through slightly clenched teeth, as was his habit when someone attempted to give him an order. Something he would have to change; one of many things. He would try. That was all he could do.

Perhaps this would be the lifetime. Perhaps this would be his salvation.

And perhaps it would be a waste of his time. He had time. He told himself that, staring down at her face. He had time. She, on the other hand, willful, defiant, foolish in the certainty age lent her, might not. He understood why power was needed; what he didn't understand, given her outburst, was how Ellerson thought she would survive to attain any rank or stature. She stank of the sincerity that led most easily to death.

And that, perversely, was what he would like best in her.

"You will listen to me in emergencies; you will do as I say and you will allow me to protect you as I see fit."

"Don't even start," she replied, her teeth on edge.

The magic came, rose at the tone of her arrogant little voice.

She snorted, as if she could see it, and see what lay beneath it. She probably could.

A guard came to lead her away, and she allowed it; they had their battles laid out before him in a gridwork that he could see more clearly than she.

He thought about his conversations with Ellerson; he could not see a clear path from them to this girl. But there was something here; he was almost afraid to touch it. Love? Perhaps. Or perhaps something more precious still.

~

That night, the mountains rose in the distance of dreams. He rose with them, taking to air as he seldom did in these latter centuries.

The woman who had sent him from the mountain paths met him halfway up, her robes a billowing darkness that might be mistaken for cloud if seen from below. "Avandar Gallais," she said quietly.

"You have the advantage."

"I will not always have it, and you have advantage enough. Forgive me if I wait before making my formal introduction. You have come farther than I thought you would."

"Do you think," he said, because it was a dream, and it was not a nightmare, and the ghosts were miraculously silent in the shadowed night, "that I will walk far enough?"

"Who can say? You are a warrior, and in service, you are *still* a warrior."

She bowed her head. "I have served my life under the geas of a god, and it is only to end the geas that I continue the service."

"My god is a dead god."

"Mine is not."

"I see." He turned away from her. "Do they stop screaming, the dead? Do they rest in peace, do they slumber? Do they…forgive?"

When he turned, she was gone; he was alone in the night air.

But her voice at the distance of dream's edge, of waking, said, *You will have the opportunity to ask that question yourself.*

And for a moment, before the day broke, before life called him back to its endless demands, he felt a tremulous peace.

The Memory of Stone

Introduction

I am very fond of this story.

I am often fond of certain stories. I have never, however, been any capable judge of how those stories will work for readers. The stories I've often loved best work the least well, although this isn't always the case. I learned early on not to second guess my readers; instead, I focus on the story and the characters and hope that when the story is finished, it will speak to others as strongly as it spoke to me.

Sometimes it does. This one seemed to. But if you asked me why this one worked better than any of the others I've written, I honestly couldn't tell you.

This was written for a 30th anniversary celebration—in this case, my publisher's. DAW put out one fantasy anthology and one SF anthology; I was invited to write for the fantasy book because that's what I write for DAW. When I received the invitation, I called my editor and said, "Do you *really* mean six thousand words maximum?"

"Yes. We've got a lot of authors."

"Oh. Ummm. If you want a story that isn't connected to my novels, I can probably write one that length." This is, by the way, completely unfounded optimism on my part. Luckily, I have an editor who understands my writing very, very well. "But if you want a story connected to the novels, I don't have a hope in hell of writing one that comes in at less than ten thousand words because I've never managed to do it before."

She preferred a story that had some connection to the published novels, and it seemed more fitting to me that I write one connected to that universe, so we agreed on ten thousand words. Which, as it turned out, was also unfortunately unfounded optimism.

But I *thought* I would have a chance of writing something that length if I chose to write about characters who never appeared directly in the novels, with small cameos by characters who did—and I had always wanted to write a story about the Guild of Makers, and in particular, the Artisans—the half-mad makers who weave magic into all of their work the way painters in this one use color.

So I started the story.

But it had two viewpoints. At about fourteen thousand words—with a story that wasn't finished—I phoned Kate Elliott. I asked her how long her story was, because both she and I tend to think structurally, and not in terms of length, and hers was shorter than mine. Being the *only* person to muff the given length limits so badly didn't have a lot of appeal. Oddly enough, my pleas for Kate Elliott to write a *longer* piece fell on deaf, if amused, ears, and I continued to write. I decided that I would cut it to pieces once I'd finished, because at that point I would know the shape of the story, and I could more easily pick out the unnecessary elements.

At length (no pun intended), I decided that the only way to bring the story in at its agreed on length was to cut one of two viewpoints. So I sent it to my editor. She read it and liked it a lot, and I told her that I couldn't bring it in at ten thousand words unless I lost one of the two viewpoints; she said, "but it would be half the story in every possible way." And I said, "That's what I thought, too."

So she generously let it stand.

The Memory of Stone

THE GUILDMASTER commonly acknowledged by The Ten Houses to be the most powerful man in Averalaan stood in front of the long window by which he might survey the eastern half of Averalaan Aramarelas. He had no throne, no place in the Hall of Wise Counsel, no direct route to the ears of the Kings, the two men who ruled the breadth of the Empire of Essalieyan. But money counted for much in the Empire; what The Ten owned in the political realm, he rivalled by the simple expedient of wealth.

He was not a young man, nor a particularly tall one, and his hair, on those days when he had no onerous public duties, fell in a white plume down the back of his head.

On this particular day, it was a solid braid.

He glanced out of the window, his eyes skimming the surface of the ocean beyond the seawall. Light sparkled there, in a pattern the makers of the east tower were doubtless attempting to capture. It reached his eyes, but no more; he looked away.

The ocean's voice was strong. The strongest of the voices that he heard. "Master Gilafas."

Certainly the most welcome.

Gilafas was an Artisan. But in truth, he was only barely that; the weakest, the most insignificant of the Artisans the guild had produced in centuries. It galled him when he thought on it, and he was a maker: he could dwell upon any fact, without pause to eat or drink—or sleep, for that matter—for a full three days.

The man who had spoken knew it.

But he was called The Lord of the Compact, the leader of the *Astari*, the men who served in the shadows the Kings cast. Although the Lord of the Compact understood Artisans as well as any not makerborn could, he was not by nature a patient man. Nor was he a man that anyone angered without reason, and that, a good one.

Gilafas ADelios turned. He did not bow; Duvari's rank did not demand such a gesture of respect. Indeed, his presence today almost demanded otherwise.

"Master Duvari."

"Duvari."

"Duvari, then. How may I help you?"

The insincerity of the question was not lost upon the *Astari*, but it brought a cold smile to his lips, his austere face.

"You may help me by tendering the Kings their due."

"You've become a tax collector, have you?" Testy, testy words. The door opened. Sanfred, Gilafas' assistant, and a Master in his own right, froze beneath the steepled wooden frame, his robes swirling at his feet. Clearly he had run the length of the hall.

He had the wit to bow instantly. "Guildmaster."

"I am afraid, Sanfred, that we will begin the testing late today. Tell the adjudicators to stand ready."

Sanfred was not a subtle man. He hesitated. But he was not an Artisan, either; the only madness that possessed him, possessed him when he made, and none of the Makers worked without the leave of the Guildmaster during the testing. "There are—"

"Not now, Sanfred."

"Yes, Guildmaster."

The doors swung shut. Gilafas turned to face the man who ruled the *Astari*. "The applicants are waiting in the city streets."

"Indeed."

"The adjudicators will not begin without me."

"Then I will be brief."

"Good."

Again, the winter of Duvari's smile crept up his face. Gilafas wondered idly if Duvari possessed a smile that did not make his expression colder and grimmer. The guildmaster was not, however, a simple noble, to be intimidated by a mere expression. "The Astari had heard that you were to personally oversee these applicants. A highly unusual step for a man of your rank, is it not?"

"Your business, Duvari. Please."

"It is my business."

"You overstep yourself. It is guild business; an entirely internal matter."

"May I remind you, Guildmaster Gilafas ADelios, that in the history of the guild annals, the guildmaster has only presided over the testing when he has had reason to suspect that among the applicants, he will find someone … unusual?"

Gilafas shrugged, and considered, briefly, the folly of giving himself over to the ocean's song. As Artisan, he could almost do so without giving offence. Frowning, he lifted his hands; they were shaking. He had not expected that. "A moment," he said, more curtly than he had intended. He reached out and gripped the edge of curtains heavy with the fall of chain links. They snapped shut audibly at the force of his pull.

"Guildmaster, is there any chance that you seek your successor among the applicants?"

Gilafas chuckled. "No chance whatsoever, Duvari. Is that all?"

Duvari did not move.

They stood a moment, two men assured by their successes in life of their rank, their power.

To Gilafas' surprise, it was Duvari who spoke first.

"I was sent to tell you," he said stiffly, "that the orb in the Rod is now white."

Ah. Gilafas closed his eyes. Were he any other man, he might pretend that the words had no significance; he might ask, in a pleasant, modulated tone, *what rod, what orb?* But that game was not a game he could play. Not against Duvari; Duvari served the Kings.

Behind the shell of closed lids, he could see not the Kings, but the hands of Kings, and in them, the items gifted their line by an Artisan centuries ago: the Rod and the Sword. Wisdom. Justice. Weapons for the oldest of the Empire's many wars, and the most important: the war that was its founding. Magic lay within them and upon them, bound to the blood of the godborn.

He had never touched them, Rod or Sword. Had prayed that he never would. He could not say what force they summoned, what spell they contained, but he knew them for more than simple ornament. They were weapons against old magic, old darkness, old wars.

And they had slept for centuries.

When he opened his eyes again, Duvari was closer; he had closed the distance between them without making a sound. "You expected this," he said softly. It was the first accusation he had made.

"Aye, we expected it," Gilafas replied, weary. Why now? Why today? He brushed nonexistent hair from his eyes. Yes, his hands were shaking; the pull of the ocean was stronger than it had been in weeks, and he would have to take care.

"What of the Sword, Duvari?"

"The Sword?"

"The gem in the Sword's hilt."

"It is as it has always been."

"And the runes upon the blade itself?"

"The King has had no cause to draw the Sword."

"He has cause," Gilafas said, forcing strength into words that wanted to come out in a whisper. "Tell him—ask him—to draw the blade. Read what is written there. Return with word of what it says."

"I suspect, from your demeanour, that you already know." Duvari held his gaze, and that, too, was a threat. "Very well. I will return with your answer." He walked away, and only when he reached the doors did he turn and proffer the most perfunctory of bows.

Gilafas waited until he left, and then made his way to the grand desk that served as this great room's foundation. There he paused, running his hands over the surface of a very simple box. It was a deep, deep red, and the carvings across its face were not up to the standards of the least of the guild's Makers.

But he had been told what lay within.

~

Cessaly stood between the twin pillars of her mother and her grandmother, her knuckles white as the alabaster statues in the distance.

Distance was a tricky thing to measure. There were men who could do it; they could tell you things by the length of cast shadows, the rise of buildings beneath the fall of sunlight some arcane measure of the shape of the land. Or so her father had once said. He had stayed in the Free Town of Durant. Said his good-byes at the edge of the fields that had yet to be tilled and planted, his face dark, his eyes squinting against the light. Except that the sun had been at the back of his head, a shining glint over the brim of his weathered hat.

Her brothers, Bryan and Dell, had hugged her tight, lifting her in the twirl and spin of much younger years. They hadn't said goodbye. Instead, they had offered her the blessing of *Kalliaris*, asking for the Lady's smile, and not her terrible frown.

She had offered them gifts. Wooden carvings, things made from the blunt edge of chisel and knife. To remember me by, she'd said. In case I don't come back.

A bird. A butterfly. Nothing useful.

But in those two things, some quickness of captured motion: tail-feathers spread for flight, beak open in silent song; wings, thin and fine, veined and open, devoid only of the color that might have lent them the appearance of life.

Dell had handled the butterfly as carefully as he might have had it been alive; his clumsy, heavy hands, callused by the tools of their father's trade, hovering like wings above wings, membrane of wings, afraid that his grip might damage the insect flight.

Her father had taught them that, each in their turn, and butterflies sometimes sat on the perch of their steady fingers, wings closed to edge, feelers testing wind. Birds had been less trusting, of course, and they were predators in their fashion, beaks snapping the skein of butterfly wings in a darting hunt for sustenance.

Cessaly loved them, hunter and hunted, because they were small and delicate when in flight. She had never been large.

Her brothers took after their father; they were broad of shoulder, silent, slow to move. But they put their backs into the labor that had been chosen for them, taking comfort in the Mother's season.

Cessaly had tried to do the same, she a farmer's daughter. But the hoes and the spades, the standing blades of the scythes, often spoke to her in ways that had nothing to do with the Mother. She might be found carving mounds of dirt, or fallen stalks of wheat, into shapes: great fortresses, sprawling manors, even small castles—although the poverty of her splendor had become apparent only when she had reached the outskirts of Averalaan.

They thought her clever, then.

Her father would often cry out her mother's name, and the deep baritone of his voice, cracked by the dry air of the flat plains, returned to her. *Cecilia, come see what your daughter has made!*

Even her mother's habitually dour expression would ease into something akin to smile when she came at her husband's call, and they would stand, like a family of leisure, for moments at a time, oohing and aahing.

She had loved those moments.

But those moments had led to this one.

"How long," her grandmother said, when the man in robes came out from the distant building and walked down the streets, a pitcher of water in hands as callused as her father's. She asked it again when he was ten feet away; repeated it when he was before them.

His face was lined with shadow, eyes dark; his chin was bereft of beard. But he smiled, and if the smile was curt—and it was—it was also friendly. "I fear, good lady, that it will be some hours yet. You are not at the halfway mark."

"You're sure that they'll see us all?"

Again, he offered her a curt smile. "Indeed."

"We've brought some of her work," her grandmother said. "If you'd like to see it."

"I would, indeed." His tone of voice conveyed no such desire. "But I fear that my opinion, and the opinion of the guildmasters, do not have equal standing here."

Her grandmother frowned and nodded, allowing him to pass. There were others in the line who were just as thirsty as they were, after all, and if she was anxious, she wasn't selfish.

"Cessaly, stand straight, girl."

I was, she thought sullenly, but she found an extra inch or two in the line of her shoulder, and used it to silence her grandmother's nervous edge.

Her mother had not spoken a word.

~

The halls of the guild's upper remove were unlike the simple, unadorned stone that graced its lower walkways. They were also unlike the halls in which the Makers worked, for those stone walls were decorated, from floor to vaulted ceiling, with the paintings and tapestries, the statues, the interior gargoyles, that were proof of the superiority of the artists that had guild sanction.

No; in the halls of Fabril's reach, the walls were of worked stone. These contours, these rough surfaces, these smooth domes, took on the shape of trees, of cathedrals, of Lords and Ladies, of gods themselves; they began a story, if one knew how to read it. There were very few who could, in the history of the Guild of the Makerborn, for such a reading could not be taught; it could be gleaned if one had the ability and the time.

No, Gilafas thought, with a trace of bitterness. It was the ability that mattered; time was what the inferior could add, if they lacked ability in greater measure.

Guildmaster Gilafas, to his shame, was only barely an Artisan. No Artisans had survived in the generation that preceded him in the maker's guild, and no men remained who might have seen the spark of his talent in time to kindle it, to bring it to fruition.

Or so he had told himself. It was not his fault; it was not his failing. And on the day that he had been completely overtaken by the voice of the ocean, on the day that he made, out of crystal, a decanter that returned to the waters of that great body the clarity and the purity of its essential nature, the acting guildmaster had cried tears of joy.

There is magic here, Gilafas. Look. He had lifted the decanter to the eye of the sun. *The waters placed in this vessel can safely be drunk. Do you understand? You are not a simple maker—you are an Artisan.*

The old man had, with great ceremony, ordered the opening of the upper remove, and installed the young man within its stone folds. *What you need to learn, you will learn here. Or so our history says.*

Aye, history.

That old man had been dead twenty years. Dead, a year and twelve months after the day he had made his joyful discovery. Gilafas had attended him for the two weeks he lingered abed with a fever that he could not shake. Healers had been sent for, and healers had been turned away; the Guildmaster would have none of them.

"I'm an old man," he had said, "And close to death, and I'll not drag a healer there and back for the scant benefit of a few more months of life." His hair across the pillows was his shroud, his chosen shroud. "And I'm happy to go, Gilafas. You're here. You're Artisan. You will guide our guild."

"The Artisans," he had said, "all went mad, Nefem."

"Not all."

"All of them."

"Not Fabril."

"I'm not Fabril, Nefem."

"No. But you *will* be Guildmaster. You are an answer to the only prayer I have ever made. I give you the responsibility of the guild, and its Makers. They are fractious. You've seen that. But fractious or no, there is no greater power in the Empire." He lifted a hand. "Say what you will. The mages can kill men; they can raise them to power. But they cannot accomplish what we have built here."

"The Kings—"

"Even the Kings, when they choose to come here, come as supplicants. Be the Guildmaster, Gilafas. While you are alive, the guild will have no other. Listen to the halls in the upper remove; hear the voices that we *cannot* hear. You have the ability." His cheeks were wet. "Protect what *I* have built."

The Maker's cry. Protect what I have created. Never 'protect *me.*'

Gilafas had become a Maker without parallel, and in the streets of the city, in the streets of the Holy Isle, that counted. But here, within the stretch of the great hall in which the Artisans, since the founding of the guild, had lived and worked, he was almost inconsequential. The walls spoke to him seldom, and when they did, they spoke in a language that was almost entirely foreign. Until the day the demon voices had filled the Old City with the cries of the dying.

The halls had been dark as thunder-clad sky when he had come to them, gasping for air, desperate now for the answers that his meager talent denied him. He had starved himself of all sustenance: company, food, and water. For three days, while the moon rode high in the harvest sky, while the winter waxed with the bright, jeweled ghosts of the Blood Barons and their legacy of indulgence and death, he had had for company, for clothing, for sound, nothing but the walls themselves.

The walls. He had traced their passage from one end of the hall to another, over and over, creating a maze of his movements. Closed eyes, open eyes, breath creaking through the passage of a tight, dry, throat, he had lost his way. Become lost in his home of decades. Lost to stonework. Lost to the hand of the Artisan.

And lost now, absolved of all dignity, of all power granted him by the accolades of other men, he had come at last to the altar.

It was in a room that did not exist. Sanity knew: Sanity had denied him egress. Some part of his mind, stubborn, sane, anchored to the world of his compatriots, could not be dislodged, but it had been shaken so thoroughly he had at last his proof of the truth of his existence.

The halls had opened the way, for him, and he had walked it.

And he wept, to think of it now; wept bright tears, salt tears. Ocean tears.

For he had come across the broken body of a young woman, her pale, pretty face scarred in three places by the kiss of blade's edge—her only kisses, he thought, the only ones she had been permitted. Hands bleeding and blistered by some unseen fire, she was the sacrifice.

Demon altar. Dark altar.

And upon it, across the naked skin of her pale, upturned breasts, she clutched them, broken: the Rod and the Sword of Kings.

He heard laughter; could not think that it could be hers, she was so still. This was a monument the Barons would have been proud to own.

When Sanfred and Jordan found him again, wandering naked, bleeding, skeletal, they had taken him in silence to the lower halls, and he had made good his escape.

But in escape, he carried knowledge: The Rod and the Sword would fail. The orb would be shattered, and the runes on the blade would speak in the tongue of an accusation he understood well: They were hollow vessels, their metal and their finery too superficial for the task at hand.

~

The line stretched on forever. Grandmother, mother and daughter, they faced it like a family faces drought: grimly, silently. Cessaly was uncomfortable in the present, and she was young, adept in ways that her elders, too slow and rigid, could no longer be. She sought the past. Found it.

Cessaly's father, his pride contained by the scarcity of his words, had taken some of the things she had made to market when the merchants began their spring passage through the Free Towns on their way to the Western Kingdoms, those lands made distant and mythical because she would never set eyes upon them.

She had been younger, then; a good five years younger, and still prone to be mistaken for a boy whenever she travelled in the company of her brothers. But she had gone with her Da when he took the wagons into the common, and she had stood by his side while he offered the merchants—at some great cost—the fruits of her half-forbidden, half-encouraged labor.

She had made horses, that year. Horses fleet of foot and gleaming with sunlight, manes flying, feet unfettered by the shod hooves that the merchants prized.

"You made these?" the merchant asked, lifting the first of the horses.

Her father shrugged.

"These are Southern horses. You've seen action, then?"

He said nothing. The Free Towners knew that her father had been born on the coast; knew that he had survived the border skirmishes that were so common between the North and the South. They also knew better than to ask about them.

"You've a good hand," the merchant continued, eyes narrowing slightly. "What do you want for them?"

Her father named a price.

The merchant's brows rose in that mockery of shock that was familiar to any Towner who had cause to treat with him.

They had bickered, argued, insulted each other's birth place, parents, heritage. And then they had parted with what they valued: her father with the small horses, the merchant with his money.

It might have ended that way, but Cessaly, impatient and bursting with pride and worry, had said, "What'll you do with 'em?"

The merchant raised a brow. "Sell them, of course."

"To who?"

"To a little girl's parents in the West. Or in the East. They are ... very good. Perhaps if you had paint," he had added, speaking again to her father. "For a price—a good price—I might be able to supply that."

"You wouldn't know a good price if it bit you," her father replied, mock angry.

"We want the paint," she'd answered.

And the merchant turned to look at her, at her eager eyes, her serious face.

"What will you do with paint, child?"

She smiled. "I don't know."

And then he frowned. "Did *you* make these?"

"Yes."

"By yourself?"

"Yes."

"And who taught you this, child?"

Her turn to frown, as if it were part of the conversation. She shrugged.

The merchant went away. But when he came back, he handed her—her and not her father—a small leather satchel. "You can keep these," he told her, "if you promise that I will have first pick of anything you make with them."

"If the price is right," her father told the man. "If we don't like the price, we're free to take them elsewhere."

"Done."

~

To find sunlight again was a blessing. Master Gilafas paused at the foot of the steps and bowed. Sanfred was at his side before his stiff spine had once again straightened. He felt the younger man's solid hand in the crook of his elbow, and was grateful for it: the memories of that early passage through Fabril's reach had teeth, fangs, gravity. To struggle free of them today was almost more than he was capable of.

Once, that would have pleased him. And perhaps, if he were honest, it pleased him in some fashion today. But triumph gave way to horror, and horror sent him scuttling away like insect evading boot.

He cleared his throat. "The applicants?"

"Waiting, Guildmaster."

"Good."

Sanfred had never once asked him why he had chosen to oversee this testing. No one had.

By unspoken consent, the Makers, fractious as only the creative could be, granted him the privacy of their admiration. What he could make—in theory—no one among them could ever hope to make.

A mage could, he thought, irritable. *A mage of lesser talent and no ambition.* But he had too great a love for his own authority to speak the words aloud.

"Take me."

"Yes, master."

"And bring the box on that desk. I do not need to remind you to handle it with care."

~

After that day, Cessaly's size was no longer a problem. Her father spent some part of the summer building a small addition to his barn, and he placed her tools, her paints, and the pieces of wood that he found for her use, beneath its flat roof. He had no money for glass, but the doors themselves opened toward the sun's light, and Cessaly worked from the moment it crossed the threshold of the room, ceasing when it faded.

The merchant returned three times in the year, bringing different tools, different materials, different paints. He asked if she had ever seen metal worked, and when she shook her head, he offered to take her to a jeweler in the largest of the Free Towns. It was an offer that was flatly rejected by both her father and her mother.

They were very surprised when, two years later, that jeweler made the trek at the merchant's side when the caravan returned.

"This had better not be a waste of my time," he said curtly to the merchant.

"I'm paying for your time," the merchant had replied, with a very small smile. "But I know my business."

"Where is your young paragon of creativity, Gerrald?"

"In front of you."

"What, this girl?"

"The very one."

The jeweler frowned. He was balding, and the dome of his skull seemed to glow. "How old are you, child?"

"Twelve."

The frown deepened. "Twelve. And you've never apprenticed to anyone?"

She shook her head.

"Well. I'm not sure that I can offer you such a position—I've heard that your parents won't hear of you travelling, and this town is not my home. But Gerrald has offered me much money to teach you for the summer, and I admit that the offer itself is unusual enough to have piqued my curiosity. If you are willing, I would teach you some small amount of my craft."

He brought with him gold and silver, sparkling gems and glossy pearls, opals and ebony, a small dragon's hoard.

But he brought something better, something infinitely more alluring: fire. Fire, in the heart of the rooms her father had built.

She had waited for her father's permission, and her father had granted it.

The man in robes came again, three times, the water jug heavy in his hands. She watched his shadows against the cobbled stones, and her hands ached. Her grandmother's hands ached as well—but she blamed that ache on the ocean Cessaly could taste when her tongue touched her lips.

Cessaly had not yet seen the ocean; she had seen buildings, horses, and streets that went on for as far as the eye could see. There were white birds in the air above, birds with angry, raucous cries; there were insects beneath her feet among mice and rats; there were cats sleek and slender, and dogs of all shapes, all sizes.

There was no workshop; she had been forbidden all of her tools. When travelling along the road, she had been permitted to idly carve the pieces of wood she had taken from the farm; they were gone now.

She wanted them.

There was no dirt beneath her feet; there were stones, smooth and flat, longer than she was and at least three times as wide. There were fences, too, things of black iron or bronze. Nothing that she could work with.

She plaited her hair instead, until her mother caught her at it, and grabbed both her hands, stilling them.

"Not here," she had said, severely. "Not here."

Her hands began to ache; her eyes began to burn. She could not wait forever.

The jeweler stayed in the town of Durant for four years. He bought a house for himself, very near the common; he built his workshop, sent for his apprentices, and brought his business to the town. He also made a room for Cessaly, and her mother brought her to it, and took her from it, every day except for the Mother's day.

Cessaly worked with gold, with silver, with platinum. She handled his diamonds, his emeralds, his rubies, the blinking eyes of curved sapphires, the crisp edges of amethyst and firestone. He had begun by telling her what he wished her to achieve, and had ended, quickly, by simply giving her material to work with.

He often watched as she worked; often worked by her side, making the settings upon which he might place the results of her labor. He was not a man who was given to praise, and indeed, he offered little of it—but his silence was like a song, and his expression in the frame of that silence, a gift. Cessaly liked him.

And because of that, she decided that she would make something for him. Not for the merchant to whom all of her work eventually went, but for Master Sivold himself.

Because she wished the gift to be entirely her own, she chose wood to work with; wood was something that she could easily afford. The merchants came in the spring, and when they did, she asked if they might bring her something suitable. But she did not ask for soft wood; did not choose the oak that came from the forests a few miles outside of the village. She requested instead a red, hard wood, something riven from the heart of a giant tree.

She was so excited when the merchant placed it in her hands; she was absorbed by the tang of its wood-scent, its rough grain, the depth of its unstained color. She wanted to rush back to the workshop, to begin to work right away.

But she heard its voice, wood's voice, and it bade her *wait*.

Voice? No, not voice, for the words it spoke were not quite words, and the wood offered her no more than that; she could not speak to it, could ask it no question and receive no answer of use. But she could feel it in the palms of her hands as if it were a living heart; could see it move, shrinking in size until the truth of its shape was revealed.

She waited.

Four days later, at the height of summer, during the longest day of the year, she began to carve. To cut. To burn. She worked until the sun had begun to touch the colors of the sky; worked until the first of the stars was bright.

And when she was finished, she saw that her mother was asleep in the great chair in the corner; that the lamp had been lit and rested on the table beside that chair; that the workshop itself was empty.

She was very, very tired, but she tucked the box away, hiding it beneath the heavy cloths that protected the gems and the metals from sawdust and insects. Then she woke her mother and together they went home.

The next day was the day that changed her life.

She came to the workshop later than she usually did; her mother had had a great deal of difficulty waking her, and was concerned that she might have fetched ill. But Cessaly wasn't running a fever; she didn't cough or sneeze, didn't shake much, didn't throw up—and in the end, her mother had relented and accompanied her to the jeweler's house.

There, shaking off lethargy, Cessaly ran inside, ran to her workbench, and grabbed the box she had made. It was simple, perhaps too simple for a man like Master Sivold. But it was not without adornment; she had carved a pattern around the lip of the lid that made the join between lid and box almost invisible. Only with care could she see it herself.

"What's that, then, Cessaly?" he said, as she approached him.

"Last month you said that you'd run out of space for the things—the things that you can't bear to part with."

"Did I?"

She nodded. "And I—you've done so much for me here, you've shown me so many new things, you've let me make what I—what I have to. I—"

His brow rose. "Is this for me?"

"Yes. I made it. For you. Only for you," she added. "It's not for Gerrald. And anyway, it doesn't matter if he does see it. It won't do him—or anyone else—any good."

He smiled and held out his hand. "It's very elegant, but a little too plain for Gerrald's taste. Or for his customers." He lifted it, examining the carving around its side. "Cessaly, what is this?"

His fingers brushed the trailing strokes of letters, letters hidden in the movement of leaves, the trailing fall of their branches.

"Your name," she told him.

"My name?" He frowned. And the frown deepened. "Why do you say that, child? It does not say Sivold."

"It doesn't?" Her eyes widened then, with panic and fear. She reached for the box, and he must have seen the horror on her face, for his frown eased. But he did not return it to her hands.

"My eyes are not nearly as good as they once were, and your work here is so delicate, child. Perhaps I am misreading." He shook himself and the smile returned to his face. "I didn't know that you knew how to spell or write."

She didn't. She said nothing.

After a moment, he lifted the lid from the box, and then his eyes grew wide, and wider still; his lashes seem fixed to his brows.

"Master Sivold?"

He continued to stare.

"Master Sivold?"

And when he finally blinked, his eyes teared almost instantly. He closed the lid of the box with great care, and set it down on the workbench. "When did you make this, Cessaly?"

"Yesterday."

"Yesterday?"

"Yesterday. And a little bit of the night."

He raised his hands to his face. "I knew we were doing you a disservice, child," he said, when he at last chose to lower them. "But I thought that your parents would be happier if you—if you worked in the Free Towns." He shook his head. "You must send for your parents, child. Tell them I need to speak with them. Tell them it is urgent."

~

And so she had.

They had come to speak with Master Sivold, and the closed door came between her understanding and their adult words—but she had waited just beyond the reach of the door's swing, and when it opened, it opened upon her pale face, her wide eyes.

Master Sivold was angry. Her father was angry. Her mother, grim and silent, stood between them, hands curved in fists, knuckles white as the bone beneath stretched skin.

She knew better than to ask what had been said. It was obvious that their anger had had no good place to go, and she wasn't about to provide one.

But Master Sivold's anger was pointed, directed; when he turned toward her, it smoothed itself away from the lines of his face. She almost wished it hadn't; he looked old as it left him.

"Cessaly, I want to ask you a question."

She gazed sideways at her father; his glance spared her nothing, but his nod was permission.

"How did you make the box?"

"How?"

He nodded. Gentle, that nod, as if she were a babe. She didn't like it.

"Same as I make anything else."

"Tell me," he said again. "Take as long as you like."

"I chose that piece of wood," she said, "because it was the right wood. It took a little while."

"How did you know what to carve?"

"Wood knows," she said quietly. She never talked about her work, and it made her nervous to speak now. She wasn't sure why. "I wanted to make it for you," she added. "And I started the minute I got the wood home, but it told me to wait. It told me to wait for the longest day."

"And how did you know what day that was?"

"I didn't," she said again. "The *wood knew.*"

Master Sivold turned to look at her father. Her father, whose shoulders seemed smaller somehow.

"And the sun knew," she continued, thinking about it, feeling the wood in her hand, the warmth of that sun on the back of her neck, her head, its light on the dark streaks of grain.

"Tell us what the sun said," Master Sivold told her.

She looked at his face for a moment, seeing in the lines around his eyes and lips the movement of wood grain. She reached out, unthinking, to touch him, to feel the surface of that skin, that grain.

And when she opened her mouth, when she began to speak, she left bruises there, around his lips, where her fingers grazed flesh. There, and in the dark of his eyes.

～

They kept her until the harvest's end, and then they travelled east, east to the Empire of Essalieyan. Her father and mother had argued three days— and nights, tucked in the battleground of their bed, their voices loud and rumbling, their words muted by log walls—and in the end, her mother had won, as she often did. Her brothers were to stay; she was to travel with the caravan until she reached the city, and from there she was to seek the Guild of the Makers.

"But—but Da—"

"It's your mother's decision, not mine. I don't send my kin to—"

"Father," her mother had said, clipping both ends of the words between tight teeth.

Cessaly wanted to be happy. Or she wanted him to be happy. She wasn't sure. "But if I'm a maker—we'll be rich. We'll be *rich*, Da."

"You'll be rich," he said, gruffly. "And we'll be farmers, here, in Durant."

"I don't have to live there."

He looked at his wife. His wife said nothing.

She did what any sensible girl would do. She went in search of Dell. Bryan was older, and minded his father's commands.

"Dell?"

"Aye, Cessaly."

"Why can't I live here?"

"They think you're makerborn," he said.

"But all of the makers don't live in the Empire."

"No."

"Then why do I have to?"

"Because you made that damn box, is why."

She wanted to tell him to burn the box, then, but she couldn't quite say the words. Wasn't certain why. "I did bad?"

"You did too good," he told her, when he heard the tone of her voice. "And now they're all afeared. Master Sivold—"

"What?"

He shook his head. "It's nothing. They think you'll go crazy, Cessaly."

"Then why are they sending me?"

He shrugged. "Because all the crazy people live in the Empire?"

So she hit him. Lots. He wasn't supposed to hit her back.

~

The crowds wavered like a heat mirage in Gilafas vision. The great doors had been rolled back, and light skittered off the sheen of marble and brass, abjuring its smoky green, its black, its curling greys. Beyond the open doors, the gabble of a thousand people moved and twisted like the ocean's voice; he could make out no words because he could hear them all so clearly.

"Master Gilafas?"

He lifted a hand. "I think—I think, Sanfred, that I will have my pipe. Now."

"Your—ah. That one. Yes, Guildmaster." He hesitated for just a moment, and then he waved another Maker over and relinquished his grip on Gilafas elbow, forgotten until that moment.

Everyone hovered. It was annoying. Their shadows against the floor, the fall of their feet, the drifting haze of their cloudy beards, made him think of the storm. He waved them away. *Ocean voice*, he thought. *What am I to do, today? It is not the time.*

Sanity. That was his curse. He listened to confusion dispassionately, refusing, as he had always done, to allow it reign. His brief dalliance with insanity had given him no cause to regret that decision.

The pipe came, and he lit it carefully, inhaling bitter smoke. It was not to his taste, and not to his liking, and it would be less to his liking on the morrow when he woke to the taste of something dead and stale on his tongue. But the alternative was less appealing.

"Send for them, then."

"Yes, Master."

~

Hours passed. Of the many hundreds of hopeful applicants, Guildmaster Gilafas found two he was certain belonged within the guild walls. He treated them not only with the respect of their future rank, but with the affection reserved for kin, no matter how distant, who have found their way home against almost insurmountable odds. It was not an act. There was a brotherhood among the men and women who were, by nature of birth and some quirky, divine providence, driven to these strange acts of creation.

That brotherhood buoyed him, although he was not entirely certain that some part of that warmth was not caused by the contents of his pipe.

It had been some hours since he had filled it, and he hesitated, hand over pouch, to do so again.

Looking up, he realized how costly that hesitation had been. He had never walked so close to the edge without realizing it; somehow he had stepped across it.

Had he the voice for it, he would have cried out in fear or horror. It was the only thing in the long day that he would be grateful for later; his dignity was spared.

For the doors *were* there, they were open; the Makers *were* in attendance; he was not in Fabril's hall, and the visions of that complicated, terrible place did not hold him in their painful grip.

Only memory did, but memory was enough, more than enough. He handed his pipe to Sanfred, hands shaking so much he feared to drop it before it held what he required.

And he tried to smile at the young woman who walked towards him.

In the privacy of his thoughts, he was still a coward, had always been a coward; he told himself that he was mistaken, old, befuddled, that the voices of the ocean and the voices of the Maker had grown strong because he had done too little, these past few days, to still them. He tried to tell himself that what he remembered could not be real.

But cowardice provided no shelter: he recognized the girl's face.

She had lain upon a bloodied altar in a hidden room that he had never tried to find again.

~

When Cessaly saw the man who sat behind a table that was larger than any she had ever seen—including Master Sivold's workbench—she froze.

"Cessaly," her mother said, impatient, fearful, angry.

But for once, her mother's voice was almost beneath her notice.

As if he were wood, or silver, or gold, the man caught the whole of her attention, diverting it from daylight, the vast rise of ceiling, the width and breadth of wall. Only the ocean's taste grew stronger as she met his eyes, and the inside of her mouth was dry as salt.

She should have remembered that when she approached wood, or gold, or silver, she approached first with axe, chisel, knife, fire; that the only voice allowed these things that waited transformation was hers.

She said to him, before she could think—and this, too, was akin to her movements with wood, with silver, with gold—"You make things." It lacked manners, which would have been a crime in a different place; lacked them in the presence of a man of obvious import.

But it spoke to the heart of the matter.

"Yes," he said gravely. "I make things." His hand reached out, and out again, as if he would touch her; it stopped inches short of her face, and fell.

She had seen glass in windows, although her family's home had had none until the third year of her work with Master Sivold, and she understood that the one that stood between them now was closed.

~

You make things.

"Yes. Yes, I make things."

She lifted a hand.

"I do, too."

He would never hear the ocean again, not as he had. A man's mind had room for only so much madness, and Gilafas', less than any Artisan before him.

"Sanfred," he said, rising, pipe somehow no longer a danger.

"Master Gilafas?"

"I am done for the day. This girl is makerborn; ask her—mother?—for the information we require, draw up those forms that you deem necessary, do what needs be done." He rose. Picked up the box he had ordered carried to this table with such care.

"This was once yours," he said.

She looked at it, and her expression twisted. "It was never mine," she told him solemnly. "I made it for Master Sivold." She frowned when she said it, and her face lost some of its luster, some of its terrible lure. "Are you upset about it, too?"

He nodded. Before he could catch himself—if he would ever be able to catch himself—his chin fell and rose in a sharp, jerky dip. "But for a different reason. I have not seen the inside of the box. I could not open it."

"Would you like me to open it for you?"

"If you would."

She took the box carefully, placing the left palm firmly beneath the center of its flat, legless bottom. And when she opened it, Sanfred understood what Gilafas had not yet said, because he was standing just to his right, and he was human enough to be curious.

The inside of the box itself was longer than the table at which the Makers now sat; it was as deep as a man's arm from palm to shoulder.

"He needed more room," she told him gravely, "for the things that I made. Will you give it back to him?"

"Yes," he told her gently. He knew how important the answer was; she was makerborn, after all.

~

It took some hours to settle not the girl, but her mother. She would not leave without speaking to the Guildmaster—a sure sign of her ignorance of the workings of the Guild of Makers.

Therefore Gilafas, exhausted and on the edge of compulsion, drove himself for a second time from the confines of his quarters in Fabril's reach. Sanfred was nowhere to be seen; neither was the girl, although he had been quite specific.

It was only when he reached the visitor's lounge that he realized that hours had not, in fact, passed; the sun was wrong for it—it was still in the sky. He steadied himself against this dislocation as Sanfred appeared. Sanfred who could hide mortal concern behind a placid, workman's expression.

He sat in front of this dour woman, and she beside an older, dourer one. They formed the sides of a triangle; Sanfred, attending, was simple shadow, and moved like a trick of the light.

Master Gilafas had only one desire when confronted with this woman, and it was strong, terrible, as visceral as any need to make, or make again, had ever been.

Take your girl, take her as far away from this place as you can, and still live. Go North, to the barbarians; go South to the slavery of the Southern Courts; go West, to the kingdoms of which I know so little. Leave her anywhere but here.

But he did not.

"Will you take care of her?" the woman said. She was fidgeting now.

"I assure you, there is not another place in all of the Empire where she will be—"

"Because she's always been a bit odd." The woman, having said the words, lost half a foot of height. Her hair, dark with streaks of grey, seemed to frame a face too pale to carry it. "She's more than a bit odd now. We're her kin, we know what she means when she speaks; we know there's no harm in her wild ways. She's a good girl. She's an honest girl."

He started to speak, but she had not yet finished.

"She won't thieve, mind, not for herself. But she takes a fancy to things she sees—bits of wood or stone, mostly—and she'll pick 'em up."

"We understand that, here."

"And she'll work funny hours, if you don't stop her. It's hard, but she needs to eat." Care had worn lines deeply into the material of her face. "Don't forget it: she needs to eat. And drink. And sleep. She's got to be reminded; we let her work once, thinking she would stop in her own time. Waited to see how long that was." Hands were clenched, now.

He stared at her. To his surprise, he wanted to offer her comfort. "She will be treasured here in a way that you cannot envision. Sanfred, the man who is hovering, was trained to do two things: he is a painter, here, one of few. And he is a … baby-sitter. We *all* work the hours that your child would work, unminded. And we have learned to watch out for each other. She will not go hungry; she will not go thirsty. Sleep is harder to dictate."

She wasn't satisfied. He could see it.

He said, simply, "There are things that she is beginning to learn that she should not learn on her own. The box—you saw it—is only the first sign of that. There are other things she might have made. In our histories, a boy much her age walked into the blacksmith's forge shortly after a bandit raid. The raids that year were fierce and terrible, for most of the land had seen little rain, and the fields would not take.

"He made a sword. It killed. That was all it did. It was his rage and his desire; he wielded it. It sang. He carried it to the bandit's home, and he had his revenge, and it was bright and bloody.

"But he had *no* sword skills, and he was not a large lad; the sword itself contained both the desire to kill and the ability. In the end, the bandits themselves were not enough to slake its thirst, and he wandered into the village he had loved. Hundreds perished before the sheath that would hold that sword was created."

She was pale, now, pale as light on his beloved ocean. But she said, simply, "what happened to the boy?"

A mother's question.

"He was mad," he replied. "And he remained so."

"They didn't kill him?"

He hesitated. "No," he said at last, and gently, "they did not kill him. They gave him, instead, to *our* keeping."

Before she could speak, he raised a hand. "And in our keeping, in the safety of these walls, or in the stewardship of those best suited to such a task, he made such things as Kings wield, and his work helped to change the face of the lands we now call the Empire. He was honored, he was revered. In his fashion, he was loved."

She closed her eyes. Opened them. "I can't take her home," she said, the statement a question.

"No."

She rose, then. "Let me say my good-byes, and I'll not trouble you further."

But she would. He could see it in the lines of her face, the depth of her concern. She would go home, to Durant, and the fate of her daughter would draw her out, again and again, to this vast, intimidating place. She would see a stranger in this daughter, and the daughter—he was not certain what the daughter would see.

Because he was sane. Because he had always been blind, that way. He rose and offered the woman his hand; she accepted it as if it were an anchor on a short chain.

～

To be a failure was something Gilafas had contemplated for the better part of his adult life. But he had contemplated it in the temple makers made of quarters an accident of birth had granted him. To do penance for his failure, he had strengthened the guild immeasurably, giving it the steady guidance of which a madman could never have conceived. This, he did for the old man whose joy he had not the strength to live up to.

If he could not increase the mystery of the guild, if he could not add to the grandeur of its legends, he could at least do that. And he had thought himself an honest man; had thought he had completely accepted his paltry ability for the better part of a peaceful decade.

Now, his meager gift was once again unbearable.

The girl—Cessaly—had been moved to Fabril's reach the moment her mother had left. He might have assigned the duty of settling her to Sanfred, or another of the Makers who served him directly, but cowardice prevented it, presenting him with the first of many menial tasks he was to adopt.

Sanfred would not fail to see in the girl what Gilafas himself lacked. How could he?

So it was that Guildmaster Gilafas ADelios led her to the winding tower stairs that led to Fabril's reach.

She had taken the steps timidly at first, her hands faltering upon the fine rails beneath the grand sweep of open tower, the fading light. She had no experience of this world, save in story—if that—and her fear made her precious to him, for he had no children.

But the fear itself was fleeting.

The light in her eyes was not; it was fire, of a sort, the fire of a forge, the fire of one makerborn who sees into the world of mages. Or gods. He could not himself say, although he had walked that path.

But he knew the moment that she lost fear to wonder; he could see it in her. Could hear it, in the whisper of moving strands of her hair, taken by a breeze that did not—and had never—touched him.

She carved birds; he remembered that the grandmother had mentioned it to Sanfred. Birds, butterflies, creatures not bound to the earth. And he? He worked water, and whales, dolphins, things of the deep that might break the bounds of their element in fleeting steps, with will and joy.

So she flew. Up, up and up. She knew where the doors were. Were she not small, were her step not contained by the reach of short legs, she might have evaded him utterly. He could not let her do it. He could not let her make herself at home in Fabril's reach.

Was ashamed of the inability.

We are not judged by what we create; we create. Maker's motto. And what use that motto now? It was a lie.

Vanity had its use.

Cessaly stopped two thirds of the way up the stairs and placed her hand gently upon the wall. A recess in the smooth stone caught the shape of her palm, moulding itself to her fingers as if the stone were liquid.

He heard the ocean's voice, then. A roar, a roar of water breaking stone and wood, rending cloth, burying men. She opened a door that he had never found.

And turned to stare at him, her eyes wide, her brows lost beneath the edge of poorly cut hair. Honey eyes, he thought, a shade too brown to be the eyes of a child of the gods. "Master Gilafas?"

He shook his head, lifting hand to clear his vision. "I hear the ocean," he told her bitterly. "Only the ocean."

"Can you hear me?"

He stopped then, turning the full of his attention upon her, upon the question she had asked. She was a child. By age, she could be counted among adults, but there was nothing of that in her expression; she was made of curiosity, insecurity, joy and fear.

"Yes, Cessaly. I can hear you."

$\sim$

His answer was important, because she could hear him. She could hear the ocean in his voice, could see it in his eyes, her first glimpse of the blue surface against which sun scudded. She smiled, her hand against something soft and warm. "I can hear stone," she whispered. "I can hear wood growing. I can hear wind in the leaves, and the rain dance. I can hear the birds, seabirds, great birds. I can hear the sun's voice."

She had heard these things before, in the dells of Durant, in the furrows of her father's fields, in the quiet of log and peat and moss, yards from the river's edge, where the water pooled before resuming its passage.

"I can hear silver," she told him. "And gold. And the voices of rubies and diamonds. Sapphires are quiet." She stopped. She had never said so much before. "But I hear other voices. There, past the door. Other voices."

"Open the door, then, Cessaly."

She started to. Started, and then stopped. She felt the cold in the cracks between stone. The voices she knew fell silent, one after the other; the cold remained, and she began to understand that it had a voice of its own.

Death. Death there. The death of all things.

She drew back. Shook her head, although it was hard; all of her was shaking. "Cessaly?"

Her hand fell away from the wall. "No," she told him sadly. "The cold will kill us." She turned to look at him, and she saw the shadows that the walls contained, straining for freedom, for something that might have looked like flight to a person who had never seen birds. Never made them, inch by inch, never carved the length of their flight feathers, the stretch of their pinions.

It was dark now. The world was dark.

But Master Gilafas was still in it.

～

He caught her hand; it was blue.

"Come," he said gently. "We are not yet there, and there is no cold in Fabril's reach."

"Where is Fabril's reach?"

"Up," he told her gently. "Up these steps."

"I can't see them."

"No. Sometimes they are hard to see." The lights in the wall sockets were bright and steady; they had never failed, and he was certain they never would. Fabril had made them himself, had made this tower, the reach.

"Will you take me there?"

"Yes, Cessaly. Can you feel my hand?"

She appeared to be thinking, as if thought were her only vision. He waited.

"I can feel it."

"Good. You have never made hands," he said. "But when we arrive, I will bring you wood and tools, and you must try."

"Just hands?"

"For now, Cessaly. Just hands." Speaking, he began to walk, the steps as solid and real as the fading light of day, the passage of time, the Holy Isle.

～

After she had made her way up the stairs—and in his estimation it took some two hours—she had to face the gauntlet of the great hall.

It was in the great hall that his envy, his bitterness, his resentment gave way to something more visceral: fear.

She screamed.

She screamed, and pulled away from him. Pulled back, turned to flee. He lost her, then. The hall swallowed her whole. She was gone.

He cursed as he had not done in years, the reserve and distance of age swallowed whole by the intensity of emotion.

~

She heard the voice of stone. The voice of mountains, old as the world; the voice of the molten rock in the heart of its ancient volcanoes; the voice, insistent, of its cracking, sliding fall. All the voices she had heard in her life were made small and insignificant; she lifted hands to capture them, and they came up empty.

She had no tools. No way to speak to stone with stone's voice, no way to soothe it.

But that didn't stop her from trying.

Trying, now, clawing at things too heavy and solid, her arms aching with effort, hands bleeding.

~

Past midnight, the fear left him, sudden as it had come. He was drained of it, like a shattered vessel of liquid, and what remained was the residue that had haunted his adult life.

Think. Think, Gilafas.

What a Maker heard—if a Maker heard what an Artisan heard at all— did not destroy the world; it did not unmake a reality. Fabril's reach, in all its frustrating, distant glory, was there before him. And he knew that the girl had come with him, slowly and hesitantly, eyes wandering across the face of its carved, misshapen walls.

And what of the door, Gilafas? What of the door that did not exist until she placed hand against wall?

It did exist. It always existed. I never found it. I never thought to look. I knew what the shape of the tower was—and is—I knew that such a door at that place could not exist.

Think.

He ran to the closed doors of his workrooms, those vast, open spaces in which light dwelled when there was any light at all. He opened drawers and cupboards, looking for chisels, for the knives which woodworkers used; wood was not his medium, but all Makers of note often dabbled.

When he dropped a drawer on his foot, when the slender tubes made for blowing glass shattered about him, he paused long enough to avoid their splinters. Just that.

He did not think to call Sanfred, and would wonder why later. For now, he continued to search until he found the oldest of his supplies; blocks of wood as long as his forearm.

Thus armed, he paused again. *Think, Gilafas. Think.*

No. Not think.

Listen.

~

By dawn, he found her, and in finding her, he found a room that he had never seen.

It lay behind the stone work on the west wall, between the arch made of the raised arms of two men whose likenesses were said to be perfect: the first Kings of Essalieyan. They were not overly tall, and the space between them just large enough to fit a small girl with ease. A large man would not have been able to follow that passage, and if he had never felt cause to be thankful for his lack of physical stature before, he was grateful now.

The passageway was narrow and poorly lit; it was cold with lack of light, and almost silent; his breath was captured by folds of cloth, muted.

He could not have said why he chose to follow this path. But having begun, he heard her, and hearing her, saw her clearly, small, fine-boned, clear-eyed. He thought of what she might be, robbed of color and lent the clarity of glass or crystal, and this helped; he could imagine the fires, the glass, the workroom, the movement of hands and lip, the changing contours of a medium that was fluid, as close to the ocean in texture as anything solid could be.

He had never had to work so hard just to walk in Fabril's reach.

Fabril's reach will teach you everything you need to know.

For the first time in years, he turned those words over in his mind's eye, blending them with Cessaly until they were a part of her, a part of his making. *What, Master Nefem, do I need to know? And if this is a part of it, why do I need to know it?*

The hall ended; it opened into a room that had windows for a ceiling, a dome of fractured light. Crystal cut its fall into brilliant hues that traced the sun's progress.

She huddled in their center, her hands scratching the surface of the floor. She did not see him; could not see him. What she saw, he could not say, but he knew that she would see it until she found some release from it, until it was exorcised.

He could see what she could not: blood, dried and crusted upon the palms of her flailing hands.

He did not touch her. Instead, he knelt by her side and placed those tools he had found into the hands that were so ineffectual.

For the first time since he had entered the room, her focus changed. He placed the wood before her, but above the flat, smooth surface of stone.

He would take her from this room, in time. But that time was not yet come.

"Cessaly," he said, although he was certain she wouldn't hear him, "make what you must; I will return."

~

She loved the sound of Master Gilafas' voice.

No one had ever had a voice like his, and she marveled at it, for there was a texture beneath the surface of his words and his emotions that moved her to listen. She had thought to miss home; to miss her Da and her mother; to long for Bryan and Dell, the two people who had brought her close to flight in the days of her childhood.

She forgot that longing quickly. The soles of her feet forgot the earth and the tall grass; forgot the slender silver stream; forgot the soft mosses, the heavy leaves of undergrowth. The stone spoke to her in a voice that was so close to her own she felt it as a part of her. To lose that would kill her.

And the only person with whom she could share this strange home-coming was Master Gilafas. His friends, Sanfred and Jordan, were as deaf as the man who had helped to birth her.

Master Gilafas understood her. He came to her with bits of wood, smooth stone, raw gems; he gave her room in his workshop, and brought to her the glass that he loved. She did not love it, but she listened to its voice as it spoke to him, and sometimes, when the world was peaceful and her hands could be still, she would sing a harmony to its quiet voice.

But at other times, the stones would lead her to rooms that Master Gilafas could not find on his own. She was afraid of the stone, then; afraid of being alone. She hated the darkness that lingered at its edges; it hurt her, and it promised to hurt her more.

She knew it, because she heard what the stones said to *him* when he walked by her side. She would glance anxiously at his face when the stones spoke in their sharp, cold voices.

Sometimes she would ask him about the voices.

And he would take her hands in his and smile gently. "Yes," he would say, "I hear them. But they are only words, Cessaly. Pay them no heed."

And she would see her death in these stones, but his words and his voice were stronger.

~

He was reduced, he thought, to being a babysitter.

He had, in that first month, attempted to foist that duty upon Sanfred's broad shoulders, and Sanfred was more than willing to accept it.

But the greatness of the talent that all but consumed Cessaly was denied in its entirety to Sanfred. He could not hear what she heard. He could not see what she saw. Instead, he heard madness, and only madness.

The stories were there, of course. Every apprentice, every young journeyman, every man who desired to be called Master—and there were not a few of those in the guild—knew the stories.

The Artisans were mad. Gloriously, dangerously, mad. Only madness could conceive of a small jewelry box in which the whole of a room might be contained. Only madness could create Fabril's reach, bending the fabric of the real and the solid to the vision of its maker. Only madness, yes.

But madness had created more, much more.

And Gilafas was doomed to understand it. To see what he could not be; to almost touch what he could not achieve. His curse.

Sanfred lost Cessaly for two days. He came to Gilafas, ashen and terrified, and all but fell in a groveling heap at the Guildmaster's feet, weeping. Two days, Gilafas searched; two days, he listened.

He found her at last in a room he had visited once in nightmare, standing before the effigy of an altar upon which her naked body lay, cradling Rod and Sword. What he found a second time in search of Cessaly, he was never allowed to lose again. It waited, that room.

He had carried her from it with care and difficulty; she had in her hands the softest of stones, and powder flew from it as she carved and polished its face, her eyes unseeing, her ears bleeding.

Two days later, she begged him for gold. He brought that, and more besides: gemstones, large as eyes. She was thin as a bird; lifting her, he could believe that her bones were hollow. She said, "I'm flying, Master Gilafas. You've made me fly!" And laughed, delirious. Insane.

He loved the sound of that laugh, and he understood, when he called Sanfred again, that Sanfred not only did not love it, but was in fact terrified by it. The fear galled Gilafas; the pity and horror that Sanfred could not hide when he next saw Cessaly enraged him. He had not expected that. Had he, he might have been more temperate.

More cautious.

"Do you not understand what you have witnessed?"

Sanfred was mute in the face of his words.

"The guild has not been graced by a talent as pure as hers since its founding. Do you not understand the significance of her presence?"

An ill display indeed, for he knew the answer. No. How could he?

"You ... are not ... as she is."

"No, Sanfred, I am not. To my profound regret, I am not. Get out. Get out; I will tend her myself."

~

He was her captive. He came to understand that. The whole of his life, his authority, his stature meant nothing to her. And where was the justice in that? For his life revolved around her. The hours of his rising, the hours in which he might sleep, were dictated by hers, and she slept the way a newborn does: unaware of the strictures of day and night, light and darkness.

She took food at her whim, and when that whim was weak, at his; she drank because he demanded it. Sometimes, when he was exhausted beyond all measure, he went to the apothecary and fed her bitter brew; it dulled her for some hours while he slept.

Sanfred, unable to champion Cessaly, became in all things Gilafas' ears and eyes. Only upon royal command did Gilafas choose to leave Fabril's reach. He had lost Cessaly for two days. He did not intend to do so again.

Captivity breeds either hostility or resignation, and in Gilafas it bred both.

He was surprised, then, to find that in the stretch of the days from summer to Henden, he had learned to love the cage.

~

He discovered it thus: Duvari came to visit.

It had been months since their first meeting in the heights of Fabril's reach; the *Astari* had sent no word, and by its lack, Gilafas understood that the Sword at least was whole. But when Duvari appeared in the doorway of his workroom, he knew that the lull had ended.

Cessaly was in the corner, by the cooling glass. She had, in her fashion, been singing, and together they had blown a bubble in which one of her butterflies was encased, its lines brought out by light. They had learned to work together in this fashion, Gilafas the hands behind their mutual will.

"Remember, Cessaly, not to touch it yet. It will burn your hands, and you will not be able to make until they are healed."

She nodded, too absorbed to look up.

Trusting her then, he stepped away.

He was not dressed for an audience; indeed, he wore the oldest of aprons, the most worn of gloves. The glass that protected his eyes sat upon his head like a wayward helm; he almost lowered it when he saw Duvari. The threat in his presence was palpable.

But he did not do it. Cessaly was sensitive to gesture this close to making's end, and she was always sensitive to the tone, the texture, of his voice.

"I would speak a moment in private," Duvari said quietly.

In that, they were of a mind. Gilafas nodded politely. "I … would prefer … to remain in sight of her."

"It was not a request. The matter is of a sensitive nature."

"As is she," Gilafas replied evenly.

Duvari frowned. The frown was unlike the one that normally adorned his features, and Gilafas instantly regretted his words.

"Very well, Guildmaster. King Reymalyn has sent me with a message."

"And that?"

"The Sword," he said softly, "was drawn this morning."

Heart's blow. He lifted a feeble hand to ward it, but it was far too late.

"I confess that I could not read what was writ in the runnels, although the words were clear to me. The King Reymalyn labored under no such handicap."

"The Sword was forged by Fabril," Gilafas said, the words leeched of the pride that once might have lodged within them. "If I were to guess, I would say that no one but the King Reymalyn—with the possible exception of the King Cormalyn—might read what is written there."

"You are correct."

"Why have you come?"

"If you must play at ignorance, I will indulge you. I came—"

"Gilafas, look!"

Cessaly had run from the room's corner, her eyes bright. She reached out and caught his apron, tugging at it insistently. "Come, look, look!"

He obeyed her, aware that he risked Duvari's wrath. Like a shadow, the Lord of the Compact followed, dogging his steps. Gilafas, mindful of this, pried her fingers free, replacing cloth with the palm of gloveless hand.

In the circular globe, the butterfly hovered, wings flapping. They brushed the concave sides of the glass, and the glass trembled in response.

Duvari said quietly, as if there had been no interruption, "The Sword must be reforged, the Rod remade. They were meant to stand against the Barons; they were not created to stand against the darkness."

"Then you are doomed," Gilafas said, but without hope, "for the man who made those emblems of the Kings' power is long dead."

"Indeed. But it is not by his hands that they must be remade."

Gilafas stiffened. He was surprised, but he shouldn't have been. The Lord of the Compact, it seemed, made all secrets, all hidden histories, his business.

"I had thought it might be by yours, Guildmaster." Duvari bowed, and when he rose from the bow, his face was as smooth as the surface of the glass that now contained the floating butterfly.

Gilafas had a moment of clarity, then, standing before the most feared man in the Empire. He saw the pity in Duvari's face; the pity and the ruthlessness.

"It is trapped," Duvari said, speaking for the first time to Cessaly.

"Oh no," she said, eyes round, face serious. "It is *safe*." And then she frowned. "I have something for you," she told him. "Can you wait here?"

He nodded gently. He, who had never done a gentle thing in his life.

Cessaly floated from the room, bouncing and skittering around the benches, her arms flapping.

"Understand," Duvari said quietly, when she had vanished, "that the Kings have no choice in this. The darkness has risen, and it is gathering. The Kings cannot go unarmed into that battle, and they *will* go."

"She is a child," Gilafas replied.

"She is an Artisan, and if I understand the hidden histories well enough, she is the Artisan for whom Fabril built the reach. What she needs to learn, she must learn here, and she must learn it quickly."

The Guildmaster closed his eyes.

"Because if I am not mistaken, she will not survive long."

"She is not the power that Fabril was."

"She does not have his knowledge," Duvari replied, "nor the allies with whom he worked so long and so secretly. But the power?" Again, something akin to pity distorted his features. "Affection is a dangerous burden, Guildmaster. We go, in the end, to war, and the chance of victory is so slight we can afford to spare nothing."

"It is not in my hands," he said stiffly. That was his truth. It was not, it had never been, in his hands.

"Is it not?"

She came then, before Gilafas could frame answer, and her hands, so often spread wide to touch the surfaces of the world around her, were clenched in loose fists. Sunlight caught the edges of gold, the brilliant flash of diamond.

She walked up to Duvari without even a trace of her usual caution. "These are for you," she told him gravely.

"For me?"

"Well, maybe for the Kings."

He held out his palms very slowly, as if she were a wild creature. She placed in them two pendants. They were eagles, the guildmaster thought, wings spread in flight, flight feathers trailing light. At their heart, large as cat's eyes, sapphires. To Gilafas' eyes, they glowed.

"These will help," she told him quietly. "With the shadows."

"The shadows, Cessaly?"

She nodded. "We have them here, and I *don't like them*. I made one for me, too. When I wear it, I don't hear shadow voices. Only the other ones. The stones," she added, by way of explanation. "The wood, and the gold— the sapphires are quiet, but you need the quiet—and Master Gilafas."

"You hear the shadows here?"

"Don't ask her that!" Gilafas cried out.

But her face had turned, from Duvari, from him. Skin pale, her eyes darted along the workroom's walls. Here, the voices of nightmare were weakest; this *was* Gilafas' space.

But the nightmares had been growing stronger; there was now not a single moment in which she could safely be left alone without some sort of work in her hands. She jerked twice, as if struck, and then turned and fled the room.

Gilafas, prepared in some fashion for these episodes, ran to the workbench and swept up the satchel in which the most portable of her tools were contained.

"Guildmaster," Duvari began.

"Not *now*, Duvari."

He did not expect argument; he did not receive it. But he was angry enough that he could not stop himself from speaking as he strode to the door. "If I have lost her again, you will pay. One day, she will go someplace where she *cannot* be found; she will be beyond us, working until she starves. If that day is today, I swear to you—and to the Kings you protect—that the Guild will never again serve at your command."

He did not wait for the reply.

And perhaps he would have been surprised to know that none was made.

~

Cessaly did not run far.

Had she been afraid of Duvari, she would have, but she found herself liking the man; he was very quiet. He wasn't cruel, but he wasn't kind; he was almost like the stonework on the walls: made of a single piece, and finished. He needed nothing from her.

The shadows were not afraid of him either. The moment he mentioned their voices, she heard them clearly, and they were some part of his. But although they touched him, he somehow did not touch *them*.

Important, that he never heard their voices.

She had used sapphires to capture quiet, and diamonds to capture light; the eagle was simply the ferocity of a flight that did not necessarily mean departure. She had made those in the round room because she had been afraid. But she had made *three*. One, she wore; because she wore it, she could now find her way up—and down—the winding stairs that led to the below.

But two she had simply held, and when she had seen Duvari—when he appeared at her side as the butterfly began its flight—she knew why: they were for him.

But she didn't like his thank you very much, and she wasn't certain if she wanted to see him again.

Maybe. Maybe she wanted to be able to see *him*.

She frowned. Things she had not tried now suggested themselves in the brilliant hues of the floor of the round room. She had her stone, of course, and she carved while she paced the floor, a hollow feeling in throat and stomach. She would ask Gilafas for what she needed. He always gave her what she needed.

~

He found her almost instantly, which should have stilled his anger; it did not. She was working, although not in a frenzy, and when he entered the chamber—her workroom, as she often called it—she offered him a smile at home in the deep, soft rainbows cast by sun.

"Master Gilafas," she said, as he bent a moment and set his knees against those colors, "could you bring me a loom?"

"Yes. Yes Cessaly. After lunch, I will bring you a loom." He did not tell her that such an undertaking would take more than a single morning, and did not ask her where the loom should be set; he did not speak to her of cost, the responsibility of expenses, the things that had always balanced his momentary frenzied desires.

She did not care; could not.

And in truth, neither did he.

~

The loom should have been foreign to her; the working of metal was a gift that had been taught over the course of months. But he was not surprised to hear the clacking of the great, wooden monstrosity that now occupied some part of his workroom. There were no other rooms that could house it in Fabril's reach—at least none that he was aware of, and if Cessaly knew otherwise, she did not choose to enlighten him.

He considered her carefully as he worked, and he *did* work; the voices were upon him, and they rode him unmercifully. He no longer knew if ocean's voice drove his hands, or if hers did—or worse, if his own now moved him, with its anger and its self-loathing. Not good, and he knew it; not good to be driven by that last voice. Men died for less, grabbing in a frenzy at those things that might still it—and not only the makerborn; all men with hollow power.

But it drove him.

Glass was before him, broken, colored, and around it a skein of lead; the things he knew better than he knew himself.

The loom was wracked with the passage of her hands. It seemed fitting that they should work in this fashion. He was surprised that he was aware of her at all, for he knew by the feel of the glass in his hands that he should have been beyond her.

He failed in his duty, this day; he forgot to feed Cessaly. Forgot to feed himself.

Was not aware, until Sanfred forcibly removed his hands from his tools, of what he was *making*.

But Sanfred, having wrested the cutters from his hands paused, frozen, in front of his mosaic.

For the first time, Gilafas permitted himself to see what the glass contained. Cessaly.

Cessaly, who, in bleeding hands, carried two things: A rod with a crystal orb that must deny all hint, all taint, of darkness, and a blade whose edge glittered like the diamond wings of her eagles.

And he looked at the sky, red and dark, sun bleeding into the night of the horizon. Three days, for three more days, the light would wane early, the night sustain itself. The heart of the month of Scaral would arrive, and with it, the longest night.

~

Duvari returned two days after his first visit with Cessaly. He came without warning, which was wise; had he offered warning, the Guildmaster would have forbidden him entrance, and would have personally dismissed anyone who disobeyed that order.

But he offered no such introduction; worse, he did not come alone. The companion he had chosen to bring to the guildhall had caused concern and quiet outrage long before the two men had mounted the stairs that led to Fabril's reach.

Gilafas understood why the instant he laid eyes on the second man. His hair was long and white; it fell across his shoulders like the drape of an expensive cape. He had not chosen to bind it, which was unusual; Gilafas had never seen that hair escape the length of formal braids.

"Guildmaster," the man said.

"Member APhaniel," he replied coolly. "To what do I owe this … singular … honor?"

"To the busy schedule of Sigurne Mellifas, alas. The Council of the Magi occupies all of her waking time at the moment."

"I had heard there was some difficulty."

Meralonne APhaniel shrugged broadly. "Among mages, there is *always* difficulty."

"Among Makers, the same can be said." But only grudgingly. "Although I confess that I have seldom had cause to resent the difficulties that keep Member Mellifas away, I resent them this day."

A pale brow rose in a face that was entirely too perfect on a man of Meralonne's age.

"It is understood. Sigurne is better at handling difficulties of this nature. In all ways. But perhaps I am not entirely truthful."

Gilafas snorted. "Of a certainty, you are not entirely truthful."

"No? Ah well, perhaps my reputation precedes me." A glimmer of a smile then. "And one day, when we both have time, you must tell what that reputation *is*. The dour and incommunicative Duvari cedes not even the most paltry of rumors to the mageborn. He is significantly less … suspicious of the makerborn."

"Not, apparently, their guildmaster."

"Well, no, of course not. The guildmaster actually possesses power."

"Gentlemen," Duvari said coldly, "may I remind you of the scarcity— and therefore the value—of our time?"

Meralonne reached into his robes and drew from it a long-stemmed pipe. "May I?"

"Of course."

"You might join me, Guildmaster."

Gilafas started to say that he did not smoke, and thought better of it. He did, and he guessed that the mageborn member of the Order of Knowledge knew exactly what it was that burned in his pipe when he chose to bring it to his lips. He reached for pipe, box, and bitter, bitter weed. Spread dry leaf in the flat bowl of his pipe.

"I have seen the work of your apprentice," Meralonne said, when smoke lingered in the air. "The two pendants."

"And they?"

"You must guess at what they do, Guildmaster."

"I confess that I have not the resources—or the desire—to test them. They are effective in some measure against the—against our enemies?"

"Yes." Meralonne's cheeks grew concave as he inhaled. "I had not thought to see their like again, not newly made. But yes." He turned, then, to the corner of the room in which Cessaly lay sleeping. In sleep she was much like a cat; she found it as it came, and took it where she sat, stretching out against floor or chair.

"She is young," he said at last.

"She is."

"Do you understand what it is that is asked of her?"

Gilafas could not find the words, but for once, he didn't need to. He turned to his bench, and lifted the gauze he had placed across his work, setting it aside with care; he wanted no dust, no wood shavings, no metallic slivers caught in its threads. Then he lifted the glasswork, the mosaic of transparent color, and he turned its bitter accusation toward the Magi.

Through the wild skein of Cessaly's hair, he saw the golden skin of Meralonne APhaniel.

"I see," the magi said quietly, "that she is not the only Artisan to busy herself in Fabril's reach."

"I have always worked in Fabril's reach," Gilafas said, dryly.

"Oh, indeed. But you have only twice created something that blends the skill of the Maker with the deeper, wilder magicks. Ah, I stand corrected; this is the third, and if I were to guess, the most subtle, the most powerful, of the three."

It was Gilafas' turn to be surprised. "Is it?"

"The most powerful?"

"A work."

"Do you not know?"

He said nothing.

"Magic—such as mine—is not sanctioned within these halls, Guildmaster, but were it, I am not certain it would be capable of divining the purpose behind your creation. Certainly it will not tell me more than you yourself know. But I will say this, and perhaps I say too much. I am not Duvari. I am aware of what is asked, both of you and your apprentice. Duvari accepts all cost and accrues all debt in the cause of the Kings. I? I do not believe that debt ever goes unpaid, and I am loath to accumulate it.

"And I believe your apprentice is waking."

Gilafas frowned; he had heard nothing. But he did not doubt the Magi. He turned to see that Cessaly had taken to her feet. She was smiling shyly.

"Have you come to see my work?"

"I have," Meralonne replied. "And I have come to bring you something. Which would you have me do first?"

"My work." Her smile was unfettered by such things as caution or suspicion. She walked over to the closet Gilafas had emptied for her use, and drew from it three bundles of cloth. One was as blue as cloudless sky, one as dark as midnight, and one the color of light seen through the fog of cloud. "I made these," she said, as if it were not obvious.

"Did you make them for anyone?"

"I don't know. But I made them. They are all too large for me. The loom moves quickly and the cloth chatters."

She handed him the darkest of the three, and as he unfolded it, Gilafas saw that it had a hood. A cloak, he thought.

"Put it on." Her little, imperious voice was the only one in the room.

Meralonne did not hesitate. He laid hand against the weave of the cloth, and ran his fingers across it, his eyes wide. "Child," he said softly. Just that. But there was no mistaking the longing—and the wonder—in the single word. "You remind me of my youth." He caught the cloak by its upper edge, and twirled it backward until it fell over his back, obscuring the length of his hair.

He raised the hood, and then, with a smile, fastened the silver clasps that hung at his collar. Gilafas was not surprised to see him vanish.

Cessaly clapped her hands in glee.

The hood fell, and the man reappeared. "My lady," he said, and he fell to one knee before her laughing face. "We have come to beg a boon of you."

"Member APhaniel—"

"We have brought, for your inspection, two things." He gestured. Magic, the Guildmaster thought.

"I have the Kings' writ," Duvari said evenly, before Gilafas could voice even token outrage.

A bundle appeared in Duvari's outstretched arms. He brought it to Meralonne APhaniel, and the magi unwrapped it with care, until he was left with two things.

Gilafas bore witness; he could not bring himself to move.

Cessaly came to Meralonne as if she could no longer see him, as if she had eyes for only what he held. Bright, her eyes, like liquid, like the ocean in summer. And dark, like its depths.

She took them from his arms and did not even notice their weight, although she buckled beneath it. She brought her knees the ground, as if in obeisance, and touched the dull white of the broken orb, the black and gold of the sword's scabbard. Her lips opened and closed, and Gilafas knew a moment of pride, for he could hear her voice, and he was certain the others could not. After a moment, she raised her head, and she looked at Meralonne APhaniel, all joy in the lesser creation gone.

She said, "You should not have brought these here."

"We had no choice, Lady."

She rose, staggering; she would not allow him to touch their plain surface. "But the demons will come, now."

"Yes."

~

She woke in the dark of the night, in her bed, alone. She had gone to sleep there, her hands absorbed with the beads she had asked for, the strings upon which to place them almost full. Her fingers were stiff with the damp and the cold; she knew that she had worked them while she slept. Master Gilafas would worry. She knew it.

It was why she had forced herself to walk the halls, to come to this room, to let sleep take her while he watched. He only left her when she slept, and only when she was here.

But she had work to do; she knew it. The days. The days had gone; the nights had slowly devoured them. They waited above her head and beneath her feet, gathering the shadows and the darkness. All the voices were strong.

And steel's voice strongest of all.

She slid her feet out of bed; the floors were cold but she dare not wear shoes. She wanted no light, nothing to see by, and without it, her feet were her eyes; they knew the halls at least as well as her eyes did.

Beneath her bed, she found the Sword; found the Rod. Her hands knew them by more than their weight, but it was their weight that troubled her, for the Sword was so long it *would* drag on the floor, the metal of its sheath creating sparks and noise.

She struggled alone.

She understood, dimly, that she was not a simple child, but the child in her was often the only element that could survive the arduous task of making. The understanding clung to her as she struggled: she was not a child. She had come to Fabril's reach *because* she was not a child, and she had remained because no one—not even her beloved Master Gilafas—could hear the voices of the wild as well as she.

But she was grateful; had she been at home, had she been in Durant, she was certain the Town would have perished this eve. It was *Scarran*, the longest night.

She was not dour by nature; not grim. Master Gilafas, haunted and tired, was both of these things, but she understood that he had come to love her, and because of it, she knew she must leave him. She understood the whole of Fabril's intent, and had, from the moment she had found the room Master Gilafas so hated.

The Rod and the Sword were vessels; they were vessels, and those vessels had long lain empty. She had listened to the ocean in Master Gilafas' words. She understood vessels, and what they contained, or could contain, because of that distant voice.

She was not so old that she had forgotten fear. In the dark of her room, she armed herself: she fastened the clasp of the pendant she had made, cold sapphire resting against the hollow between her collar bones. She drew cloak from an armoire that was otherwise empty, and ring from the box at her desk. She took no gloves, and paused a moment before the silver sheen of dark mirror.

In the dark, she drew the blade. She was not a swordsman; it was an awkward action. But she must do it; she must leave the sheath here. The blade, the rod, they must go where she travelled.

The moon was high. Fabril had loved light, and if gold was the color of day, silver shone now, radiant and cool. Enough light to see by, but she did not need it; she could see in the shadows.

She hesitated for just a moment, on the edge of the Master's workroom. And there she laid down her burden, and ran lightly across the darkened threshold. Moonlight came through glass in all its muted color; she passed it by, again and again, until she reached the delicate globe of blown glass Gilafas had given her.

Inside, floating and fluttering, was her butterfly.

She pursed her lips, touched the cool glass, and with a simple word, set the butterfly free. It broke the meniscus of glass surface as if it were liquid and passed above her, circling her head three times.

She let it go and turned again to her task.

The Rod and the Sword had been forged and quenched in the whole of a single day. She knew it, by touch; understood what not even the cold man understood: that Fabril had made these in the light of the longest day, a measure of, and containment for, the Summer. It was, as her simple jewelry box had been, an act of affection, a desire to help those he had loved and respected. And in Summer's season, the Rod had served the son of Wisdom, and the Sword the son of Justice: the Twin Kings who had, for centuries, given their lives to the Empire of Essalieyan.

But all things living know time and its passage, and all things living know the shifting of seasons. Summer had passed, the season so long for these crafted items that Winter had been forgotten.

Aiee, she hated the shadows, the sibilance of their terrible whisper.

But what was forged in the grim stillness of Winter, what lived in its ice and its blankets of pure, cold snow, was strong in a way that the Summer itself was not strong, and that strength, cold and terrible, existed beyond the shadows.

Terrible power, scouring and lonely.

She had heard of men who had died steps from their homes when the blizzards had come; they could not see their way to safety, and what love and hope they carried as they struggled ended there.

Kalliaris, she thought, for the first time since she had come to Fabril's reach. *Kalliaris, smile.*

She walked the long hall, seeing the frozen stone about her, fitting company, and silent, for this last journey. She was afraid of only one thing: That she would finish what she had been born to finish, that she would remake the Rod and the Sword that would be so necessary to the Twin Kings upon whom the Empire depended, and that there would be no one to bring them home.

Other fears would come later, to keep her company and ease her loneliness, but this fear was the wisest and the strongest.

She could not make anything while she walked, and she felt the gnawing hunger take her hands, felt this scrap of reasoned fear, this almost adult comprehension, fray about the edges, pulled like the loose thread in a weaving from her loom. So she cradled the blade with care against the cloak that protected her from the sight of men, and she ran her fingers, over and over, across the surface of what was writ in its runnels.

She began to descend the stairs, and it was hard: the floor was cold, and the steps steep. The lights that existed against the walls were dim; they no longer spoke a language that her eyes understood. But she did not need them; she knew where she walked, and when she reached the halfway mark, she set her hand against the wall and waited.

The door opened.

The door opened into the Scarran night, and the Winter road wound from its step into the hollows of the ancient, wild way.

~

Gilafas could not say what woke him, not at first.

He sat up in bed as if struck, the full face of the moon framed in the windows of his chambers. The night was silent; he listened a moment and heard the distant thrum of ocean voice. It was not insistent.

He rose, clenching fists, and cried out in shock and pain; his left hand burned.

He spoke a word and mage-light flooded his vision, forcing his lids down; when they rose again, he stared at the open mound of his hand, his left hand.

In it, in the light, were shards of delicate glass, the broken form of butterfly wings above crescent pools of blood.

He listened, and he heard the ocean, and only the ocean, and then he understood.

~

He dressed like a madman, taking the time to don jacket over his sleeping robes. He grabbed dagger, although it was futile; tore light from the wall and clutched it in his bleeding fist.

He took no care to be silent; silence was not his friend, and the noise was a distraction, a welcome one. He ran to his workroom, commanded light, banished moon. There, on the furthest reach of his personal bench, he saw what he had dreaded: the globe in which he had encased Cessaly's butterfly. This was their only common work, and it was empty now; what she built, he had in the carelessness of sleep destroyed.

What night? What night, he thought, frenzied. Was this the longest night? Or was it past him, was it gone?

But no: for once the darkness was blessed, for it lingered, deep and forbidding.

He began to search for Cessaly.

The first place he looked was her room, but it was empty; there was no trace of her presence in it at all, although the sheets were turned back. Her cupboard door swung open as he approached.

The halls were long. He knew all of her rooms, for once she had opened the ways, they could not be closed. And he knew his own: the room in which her death was carved in stone, the obscenity of it stronger every time he chanced upon it.

He visited them all. All of them, and he found her in none, although his own horror waited around every doorway and ever corner.

He had left her. In his exhaustion, he had chosen to leave her. If he found her, he promised whatever capricious god might be listening he would never leave her again.

No, Gilafas, fool. No. *Think.*

But thought eluded him, deluded him, sent him in circles that ended, always, with the workroom.

But the last time, the last circuit, had finished him; in agony, he retreated into the moonlight, his hands shaking.

The lights were dim; he could not remember dimming them. He started to speak, and lost the words as he turned to the great windows that formed a casement for the moon. No; not the moon, but some light that was much like it: radiant and cool.

In its heart, standing in robes the color of night, stood a ghost, a demon. He had brought the wind with him, and it was a foreign wind, devoid of the taste of salt. He turned, and the light turned with him, and when at last this intruder faced Gilafas he saw two things that he recognized.

The first, the least, Meralonne APhaniel, shorn of the emblem of the Magi, the decorations of mageborn rank. His hair was white and long, his eyes the color of new steel; he wore no sword, no shield, no armour, but he was dressed for war.

The second, the source of the room's light: the mosaic he had made in the likeness of Cessaly. Golden hair, honey eyes now shaded to the green that was either trick of light or whisper of power, blue dress, and red, red blood, these burned in his vision. The lead that held the glass was grown insubstantial and weightless, or perhaps it was fluid; he could not see it clearly. Did not try.

"You asked," Meralonne APhaniel said softly, "what purpose this Work served, and I believe I have divined it. It is of glass for a reason, Guildmaster.

"It is a window."

A window. Gilafas stepped toward it, and faltered in the glow of its light. "Why did you come?"

"I told you. I am not Duvari."

"You are not truthful."

"Not entirely, no. This is Fabril's reach. Fabril was not seerborn; that was not his gift. But it is myth that he created the whole of this wing; he made it his own, but he chose it for a reason.

"For the Summer, Guildmaster, and for the Winter." He eyes were unblinking. "You do not hear the Summer voice; you do not hear the Winter. That is both your gift and your curse. What Fabril wrought does not speak to you. But it speaks to her, to your apprentice, and this is the longest night, the Scarran night.

"And I believe that *she* speaks to you."

Truth, Gilafas thought, but not enough of the truth.

"Why did you come here, mage?"

Meralonne was silent a moment, and then he said, "I believe that she will be drawn to the Winter road, and if she enters into a great work upon it, she may never return.

"But her work *must* return. Do you understand?"

Gilafas said nothing.

"Guildmaster."

Silence.

"The Guild of Makers has been waiting for longer than you can imagine, guardians against this age. It has waited so long, there have been those among you who have come, over time, to believe the wait has been in vain, a thing of child's story. But you know, now. And I, and the Kings. Open the window. Open it, Guildmaster, for I cannot."

∼

He cursed his gift for the first time in his adult life. Cursed himself for a fool for making this window so small, although it was the gift itself that had guided the making. His hands shook as he approached her, trapped in glass, circled by lead. Her eyes were now closed.

They had not been closed when he had made her, for the width of her eyes were, among the many things about her, the one that he had come to love best.

He cried out in fear and reached for the glass, and his hands passed through it as if it were mist, or smoke, or veil.

The winds tore past him, then, and in their folds, they carried the screams of the dying, thin high ululations, the keening of the damned.

His eyes teared at once, and his cheeks froze; the wind was dry and cold, and it allowed for no liquid. Ocean voice denied him, then, and just as well. He saw darkness, felt it across the length of his arms. Frost formed in the folds of his jacket; flakes gathered against cloth and found purchase there.

Bodies lay aground, some writhing, most still. He saw an arm, a jerking hand, a fallen blade; saw a broken bow, its curve shattered, saw the spill of hair across snow, white upon white, with the thinning pink of spreading blood beneath it.

He could not count them all; he did not try. Once, in the whirl of the angry wind, he saw the pale skin of an upturned face, its eyes wide, lashes made of snowflakes. Too beautiful, he thought, although clearly the man was dead. To beautiful to be a demon.

He moved, although he could not say how; he knew that the window itself was too small a passage for a man of his size. Could not regret it, either.

Until he saw her.

He knew her at once, although he could not see her face, for her hair was short and golden; not even the snow that clung there could obscure its color. He knew the bent shape of her shoulders, the moving jerk of elbows at play; he knew the shape of her back, even seen now, beneath heavy folds of cloth that obscured it. He knew the soles of her feet, for in the vastness of Fabril's reach, she never wore shoes.

Had not, he saw, worn them now. She would freeze to death, she would freeze in the wailing storm, and he thought her unaware of it, for the madness was upon her.

He could hear it so clearly he almost forgot himself.

But she was not alone in that clearing; the trees themselves, like wrought iron fences, surrounded her, and in their shadows a shadow rose, tall and slender and perfect.

It made a poverty of any beauty he had ever seen, and in the guildhall, he had seen much of it. He was humbled, instantly, by the presence of this stranger, this Winter Queen.

She looked up, then, and she smiled, and although she was beautiful, and the smile a gift, he was chilled by it in a way that not even the slaughter had chilled him.

"Yes," she said softly, "I am the Winter Queen, and you are bold, to come here on this night."

He could not speak; his legs would not hold his weight and he felt himself begin to bend so that he might place his life where it properly belonged: at her feet. Or beneath them.

But something held him up, something sharp and sudden.

"I do not walk the Winter Road," he told her, the words flowing through him as if they belonged to another. "I have placed no foot upon it, and I have taken nothing, touched nothing, that belongs to the Queen who rules it."

Her smile deepened, and it was chilling; there was no pleasure in it. "You are wise, who appear to be a simple, mortal fool."

"I am not wise, Lady, or I would not be here, witness to Winter; the mortal seasons are not your seasons."

"No, indeed they are not, and mortals themselves are so fleeting." And her gaze, the gaze he coveted and feared, slid from his face to the shuddering back of Cessaly. "But not all that is mortal is beneath my interest. You have come for the girl."

"I have."

"Ah. But she has not your wisdom; she has set foot, unencumbered foot, upon my path, and she has taken the lives of those who serve me." She stepped toward Cessaly, and Gilafas followed. Somehow, he followed.

He wanted to shout, to give warning, to raise alarm; he was mute. The words that were not his words failed him.

The Winter Queen laughed in the wake of his silence, and her laughter was almost genuine.

She turned to him, then. "Has it come to pass, little mortal? Have the gates been opened, and the covenant shattered? Does the darkness stride the face of the mortal world once more?"

He was mute. Mute, still.

"Leave," she said. "Leave while I am amused and may know mercy."

"It is not for your mercy that I have come."

"Oh?"

"What the child carries belongs in the hands of the godborn; no other might wield or claim them."

"The hands of the godborn do not trouble them now," she replied, but amusement had left her face, and her lips were thinner. "And they have been made, remade, in *my* realm."

"They have been made and remade in the wild realm, Lady."

"And the wild realm knows no law but power."

"The wild realm knows no law but yours, it is true. But your vow is law in the realm, be your oath ancient, so ancient that it is forgotten upon this plane. You cannot lay claim to the Rod or the Sword until those vows are fulfilled, and Lady—if you seek to retain even one, they will never be fulfilled, and your power diminished by the binding."

Her hair swept past her face; the gale had returned in the clearing.

"Perhaps," she said, one hand falling to the hilt of the sword she carried, and the other to the horn. "But so, too, will yours, and the mortal kingdom will surely fail. The Sword and the Rod came to me."

"Indeed."

"And they might lie here, unclaimed, until the seasons turn."

He fell silent again, the words stemmed.

And then she smiled. "I sense another presence, mortal. And perhaps this means that you do not understand what it is that you risk. What do you desire?"

His mouth opened. Closed.

Her eyes, her dark and golden eyes, flared; he felt a trickle of fire along his cheek, a caress that would leave a scar. "Speak," she said again. "And speak freely."

"I want the girl," he said. His words now. His own.

"Let me grant you a gift," she said coldly, "a gift of vision." She lifted her arms, one to either side; in the wake of the moon's light across the fine, fine mesh of chain shirt, the world darkened.

Dark, he knew it: it was his own. He saw the spires of the three cathedrals, raised higher than even *Avantari*, the palace of the Kings. They burned; circled in air by winged beasts and their riders, besieged by wind and shadow. They were empty, he thought; empty, he prayed. Beneath them, in the streets below, the flash of magic, the clash of armies.

Small armies, pockets of futile resistance.

The vision shifted as the wind changed; he flew over the dying city to the fields of Averalaan, and there he froze, for there he saw what they did not name.

Lord of Darkness.

It is not possible. It cannot be possible.

"Look well," she told him softly, "for you will see no Kings upon the field, and few armies. All of the bodies are yours; the Lord of the Hells has risen.

"I cannot say that the Kings would triumph had they the Rod and the Sword for which so much has been offered. But you have not even the hope of that: the Kings perished in *Avantari*, bereft of the power granted them by the artifacts of Fabril. Yes, even with her hand upon them, they are his."

She lowered her arms slowly, and the smile returned to her face. "I understand some small measure of mortality, Gilafas ADelios. It amuses me, and in this long, long Winter, very little does.

"So I will give you what I have given few: a choice. You may take the child, or you may take the artifacts. But you may not take both. Choose," she said softly. "Choose; I will not intervene as long as you take only one thing when you depart. Either—she, or they—will be of interest to me."

Gilafas was consumed by the Winter, the Winter's chill.

"The dawn is coming," the Winter Queen told him. "In your world, in the world in which you now stand, the sun will soon rise. Delay, Gilafas, and you will have neither."

He reached out to touch Cessaly; his hand gripped her shoulder. He had thought she would not notice, for she often didn't.

But she turned to him, turned at once, snow spilling from her lap. Her hands were dark with blood, but he could see, as she lifted her palms, that that blood was not her own. She had never been so still, in all the time he had known her. In all the brief time.

"Cessaly?"

Her face was a young woman's face, her eyes round and dark with exhaustion and fear. She lifted her chin, and met his eyes, and he realized that she had poured so much of herself into *this* making that she could at last, for a moment, know sanity.

It was terrible.

I will not do this, he thought. *She is Fabril's equal. She is his superior. What Fabril made, she can make again, and better. If we have her. If only we have her.*

But he did not believe it. Desired belief more than he had desired anything, even the mantle of Fabril's legacy.

Cessaly touched his hands, pulling them from her shoulder. She was so cold he would not have thought her living had she not moved; her lips were blue.

And her eyes. Blue, he thought, and reddened.

"You can only take one thing," she said softly. She raised the Rod; its orb was whole and glowing with fractured, colored light, a dance of fire, a thing not of this Winter place, although it had been born to it. "These."

"Or you," he said, and the words cut him. Guildmaster. Keeper of Fabril's legacy. If she were gone, he would again be the only Artisan to grace the guildhalls.

She said, "I have made these. They are your responsibility and mine. Protect what I have made, Gilafas. Protect my making."

Maker's words. Maker's ferocity, in her sanity.

He shook his head. He knew; he knew what must be done. The Winter Queen had shown him the truth of that need.

"No. No," he whispered. "Cessaly—"

She smiled, her jaw shuddering with the effort of maintaining that expression. "Thank you," she told him softly. "I know what has to be done … but … thank you."

Then, before he could speak, she placed the Rod and the Sword into his arms, and she rose, quick and cat-like, and she pushed.

~

Meralonne APhaniel was not Duvari, as he had promised. He restrained the guildmaster when the guildmaster almost threw himself into the window again; he forced him—as gently as one could a man made wild and frenzied with grief—to see that the window had closed: he had a mosaic, some proof of the existence of a girl he had foolishly learned to care for, and that was all. To run at it would simply shatter it.

At the time, that would not have been a loss.

"You have what you want," he had said. "Get out!"

But the magi had carried the stained glass to the window, and he had gestured there a moment, and when he had stepped back, it rested securely against the greater glass.

"This will not comfort you now," he said softly, "and perhaps it never will. But I will say to you that the Winter Queen has always had an interest in the Artisans; that their madness in the end is proof against the madness she would cause." He bowed. "I am sorry, Guildmaster."

He looked up. "What did she mean?" He asked, dully. "When she spoke of the turn of seasons, what did she mean?"

"Nothing," Meralonne replied. "For she speaks of the Summer Road, and it has been forbidden her for so long, I do not know if it will ever return."

"And Cessaly?"

"She will never return."

~

He was required to come up with a story that might explain a young girl's disappearance, and he did, but Duvari judged the explanation itself unwise, and in the end, in disgust, he accepted the Lord of the Compact's version of events and burdened Sanfred with its spread.

He labored in Fabril's reach in a fruitless search for a door, or a window, into the Winter world, and the days passed, spring becoming summer, summer fading into fall, and from there, the rain and the shadows of Scaral. He counted them, and lost count of them as he toiled; he spoke with the wise, and when the wise gently turned him—and his money— away, he at last surrendered.

He did not accept her loss.

And perhaps because he could not accept it, could not accept the terrible silence of the absence of her voice, it was a full year before he chose to leave the guildhall, to take the road that led to the Free Town of

Durant. This was not his penance; it was his duty.

To the mother, he carried word of her daughter's greatest act of making, but the mother had no desire for the comfort of the accolade. Hero was a hollow word.

"You promised," she said.

And he had bowed his head, old now, and shamed beyond the simple use of words.

"How long?" she had demanded, her voice rising, the tone fierce and terrible. "How long have you known?"

He could not answer.

"Why did you not come sooner?"

Why?

Because to come here, to make this pilgrimage, to stand before her just and terrible fury, her keening loss, was to acknowledge what he had so desperately refused to acknowledge. Cessaly was gone. Cessaly would never return.

"She is not dead," he told her.

"How can you know that?"

He met her eyes, her wide, reddened eyes, and he bowed his head. "I know it," he said bitterly. "And I had hoped that you might know it as well. She was your daughter."

~

Fabril's reach was no longer a cage. It was his home, the place from which he ruled the guild in the splendor due his rank. Empty splendour, as it had always been, but empty now in a different way. He heard the ocean, and only the ocean, and sometimes, in anger and desperation, he gave himself to its voice. More often, he gave himself to the numb detachment of bitterweed, and the business, the empty, hollow business, of the Guild.

And then, one quiet morning, he felt it: something familiar, some hint of strangeness in the tower walls. He rose slowly and dressed, and then he walked the hall, fingers trailing the rounded surface of stone until he reached his workroom.

He opened the door, and as he did, something darted past him and down the hall. Had he been in any other place, he might have thought it a bat; in the heights, they were common.

But its flight was too delicate, too much the drunkard's spin, and he frowned as he stepped through the door.

Froze there, in wonder. The upper reaches of his room were thick with butterflies. Butterflies of glass, blown in every conceivable color; butterflies of silver and sapphire, of gold and ruby, of wood and stone. Among them, smaller than life, were birds, and the birds, too, were the hatchlings not of egg and warmth, but of the things with which Cessaly had loved to work.

He turned to the window, to the stained glass, and his smile, in this room, was the first that had not been tainted by bitterness in a decade. He lifted his hand to touch it; felt glass, and only glass, beneath his palm.

But the butterflies landed upon his shoulders, his head, his arms; they rested lightly upon the back of his hands, and they spoke to him, and each of their voices held some echo of hers.